KILLER
OF
ORCHIDS

KILLER
OF
ORCHIDS

Ralph Ashworth

STATE STREET PRESS

KILLER OF ORCHIDS
A novel

Published by special arrangement with:
The Cadence Group
5 Broadway
Suite 201
Troy, NY 12180
United States of America

ISBN: 9780681476301
Library of Congress information on file with Publisher

Printed in Canada

The characters portrayed in this book are works of fiction and do not represent or reflect any persons, living or dead.

This book was set in Adobe Caslon

Cover design by Anne LoCascio
Cover photo © Jupiter Images
Interior layout by Anne LoCascio

FOR
GREGORY WEIDNER

1.

Marshall Chester opened the collar of his shirt.

Unseasonably warm for a December night, he thought. He felt clammy and sticky in his heavy gray overcoat. *Nothing seems right anymore. Everything is backward. Nature is turning in on itself.* He opened another button. *I should go back home. I should see Vernon another time. Or not at all.*

Marshall ignored the supernatural warning inherent in weather anomalies. He ignored the repeated warnings from the voice in his head to turn back, go home. He walked on. He walked on, sweating in his winter coat. Just another block to Talvert Street.

Just go through with it. Get it over with. Picture how it will be this summer. My job secure, my career path in tact. Summer at the beach. Elenora healthy again. Perhaps at the beach, in the summer, our finances certain, we can rediscover the passion in our marriage. Yes, just focus on that. Focus on the future. Elenora on the deck of our summer retreat, happy again.

He spotted Vernon leaning against the cement wall in front of the old Homeopathic Hospital. *What an odd place to meet,* Marshall thought. *This borderline derelict neighborhood.*

Vernon looked at him in an offhanded manner.

"Let's walk this way," Vernon said. He took Marshall's arm and led him across the street toward Center Avenue.

A final distillation of dusk cast a pall on the people and the cars around them. Although quite dark, there was still enough light to make out general shapes and a few bright colors. A businessman's white shirt, a woman's yellow dress. Vernon moved him along quickly.

Marshall's head filled with a terrible, loud noise. His heart beat fast. He hoped his heavy winter coat muffled the sound. He didn't want to appear afraid. The situation required a certain degree of command. He dared not allow Vernon to decide everything. It was Vernon's way to push, to take action, to decide. Marshall was going to have to exert a little influence, let Vernon know that he, Marshall, would not do just anything.

They entered the parking lot of a Wendy's restaurant. Behind the restaurant the speaker monolith advertised larger than life food. Why here? Did Vernon mean for them to sit down and talk over hamburgers and fries? Maybe it was that simple. They would talk it out; maybe just let it all go. That would answer at least half of his prayers.

Vernon tightened his grip on Marshall's arm. The walk from the old Homeopathic Hospital hadn't seemed all that long. How much time had gone by? The noise in Marshall's head scrambled reality. He was losing his sense of time, his sense of real and not real. Vernon did this to him. His old friend Vernon. His best friend since first grade.

Vernon gripped his arm so tightly it hurt.

Then Vernon pushed him. Pushed him away, around, away. Marshall wasn't facing the restaurant now. Vernon pushed him away and it was confusing and frightening.

Out from behind a car. Out from nowhere. It was a figure, a man. Who was he? What was he doing here? The man was dressed in a costume. What was he supposed to be? A samurai warrior? That's what he looked like. A samurai warrior. Dressed in a blue and gold embroidered cloak. The samurai screamed something at Vernon. Screamed something incoherent. He held a sword, a large sword. In the dull, windless night the sword gleamed as if lit up from within, gleamed with a supernatural light, the only object of importance in the world, lit up and swinging high and around.

With ferocious power the blade swung down on Vernon's neck. Marshall watched spellbound as Vernon fell to the ground. It seemed to happen in slow motion. Marshall couldn't hear anything anymore, not even the noise in his head. The man in the samurai costume lifted the sword again, high, high, lit from within, so bright, so sharp. The samurai screamed. In the real world, in the Wendy's parking lot, right in the middle of Marshall's sane and customary existence, the samurai brought the sword down into the precise spot of the previous cut in Vernon's neck. The samurai lifted the sword and struck down again, like a woodsman hacking away at a tree limb.

The samurai struck one final blow with such brilliant force that when he lifted the sword into the air Vernon's head came with it. Right there in the Wendy's parking lot in front of the speaker monolith. Vernon's head lifted with the movement of the samurai's sword then hit the pavement and bounded across the lot. Vernon's face, locked in bitter pain, dissected now from his body, bounced and then rolled across the black pavement and stopped.

Marshall knew he should run. He knew he should have been running already, a long time ago. But he hadn't been able to move then and he couldn't move now. It was as if he wasn't there, not really.

The samurai turned toward him. He lifted the gleaming sword, stained now with Vernon's blood. As the samurai lifted the sword high into the air, blood sheeted off the steel blade.

"Please don't do it," Marshall heard himself say. "It was Vernon. I had nothing to do with it."

A sensation came into his legs. Energy, power. He felt his legs move. He started to run, vaguely aware of people in the restaurant watching him through the windows. He started to run, one step, two steps.

The samurai brought the sword down swiftly on Marshall's left knee. It cut deep into the flesh and through the cartilage and bone, producing a searing pain. Marshall stumbled forward, still possessed of the urge to run, to escape. The glistening sharp sword rose high into the air, turning gracefully in the master's hand. In an instant the samurai reached behind Marshall Chester and cut the hamstrings of his right leg. Marshall fell forward onto all fours, struggled to crawl, but he was unable to progress.

"Leave me alone," he screamed at the samurai. "I didn't do it. I wasn't a part of it. It was all him. I am innocent. I am an innocent!"

Heroically Marshall lifted his torso. He looked pleadingly into the eyes of his adversary. The samurai lifted his sword.

"Please."

The samurai lowered his sword. In a commanding yet soft voice he murmured, "I will be merciful."

The samurai ran his sword through Marshall's solar plexus, quickly pulled the sword out and thrust in again, this time through the man's heart. The samurai withdrew his sword one final time. Marshall's body pulled up with the blade. His winter coat in the warm December night showed a small but deepening spot of blood. Marshall was dead but still his body manifested energy, the last remnant of the will to continue, to live yet another moment and then another. Then this last energy dissipated. Marshall's body fell forward onto the pavement.

The police arrived. The restaurant manager unlocked the doors. Statements were taken. Several people saw the direction the samurai used to make his escape. The police looked in that direction. They raced down neighborhood streets in cars with blinding lights and screaming sirens.

The samurai was not found.

He got away clean.

2.

Xander Pooka left the house quietly so as not to wake his mother. Saturday morning. The weather was great. Not cold like it usually is in December, but warm like spring. And he had news. All the news that was fit to print.

Xander devoured all forms of reading material. His mother liked to tell her friends that he popped out of the oven asking for C.S. Lewis. He left Kiddie Lit behind at an early age and became a fan of the oversized DK intermediate books on every subject from dinosaurs to gemstones to Native American culture. Xander spent the bulk of his library time in the reference room reading at random from adult encyclopedias. Every so often the reference librarian, Mrs. Claudus, allowed Xander into the climate controlled rare book room for a peek at some of the older compilations, like Diderot.

Nothing in the Pooka family history presaged Xander's extraordinary intellect. The word savant had been kicked around. Budding genius. Smart shit. He immersed himself in what he considered adult fields of learning. Last year it had been calculus. This year language—especially vocabulary. His favorite new word was "synchronicity."

Even though he was only eleven years old, Xander read the *New York Times* every morning. If he were being honest, he would tell you that most of what he read in the *Times* went over his head. On this particular morning, however, it wasn't something in the *Times* but a news article in the *Pittsburgh Post Gazette* that put the match to his highly combustible mind.

Xander walked to the end of his street and started down the next. He spotted Mrs. Wightman, the neighborhood nebbish, walking her cat on a leash. Mrs. Wightman lived alone in the biggest house in their suburban plan. Her husband had died so long ago that no one else in the plan seemed to remember him. She spoke with a thick eastern European accent—

Hungarian or Romanian, maybe even Russian. Mrs. Wightman refused to talk about her origins, so nobody knew for sure.

"Hello Mrs. Wightman," Xander called, crossing to the other side of the street.

"Xander Pooka," she intoned in a hooting sort of high-pitched voice. "Where are you going so early and in such a hurry?"

"I'm going to see Jeff," he replied. Xander walked purposefully so he wouldn't have to stop.

"That man is still sleeping in his bed. Why don't you leave him alone for a while? Play with your little boy friends." Xander ignored her. "Do you hear me?"

"I have to see him about something important."

"Your Mr. Jeff spent the night up in his attic. Until past 3 a.m. he worked on that computer of his."

"And how do you know that, Mrs. Wightman?" Xander knew that Mrs. Wightman liked to spy on Jeff.

"Don't you get smart with me, little boy." Mrs. Wightman collected her dignity. "I am your elder. To me you pay respect. It so happens I know on account of I walked my kitty late last night. Out on the street. Past his house I went." She flung her fingers up at the sky. "All his lights were on in that attic. Like a lighthouse, it looked. Like a blazing lighthouse. I saw him there typing. You tell him if he don't want people looking, don't have such big windows."

Xander wondered briefly if Mrs. Wightman was one of the brigade of neighborhood women who spied on Jeff with binoculars hoping to catch a glimpse of him in the buff. Oh well, it didn't matter. Xander stepped up his pace. Mrs. Wightman had a special talent for talking without breathing. Once trapped in a conversation with her there was no easy way out. He liked Mrs. Wightman and he knew she was lonely, but on this particular occasion he was on a mission.

"Stop moving when I talk to you," she demanded.

"I can't, Mrs. Wightman. I'm late. I've got to hurry." Xander broke into a trot, effecting what he thought was a discreet escape.

He pretended to be out of earshot of her next words, which were: "You're not as smart as you think, little boy. One day you'll fall running away from me."

At one time Jeff's house looked like every other two story house in the plan. Shortly after buying the property, Jeff initiated a series of architectural alterations. He removed the teeny tiny attic crawl space and the teeny tiny dormers and the gently sloping shingles that constituted the roof and added in their place an airy, modern attic loft featuring a hub and spoke design. The hub itself was shaped like an octagon. The hub roof, made entirely of glass, created an immense skylight.

The four panels on the corners featured rectangular rooms, each culminating in a floor-to-ceiling window. Jeff had located these windows on the corners of his house so that he could take in the panoramic view of the plan and the surrounding countryside rather than look directly into the homes of his immediate neighbors.

This revolutionary attic loft created a sensation in the otherwise quite ordinary suburban plan. It even got written up in the *Tribune Review*. Of course, it was customary for a new resident to elaborate upon a modest deck or outfit the kitchen with modern appliances or transform a cement basement into a game room. But this attic loft business pressed the envelope of community standards. It was bold, it was…well, bold.

But Jeff didn't stop there.

Following the completion of the attic loft, Jeff knocked out the southwest corner of his house, facing the woods, and installed in its place a multi-colored red brick turret. You see, he had always wanted to live in a house with a turret. The turret rooms, though small, were among his favorites. He liked to sit in them and read, or sit in them and contemplate, or just sit in them. His neighbors didn't know what to make of it. Jeff's turret, so far as anyone knew, was the only turret in all of Wexford.

For a time the men of Wexford wondered if they, too, should build turrets onto their homes. Sharon Beineke's husband, Tom, broached the subject to Jeff one weekend afternoon.

"What is that for?" Tom asked.

"It's a turret," Jeff told him.

"I know that. But what does it do? What is its function?"

"In medieval times turrets encased circular stairways. They functioned as lookouts to guard against enemy encroachment. But here in Wexford it just looks cool."

Tom pondered this, looking sideways at the ground. "Does it increase or decrease property value?"

"I'm never selling this house, Tom. They'll take me out of here feet first. After that the house can sell for a buck."

Tom took that to mean decrease. Wexford was saved that fateful afternoon from becoming known as "the community of turrets." The path not taken.

Xander stood in front of Jeff's house and yelled up at the bedroom window.

"Je-eff! Je-eff!"

Jeffrey Redwing was, in fact, still in bed just as Mrs. Wightman had predicted. A big, fat king-sized bed with big, fat goose down pillows and a big, fat goose down quilt. Not to mention fresh cotton sheets that were nice and warm from his body heat. He liked his bed. There were times when he thought of his bed as a kind of goose down sanctuary to which he could retreat from the world, his neighborhood, even the other rooms of his house with all their implied responsibility. He could crawl right into this sanctuary and never make another mortgage payment, never recycle another aluminum can, never ponder another software problem, never have to show up for events in appropriate clothing. He didn't agree that a dog was a man's best friend. No. A man's best friend was a big, fat comfy bed. And he had one. Yes, indeed, he had a best friend.

"Hey Je-eff!"

'Oh, no. Oh, no. Noises from the outside world. Xander-type noises. He can't be here already. It's still dark outside. Oh, no. He's got all the neighborhood dogs barking. I can't pretend I don't hear him. I'm going to have to get up. I hate getting up. I just hate it. What time is it? Oh my God, it's only seven o'clock. I bet he's been up since six. I'll bet he waited for the stroke of seven to call on me. I'm going to have to convey to him some notion of what it's like to be in your thirties. I have a darker view of things. I don't look forward to the crack of dawn.'

"Je-eff!"

'Okay, this is it. I'm going to have to get up now or they'll start a petition to kick me out of the neighborhood. I don't know why he can't just ring the bell. All right, body. Are you ready to boot up?'

Jeffrey pulled aside the goose down quilt and flapped open his cotton sheets. The weather was warm for this time of year, but not as warm as Jeff liked it. Once the cold morning air crept into his sanctuary, once it invaded his sheets, the spell was broken. There was no going back to bed.

He walked to his bedroom window, opened it and leaned out. It was, in fact, still dark outside but he could make out the shape of his friend.

"You're going to wake up the whole neighborhood. Why didn't you just ring the bell?"

"Because you would ignore me," Xander replied. "I can't believe you're not up yet."

Jeff waited, then pronounced with appropriate solemnity, "It's 7 a.m."

Xander put his hands on his hips. "I'm eleven years old. I can tell time. You know, I wish I lived with you. We could get an earlier start on weekends."

Jeff rubbed the sleep out of his eyes. "An earlier start," he mumbled.

"Yes. I've read the paper this morning. That's what I want to see you about. There's something in the paper. Have you read it yet?"

"No. I haven't had a chance."

"I bet it's still in the vestibule. Let me in. I need to see you."

Jeff wiped a little more sleep out of his eyes and sauntered downstairs. Xander met him in the vestibule with paper in hand.

"You're still in your pjs."

"Believe it or not you got me out of bed. Saturday is a recovery day for me. I like to sleep in on Saturday morning. Left to my own free will I would probably not rouse until noon."

"Get real. You don't sleep, you hibernate. Left to your own free will you wouldn't get up until next week. You know I like to get an early start on Saturday. Why don't you set the alarm or something?"

Jeff's mind wasn't functioning just yet. He didn't have an answer for his young friend.

"Can you start the coffee?" Jeff asked.

"You bet."

"I'll take a shower, put on some clothes."

"I'll make the coffee extra strong."

"Not too strong. I already have hair on my chest."

"I want you alert this morning," Xander said. "Wait till you read what's in the paper."

Jeff grabbed at the paper, but Xander put it out of reach. "Not till you're awake and dressed," he said. "Now hurry up."

While Jeff stumbled up the stairs, Xander prepared the coffee. Xander didn't drink coffee; the taste put him off. But he had a knack for making a great cup. He withdrew the beans from the airtight canister. Jeff's research taught him that the best beans came from places like Africa and Indonesia, but he had recently stumbled across an organic dark roast from Nicaragua that he particularly liked. "The very best beans sell at auction to France," Jeff had told him a year or so ago when Xander was first learning to brew the caffeinated elixir. "That's why a cup of coffee in a Parisian restaurant can cost as much as five dollars a cup." Xander couldn't imagine paying five dollars for a cup of liquid so bitter. "The next best beans go to Turkey and Greece. Then Spain and Italy and various places in the Middle East. These are the countries that value good coffee."

"What kind of coffee do we buy in the United States?" Xander had asked.

Jeff shrugged. "The gourmet roasters in the U.S. buy the best of what's left. It's relatively cheap. There are exceptions, of course. Our national taste buds are evolving. You can taste test coffee by chewing one of the beans. That's how professionals sample batches. Here, taste one."

Xander vividly recalled the chalky, bitter taste of the bean as he ground it between his molars. Jeff and his research! Jeff researched everything, every detail of life. The pleasure Jeff took from his first cup of morning coffee came as much from the pleasure of his research as it did from the perfect brew. "We can live better than Louis XIV," he once boasted to Xander, "if at first we are willing to do a little research."

The coffee dripped slowly into the pot. Xander decided to speed things along by making Jeff's bed. Jeff was a neat freak. He couldn't start his day unless the bed was made—hospital corners.

The shower water stopped. A long, sorrowful cry such as might come from a lovesick moose sounded out from the shower stall. This was followed by another cry, deeper and longer, that seemed to carry in its tone the weight of a thousand guilty souls. And then a third: dark, forsaken and bitter. An unseasoned listener might have rushed into the bathroom expecting to find blood and a withering corpse. But these sounds brought a smile to Xander. Jeff rode these resonant tones from the lethargy of somnolence to the zest of wakefulness. To Xander it signified the passing of adult tiredness from Jeff's body. Now they could play.

Jeff entered the room; he had slipped into cords and a tartan patterned flannel shirt from L.L. Bean.

"Coffee smells great," he said, toweling his hair dry.

He fired a quick quiz at Xander. "What did John Lennon say?"

"There's nothing you can see that isn't shown."

"That's right." Jeff sat on the edge of the bed to put on a pair of Argyle socks and Bean penny loafers. "What else did he say?"

"There's nothing you can know that isn't known."

"Right again." Jeff casually walked to the windows and opened the slats. He turned to make the bed and noticed for the first time that it was already made. "I must have really been groggy this morning. I made the bed in my sleep."

"I made the bed, you idiot."

"Hospital corners?"

"Wrapped tight enough to hold psychos."

"That's the way I like it." Jeff smiled devilishly. "Now where's this newspaper?"

3.

JEFF TOOK A SEAT AT THE KITCHEN TABLE. XANDER PUT JUST ENOUGH cream in Jeff's coffee to make it look like mud. No sugar. Jeff took two sips, long and slow, savoring the flavor. "The best," he muttered, cupping the mug close to his face, allowing the vapors to give him a steamy facial. He closed his eyes, breathed in deeply, and then let all the air out slowly, waiting until just the end to open his eyes again.

Xander spread the paper out on the table in front of him. "Take a look at that," he said, pointing to the headline. It read: TWO MEN MURDERED BY MYSTERIOUS SAMURAI.

"Oh no," said Jeff. "Another murder."

Xander, considerably more excited, waved his arms about. "Another murder. Yes! A wonderful murder. A fascinating murder. An intriguing murder." Knowing his friend's particular weakness, he added, "And a great puzzle."

Jeff declared flatly, "You're not involving me in another one of these Jessica Fletcher escapades."

"This one is better," Xander insisted, pushing the paper a little closer. "This one is so much better. Read it. You'll see."

Jeff covered his eyes with the palm of his hands like the See-No-Evil monkey. "No, I don't want to read it. My life has been good lately. No guns held to my head. No sergeant detectives threatening to put me in jail for the rest of my life."

"Don't be such a wuss." Xander pulled Jeff's hands away from his eyes. "At least read the report. It's good. It's really good." He put a little extra coffee in Jeff's mug. "Take a swig first. That'll help."

Jeff downed the coffee like pirate's whiskey in one great gulp. He took up the newspaper.

TWO MEN MURDERED
BY MYSTERIOUS SAMURAI

At 5:40 p.m. two men formerly of Butler were brutally murdered outside the Wendy's restaurant on Center Avenue in Shadyside. Vernon Roman (43) and Marshall Chester (44) approached the restaurant from the parking lot entrance. They were surprised by a man carrying a long, curved sword. Eyewitnesses described the attacker as a tall, athletically built man dressed in the traditional robes of the samurai warrior. The alleged samurai struck Roman repeatedly in the neck with the sword, severing Roman's head from his body. The samurai then cut both of Chester's legs, rendering him immobile.

As Chester, a family man, pleaded for his life, the samurai plunged the sword twice through his torso.

According to reports, the samurai then fled in the direction of St. Stephen's church.

Roman and Chester were both reported dead at the scene.

Jennifer Hafney, a Wendy's employee, witnessed the attack. "I was bussing tables when I heard a customer scream," recalls Hafney. "This samurai guy went after those people like they'd killed his mother. It was wild. He hacked and he hacked at that first guy's head until it just flew off. That was amazing. Like watching television. Blood shot up out of his neck like exploding champagne. It was really gross. We all screamed, even the manager.

"Some of us yelled for the other guy to run. He just stood there, like paralyzed or something. Our manager even stood at the door and yelled for him to come inside. But he didn't move.

"Then this samurai cut the second guy behind his leg with the sword. The guy fell to his knees. He looked like he was begging for his life. We couldn't hear from in here. Then the samurai ran the sword twice through his body. It had to be a really sharp sword, because this guy had on a heavy coat.

"That's when our manager locked the doors because we didn't want the samurai coming in here next.

"But he never even looked in our direction. He ran off toward the old church. Some people say he stopped and picked up the head, but I didn't see that. I was too upset."

Sister Anna Marie Beck crossed paths with the alleged samurai in front of St. Stephen's church. "He almost knocked me down he was running so fast," said octogenarian Sr. Beck. "I thought maybe he was a martial arts student. He looked like he was dressed for karate. He ran down Liberty Avenue toward Bloomfield and then seemed to just disappear. Poof. Like magic."

Police are uncertain as to motive. Was the attack premeditated or just another senseless act of violence so common to the East End in recent months?

Roman, unemployed, was a long-time resident of Woodlawn Road. He is survived by his mother, Rose, and three sisters. Chester, a teacher at Upper St. Clair Academy, was a longtime resident of Upper St. Clair.

He is survived by his wife, Elenora, and seven children.

Roman and Chester were reputed to be longtime friends.

Police have no leads in the killings. No trace of the alleged samurai has been found. Police are still searching the area for Roman's head.

In the Japanese language samurai means "one who serves." The samurai warrior dominated Japanese military life from the twelfth to nineteenth centuries. Loyalty, service, and family honor characterized the Samurai Code known as the Way of the Warrior.

Police are checking with regional Japanese culture centers for clues to the mysterious samurai's identity.

Xander, who had been reading the article over Jeff's shoulder whispered, "Poof. Like magic."

"It's intriguing," was all Jeff would say.

"Research," Xander whispered yet again. "Imagine the fun we could have tracking this one down."

"Hey, this guy Roman had his head chopped off. That's decapitation, buddy. Decapitation is very low on my list of favorite ways to die."

"Favorite ways to die?"

"Yes. I have a list. This is one of the things older people do. We compile lists of how we prefer to go. First is dying peacefully in my sleep at an age when I'm good and ready. After that the options become less appealing."

"What's on the bottom of the list?"

"I don't speak it. If I don't speak it, it won't happen. I'm superstitious about death. But, it's safe to say that decapitation is close to second from the bottom. Especially slow decapitation. What did this girl say? 'He whacked and he whacked until it just flew off.' Whacked and whacked. That means this poor Roman character had a couple of whacks to think about it."

Xander paced behind Jeff's chair. "I have a feeling," he said, "that this samurai is a good man."

"Good man? Gandhi he's not. We're talking decapitation here. We're talking skewered people."

"He's a good man by modern standards."

A set of standards that allowed for any kind of murderer to be considered a good man troubled Jeff. Xander spoke like this from time to time. It troubled Jeff not because Xander was coldhearted or mean-spirited but precisely because Xander represented the best of his generation. Just two decades away the view seemed sometimes calculated and cynical. Jeff remained silent for a moment.

"It was just a thought I had," said Xander. "Maybe he's as evil as he seems. But why commit murder dressed in the robes of a samurai warrior? Why commit these murders so publicly? Why not do it with a gun in the dark? So much easier to do. So much easier to escape detection. It seems to me the person in the samurai costume was making a point."

Jeff considered this, drawing slowly on the coffee. "It's possible," he conceded. "It's also possible this guy is a homicidal psychopath who's seen too many Japanese action films."

"C'mon Jeff. Think about what the girl said. The samurai went after these guys like they had killed his mother. Only that's not really true. The samurai kills Roman first and kills him viciously by hacking and hacking at the head until it comes off. Gruesome. Painful. Must have been a horrible way to die. Chester gets it quick through the heart."

"After his hamstrings have been cut."

"That's so he won't get away. After all, Chester probably suspects the identity of the samurai."

"Maybe."

"The hamstring cuts prevent him from escaping. But then the samurai runs him through the heart with the sword. That would be a quick death. Right?"

"Almost instantaneous. So I hear. Why run him through twice?"

"To make sure he's dead. He was wearing a heavy coat. Hard to locate the heart exactly through a heavy winter coat."

"You smart shit. So you're saying the first murder, Roman, is an act of vengeance or justice or something in that order. He kills Chester expeditiously, almost mercifully. If the samurai were a psycho he would have killed them both the same way."

"The second killing is a necessity. There is a kindness in it."

"Kindness!"

"I think the samurai made moral distinctions. He chooses the robes of tradition and honor to make his statement. The murders are deliberately planned and executed."

"Don't you mean cold blooded?" Jeff asked.

"But the samurai acts out The Code of the Samurai. The Way of the Warrior. He is not completely ruthless. To tell you the truth, I don't think he would skewer an innocent eleven-year-old kid."

Jeff considered for a moment the possible between-the-lines moral distinctions of the samurai. "I think he would," Jeff concluded. "I think he'd skewer your innocent little ass in a nanosecond if you crossed the wrong line."

"But I wouldn't. I'd never cross that line. I'm not Roman. I'm not guilty of Roman's sins. I'm on the same side as the samurai."

"You don't know that," Jeff said. "You don't know what side the samurai is on."

"C'mon Jeff. Can't we just puzzle it out?"

"It's too dangerous. You know what happened the last time."

"That was different."

"Yeah. It didn't involve violence. It didn't involve death by decapitation."

"C'mon Jeff. Don't make me whine. I've read this article a hundred times this morning. It's a great puzzle. Two old friends. One is unemployed and lives in a poor part of town. The other is a teacher at a private academy in an uppity suburb. One is single, the other has seven kids. One is decapitated, the other killed mercifully. There's a samurai. A nun. The head is missing. Jeez. We could have a lot of fun."

"We could have just as much fun at the Science Center. We could check out the *Star Trek* exhibit."

"I want to solve the murders."

Jeff laughed, albeit nervously. "I'm sure you do. But it's too dangerous."

"We'll treat it like a puzzle. We won't get near any dangerous people. We'll stay out on the edge, invisible to the evil eye. If we discover anything we'll send an anonymous letter to the police."

"I'm supposed to be your Big Brother. Your mother thinks I'm taking you to baseball games and the zoo and the museum."

"You take me to the library."

"So we can research rare African poisons. I don't think that's what your mother has in mind."

Xander sighed. "Let's face it. My mother's a wonderful person, but she lacks imagination."

"Do you know what would happen to me if anyone, any government agency, found out that you and I spend our Big Brother/Little Brother time investigating blood thirsty murders? They'd build a special jail cell just for me and fill it with sex starved weight lifters."

"You're being melodramatic," Xander said quietly. "It's just a puzzle. A simple puzzle. But if you'd rather go to the Science Center—"

Xander did his best to appear crestfallen. Jeff stared blankly out the kitchen window, saying nothing. The eyes of the cat clock on the wall shifted back and forth.

Xander refilled Jeff's coffee, adding ever so adroitly just the right amount of cream. His movements affected a butler-like supplication.

"That was pathetic," Jeff said.

"I'll shine your shoes. Whatever you say."

"All right, all right. Look. We will engage in a teeny, tiny bit of very private puzzle solving."

"A tiny bit," Xander echoed, willing to take anything. (He could stretch it to more later.)

"We will keep an extraordinarily discreet distance from anything that even remotely resembles danger."

"No danger," Xander reiterated. "I don't like danger anyway."

"We get anywhere near danger, we stop. No matter how close we are to solving the puzzle."

"Agreed."

"And you're not allowed to talk me out of this agreement," Jeff added emphatically. "You're a clever little lawyer for an eleven year old."

"I'll just be a regular kid on this one, I swear."

"All right then," Jeff said, enthusiastic, despite his reservations, to have a puzzle at last. "Let's get started."

"Up to the Cloisters?"

"Yes. Up to the Cloisters. We'll begin with the relationship between the two murdered men. The Butler connection. Remember? The paper described them as two men formerly of Butler."

4.

Time, Dear Reader, for just a tiny sidebar. I feel compelled, as the official chronicler of the Jeff and Xander mysteries, to draw attention to a character trait, some might say a character flaw, in our man Jeff. He likes to hide. Retreat, burrow, hibernate. Squirrel away. Lose himself.

I have voted him most likely to leave a cocktail party without saying goodbye to his hosts. Even though he graduated at the top of a distinguished class of Carnegie Mellon computer science students, he did not bother to attend graduation ceremonies. And he has virtually exiled himself from his People by moving to an antiseptic, lawn obsessed hamlet called Wexford.

Which People you might ask?

City People specifically. The People who inhabit the magical concrete kingdom of Jewish delis, Asian grocers and imported cheese emporiums. But it could also be said that he is hiding from a variety of subsets of People to whom he belongs: Cherokee People, Gay People, People of Intellect, People Who Are Social with One Another, and, of course, Computer Geeks. Hiding from us all.

And what have we done to offend? We've winked in his direction. We've pinched his bottom a time or two. Really, what else is one to do with a man so sinfully, so unjustly good looking? Swarthy handsome. Death-black hair. Exotic ice blue eyes (unusual for someone with Cherokee ancestry). And that complexion: crème de cocoa lit up from deep Moroccan red highlights. I'm not a big fan of L.L.Bean clothing, yet draped over Jeff's tall-ish, rugby-player physique it must be said that the Stewart plaid shirt and the comfy cut chinos and the oxblood penny loafers look yummy.

And there he is in Wexford.

Hotter than a chili pepper in the Alabama sun.

Single.

Not divorced single, which is perfectly acceptable in the suburbs. After all, one should not have to leave one's home and friends just because one's pint of love has curdled. Not dating single with a frequently spotted girlfriend or better yet fiancée. Not even single with a boyfriend or a male partner, which can be acceptable in the suburbs given the right boyfriend, the right partner.

No. Jeff is just plain old unattached single. With the kind of physical beauty that makes people stop while in the middle of important work, stop while in the process of driving a car, stop while in the process of kissing one's husband goodbye for work. Jeff moved his careless, unselfconscious beauty into a nearly innocent, almost sleeping suburb of mostly Republican voters. The men of Wexford and even some of the women thought it was a lot like a wolf choosing to make a little home in the sheep pasture.

Tired of the hunt. Just taking up a little corner, you know. Pay me no mind.

Worse, he took a perfectly normal two-story-with-tiny-attic home and added a third floor. That wouldn't have been so bad if he had constructed a normal set of rooms, but no. He turned the entire floor so that the corners hung out over the sides. Where the corners should have been he installed, floor to ceiling glass. Then he added a turret! (But we've already discussed the turret.)

Once this domestic oddity had been constructed, Jeff initiated the slow and, to some, maddening process of moving in. It took on the aspects of a great unfolding. Every couple of days Jeff drove up in his car, paused in front of the house or across the street from the house or down the road a bit, and looked the thing over. He considered it. He pondered it.

Until one day he actually got out of his car. He paced back and forth, a block this way, a block that way, until settling finally on the sidewalk across the street from the gleaming edifice. Each day, for a couple of hours, Jeff sat on the curb across the street from his house and just looked at it. Every so often he entered his house, turned on a light in one of the rooms, then returned outside to resume his vigil.

At first the good citizens observed him from the safety of their windows. After a few days of Jeff's odd behavior, this citizen and that citizen decided to take a stroll along the sidewalk to investigate. Tom Beineke made a point of introducing himself as it was his sidewalk that Jeff chose as his viewing perch.

"How many children do you have?" Tom asked in as casual a manner as he could manage. "When will your wife be joining you?"

He didn't like the answers Jeff gave to these questions.

Tom's wife Sharon, for her part, enjoyed the dark handsomeness of the man on her sidewalk. She brought him coffee and fresh bakery rolls. She invited him to sit on the Beineke lawn. It might be more comfortable and offer a better vantage point. Jeff declined the offer. For him the curb offered the best possible perspective.

The Beineke children, Sarah (four) and Julian (six) sat with him from time to time. They plied him with questions.

"Hey Mister," started young Sarah, "what are you doing?"

To which Jeff replied, "I'm looking at my house."

"But why?" asked Julian. "Aren't you allowed inside?"

"I'm not quite sure why. But I am, in fact, allowed inside. I can go inside any time I want."

"Would you like to play with us?"

"Not just yet."

Mrs. Wightman took her turn with Wexford's enigmatic presence. At first Jeff reacted politely, if curtly, to Mrs. Wightman's all too personal questions. But Jeff had already decided to give very little of himself away to his new neighbors. (While hiding from his Old People he had also decided to hide from the New People.) He offered little more than the chitchat version of name, rank and serial number.

After several days of getting no answers, Mrs. Wightman gave up on prying. Instead, in the course of taking her daily constitutional, she passed the Beineke sidewalk, stopped behind Jeff, and made pronouncements.

"This sidewalk is not a lighthouse," she said one day.

Another time she warned, "You're not making any friends here."

This, after considerable frustration: "I come from Eastern Europe. We know our way around an interrogation."

None of this fazed our man Jeff. For clearance purposes he had been investigated and interrogated by intelligence professionals. Besides, he had access to records. He knew a little bit about Mrs. Wightman. She would be the last person to advocate illegal or cruel methods of investigation into personal and private matters. He smiled in the midst of her pronouncements as if to say, "Thank you for sharing your thoughts with me."

Jeff burrowed into Mrs. Wightman's psyche. She thought about him occasionally throughout her day. He even starred in a few of her nocturnal dreams. In one dream she was a much younger woman. She was not in Wexford, but back in her parents' home. It was her wedding day and she was dancing, dancing, dancing so gaily with her husband and with some of the other young men and a few of her girlfriends as well. Dancing and dancing and off to the side she spotted Jeff. He was wearing a suit too big for him, but he looked handsome just the same. He was not dancing and she thought, in her dream, I will go over there and dance with him myself. In the dream she walked over to him. She saw her hand reach for his hand and just when she felt the warmth of his palm, she woke up.

"I know just what to do," she said out loud in her bed.

That afternoon she approached Jeff on the Beineke sidewalk with a bottle of champagne in her hand.

"It's a house," she said. "You're not supposed to look at it, you're supposed to live in it. Come with me, Mr. Jeff." She led him across the street to the closest corner of his multicolored brick abode. She handed him the bottle of champagne. "Here, you break. Shake it up good first, it makes a better explosion."

Jeff gave it a good shake and broke the bottle against the brick. It erupted with great fizzle and foam all over the brick and himself and even a bit on Mrs. Wightman.

"There you go," she said. "Welcome to the neighborhood. You pick up the glass."

5.

JEFF ACCOMPLISHED HIS MOVE IN A SERIES OF INSTALLMENTS PACED OUT OVER several months. He started with a simple cherry-lipstick red Scandinavian chair, not particularly comfortable, intelligent but bone hard. The chair reflected Jeff's personal philosophy toward community room furniture, to wit: visitors should not get too comfortable or stay too long.

The day after Mrs. Wightman's champagne, he drove this erstwhile chair up to the house in a rented U-Haul. With a great banging of handles and levers Jeff opened the back of the van. He peered inside, glanced over at his front door, looked back inside the van as if working out complex geometric equations. Neighbors watched through slatted blinds with anticipation.

Jeff eased out the one chair. He carried it in outstretched arms like an offering, a lamb to appease God. He placed it in the room on the right facing the street. His neighbors witnessed The Placing Of The Chair easily enough through Jeff's naked windows. He set it down, stepped back to regard it, moved it eight inches further back into the corner, stepped back to regard it again.

That was it. He left the house, locked the front door, banged the U-Haul doors closed, and drove away.

"It was just one chair," Marlena Peresky observed to her husband.

"Just one chair?" A curlicue of smoke arose from Stan Peresky's pipe. "Was it a special chair?"

"How special can a chair be?"

"Could be a barber's chair," Stan offered. "Maybe it's an heirloom. Maybe his father was a barber."

Marlena looked at her husband as if she had just witnessed the disappearance of his last brain cell. "It's not a barber chair. It's some horrible looking thing without any padding. The cat wouldn't want to sit on it."

"Maybe he hasn't got a cat." Marlena's husband hadn't grown up in the suburbs. He espoused an easygoing, live and let live attitude acquired during a childhood spent in New Jersey.

"You're missing the point entirely," quipped Marlena. "He didn't move in a house full of furniture. He moved in one ugly chair."

"I think the women of this neighborhood are paying entirely too much attention to this man. He's a bachelor. He's quirky and odd. He hasn't had his character snuffed out by responsibility like the rest of us."

"You've got plenty of character," Marlena warned, returning her gaze to the window. "I'm not paying too much attention. I'm paying just the right amount. I want to know who is moving into my community. I have children. It's a healthy concern. Do you know that his last name is Redwing? Did you know that? He's an Indian. All the Indians were chased out of Pennsylvania over a hundred years ago and yet here he is."

"A couple of Indians always manage to stay behind," Marlena's husband observed, as if quoting a study. "He wears penny loafers. How threatening can he be?"

"Yeah, well…. Maybe he's adopted our ways, but you know what they say: once an Indian always an Indian."

"I think they say that in old John Wayne westerns. I'm not listening to you anymore. I'm smoking my pipe. Leave the man alone."

"He'll be bedding down the discontented women of this neighborhood. You watch. Or maybe a few of the men. Larry Carnisky looks at men's butts and I don't think his wife knows it."

"I'm smoking my pipe."

"He might be a drug dealer. Have you thought about that? My cousin Sheila has a drug dealer in her plan. You move to the suburbs to get away from these people and look what happens—they move in with you."

"What people did we move here to get away from, Marlena?" asked Stan. "I thought we wanted a good school district. Never mind, I'm smoking my pipe."

"Drug dealers, bachelors. Those kinds of people. You know, Sharon Beineke says there hasn't been a bachelor in America since the fifties. That alone arouses my suspicion."

"I'm smoking my pipe. I can't listen and smoke at the same time. Leave that man alone."

"I'll leave him alone," Marlena said slyly. "But I'm keeping my eye on him."

Much of Wexford kept an eye on Jeff as he moved in one stick of furniture at a time. This piecemeal moving-in process became something of a game for the children of the neighborhood. Whoever first spotted the familiar van spread the word and within minutes an audience assembled on the Beineke lawn. Mrs. Wightman usually joined the children. Sharon Beineke continued to bring Jeff refreshments.

Xander rode up to the scene on his bicycle, pumping his brakes with a flourish as he eased up into the group. Most kids liked and respected Xander. Early on some of the older kids tried to harass Xander Pooka, the brainy boy with two peculiar names. There are children who shut down in the face of peer harassment, becoming quiet and studious and evasive. Others lash out and toughen up. Xander made it clear he took shit from no one, including adults. He didn't become mean—just certain.

Xander felt drawn to the quirky man with the Indian name. Since the age of four he had been planning to adopt a father. Here was someone clearly out of the mold. Xander observed Jeff on a number of occasions and then decided to take action. He pulled his bike up to the back of Jeff's van and studied him up close as he unloaded a box of books.

"Hello," Jeff said. He recognized a familiar style in the boy.

"You carried books in yesterday," Xander observed.

"Yes."

"You must like to read."

"A fair assumption. Do you like to read?"

"I live for it," Xander replied, leaning back on his bicycle seat. "Can I see what you've got in there?"

Jeff tilted the box for viewing. This particular armful contained a year's worth of old *Spy* magazines and three hardback books: *How To Break Almost Any Lock; Computer Codes—How To Make Them, How To Break Them; New Infectious Diseases—The New Retro-Viruses*. Not exactly the throw away gossip/trash his mother liked to read.

"Can I help you carry stuff in?"

"Not today," Jeff replied. "Maybe tomorrow."

The next day Jeff still wasn't willing to allow the boy into his house, but they exchanged pleasantries.

"Jeff," the man offered his name.

"Xander," the boy replied. "I live, well, you can't see it from here but it's up the street a ways and around a bend and then a couple of houses down. It looks like eight other houses in the plan. Not really cool, like yours."

Jeff leaked a barely perceptible smile, not willing to give himself away. "Alexander?"

"Technically speaking, I prefer Xander."

"Why is that?"

"I like having a name that begins with an X."

Jeff smiled again, letting it linger this time. "I'm curious about something, Xander. How old are you?"

Xander came to an upright position on his bike pedals. "I'll tell you tomorrow," he said, pedaling away. "I have to go home and make dinner for my mother."

Clever tactic, thought Jeff. A chess move of a certain kind. Jeff had forgotten much of his Piaget, but it seemed Xander exhibited cognition skills atypical for his age group. A possible prodigy.

On the third day of their friendship Jeff moved his mainframe into the house. This turned out to be quite a spectacular chess move. The mainframe was too big to be carted up the stairs. A crew of men arrived in Wexford that fateful morning with a crane. They lifted the impressive piece of technology up to the third floor.

"He's going to blow us all up," Mrs. Wightman announced to the largest group yet assembled on the Beineke lawn.

Xander sat back on the seat of his bike impressed to the max.

"But can you use it?" he asked teasingly.

"I helped design it," Jeff boasted. "I've fed the wisdom of the world into that machine."

Together they followed the progression of the giant metal rectangle through the air. It's great bulk blocked the sun for a moment, encasing them in shadow. With the aid of hooks and heavy duty straps the workers maneuvered the computer in through one of the floor-to-ceiling windows.

"I call her Georgie," Jeff said. "Let me show you where she's going to go. See if you think it's the right spot."

In that way Jeff invited Xander into his house and into his life. It was a private house and an equally private life. Many people tried to talk their way into both, but only Xander, and later Xander's mother, managed to get an invitation.

6.

I know you're anxious to return to the Chester and Roman murders. And that intriguing little business with the samurai. Is he cruel or is he (sword and blood notwithstanding) the kind of person who would never harm an innocent child? Is this a random inner city street killing or is it justice as street theater? Dear Reader. You know damn well we wouldn't be going to all this trouble for a random killing. As a veteran of the mystery tale I'm sure you've figured that much out already. But justice as street theater—that might keep us occupied for a page or two.

And I promise we'll get there. But in the meantime we left Jeff and Xander racing up the stairs to the Cloisters. And you don't even know what the Cloisters are. Well, I haven't told you. It's Jeff and Xander's nickname for the entire third floor of Jeff's house. But why? What is up there? Why did Jeff go to all that trouble to build an extra floor with fourteen-foot windows on the corners and an atrium in the center?

As it turned out, Georgie fit nicely against the length of one wall in the southernmost room. Later that day Xander helped Jeff place a PC and an iMac into that same room. In the evening he helped Jeff assemble a small library of DVD's, CD-ROMs, and floppies.

Electronic gadgets went into the western corner room of the Cloisters. Xander helped assemble and connect an oscilloscope, a voice decoder/analyzer and another formidable, crane-delivered item called an electron microscope. "Yes," Jeff assured him, "the floors have been reinforced." This was in addition to any number of vacuum tube items with color-coded jacks whose purpose Jeff left unexplained.

In the northern room Jeff created a recording studio that featured a Sony 48-track mastering deck and all manner of microphones, effects processors and outboard synthesizers. Throughout the room he scattered an assortment of musical instruments ranging from an original Fender Rhodes electric piano to a Mickey Hart-like array of peculiar percussion instruments gathered from around the globe (including two human leg bones that made an interesting sound when clacked together). A glimpse into this room might lead one to suspect that Jeff possessed at least some small degree of musical talent. But no. Let me assure you Jeff possesses no musical talent whatsoever. He basically makes bumpity little batches of purposeless (often annoying) noise which he diligently records in Hi-def digital sound while dreaming, dreaming, dreaming of Mickey Hart, John Lennon and, perhaps closer to the mark, Stockhausen.

The final corner room, the easternmost room, the room from which one might look east and east some more until spotting ancient Alexandria itself, this room housed Jeff's impressive library of research materials. Filing cabinets along one wall held articles cut from newspapers and magazines on such topics as Bucky Balls, the mysterious disappearance of frog species, the human genome project, the acoustic properties of Steinways versus Yamahas. It was all there.

A set of long, wide drawers originally designed to store art prints contained microfiche, some of it of a sensitive nature. Here one might find government documents from the National Archives, corporate blueprints, and diagrams/schemata/code relating to the wonderful, competitive world of computer software design. Most of it incomprehensible to the average citizen. How did our man Jeff acquire such sensitive materials? He would never tell, of course. But I can tell you that some were purloined for him by agencies of government spying on branches of government. Some he acquired on the dark alleys of the Internet. Yet others Jeff "discovered" and liberated after breaking corporate, government, even private computer codes—breaking codes being something of a specialty. Rounding out the microfiche drawers was a roll or two featuring the scores of the great composers.

Once the four corners of his universe had been assembled, Jeff created the center room: the atrium. Under a six by six skylight he positioned a big fat paisley upholstered comfy chair, the kind that reclined to a full horizontal position should Jeff decide, mid-read, to take a nap. Two massive oak tables flanked the comfy chair. On these great wings rested massive stacks of magazines, books, brochures, and newspapers. These stacks grew and grew and grew until, as in nature, they toppled and started new stacks. A floor lamp in the shape of a graceful arc cast a warm, inviting light over the chair. Palms and ferns and orchids and lilies and other botanical lovelies filled out the rest of the atrium. Marlena Peresky would certainly have considered it the most livable room in the house—had she ever been invited inside.

To Xander this electrical, scientific, botanical, and, yes, musical assemblage of rooms felt mysterious, even religious. Jeff was its lone (lonely) monk. On the morning after the killings at Wendy's, Jeff and Xander retreated to that third floor space—nicknamed by Xander The Cloisters —and took up chairs at the iMac.

7.

"What do we have so far?" Jeff started.

"Start with Butler County," Xander replied, consulting the newspaper article he had already committed to memory. "The newspaper says they were both originally from Butler County."

Jeff called up a series of regional maps. A few mouse clicks and there it was: Butler County.

"Just north of us here in Wexford. Rural but under development," said Jeff. "Or should I say under assault. When Chester and Roman were kids it would have been all corn and cows. Farm people, a handful of rich people living in the more isolated areas. The occasional ghastly mall plunked down along major arteries. Schools, maybe even just one school, would have contained a mix of class and occupation groups."

Xander continued, "Looks like one of them, Chester, recently lived in a place called Upper St. Clair. I've heard of it, but I don't think I've ever been there."

Jeff clicked to a map of the greater Pittsburgh area.

"As you can see, Upper St. Clair is as far south of Pittsburgh as Wexford is north of it. Butler is further north still. What can you deduce from that?"

"Well...this Marshall Chester guy chose to live pretty far away from where he grew up."

"That's right," said Jeff. "He didn't move as far away as Australia, but he put some distance between himself and his past. In a city of mountains, hills and river valleys he might as well have lived in the next state. Didn't the article say he was a teacher?"

"Upper St. Clair Academy. Is that a prep school?"

"No." Jeff pulled up the Website for the Academy. The web page included a photomontage, some basic information about location, history and class size. There was a tab listing teachers, their degrees and accolades; there was another tab listing graduates who had gone on to jobs of distinction.

"It's a fancy suburban high school. You have to have some money to live in Upper St. Clair. The considerable property taxes go primarily to the school." Jeff clicked through photos of the school buildings, the wooded surroundings, the elaborate football stadium, and the state of the art auditorium. "Kids are groomed for college and the inevitable professional career. Our friend Marshall had something on the ball to teach there. Not enough on the ball to teach at a university."

"Maybe he likes high school kids," Xander remarked. "My favorite teacher, Mr. Manese, says all he ever wanted to do was teach sixth grade."

"Maybe," said Jeff. "But high school kids are difficult. Most teachers have to put up with a lot of crap. But you don't have to publish or perish in high school. You just have to get in and ingratiate yourself. But you're right. We don't know enough about him yet to pass judgment. What else do we know about him?"

"He's the father of seven boys."

"He's a family man. A big family at that. These days most people stop at two children, but this guy does the old Catholic thing."

"What's that mean?" asked Xander. "What's the old Catholic thing?"

Jeff started a search for Catholic and birth control.

"The Catholic Church forbids birth control. It considers wasted seed a certain level of sin—I've forgotten which level."

"Wasted seed. Is that semen not aimed at an egg? Left behind in a Trojan? Little men hacked to death on the battlefield of the uterus?"

Jeff, squeamish around the subject of sex under the best of circumstances, looked down and shook his head as if to say Lord help me with this little smart-ass scientist.

"C'mon, Jeff," Xander continued, loving the opportunity to press Jeff's buttons on this issue. "I've already had sex education. I know all about the little men marching to the egg."

"Well, to the point, Catholic families are encouraged to have lots of children and it's more likely to happen if birth control is a sin. The thing that I want you to realize is that there are often ulterior motives lurking behind ideology. Back in Biblical times the Jews had a lot of competition. It was important to have as many Jews as possible. The more Jews, the more Jewish power. Women must reproduce. Marriages are arranged so that all the women get married and make babies. Men die early. They die working, they die in wars. Those that don't die can have multiple wives, again so we're not wasting any of the women. Birth control of any kind is a sin; men wasting their energy with other men is a sin. Making as many Jews as possible is a priority for not just the survival of the race but the power, the control of land and resources. So tell me. What do the Jews have to do with the Catholics?"

"The Old Testament is also the Jewish Bible. Catholics also want to be fruitful and multiply. The more Catholics the more Catholic power," Xander answered.

"Did they teach that in your comparative religion class?"

Xander shook his head.

"I didn't think so." Jeff smiled. "So look. As far as Chester is concerned, he might be a devout Catholic. His wife might be a devout Catholic."

"Or," said Xander, "he just likes big families."

"That's right. He likes children. He likes a big family. Could be all those things. We don't know yet. But he's a career teacher, he's got a large family. He loves kids and if the murder was premeditated then kids factor into it somewhere."

"Cool," said Xander, scanning the article once again. "So what about this Roman guy?"

"Wait. Not so fast. There's one more thing about this that's odd. Chester is a suburbanite. A suburbanite in a far off, rich suburb."

"Right!" said Xander, realizing the point Jeff was making. "He was murdered in the city."

"Not just in the city, but in a part of the city known for gangs, drugs, prostitution, mob activity. You know what people are like in our little corner of suburbia. They don't venture into the city, even safe parts of it, unless to see a Steelers game or go to the symphony. What was this arch suburbanite-school-teacher-family-man doing in this part of the city? He was murdered in an environment alien to him. It's peculiar, that's all. Now, tell me about the other guy."

"Vernon Roman," Xander read. "Unemployed. From Woodlawn Road. Doesn't say where."

"That means the journalist was rushed. He had time to track down a street address but not a neighborhood. If the ID came from the unemployment office, the welfare office, even from an ID card, the journalist probably had a zip code but couldn't discern the neighborhood. Do you know why?"

"No, I don't."

"It's a city zip code. In the city, zip codes cross neighborhood lines. You can have a rich neighborhood and a poor neighborhood in the same zip code. I'm going to deduce that Roman lived in the city."

"Maybe that's why Chester was in the city—to visit his old friend who lived there. And! I'll bet Woodlawn Road is within walking distance of the Wendy's."

"Why is that?"

"Because Vernon is unemployed. My mom says that our car costs about a third of our after-tax income. This guy wouldn't have been able to afford a car. So Chester drove into the city to see his friend, parked his car, then they both walked to the Wendy's."

Jeff knew the payments on the Pooka family Chrysler sedan couldn't be more than $350 a month. Sally Pooka didn't make much money by suburban standards. Now Jeff knew just how poor they really were.

Jeff took a deep breath. "If we add it all up, Chester drove to Shadyside sometime after school let out. Let's say he leaves from school at 4 p.m. That would put him in the East End a little after five o'clock. Five fifteen? He parked his car somewhere other than the Wendy's parking lot because the two men were seen walking together into the lot. They met somewhere else, then decided to walk to the restaurant together."

"Where a Japanese samurai jumped out at them and killed them both."

"Right."

Jeff looked out his floor-to-ceiling window to the woods beyond. Xander studied Jeff. Some time went by. A dog barked. The neighborhood opened one eye to the day.

"The solution to this puzzle," Jeff said, "lies in the relationship between the two men. They live in completely different worlds. One suburban, one city. One with a career, one unemployed. One with a large family, one with no family—at least no family the journalist was able to uncover."

"Maybe they were lovers," blurted Xander. "Maybe Chester was slumming it with his low-life leather daddy."

"Oh, please. Where do you get this stuff? Do you hear me talking about leather daddies? I'm gay and I don't think I would know one to see one."

"They're on cable. They're right there in your little computer. I've read all about it. I've visited some of the Websites."

"Don't tell me this."

"Oh yes. I know more about your lifestyle than you do."

"Leather daddies are not a part of my lifestyle. And I dare say they should not be a part of your vocabulary. Now, I will admit I thought about the love angle. People can love each other without leather being involved, you know. There might be a love angle. When the classes mix it's often for sex or drugs. But if they were having a liaison, why go to Wendy's? It would have taken him an hour or more to get to Shadyside after school. Add time for parking, time for meeting up, time for walking to the restaurant, and you get the time of the murders. People don't usually eat and have sex on a full stomach. And under most circumstances, Chester would have been expected at home to have dinner with his family. That means he had just enough time to meet his friend, have a quick chat, then get home for a late-ish dinner."

"Maybe his wife works at night," said Xander. "Maybe she works at Borders until 11 at night like Barry Caffrey's mom."

"Not likely. You can do that with one kid or two kids, but not when you have seven kids. I'd bet my turret Mrs. Chester is a career mom."

"So if it wasn't sex and it wasn't drugs, what was it?"

Jeff closed his eyes, pondered.

"The article says they were both formerly of Butler County. So that's where they met. That's how they know each other. They probably went to school together, maybe lived close to each other. But they grew apart. Somehow...somehow they came back together again. Maybe this Vernon Roman knows something that Chester wants to remain unknown."

"Blackmail," whispered Xander.

"That's right." said Jeff. "When we know what they met to discuss we will know why they were murdered."

8.

PENNY ENGLISH KNEW SOMETHING ABOUT MARSHALL CHESTER.

He was a simple man. No guile, no duplicity, no rear corridor gossipy backstabbing machinations. Just a simple man with simple needs.

First came work. He needed important work, work that nurtured, work that left him exhausted and satisfied at the end of the day. Teaching addressed this need. Supervising within the teaching environment, coaching the volleyball team. Healing the wounded students so that they graduated and got ahead in life and came back years later to shake his hand. And he was just enough of a child himself that he needed the assurance of appreciation—from his students, from his fellow teachers, from the administrators, from the Board and ultimately from the community. Job Well Done, Marshall. The occasional back pat, notice, reward, mention in the paper. Teacher of Distinction.

Next came the need for love. Close to appreciation, but more substantive. He craved love for the spirit, the soul, the being. He craved love for the man as well: the skin, the hair, the torso, the fingers, the sex. All of it. Immersion. Hold me, he said in the dusk of her bedroom. Kiss everything. And Marshall possessed the need to survive. He required a decent income for his wife and children. College for the seven boys. The all-important, always-there paycheck. The paycheck that acknowledged his hard work, his commitment, his passion.

He needed promotions with the ultimate prize at the end: Principal. Principal Chester. Eventually, in retirement, a seat on the Board. Some teachers were content to collect a check and have the summers off. But Marshall followed an ambitious path that led to accolades, modest riches and maybe a few distinguished words on the headstone. And if he was willing to work hard, bring purpose and courage day after day to the classroom, shouldn't he have the rewards?

Penny looked out her picture window at the browns and blacks of the Allegheny River Valley below. We don't set ourselves up to meet our needs. No we don't, she thought. If we did, then Marshall's wife would have understood. It wouldn't have been a problem. We all could have gotten along fulfilling important needs without the anger, the threat of divorce, the hint of suicide. It's just the fulfilling of needs, Elenora. Just that.

And Greta Fields. That vicious cunt. In a just world where decent people could pursue quite reasonable, even traditional, dreams, Greta would have been an outcast. And Vernon Roman would be a distant memory, a detail from tenth grade.

Oh God, she thought, I will have to see Elenora. Marsh used to say her name over and over again like a mantra. Elenora does such a nice job with my shirts, Elenora made the most delicious duck with figs for the holiday. Elenora, Elenora, Elenora. When Penny said *Hello Elenora* at social gatherings, had it come out sharp and bitter like it felt? It must have. Oh hell, it must have.

Well, she would say *Hello Elenora* at the funeral. Penny would attend all three days just like the wife. She would say *Hello Elenora* at least three more times in her life. The widow might even comfort her. They shared the same loss, after all. Penny imagined an embrace laced with softly spoken words of forgiveness.

A tear traced a graceful line down the freckled porcelain of Penny's face. A tear for her dear friend and sometime lover Marshall. And his failed life. One tear more for her lonely self. Her one true friend gone. Just acquaintances left now. Her students and colleagues. And the men, of course, who enjoyed her freckled porcelain and her long wavy red hair.

Penny stared blankly at her half-there reflection in the glass of the window. Her analyst once advised *If an apparition comes at you in the dark reach out and grab it. If it is a product of your tortured imagination, it will turn to vapor. If it is real, you will hold a monster in your hands.*

I murdered that lovely man, she thought. Death seeped from the tips of her manicure, leached from the rationalizations of her good intentions. How would she live with herself? How would she manage to dress for work in the morning, apply her makeup, stand before class, when she knew she murdered this simple, innocent man?

How would her voice sound when she said *Hello Elenora* at the viewing?

9.

Rose Roman wept openly, loudly, with great exaggerated gestures. She played to the cheap seats in a capacity house.

"He always had a hard life, that kid," she cried. "Since he was four years old and he fell down eight flights of city steps and broke every bone in his body. They put him in a plaster cast, Eddie, so he couldn't move. I had to help him with his bowel movements. I carried his little poop away and washed him clean."

"For Christ's sake, Rose," Eddie objected in his gruff voice.

"His father beat him, beat him every day of his life. Beat him with his fists and beat him with his mouth. Told him he was stupid, told him he was ashamed to be the father of such a child. My boy had such a hard life. And now! Now! How could it be worse? Can you tell me that Eddie? How could it be worse?"

Eddie was Rose Roman's boyfriend. Eddie was fifty-six years old and qualified more as a man friend, but Rose still introduced him with the term she used as a young girl when she dated "the mistake" that later became her husband. Eddie kept a small room in another neighborhood, but mostly stayed with Rose. That morning he had put on pants for the police, but after they left he stripped back to his usual morning attire: BVDs and an athletic T-shirt. He sat at the kitchen table, unshaven face suspended over a mug of steaming coffee.

It could only be worse, Eddie thought, if the boy was still alive. But he dared not voice that opinion.

"I can't identify my own son's dead body because he has no head," Rose shrieked. "His girlfriend has to go identify his body naked on a slab. They're going to slide out a stainless steel shelf with my son on it and pull a cloth down past his dinky so she can say, 'Yes, officer, that's him. That's my Vernon's dinky.'"

"For Christ's sake, Rose."

"It's not fair. There's no dignity in it for him. He had no dignity in his life. And now he's in the newspaper with no head."

Eddie thought, Wait until the police get a look at his girlfriend. Talk about a life with no dignity. But instead he said, "They'll identify him by moles or something."

"He doesn't have a mole. My Vernon did not have a mole on his entire body."

"So they'll identify him by a birthmark."

"He doesn't have a birthmark. My Vernon's body was flawless. Flawless!"

Eddie thought, He had a big ass, didn't he? Maybe they'll roll him over and identify him by his big ass. Eddie almost laughed out loud at the joke he made in his head. Was it hard-hearted of him to be grateful the boy was dead?

"We should have a ceremony for him at home," Rose announced. "I don't want my boy laid out in some strange funeral parlor. We'll have him here in the house where he grew up."

Eddie pictured for a moment Vernon's headless corpse laid out in the living room. With his head gone he'd probably just fit across the blonde mahogany stereo console. Eddie had to be careful here. Rose was grieving out of her mind. She might just pull it off.

"Rose, it's no good. It's not legal."

"I'm his mother," she said, shaking her fist at the air.

"It doesn't mean you can bury him in the back yard, Rose. There are laws."

Wrong thing to say. He knew it. She'll never forget that. One night we'll be fucking and out it will come, the bury-him-in-the-backyard thing.

"You don't care," she said, calm, almost matter-of-fact. "You hated Vernon. I know that."

"I didn't hate the boy, Rose. I thought he used you. I thought he used your love for him."

Rose paused for a moment, then quietly replied, "He had my permission to use my love."

"Rose—"

"He understood that he could always come here, no matter what he did. If he committed murder, even, or raped a child. I had unconditional love for him. Unconditional love. Money, a place to stay, a place to hide." She added, "It wasn't a one-sided relationship."

Eddie blew across the hot coffee, sipped. There was a hole in the back of his T-shirt. He was used to holes in his clothing, but it bothered him at that moment that she could see through to the skin on his back. He hunched his shoulders and sat back in the chair to casually bunch up the white cloth around the hole.

"I'm sorry your son is dead, Rose," he said softly.

"It's all right," she said. "I killed him. I will have to live with it."

"Now Rose—"

"Every time a child dies young the parent is guilty." Before Eddie could object, Rose quickly added, "Lovers are guilty, too. You'd better watch your back or I'll kill you just like I killed him."

She turned from Eddie. All morning she had been going from floor to floor in the house. The attic, the basement, the boy's old room. Turning things over. Examining old clothes and abandoned possessions. Each time she took something up in her hands she cried out with the anguish of a full Greek chorus. The neighbors heard. The neighbors were meant to hear. This was a mother whose son was dead, his story in the papers, his headless corpse on a slab at the morgue.

Eddie loved Rose with all his heart. He prayed that she'd be able to express her grief completely and then return to being the person she was before. Better for the loss of the horrible son, the drain.

And when everything was settled, when her old self returned, he would have to make it clear that when he died he did not want to be received in the living room.

10.

THE POLICE SO DISTRACTED ELENORA CHESTER THAT SHE HARDLY KNEW what she was saying. They had occupied her home most of the previous evening—only leaving sometime after one in the morning, and here they were again. Asking questions, hour after hour, expecting some vital piece of information to leak out.

Two detectives spoke with her, a man and a woman. The woman asked most of the questions, affecting a sympathetic attitude. Her name was Detective Winters. Her counterpart, a portly black man, took copious notes, even when no one was speaking. He had introduced himself the night before as Detective Carlton Lyons, stressing his Christian name as if saying it was a right he had earned. She rewound and replayed Detective Lyons' introduction to the exclusion of other thoughts, like a song she couldn't stop humming. Detective Carlton Lyons, ma'am. Detective Carlton Lyons, ma'am. Where was her dead husband in all this?

"We can see that you're distraught," said Winters. "Wouldn't you like to call a friend to come and stay with you?"

"My brother is here," she heard herself say. Her voice sounded far away, not belonging to her.

"Oh? Your brother? Where is he?"

Lyons wrote more words in his notebook than people were speaking. He just went on and on. Were the drugs making her say wise, insightful things she couldn't remember saying?

"Your brother, Elenora?" Detective Winters reminded.

"You met him last night. His name is Jeremy. Jeremy Richer, which is my maiden name. Richer. I guess that makes sense."

"Yes, it does. I remember him now. Cute guy. Strong family resemblance. Is he single?"

Detective Carlton Lyons rolled his eyes.

"Single?" A disassociative thought. Single. Married. What strange concepts these seemed under the circumstances. "I believe he is single."

"You believe? Don't you know?" Winters smiled. Nice. Friendly. But it was an act.

"Yes. He is single. Does it matter?"

"I always want to know if guys are single." Winters laughed. "Too many single guys in the world. It's an injustice I intend to correct with at least one of them. Who knows, maybe it will be your brother."

Elenora laughed. She couldn't help it. It was a bit of laughing that got away from her. The drugs again. She couldn't control it.

"I'm not aware of my brother's dating habits," she giggled. "I know he once considered the priesthood." Elenora looked slyly at Detective Winters. The next part she just couldn't stop. The words just rolled out of her. "So of course he's gay as last year's Christmas tree." Elenora shook, laughing so hard that finally she couldn't breathe. Winters helped her to the sofa. When Elenora finally calmed down she started to cry and then just wept in Detective Winter's arms. "I'm so sorry," she said. "I'm so sorry."

"Don't you worry about it, hon."

"My brother was very serious about the priesthood. I didn't mean to make fun of him. He was young then. He went to Vincentian, you know. It's a monastery with a school attached. He was a monk for a while. Robes and everything."

"So you're a practicing Catholic, Mrs. Chester?" asked Winters.

"Yes. My whole family. My husband and all the boys. We attended the 8:30 mass on Sunday mornings without fail."

"A man who goes to church with his family every Sunday. This is a rare thing in today's world, Mrs. Chester. We know your loss is a great one."

Elenora nodded. "I want you to find my husband's killer before he kills some other woman's churchgoing husband." She heard how stupid she sounded. And it wasn't anything she meant. It sounded like something she heard on a hundred TV shows. She felt numb. She didn't care if they caught her husband's killer. She just wanted them to leave.

"I could assign an officer to stay with you until your brother comes back," Winters said. "Does your doctor know what drugs you've taken?"

"I'll be fine. I just need to be alone for a while. There have been people, people all around me ever since this happened and I'm getting claustrophobic. I need some space. Maybe I need to take a nap. A long one."

Detective Carlton Lyons just perceptibly giggled. Elenora caught it and thought, no control, no professionalism. He had obviously not been to acting school. He was not properly prepared. Shouldn't detectives be actors? These two were so transparent.

Winters put her arm around Elenora's shoulders. "Look. You've been through an ordeal. Go easy on yourself. And go easy on the drugs. I know you don't want to hear this, but in the end it's better to feel your pain. You have to feel it, feel it deeply, feel it completely, in order to arrive at a point where you don't feel it anymore. Now." Winters stood. "We're going to leave you in peace, but I want you to know we're going to have to ask more questions at a later date."

"The drugs are just for today. Just…for today."

"We understand. You have my number. If you think of anything, call me. I work out of the Public Safety Building but I'm out in the field a lot. If I'm not in, believe me, someone can find me. Just call."

Elenora nodded. Go. Go away now.

"Where is that cute brother of yours anyway?"

"He went out shopping for me. Today is the day Marsh and I would have gone food shopping."

"You did your food shopping together."

"Yes."

Another detail from their marriage out loose in the world, a matter of public record, recorded in Detective Carlton Lyons' notebook. "We have no food in the house."

"And seven children and who knows what other family members on their way here. I feel for you, Elenora. You hang in there. Call me. Anytime. Four in the morning. Anytime."

Elenora gladly shut the door behind them. No more police, no more interrogation. As if she didn't know what lurked under all that false sympathy. Terrible acting. She wondered how a person acquired morphine. She had heard that morphine could numb almost any painful experience. Elenora felt she needed something extra now. Maybe Jeremy would know how to get morphine. Well. For the time being another Valium would have to do.

She watched the two detectives drive away, past the reporters diligently waiting for her to emerge from the house. Fat chance. She had told the police everything. Except for the ten thousand dollars. Of course, the police already knew about the insurance policies. There was nothing she could do about that. Marsh had arranged for those behind her back.

But the ten thousand dollars. She'd like to keep that bit of information private.

Elenora walked over to the rosewood table in the corner of the living room. It held a collection of framed family photos. Many of the photos featured Marsh and the boys. One pictured the family fishing off a boat in Lake Erie. In another the boys posed together with their father at a track meet. Who took that photo? She had forgotten. In a third one, taken at the

Fox Chapel Yacht Club on their twentieth wedding anniversary, she and Marsh posed beside a two-tiered cake, smiling into the camera. They were still happy then.

Oh, and this one. The last staff picnic. Marshall eating barbeque. Taken maybe half an hour before Greta's heart attack. An odd picture to frame. Who wanted to remember a day filled with such tragedy? Penny English had taken that photo. No, no, it had been Larry Cone, Penny's leather clad boyfriend. Such a strange woman.

She never understood how Penny and Marsh had become such good friends. Perhaps he had needed a strong ally at work. Penny must have fulfilled some part of him that a mere wife with no academic pursuits could fulfill. And there was that dreadful Greta Fields and her woman friend Jane. The two women were lovers. Well, it was obvious. Greta was a flannel and blue jeans lesbian even when she dressed nicely for school events. Jane seemed nice. Yes, she remembered having quite a nice conversation with Jane. But that Greta Fields was a witch. A person like that should never have been permitted to be an administrator. No one that callous should have dominion over hard won careers. It had been such a relief when Greta died.

Well, Greta was fat. Extremely fat. She ate noting but cupcakes and potato chips at the picnic. And fatty meats. Elenora had a picture in her mind of Greta seizing a small slice of cheesecake, shoving it whole in her mouth in front of the teachers who hated her so much. Showing off for them. But showing off what? That she was addicted to fatty foods? What was the point of that? What were the teachers supposed to think? Elenora remembered having an evil thought about Greta at that moment. She had thought to herself, *Go ahead and eat that. Shove it all in. I hope the fat from that cake goes straight to your heart and kills you.*

That was the first time Elenora had ever wished another human being dead. That she could remember. And Greta Fields did die! She died of a heart attack not long after eating that cheesecake. From that point on it wasn't so difficult for Elenora to wish someone dead. She saw how it could solve problems. One day she found herself wishing that Vernon Roman would die. She pictured a horrible death for him. And he did die. A truly horrible death.

When she thought about her life and about all she gave up for Marsh, her career in the theater sacrificed to create and raise a family, she sometimes wished Marsh dead. She did. Not run through with a sword. But some, more quiet way. It was a dangerous thing, wishing people dead. She had wished three people dead and they had all died.

She would have to focus now. Get back to the theater. Resume her training as an actress. There would be money for classes once the insurance came through. Half a million dollars would provide quite an excellent training. Maybe even New York. Maybe even the Actors Studio. She could settle a stipend on Jeremy; he could stay here in this house and raise the children. Why not? He'd probably like that. Oh, she didn't know. What on earth would she do with her life now?

Had she killed her husband of twenty-six years? Had she killed Vernon Roman? She had wanted them dead. She wished them dead. Only through their death could she be reborn.

Her head ached. She was so tired of thinking. She just couldn't stop thinking. Detective Winters had asked her where she was during the exact time her husband was being slaughtered in Shadyside. She told Detective Winters she had been at home. Her brother corroborated her story. But she couldn't really remember being at home. Her life was so boring, so empty, so filled with day-to-day work that she just couldn't remember the details. Her life was one long flat plane of housework and childcare and television shows and rented movies. She didn't always remember the specific details of specific days. Her memory had been shot through with Novocain. Or Valium.

She couldn't remember anything at all.

11.

Jeff and Xander parked across the street from the crime scene. The sun cast an eerie iridescence over the Wendy's parking lot, the yellow police barrier, the gawkers along the perimeter. Xander noticed two young boys, roughly his own age, exploring the grounds of St. Stephen's church.

"They're looking for the head," Xander ventured. "Wouldn't it be great to find the head?"

"They won't find the head," Jeff said, certain of it. "Not around here. Our samurai took it with him. There is a reason why the head is missing. Two centuries ago Native Americans took the scalps of English colonists in order to collect payment from the French. They were paid by the scalp. If this is a professional killing, our samurai might need the head to collect his fee."

Jeff and Xander joined the gawkers at the edge of the yellow police barriers. From there they could see the chalk outlines of the fallen victims. One featured a straight line at the neck. "Looks like Roman was a short guy," Jeff surmised. "Maybe five-seven."

Chester's six-foot-plus outline appeared armless, indicating that he had clutched his wound as he fell forward. "He wore a heavy coat," said Jeff. "Even so he was about forty pounds overweight."

"Does that matter?"

"It confirms our hypothesis. Roman's outline: short and lean. Chester's outline: tall, overweight. Probably led a sedentary existence. A steady diet of eggs and sausage, the occasional Danish in the teacher's lounge, fatty comfort foods for dinner. The two men are a study in contrasts."

Jeff noticed two police officers in an automobile taking notes. He put his hand on Xander's shoulder and directed him toward the restaurant.

"Let's get something to eat," he said.

"But I thought we were—"

"We're being watched," Jeff said quietly. "Killers often return to the scene of their crime to soak up the reactions of other people. The police are taking notes on visitors."

It was a brisk lunch crowd for a Sunday afternoon. Jennifer Hafney, the official eyewitness quoted in the paper, held court near one of the waste stations. She was a pretty girl who infused her story with a sparkle that kept it fresh despite repeated telling.

Jeff and Xander eavesdropped during the ordering process and then took a seat within earshot.

"The one guy, the short one, he came in here a lot," Jennifer said. "I think he lived around here. That was the guy who got his head chopped off. I've been working here for almost two years now and you get to recognize some of the regulars. The other guy, though, I'd never seen him before. The police asked me to look up real close—which was gross—but no, him I never saw before."

An older woman with a too perfectly sculpted wig asked, "What was the regular guy like?"

"Um, he was a bit on the sleazy side. Sometimes he dressed like he was real poor or homeless or something. He didn't smell, though, like they sometimes do. He ate everything biggie. Big Classic and biggie fries and large frosty. Like, eight little cups of ketchup. He never put his garbage away, so I know."

A snowy haired man with pink skin said, "You witnessed a serious crime. Aren't you afraid to come to work? What if the samurai comes after you?"

"My dad and my boyfriend drive me to work and pick me up after my shift. My dad has a gun. He's an ex-Marine. He won't freeze with fear like this Chester guy did. The samurai would be stupid to come after me."

Jennifer excused herself to bus a few tables. A statuesque African American woman near the dirty tables asked, "Was the samurai black or white?"

"I couldn't tell," Jennifer replied. "His face was painted with thick white make-up. The eyebrows looked glued on. I couldn't tell what race he was. He might even have been Japanese."

Xander spoke up. "What happened to the head? Did you see where it rolled?"

"Like I told the police, it literally flew off the guy's neck. It rolled pretty far toward the parking lot entrance. But I didn't see where it stopped. We were yelling at the window to get the other guy inside the building. I can tell you the police were here lickity-split and they didn't find the head. They looked in all the nearby stairwells, inside dumpsters. They searched for hours."

The restaurant manager signaled for Jennifer to come speak with him. He whispered something to her; she turned a little red in the face and nodded. It looked to Jeff like he had told her to tone it down. Jennifer returned to work. As she passed Jeff and Xander's table, Jeff asked quietly, "How fast did the samurai run?"

Under her breath, just to Jeff, Jennifer replied, "Like a forest creature. He didn't look back. You could have blinked and missed his escape. Some nun who happened to be walking past St. Stephen's spotted him running down Liberty Avenue and then poof, he disappeared. 'Like magic,' she said." Leaning close into Jeff's ear, she added, "He must have had a ready made place to hide. Don't you think? He might be into some mysterious cult or something but, let's face it, nobody disappears like magic."

12.

OUTSIDE, JEFF AND XANDER PEERED OVER THE YELLOW CRIME STRIPS ONCE again at the crime scene. Spots of blood lining up like a Hansel and Gretel trail ended at the edge of the parking lot in a splattered ball.

"The final resting spot," Jeff surmised. "No other blood indications. The samurai meant to take the head with him. Probably had a plastic Ziploc bag tucked in his costume for that purpose."

"Or a lettuce crisper," said Xander.

A police detective strolled toward the crime scene. Jeff gently laid his hand on Xander's shoulder.

"I want to see St. Stephen's church," said Xander.

"It's probably locked up. Inner city church, plus all this excitement."

"We can try. I've never seen a real city church. It's over a hundred years old. Come on, I want to see it. Just because some priest pinched your bum when you were an altar boy!"

"For your information no priest ever pinched by bum or any other part of me. And I was never an altar boy. The police are looking. Let's start walking. Here, take my hand."

"Eleven-year-old boys don't hold their father's hand," Xander informed Jeff. "Boy, what you don't know about child rearing."

Xander, walking five feet ahead of Jeff like a real eleven-year-old son, reached the fifteen-foot tall double doors of the old sandstone church first.

"You know what?" he said.

"What?"

"Maybe the nun will be in here. The paper said she was on her way to church. Maybe she was on her way to this church. It's the closest Catholic church. Maybe there will be other people we can interview."

"Discreetly," Jeff warned. "We're not really investigating anything.

Officially we're gawkers like the rest of the people here today."

Xander hung on the giant door handle, pulled and pulled, but could not budge the massive doors. Jeff then added his considerable strength to the mix and eventually coaxed a clang and a squeal from the ancient mechanics. The great door finally swung open. It clanged and banged. These clangs and bangs echoed and amplified within the great hall of the hundred-year-old church.

Not unlike the doors to haunted mansions in Vincent Price films, Dear Reader. Very apropos because Jeff, you see, is squeamish on the subject of the church, particularly the Catholic church. Something happened, something Dreadful, possibly even Wicked, in a church. Or perhaps several churches. It might have been one particular event on one particular day or perhaps a series of events that took place over a period of time. Jeff can be annoyingly secretive when he wants to be. Hence Xander's little fishing expedition regarding the possible indiscreet pinching of the tempting Redwing posterior by those naughty, naughty men of the collar.

No, the priests of Jeff's youth did not bother much with him one way or the other. In fact I can safely say that Jeff is one of the very few adults in this world who does not seem to have been sexually abused as a child—not even by other children. A government psychologist hypnotized Jeff at one point and encouraged a confession of repressed wounds suffered at the hands of nasty aunts or uncles. Nothing. Not even a hand lingering a little long on his pre-pubescent shoulder. The aunts and uncles were all rather nice to him. They gave him, to the chagrin of the government doctors, the most un-Freudian presents. Chemistry sets and books and such. Boring, boring.

By the way, those government psychologists are very nosy people. They uncovered during one of their sessions that Jeff only discovered masturbation at the age of fifteen and then only by accident. Well, he says it was an accident. Who can say really. But fifteen is rather late, wouldn't you agree? And he reached puberty a little ahead of the other boys in his class. All of which is to say we can't blame the indiscretion of the professionally celibate for the dread fear Jeff feels when walking through the doors of the church that burned Joan of Arc at the stake and stretched poor Galileo on the rack. It wasn't sex that put him off. That's all that I can say for sure.

The great sinewy spires of St. Stephen's—its wrought iron hands reaching to heaven, brought on a hot flash or two for our man Jeff. Xander was awed by it all. Life-sized hand carved Stations of the Cross lined the sides of the hall leading to the altar. Martyrs bleeding, stuck through with swords, tortured, beheaded.

"The rich went to this church," Jeff said quietly. "The robber barons who stole the spirit of their workers and spun it into gold. They came faithfully every Sunday. I'm sure they were comforted in their greed just like they are today.

They heard from the pulpit that God would provide for their workers in heaven. Their immortal souls did not belong to this world, only the next. Not to worry. Keep that steel coming, along with your generous donations."

"Where are the worshipers?" asked Xander. "I thought there would be people in the pews praying or maybe people attending a service."

"It's Saturday. There will probably be a mass this evening. Remember, this is a city church. The rich people are certainly gone. There might not be much of a congregation left. A lot of churches don't leave their doors open. So many have been vandalized. The priest might be in his office or maybe next door listening to Jennifer tell gruesome tales."

Jeff peered into the row of confessionals. Four confessionals, so there must have been quite a large congregation at one time. Three of these had been converted to storage units, open-faced closets jammed full of crates, magazines, fabric, and church bric-a-brac. Jeff hadn't been inside a confessional since he was a child. Xander's age, maybe younger. He didn't believe in it any longer. Didn't believe in it then, really, but went along for the sake of his mother. In matters of spirit he followed more closely the way of his father's people. He felt now that he was entitled to keep his secrets.

"Teach me how this works," said Xander, popping into one of the booths.

"I don't think that's a good idea," Jeff said. "This isn't my religion any longer, but it's still sacred to other people. It would be sacrilegious to pretend."

"C'mon," Xander teased. "A god who doesn't exist can't punish you for playing with his toys."

"Little lawyer."

"Some nun made a grab for you. This is why you hate the Catholic church and it explains why you're celibate."

Jeff shook his head, thinking *This child, this child.* "Where do you read stuff like this? First of all, I don't hate the Catholic church, I'm just a little uncomfortable in this environment. Secondly, who says I'm celibate?"

"Name the last time you had sex."

"That's an adult matter. Not for little boys. You are not entitled to know everything about me, you know. Celibacy is a philosophy, a way of life, a path. Priests, at least in theory, choose this path as part of their commitment to the service of God. I, on the other hand, am merely between men."

"Evasion," Xander teased.

"Hey," said Jeff, "I was smarter than you when I was your age and I've gotten one year smarter each year since. Don't analyze me."

"Okay. But teach me about confession. Just once. Big Brother education stuff."

Jeff looked around the church. The last thing he wanted was a confrontation with a priest. Or worse, a nun. He slid slowly into the side of the confessional opposite Xander. "First you say Bless me Father for I have sinned. And I say, How long has it been since your last confession. And you say—."

"This is my first. Now, what kinds of things do I confess?"

"You're a little young for impure thoughts," mused Jeff.

"Don't count on it."

"Let's start with honoring your father and your mother. Have you dishonored either your father or mother lately?"

"Well," started Xander. "I dishonor my father all the time. He ran away from our family when I was a little kid. He left us poor. And I don't have a father around to help me out with stuff. I like having you, but I'd also like my father to be at home. So I am angry with him and I hate him sometimes."

"What about your mother?"

"I try not to dishonor her. Well, wait. If I'm being honest. Sometimes I dishonor her by thinking I'm smarter than she is."

"Whoa," said Jeff. "Excellent insight."

"Would a priest say that?"

"Not really, but continue."

Xander fiddled around with something—Jeff couldn't see what. "Excuse me Jeff," he said. "I'll be back in a minute."

"What do you mean you'll be back in a minute? Where are you going?"

An adult man entered the confessional and crossed himself saying, "Forgive me Father for I have sinned."

"I'm sorry," Jeff said. "This confessional is occupied."

"I'm sorry Father," the man said quickly. Jeff thought he smelled alcohol on the man's breath. "This little boy, what has he got to confess? In his little life so far? Father, I want to kill myself. I want to take my own life. I have got to talk to you now."

"I don't think—"

"I have done something so wrong, so vile, I stand in disgrace in the eyes of God. First, I should let you know it's been seven years since my last confession."

"Seven years," Jeff echoed.

"Unlike the little boy, I have had impure thoughts. Thousands and thousands of them."

"Well, it's been seven years."

He heard Xander giggle.

"And I've committed many impure deeds. But none as terrible as last night."

At this point Jeff was intrigued. "What, may I ask, did you do?"

"I put on a false face, Father. In my recent past there is unspeakable evil. Bloodshed. Murder."

THE KILLER OF ORCHIDS | 49

"Murder?"

"Yes." The man leaned into the grate. The man was quite handsome, really, with a five o'clock shadow and perfect white teeth. But then Jeff had to remind himself: the guy is a murderer, not date potential. The man continued, "And I've been lying to you, Father. Lying to you and this whole congregation."

"You've been lying?" Jeff leaned in further to hear.

"Because, you see," the man dropped his voice to a whisper, "I've been pretending to be a member of this congregation when in fact—."

"Yes?"

"I'm the priest who runs the whole shebang."

Jeff scrambled out of the confessional.

"Gotcha," said the priest.

"Damn," said Jeff. "I knew I'd get caught."

"Perhaps bloodshed and murder are a little strong," the priest said, extending his hand. "Father Landus, by the way. I heard your little spiel about the rich. They were definitely before my time. But we were, I confess, a little cruel during the Inquisition. A little bloodshed and murder there in our past. And we haven't been all that good to the Jews for a couple of thousand years now. But that's all over. We've officially apologized for that. Perhaps you heard the Pope's speech."

"I did," said Jeff. "It would have had so much more impact if he had said, 'And we've learned from our past, so we're not going to commit the same crimes against gay people.'"

"Ouch. Yes, well. And you are?"

"Jeffrey Redwing. This is my son, Alex."

"Xander," he said, shaking the priest's hand. "You look awfully young."

"I am awfully young, thank you for noticing," said the priest, smiling. "This is my first church. I replaced Father Lowrie, whom you may or may not know had been the priest here since his ordination twenty years ago. He died just recently."

"Oh?" asked Jeff.

"AIDS. Very sad. Blood transfusion, they say." The priest looked down and away.

"We're actually here looking for clues to the murder next door," said Xander.

Jeff shot Xander a dirty look. "Not actually looking in earnest." Jeff hastened to say. "Just idle curiosity. We happened to be in the neighborhood. It's my weekend with the kid."

Xander stuck his tongue out at Jeff when the priest wasn't looking.

"You haven't divorced, I hope."

"No, but we are separated."

"That's too bad," intoned Father Landus. "You know, counseling is my specialty. I'd be happy to make an appointment to see you and your wife."

"I'm afraid that's not feasible, Father."

"Don't you owe it to someone?" Father Landus nodded toward Xander.

"Yes, Dad," said Xander. "Make an appointment. For me? Please?"

"Father," said Jeff, changing the subject, "perhaps you could tell us something about what happened next door. Did you see anything?"

"I'm afraid I didn't. I shall have to address it with the congregation tomorrow. Vernon Roman was a member of this church."

Jeff was surprised to hear that.

"Was he really?"

"Started coming regularly four or five years ago. He was a special case to Father Lowrie. Mr. Roman expressed no affinity or interest in me after Father Lowrie died. He was a troubled man but secretive. Sat by himself. He lived near here, you know."

"No, I didn't know that," said Jeff.

"What about the Sister mentioned in the newspaper?" asked Xander. "She's the only one who got a good look at the samurai."

"Yes, the police asked me quite a few questions about the illusive Sister. So far as I can tell, she's not from this area. She's not associated with this church, that much I can say for sure. There are so many churches. The diocese doesn't seem to know who she is. She might simply have been in town visiting family."

They chitchatted a bit more. Xander feigned restlessness. Jeff used this as an excuse to take their leave.

Father Landus called after him, "The offer of counseling still stands. Let's not forget about the boy."

13.

"You should seek professional help for your problem," Xander said in the car. "That priest felt sad for you."

"That priest was irreverent," Jeff replied. "I think he was making fun of the Pope's apology."

"Maybe he noticed the same irony in it you did."

"You love that word, don't you," Jeff teased. "Irony."

"I used it correctly, didn't I?"

"That you did. Now. Shall we call it quits for today or would you like to see if we can find Woodlawn Road. We know now that Roman walked to church, so it must be in this vicinity."

Xander pulled out a well-worn AAA map. There was no listing for Woodlawn Road in the index. It was probably very small or might even be an alley. Jeff pulled up along side a pedestrian, an Indian woman. Xander asked for directions.

The woman placed her hands over her cleavage as she leaned down to speak with Xander. "I am not certain mind you, but I think it is the little road that winds beside the Athletic Hospital."

"The Athletic Hospital?"

"Yes. First there is Lebanese restaurant Khalil's, yes? Then a dealer in fancy sports cars, then the road, the—um—sports clinic. Yes? Owned by the University. A sports clinic. That's what they call it. But the road comes first. At least, I think that is the road."

"Thank you."

"Good luck to you." The Indian woman waved goodbye to Xander as they drove off.

Xander said, "I think I really like the city, Jeff. The only part of it I get to see is the library and the museums and symphony and the sports stadiums.

I like this other part where the people are."

Jeff drove past Khalil's (made a mental note to take Xander there and introduce him to Middle Eastern food). "There is more to it than nice people from foreign lands. I have a feeling you'll get to see the seedier side of it as soon as we locate Roman's road."

Just after the Alfa Romeo dealer they came to a road/alley. Just past it stood a nondescript brick building, probably a former warehouse, recently reinvented as a sports clinic. No street sign. He maneuvered past three dumpsters and a shattered pallet, then hit a clearing. Here the road wound snake-like through wooded hills spotted with decaying warehouses and rusted storage sheds. Graffiti covered every building surface.

Down the road a little further they spotted houses. Curious, Jeff thought. The highway with its fast lanes and billboards hovered just one hillside above them, barely audible. Here old two-story wooden houses aged and rotted in park-like quiet, sliding slowly downward along with the rocks and the dirt and the trees. Darkly weathered telephone poles, probably cut from primeval forest, bore lines that drooped a little too low for public safety. Here, indeed, was a good place to hide.

"What do we do now?" asked Xander.

"We'll park and walk," said Jeff. "And look for Roman's name on a mailbox. The houses are all close to the street, so we'll be able to read without trespassing."

No people walked the street—or cats or dogs or even birds. The place had an eerie science fiction feel to it, like a virus had come through and put all the living creatures to sleep. Xander spotted it first: two iron mailboxes, one with a piece of paper taped to it that read "V. Roman."

The wooden porch gave timorously beneath their feet as if the deck might disintegrate into dust before they reached the door. Through an open window Jeff and Xander heard the sound of a television game show blasting at the decibel level of a jet engine. They pushed the doorbell button repeatedly but could not tell if it actually rang inside. Jeff banged on the door a bit. When that didn't work they both yelled "hello" into the open window.

"Hold your horses," came a crusty female voice from inside. "I was in the bathroom. Let me get my pants up."

A short, quite enormously round woman opened the door. She wore a tent sized black and gold Steelers T-shirt which billowed out over a pair of grand, aged breasts. Jeff and Xander couldn't help but look at the recently referenced pants, luminescent polyester green.

"*Wheel of Fortune* is on," she said as if no person in their right mind would visit at such a time. "It's on Saturday afternoon now. Repeats. But what the hell. It's not like I remember those people."

"I'm so sorry to bother you," Jeff said in a solemn tone. "I'm Jeffrey Roman. Vernon's cousin."

"Wait, I can't hear." The woman turned up her hearing aid. "Okay. Who the hell are you honey?"

"I'm Vernon Roman's cousin. I believe he lived here."

"C'mon in."

The woman waddled back into her apartment. She reduced the volume on the television.

"Sorry," she said. "I don't like to wear out the batteries on my hearing aid so I blast the television. I'm Bertha Moore. I was Vernon's landlady."

"I see. I'm Jeffrey Roman. This is my son Xander."

"How do you do, ma'am?" Xander bowed his head just slightly, a picture of politeness in sorrow.

"What a nice looking boy," Bertha commented. "Doesn't look much like you, though. Must take after his mother."

"Actually, Xander is my stepson."

Bertha nodded. She waited.

Jeff asked, "Have the police been by to see you?"

"Heaven's yes. The police and every reporter in the 'burgh. Did a live feed this morning for Channel 4 Action News. Not bad for an old broad." Bertha smiled, then caught herself. "It's a shame what happened to him though. A shame."

Jeff nodded. "I don't suppose there was much you could tell them."

"What could I say? He was a good tenant. Quiet. Paid his rent the first of the month without fail. Never had to fix a thing the whole time he lived here. I certainly couldn't tell them about the other stuff."

Jeff shook his head as if he understood. "Certainly not."

"It would kill his mother for one thing. Poor woman. Rose Roman loved that boy like he was the only child ever brought into the world. She cried to me. Her poor baby. They have his head. Someone has his head. They have to have a closed casket because there is no head, just a neck. She insisted on seeing it. Well, she had to identify the body. She and the girlfriend."

Bertha rolled her eyes at the mention of the girlfriend.

"We haven't met her yet," Jeff said. "I imagine we'll meet her at the funeral."

"Just you wait." Bertha touched his arm. "Hey, I'm an open-minded woman. I've always said, in this world you've got to do what works for you. And Vernon loved her. Fawned on her. Powder puffed her fanny left and right. Which was strange to see because Vernon was a tough butch of a man." She took hold of Jeff's forearm, gave his muscles a little feel. "She's a doosey, this girlfriend. Dottie's her name. She'll keep you entertained. She's better than television."

Xander shifted from foot to foot. The house creaked.

Bertha let go of Jeff's arm. "So. Is there something I can do for you gentlemen?"

"Aunt Rose asked if we would come over and select something from Vernon's wardrobe. Something nice. A good suit he could be buried in."

Bertha looked at him as if he had just materialized through the back door of a time warp.

"I looked through everything with that husband of hers," she said. "I haven't found anything new."

"I know. I'm embarrassed to trouble you in this way. They asked me to look again."

"Incredible."

"She's distraught."

Bertha folded her arms across the word "Steelers" on her jersey.

"Well, you can look. Can't shoot you for looking. You won't find anything. Wait here, I'll get the key."

Bertha waddled into the kitchen, took a jar down from a shelf, and extracted a set of keys. She led Jeff and Xander down a hallway to a set of wooden stairs with a worn carpeted runner down the center.

"It's not easy for me to climb these stairs. You'll have to be patient."

"I hate to make you go through this," Jeff said. "I could just take the key and look around the apartment myself."

"Believe me, I'd like nothing better." With great effort Bertha lifted one foot onto the first step and then pulled up the other. "But I promised the detective who was here this morning that I wouldn't let anyone into the apartment, even family members, unless I was present."

"Really? What's up there that's so important?" Jeff asked.

"Nothing that I can see. That's the odd thing. The apartment is practically bare. What's there doesn't make any sense." Bertha accomplished another step. "He was a peculiar boy. And the girlfriend! Extra peculiar. I suppose it makes sense that a peculiar boy with a peculiar girlfriend would have peculiar possessions."

Xander asked, "Did the police take anything?"

"Nothing of importance. There was nothing of importance to take. You'll see."

At the top of the steps Bertha paused for a moment to take in air.

"If you tell me I should lose weight, I'll kill you," she said. "I've been fat all my life and I intend to die fat."

She put a key into the lock of an old, dark walnut door and turned the facetted glass handle.

Before Bertha could object, Jeff and Xander scattered to the various rooms of the apartment. A modest place. Big living room, small bedroom, no kitchen. Nice old woodwork throughout. Vast black and white tiled bathroom. A few water stains here and there on the ceilings. Sad old wallpaper featuring lilacs and cherubs. They both looked through closets and drawers. They found abandoned wire hangers in the closets and orange newspaper lined drawers, but no clothes whatsoever.

"Mrs. Moore, " Jeff started, "are you sure the police didn't take anything? There doesn't appear to be any clothes at all. Not much in the way of toiletries. No personal possessions other than the furniture. I mean, no television for instance. Not even a transistor radio."

"Peculiar, like I said."

Jeff didn't comment on the quality or condition of the Salvation Army furniture. You never know, the apartment might have come furnished and he didn't want to insult Bertha. There were a few Art Deco pieces in the living room. A large, oval throw rug in the center, quite worn, in which stylized silver wolfhounds chased about madly within the confines of purple thunderbolt clouds. On this rug rested a Deco sofa so long and wide one wondered how the movers got it through the door.

There was one piece of furniture that looked like it was still in good condition and might actually be valuable: an Edwardian armoire made of cherry or perhaps mahogany. Twin paneled doors in the center of the armoire held small brass keys. Jeff turned the key of the door on the right and opened it. Inside he saw four wooden shelves. Each shelf held eight to ten exceptionally large glass jars.

"What kind of jars are these?" Xander asked.

"Pickling jars," answered Mrs. Moore. "Real pickling jars. The kind people of my mother's generation used to put up large stubby pickles."

Jeff stared at Mrs. Moore. "How—"

"Peculiar. Yes."

Jeff opened the door on the left. A metal rod stretched across the top. Nothing hung from it. No clothes hangers. No clothes.

"The police took what they found on that side," Bertha offered. "Evidence, they said. Odd sorts of things. Nothing you could be buried in."

"What sorts of things?" Jeff asked.

"Costumes I guess you would call them. Strange things. Exotic. Women's costumes as well as men's. The women's costumes were all one size: size twelve. Don't know if the police noticed that, but I did. The men's costumes came in different sizes."

"Really!"

"Oh, yes. Beautiful gowns with chiffon and sequins. Fantasy gowns like you see women wear on *The Love Boat*. Halston designed one of them. The rest had Italian labels I didn't recognize."

"What were the men's costumes like?" Jeff asked.

"Things you'd wear on Halloween. A policeman's uniform, a baseball uniform, a tiger outfit—you know, fur with stripes and a tail."

"No kidding."

"Looks like he robbed a theater supply store. There was more. A pirate costume, a veiled kind of thing Scheherazade might have worn, Queen Elizabeth stuff with lace cuffs. A nun's outfit—only white like Sally Field wore in *The Flying Nun*. Big hat and all."

Jeff stared at the empty side of the armoire. If furniture could talk.

"I don't suppose they found a samurai costume?" Jeff asked.

"No. They looked for one, believe me. They took all the costumes to show to eyewitnesses. You never know. One person's samurai might be another person's Scheherazade."

Jeff and Xander hovered around the armoire. They examined it, caressed it, tapped on it. "What about underwear, Mrs. Moore?" asked Jeff. "Any normal clothes at all?"

"Some women's underwear. Pretty things. Silk in vibrant colors like orange, purple, apple red. No shoes either. Just Scheherazade's slippers."

Jeff turned abruptly to the landlady.

"Obviously there are no clothes in which to bury my cousin. I guess we'll have to get him a suit at Macy's."

"Bury him in his leather jacket," suggested Mrs. Moore. "He wore it night and day. Probably wore it to bed." 'Of course,' she thought to herself, 'it might be covered in blood.'

They proceeded slowly down the steps together.

"My aunt doesn't know his size," Jeff said. "Do you think his girlfriend might?"

"I'm sure she would. She'd be a good one to ask."

"What was her name again, Mrs. Moore?"

"Dottie. Tall like Lauren Bacall. Big feet. More than that I couldn't tell you. Never heard a last name. No idea where she lived, although I got the impression it wasn't far from here. Your aunt would know."

———

It was just about Xander's dinner time.

On the drive home they had a hot discussion about what they had learned.

"It's clear," Jeff noted, "that Roman used that apartment as an address to collect welfare checks. His real residence was somewhere else. I'm going to guess that Vernon Roman was either kept by this Dottie person or, more likely, he was gainfully employed in a sub-legal line of work."

Xander chimed in, "The samurai costume is probably the mate to the Scheherazade costume. It was probably more of an Aladdin's costume. Don't you think?

"The sword might have been part of that costume."

"I don't know. Very sharp sword for a Halloween or even a theater costume."

The bigger puzzle: why did Roman have all of those costumes in the armoire in the first place? Why just the costumes and no other clothing? And then there was the question of the oversized pickling jars.

Time to rest, thought Jeff. Time to eat. The puzzle-solving part of his brain would work on these questions while he himself relaxed in the warm comfort of Mrs. Pooka's kitchen.

14.

THE ARCHITECTS WHO DESIGNED XANDER'S PLAN, FALLING ACORN—VERY Haiku, really, created six distinct designs: a modest Queen Anne, a modest Victorian, a modest Ski Cottage, a modest Ranch, a modest Bungalow, and a modest (if you will) Bavarian Lodge. To Jeff the houses looked all alike. In the early days of Jeff's association with the Pooka family he lost so much time trying to locate Sally Pooka's modest Ski Cottage that he decided to place a marker on the lawn. He thought it quite clever: a white stone hand, reaching out from the surface of their lawn, with an index finger that pointed mindfully toward the Pooka's front door.

The hand annoyed Mrs. Pooka's neighbors. They argued it kitsched-up and otherwise devalued an upscale suburban plan. And besides, the kids couldn't resist slipping condoms over the eight inch pointing digit. Sally did broach the subject with Jeff.

"This neighborhood can't possibly be kitsched-up," Jeff replied. "It's pure kitsch to begin with. If you miniaturized the houses you could put them under a Christmas tree and drive toy trains through them. It's the only way I can find this particular house. Tell them to piss off."

"He can't find the house without it," Sally explained to the neighbors. "What am I supposed to do?"

"Tell him to memorize the street address."

"He's a genius. He can't memorize street addresses. It's the Einstein thing. Or something."

Every excuse Sally offered on Jeff's behalf seemed feeble, even to her. Ultimately she declared, "He's important to my child. The hand stays."

Guided by the magic white hand on that unseasonably warm day in December, Jeff once again navigated successfully into the Pooka driveway. On days when Jeff took Xander, it was understood he stayed for dinner.

"What's for dinner, Mom?" Jeff called as he and Xander entered in house.

Mrs. Pooka stood in the kitchen doorway, dishtowel in hand, attitude on face.

"Just a little warning," she said. "The next time I don't get a phone call with an estimated time of arrival, I make hot dogs with canned chili in the microwave. Xander, get upstairs and wash you hands."

"Yes, ma'am."

Xander took the steps two at a time. Jeff offered his hands for examination.

"Looks like you've been playing in cadaver dust," Sally pronounced.

Jeff sulked his way into the guest bathroom. His left the door open so he could continue to talk.

"Cadaver dust? Isn't that a little extreme?"

"We had a crematorium in my neighborhood when I was a kid," she explained. "They had an ash pile out back so naturally we thought this was the dust left over from the burning of dead people. We called it cadaver dust. If someone got particularly dirty they'd be accused of rolling around in cadaver dust."

"How morbid." Jeff turned off the water and shook his hands a few times over the bowl of the sink. "So, Pooka. You had an interesting childhood after all."

"Hey buster!"

Without thinking she snapped the dishtowel on his rear end. Jeff's mouth fell open. For a moment they stared at each other. Xander's mother wondered if she hadn't stepped over the formal line in their relationship.

"You snapped my butt," he said incredulously.

"It's a big target."

He laughed. "Oh yeah?"

"I'm surprised you fit through doors with an ass like that."

On a table in the hallway Jeff found a copy of Saturday's *New York Times*. Snatching it up, he slowly, dramatically rolled it into a tight paper pipe. Mrs. Pooka stepped back with each roll of the paper.

"It's the *New York Times*," he said.

"I know. We subscribe."

"All the news that's fit to print."

"So I hear."

"Bet it leaves a hell of a butt mark."

Sally screamed and ran through the hall into the kitchen. Jeff swung the paper at her with devilish glee. Sally avoided the mighty sting of the *New York Times* by pushing her butt out ahead of the rest of her body. Jeff missed but persisted, chasing her through every room on the first floor. Screaming half with joy and half with fright, Sally ran outside into the yard. Quite fleet of foot, Sally managed to outmaneuver him as she dashed from picnic table to barbeque grill, past the basketball hoop and back into the house. There she made her mistake. She dashed into the guest bathroom, closed the door behind her and locked it.

Catching up with her on the other side of the door Jeff laughed the soft but wicked laugh of certain vengeance.

"You're trapped," he said.

"I'm not coming out."

"I'm afraid you'll have to come out. Your dinner will burn. In fact, it's smelling a little crisp already."

"It's sauerkraut and dumplings," she said optimistically, knowing it was one of Jeff's favorites.

"Smells more like burnt sauerkraut and dumplings to me."

He tapped the door ever so gently with the newspaper. Sally pictured the gas burners on the stove. How high had she left them? She couldn't remember. She yelled up toward the ceiling, "Xander! Come help your mother!"

"He can't hear you." Jeff laughed. "Anyway, he might take my side. Ever think of that?"

The gall of this interloper! "You're not a very nice man," she said.

"I can be persuaded to be a nice man."

Oh, if only he'd demand sex, she thought. That was the real reason she had snapped his butt with the towel. She wanted to lay her hand on it, but didn't dare.

"Okay. What do I have to do?"

"Unlock the door," he replied. "Come out slowly."

"I can't. I don't trust you."

"You'll have to trust me. That's the main thing you'll have to do."

"Can't trust computer geeks," she said. "Everyone knows that. You people are all about practical jokes and tricks."

"Really, Sally, that stereotype is beneath you."

Sally edged out from behind the door.

"I'm sorry I snapped your butt with the towel. But it was only a little tea towel. Nonetheless, I am sorry."

"You should be," Jeff said. "For all you know I might also have been traumatized by butt smacks at an early age."

"It was done in a moment of weakness."

"Apology accepted. Safe passage. No kidding."

Sally walked cautiously ahead of him toward the kitchen. After a few steps Sally turned quickly around and pointed a finger at him. Jeff put his hands up in the air. At that point Xander came down the steps. He stopped for a moment to observe the strange pantomime being enacted by his two favorite adults. Jeff grinned sheepishly.

Sally turned around. Jeff smacked her butt with the paper.

"You hit my mother with the paper," Xander said, surprised.

"She hit me first."

Sally didn't run. She power walked into the kitchen. She banged every pot and every utensil harder, much harder, than culinary expertise required. Jeff edged into the kitchen.

"Can I set the table?" he asked, all amends.

She turned on him. "You swore!"

"I promised. A promise carries less weight."

"Obviously."

Sally vigorously stirred the pot of sauerkraut as if stirring cement.

"Oh, come on," Jeff said. "It was just a little butt smack. I didn't do it hard. And you did it to me."

She waved the krauted spoon at him. She started to say one thing, then couldn't. Started to say another thing, but sputtered. Finally she blurted out, "I hated high school! All right? I hated high school. Everyone did better than me."

"I," Xander corrected.

Sally gave her son the stink eye. "They made fun of me. I didn't have a date to the prom. My cousin took me."

Xander took the *New York Times* from Jeff's hand. He sat at the small kitchen table, unrolled the paper, and started to read. He had heard this story perhaps too many times.

"I was just having fun with you," Jeff softened his tone. "Here you've been working on this meal all day. I thought you might find it amusing."

Mrs. Pooka snatched plates from the cabinets above the sink. She power walked into the dining room, plunked the plates down hard, then returned to dramatically position the flatware.

"Xander," she said, collecting her dignity. "I made dumplings for you."

"Thanks, Mom."

"Come on now," Jeff said. "Don't be angry with me. You know I can't help it." He lowered his voice and leaned into her ear. "You know how I am."

She stopped and faced him. "I don't know. How are you?"

"You know."

"I don't know. Tell me."

"I'm like a big child sometimes. I don't always know where the line is. I go too far."

"Yes, you do."

"I'm really, really sorry. I'd never deliberately do anything mean spirited. Especially to you. You and Xander are my only real family. I know I make a big deal about being independent, but it's nice to have people around. You know. Other people."

Xander, listening on the edge of his reading, rolled his eyes.

Jeff and Sally stared sullenly at each other.

Jeff turned around slowly and lifted his butt. "Free smacks. What do you say?"

Sally lifted her hand as if intending to bring it down hard, then patted him gently. Might even have been a little squeeze involved.

"It's a big target," she said.

Jeff over reached a bit as he helped Sally carry food into the dining room. He silently chastised himself. He would simply have to learn what he could and couldn't do around Xander's mother. He felt awkward sometimes. And he could swear she copped a feel there at the end. What was that about? More dubious areas in their relationship.

"It's a well-known fact," he started, "that every human being alive had a bad high school."

"No. I'm the only one. Pamela Flowers had a fabulous high school."

Jeff lit the dusty rose candles in the center of the table. "Who was Pamela Flowers and why did she have a fabulous high school?"

"She was blonde, beautiful, loaded with energy. She was sweet to everyone, even me, so it was impossible to hate her. She was the student body president, the head cheerleader. The principal often asked her to speak at assembly and she spoke well chosen yet spontaneous words that were wise and funny and inspiring all at once."

"Shoot her now," Jeff offered.

"It doesn't pay to interrupt," Xander added quietly.

"She dated, I swear to God, the captain of the football team—who also, incidentally, had a fabulous high school. She took a beautiful picture. Her beautiful picture was all over our senior class yearbook because she belonged to and was president of every important extracurricular group in the school. She had to have three sets of her senior pictures made because literally every student and most of the teachers wanted one. I still have mine in a drawer upstairs."

"It's true. She does," said Xander.

"I look at it periodically and say out loud, 'You are living the life I am supposed to be living. Why have you been given everything?'"

"Wow," said Jeff cautiously. "You still have a lot of energy on this."

"I could live with it all," Sally continued, "and still believe in God if Pamela Flowers' life had turned to shit after graduation. But do you know what happened to her?"

"She won an important literary prize?" Jeff suggested, half expecting it to be true.

"No. She graduated Valedictorian from Sarah Lawrence. She married a doctor, a pulmonary specialist who makes so much money it grows on the side of their house like moss. She works for the Environmental Defense Fund. She's their number one fundraiser. She has personally raised over seventeen million dollars to save the world from toxic waste. I ran into her on the street one day and she whispered in my ear as if we had always been best friends, 'You know Sally, my husband and I have been married for eleven years now and we still have sex four or five times a week.'"

"Jeff put his hands over Xander's ears. "Please."

"Not only can I hear through your fingers," Xander retorted, removing Jeff's hands, "but I've heard this story so many times I can recite her lines."

Jeff asked Xander, "Have you seen this Pamela Flowers?"

"Twice. She's gorgeous. I want to marry her when I grow up."

"Watch that mouth of yours," Sally warned.

Jeff pulled Mrs. Pooka's chair out for her. As he turned to take his own chair he hummed a few bars of *At Seventeen*. Sally gave him another sharp smack on the butt.

15.

Once home that night Jeff settled into his atrium for a little catch-up reading. He scanned through an FBI report on computer encryption. College kids in Iowa broke an unbreakable code and infested essential military and strategic defense programs with a devious virus. When the moon is in the seventh house every number two converts to a number three. Simple but devastating.

Jeff designed encryption programs. He held numerous patents on search and destroy anti-virus programs. College kids and, increasingly, organized criminals spawned ingenious mutant viruses.

'Oh well,' he thought. 'At least they keep me gainfully employed.'

Jeff glanced through several trade magazines just to see if there was anything new. No, not really.

He considered going to bed. It had been a long day, after all, and he had absorbed a lot of new information. His brain would process this information while he slept. It would collate and organize the Vernon Roman/Marshall Chester details, break it all apart, put it back together like computer-generated art. Murder scenes, churches, costumes and swords. The priest. The head rolling down the parking lot entrance. Quotes from newspapers. Jennifer Haffney's vivid description. The landlady, the armoire, the sparse apartment.

While he slept, little bits of truth hiding in all these details would resonate, become manifest. Throughout the night the angels of sleep would appear, gifting him with answers to perplexing questions.

I should go to bed now, he thought.

But he couldn't. Not just yet.

The workaholic in him, ever afraid of sleep, urged him on to one more task.

He called his old friend, Jimmy Heath. Jimmy, a converted hacker, worked the troubleshooting end of the field. This is typically how Jimmy got business:

A half-baked, fly-by-night computer firm talks a corporation or, better yet, government agency into spending a vast sum of money on a custom designed hardware/software package meant to serve their needs for the next twenty years. Said half-baked, fly-by-night operation installs system, collects the vast sum. The system doesn't really work.

Under-paid and under-skilled techs from the half-baked, fly-by-night operation fiddle with the system, patch together temporary solutions, but in reality the system doesn't really work. Sniffing the warm manure of fraud, the corporation, or better yet government agency, attempts to sue. The half-baked computer firm, already inundated with law suits, files for bankruptcy.

Enter Jimmy, computer sleuth and program miracle worker. From a keyboard Jimmy talks his way behind enemy lines and reprograms the enemy's missiles. For a staggeringly immodest fee, Jimmy saves naive corporate and government bureaucracies from the effects of their own ignorance. He wins the war, then stays behind as permanent military advisor, again for an immodest and regularly assessed fee.

The new code always includes a set of back doors. Always.

No problem calling late at night. Jimmy was bi-polar and refused to take medication. He rarely slept.

"Hey Jimmy. It's Jeff."

Jeff met Jimmy in a chat room. They talked on screen for several months, then exchanged e-mail addresses, then phone numbers. That's when they discovered they lived in the same city. At one point Jeff asked Jimmy for a photo. Jimmy sent an attachment of a picture of Richard Gere.

"My man Jeff," Jimmy touted. "How's little Xander?"

"Too smart to be called little Xander."

"Are you two on a new case?" Jimmy asked.

"We're just investigating," Jeff replied. "Quietly. In the background."

"Right. Like the last time."

"I mean it. He's not dragging me into any police involvement."

"We'll see how long that lasts. I flashed your newspaper photo across the Internet. Across the galaxy, really."

"Thanks, I appreciate the attention."

Jeff's old moniker with Jimmy had been Happy Hunter, in honor of his Indian ancestry. Now Jimmy referred to him as Movie Star. He wished Jimmy hadn't seen his photo. He liked Happy Hunter better.

"I presume you need a favor," Jimmy intoned.

"Just a little one," said Jeff.

"Fill me in."

Jeff told him everything he knew about the Roman/Chester murders.

"I'll tell you what," Jimmy said. "I'll help you any way I can if you keep me up to date on your progress. Hell, I like to think about this stuff. My brain burns. I can't sleep anyway. Give me something to think about."

Jeff agreed, knowing full well he would divulge as little information as possible.

"I'll tell you what I want," Jeff started. "Marshall Chester taught at Upper St. Claire Academy. I'd like to get a look at any files they might have on him. I'd also like access to the County Board's files."

"The Board will have a copy of anything stored on the computers at the Academy. The Board uses an AS400. At the end of the day each school sends new and updated files to the AS400. Passwords are easy so the bureaucrats can remember them. They don't even change them."

"You're kidding."

"Nope. Of course, I can't give you my personal back door. But I hope I don't talk in my sleep. I get in a lot of trouble with that. I've placed ads in the personals while sleepwalking. Might even have answered a few. At least I can't get into any legal trouble while sleepwalking. When I do sleep."

"Good night, Jimmy."

"Good night, Movie Star."

They hung up. Jeff went to his computer, clicked onto the personals Website that he and Jimmy used for secret correspondence. He stopped to read some of the entries—always fun. He located Jimmy's ad:

> SLEEPWALKER wants to play a couple of tunes for MOVIE STAR. All phone numbers of dream dates. Beechwood 45789, you can call me up and get a date any old time. Remember? R-E-S-P-E-C-T, don't know what it means to me. Hey girls, TCB. Sock it to me 8 times. It's past your bedtime MOVIE STAR. SLEEPWALKER wishes you pleasant dreams and happy hunting. Love and kisses XXX.

16.

Beechwood 45789 or 23324966345789 got Jeff into the County AS400. The next set of numbers (RESPECT TCB 8) granted him access to the Board of Ed files.

From the Board of Ed he learned date of initial employment, salary history, promotions, appointments, taxes withheld, life insurance (a basic one year salary payout), wife Elenora, seven dependent children, all relevant dates of birth and medical history.

Marshall Chester taught at the same school his entire career. His salary seemed a bit high to Jeff, even for a veteran teacher in an upper class suburb. Jeff guessed that Chester took on extra jobs like coaching to extend his regular pay. His family appeared amazingly healthy, considering the number of family members. He saw no evidence of chronic health issues or major surgery.

Most of the kids were college age, suggesting that the Chester's started their family early, possibly while attending graduate school.

Wife Elenora possessed a Bachelors of Fine Arts from Carnegie Mellon. Drama. Marshall's bachelor degree in education came from Carnegie Mellon as well. They probably met in college. Chester also earned his master's degree from Carnegie Mellon. His degree took four years to achieve, suggesting Chester worked his way through school. Straight A's in grad school, so he made it count.

The Upper St. Clair files revealed more damaging information.

Jeff was able to access Chester's annual reviews dating back almost to his time of hire. In the early years the school administration absolutely loved him. Praise, commendations, superlatives amounting to purple prose. Repeatedly recommended for promotion along with the maximum increase in salary. Chester accepted additional responsibility, excelled in his new responsibilities. He was elected Teacher's Representative twelve years running. He served as Student Activity Coordinator along with someone named Penny English.

Good boy does better and better.

Then two years ago an abrupt change.

Memos appeared in Chester's file detailing substandard or questionable behavior. *Mr. Chester lax with tardy students. Mr. Chester not versed in current teaching methods—perhaps should go back to school? Mr. Chester ignoring established course guidelines, improvising without authority. Mr. Chester plays favorites with certain students, particularly buxom female students. Mr. Chester appears at time to flirt with female students. Mr. Chester's demeanor not always professional—might even prove a litigation risk to the school.*

On and on it went, memo after memo. Principal Midani defended Chester at first, then appeared to back off, then sided with the memo writer. He agreed toward the end of that first year of criticism that perhaps Mr. Chester had taken advantage of the family atmosphere provided by the school and it's administration in the past. Mr. Chester's performance, once stellar, was now perhaps below standard. Certainly the business of flirting with the students could not be overlooked.

At the end of that school year the vice principal retired. Letters appeared in Chester's file recommending him for promotion to the vacated position. It appeared that these letters were written primarily by teachers. Photostats from students also made their way into the file. They all said pretty much the same thing. Marshall Chester was an exemplary teacher who was the unfair target of a personal attack.

Penny English weighed in with her opinion. She did not bother to couch her words. She asserted that the perpetrator of the attack against Marshall Chester, apparently an administrator brought in to oversee the performance of the teaching staff, was an evil, backstabbing cow who was deliberately and with malice slandering the school's best teacher. Ms. English warned that this "overseer" (a Ms. Greta Fields) hated all men, particularly men in positions of power. It was Ms. Fields' intention to remove the most prominent male members of the Academy's faculty and promote women into the vacated positions. Ms. English warned Midani to watch his own back.

Jeff brought up the file for Greta Fields.

She had been hired exactly three weeks before the first poison pen memo appeared. Of the seven jobs listed on her resume only the most recent position was even remotely in the field of education. Before being hired by the Upper St. Clair Academy, Greta Fields had worked as an administrative assistant/teacher with the Michigan School of Industrial Engineering, Lansing. Her tenure there lasted two years. The other jobs on her resume lasted an equally short period of time, some shorter.

Not a good medical record for Greta Fields. Overweight, high blood pressure, cholesterol in the 400 range, diabetes. Regular podiatrist visits. Regular chiropractic visits. There was something else interesting about Greta Fields' medical history.

She was dead. Heart attack. July 4th.

———

Before going to bed Jeff left a note on his favorite bulletin board. *Happy Hunter would like to know if anyone is familiar with the Michigan School of Industrial Engineering. Went there, worked there. Anything. Leave ideal time for phone exchange of info. Anytime day or night.*

There, he sighed. I have done everything I can do for one day.

Jeff crawled into the tightly wrapped cocoon of his bed. The sheets soon warmed from the heat of his body. In mere seconds he drifted off to the place where reality shape-shifts into symbolic visions of madness and sometimes truth.

———

While Jeff slept, a computer service contract rep—an acquaintance known to Jeff and the others in the community as the Egg Man—read Jeff's request regarding the Michigan School of Industrial Engineering. He laughed. Boy did he know something about the Michigan School. Why didn't Jeff just write him directly about it?

He knows I'm the Man.

I'm the Egg Man.

Goo Goo Ga Choo.

17.

Across town, in the exclusive Virginia Manor area, Jane Lund moved nervously throughout her dark house.

So big, this house. This house that Greta Fields willed to her. This big, lavish million-plus dollar house with its vast rooms and its rare view of Dutch Elm trees and its proximity to other million-plus dollar homes.

Nervous, nervous, so nervous.

A nervous specter.

Jane's bone thin frame wafted past antiques, over thick wool carpets, past photos and art renderings of Greta posed with each of her four ex-husbands. Past the tiny gallery of Jane and Greta photos.

Jane hated photos of herself. She hated her look in them. Fat. Everyone told her she looked way too thin. Like a refugee, they said. But Jane saw the fat all too clearly. Inches and inches of fat on her belly, on her hips, on her thighs, even on her face. Her face was not hollow and sunken. It was filled, highlighted and contoured with fat. She wasn't even remotely thin. She wasn't going to listen to what anyone else had to say about it. No food. No food at all ever again. Just cigarettes.

Greta understood about Jane's fat. Greta had understood about everything, absolutely everything. People shouldn't feel so bad for Karen Carpenter. At least she was at peace. Karen will never again have to look at the fat in the mirror.

The Jane and Greta photos would have to be destroyed, Jane decided. Once she got rid of Greta's ghost. Greta was still around, you see—had been from the moment she died. Came straight to the house from the Fourth of July picnic. Greta would not leave Jane in peace. Greta was trying to deliver a message to Jane, but Jane didn't want to receive it.

After a respectable mourning period Jane intended to have Greta's ghost cleansed from the house. Her friends Kim and Connie performed spirit removal. For a few hundred dollars they swept through the house with fluttering eagle feathers and smoking sage. They chased unwanted spirits on to the next dimension or into the light or wherever. Jane didn't care where Greta's ghost went as long as it left the house.

Jane wafted weightlessly into the kitchen. She withdrew a half-gallon container of Butterscotch Praline ice cream from the freezer. She took a bottle of maple syrup from the pantry. She retrieved a soupspoon from the flatware drawer. At the table, in light cast from streetlamps from the next street over, Jane sat down to a meal of ice cream and maple syrup. No need for a bowl. She poured a layer of syrup into the container, ate a layer of ice cream, poured in more syrup, ate another layer.

Jane wondered about Greta's rich aunts, her dead rich aunts. How would they feel if they knew all their money had passed down to her, Jane Lund? Shy, paranoid, frightened, dysfunctional Jane. Who could not focus enough to finish school or hold a job. Who was being treated by an orchestra of doctors for a medley of disorders: fear of heights, fear of crowds, fear of the outside, fear of intimacy, Lyme disease, depression, anorexia, bulimia.

Jane. Who had attempted suicide four times. Who smoked three packs of cigarettes (sometimes more) a day. Who was Greta's lesbian lover.

'Oh, yes,' Jane thought, 'I would love to gauge the reaction of Greta's rich aunts. They're probably here in the house with Greta. They're probably really pissed.'

Jane laughed out loud. In her dark, empty kitchen, stooped over her carton of ice cream, she took another bite. And another bite. More syrup. Another bite. She laughed in short choppy spasms that rose from her stomach to her mouth like hiccups. It sounded peculiar, like the song of a bird that has never heard another bird sing. She laughed while she plundered the ice cream. She laughed until she had another thought.

If the dead aunts still inhabited the house, then the dead aunts had watched Jane and Greta have sex. The thought gave her chills. She hunched her shoulders as if in defense of the harsh cold of such a thought. Add another fear to the list. Fear of nebbish, voyeuristic rich aunt spirits.

Yes, this house should be cleansed. She planned to call Kim and Connie in the morning.

Greta's ex-husbands, all four of them, were still alive. That was a good thing. Dead husbands would be here with the dead aunts getting even with Greta for years and years of emasculating torture. Greta's father had beaten and humiliated her throughout her childhood. She treated her husbands like Daddy whipping posts.

Why did any of them stick around for it? One of them lasted six years. Imagine. What did they get out of it? Jane had seen Greta's photos from her married period. She appeared fat, ugly and mean in every one of them. Good thing the husbands were still alive. As spirits they'd be poltergeists, breaking things, thrashing themselves against walls. It was scary enough living here with Greta and the aunts.

On the day God called Greta forward to the Pearly Gates there would be only one witness on her behalf: Jane. Jane Lund. Jane—the almost-dead dog hit by a car—lying on the side of the road, eyes turned toward people who might help. Greta stopped, picked her up, and nursed her back to a close approximation of health.

Jane would never be fully healthy. She would never be psychosis-free. But after the love and support Greta showed her, Jane now took walks outside, met new people, took cabs to the supermarket, did her own shopping. She lived in this big house in the ritzy neighborhood with all the super-confident rich people. She envisioned possibly, one day, ending her loneliness by taking a lover instead of taking her life.

Greta accepted Jane's anorexia and bulimia. Greta told her early on, "I don't want you to lie to me about it. Don't sneak around, waiting until I've gone to work, keeping the gagging quiet in the middle of the night. If you're going to do it, do it. Excuse yourself, go to the bathroom, and make as much noise as you need to make."

Yes. Greta had been good to Jane. Not evil or mean spirited. Jane intended to speak on Greta's behalf on Judgment Day.

Jane polished off the last of the ice cream with the last of the syrup. She stared at the empty carton and the empty plastic bottle. What had she done? She'd consumed about twenty-eight thousand calories without even thinking.

She removed the evidence of the feast. Jane drifted out of the kitchen, wafted through the thickly carpeted rooms past all the antique furniture. She climbed the thickly carpeted steps to the master bedroom where her satin-sheeted bed awaited her, covers turned down. She had only eaten in order to puzzle out a dilemma.

Should she attend the funeral of Marshall Chester tomorrow?

She knew instinctively that those people didn't like her.

It was actually Greta they didn't like. But would they make that distinction? Greta had done her 666 number on that school and some of its teachers. Greta had targeted Marshall Chester in her sight range. Greta deliberately destroyed his reputation, slandered him with exaggerations and falsehoods. Greta had discussed her actions with Jane. Only Jane knew the personal, vindictive nature of Greta's tactics. To administrators, Greta's actions appeared objective and professional.

Jane remembered Mrs. Chester kindly. Mrs. Chester had sent flowers to Greta's funeral. Mrs. Chester, Elenora, attended the funeral. No one else from the school bothered. Mrs. Chester comforted Jane. Jane remembered that. Mrs. Chester sat with her, held her hand. She cared about Jane. She felt Jane's loss.

Perhaps it was Jane's turn to provide sympathy and comfort. Funerals could be frightening. Wasn't it the right thing to do? To offer comfort in return?

Once in the master bedroom, Jane closed the door behind her.

Jane removed the twenty-eight thousand calories from her digestive system.

She brushed her teeth, then turned in for the night.

18.

"THEY HAVE A CONFESSION."

It was Xander's voice, but it sounded far away. What was this cold thing next to Jeff's ear? He brought the cold thing under the warm goose down blankets. He planned to warm the cold thing and include it in his consciousness...eventually.

"This is Jeff Redwing," he muttered.

"This is Xander Pooka," came Xander's clear, energized voice. "What time did you get to bed last night?"

"I almost went to bed at one, but decided to do a little research. Then I almost went to bed at two, but I decided to do a little more research."

"What time?"

"About three-thirty actually," Jeff confessed.

"Jeff, we have so much to do today. You won't be awake for any of it."

"I did two hours worth of today's work last night. So I'm entitled to two hours more sleep today. Just two hours quality REM sleep. Then I'll be refreshed, I swear."

"Okay," Xander capitulated. "Two hours. But you have to call Mrs. Chester today. You don't want to wait until she has left for the funeral home."

"I know." Jeff slipped back slowly to REM-land.

"And we need to go to the Horace Miller Funeral Home sometime today. That's where Roman is laid out."

"Okay, sure. No. Wait. We can't. The police will be there."

"Not likely," Xander replied. "The police got a confession this morning. It was on CNN. The guy confessed right into the television cameras. I recorded it. Go back to sleep. I'll be over later so we can watch it together. Nighty night, Jeff."

"Nighty night, Xander."

Jeff stuck the cold thing back out into the cold. It dropped onto the thickly carpeted floor and soon drifted from Jeff's thoughts. The agents of REM-land signed him to a two-hour deal.

Toward the end of the two hours a question encroached upon the shores of Jeff's consciousness. Far, far out at first. Barely a speck of a question. It rode wave after wave, sunk under the water, crested above a wave, then sunk back again. It re-emerged larger each time until the question grew so large it overwhelmed the shoreline. Startled, Jeff opened his eyes and asked out loud, "CNN?"

———

A little after 9 a.m. Jeff dialed Mrs. Elenora Chester at her home. Busy. He programmed the phone for continuous dial, then grabbed the television remote. He tuned to CNN but kept the sound down so he could hear the phone. Busy, busy, busy, busy. He wondered why they didn't have call waiting. Probably too many calls from students.

Jeff got warm feelings in his cozy flannel robe thinking about the one teacher from grade school Jeff called (and visited) at home: Mr. Penwell. From the age of nine Jeff had been in love with Mr. Penwell, his grade school music teacher. Jeff lived to sit on the piano bench beside Mr. Penwell and take piano lessons. He willingly gave up sports, science, virtually all other pursuits to visit the Penwell home, take a private lesson, and practice, practice, practice.

Mr. Penwell was so handsome. Tall, square shouldered, lean with nice sinewy arms, cocoa brown hair, five o'clock shadow. When Jeff performed particularly well, Mr. Penwell wrapped his arms around Jeff, pulled him into his chest, and rubbed his head in a manly, playful way. Mr. Penwell wore an aftershave people don't wear today. Just a little bit. Jeff closed his eyes and remembered nestling into Mr. Penwell's embrace, breathing in his aftershave. Such a beautiful man.

As a boy Jeff often fantasized that Mr. Penwell left his dolt of a wife and adopted him—or something. At such an early age he couldn't quite grasp the implications of tender feelings for a man teacher. The feelings were real, but he couldn't imagine what they meant or where they led. Still, how sweet it had been, in retrospect, to be in love at the age of nine.

The phone rang, breaking Jeff's reverie.

A gruff male voice answered. "Hello?"

"Hello," Jeff answered. He hesitated, then continued. "This is Jeffrey Redwing. I'm an old friend of Marshall's. From Carnegie Mellon."

"Oh."

"I knew Elenora only just a little," Jeff said. The word "Pittsburgh" appeared on the TV screen below what appeared to be a police press conference. He couldn't turn the sound up, but watched while he continued on the phone. "I don't know if she'll remember me. I was mostly Marsh's friend."

"I see," came the gruff voice, distinctly unsympathetic.

"Are you one of Marsh's children?"

"No. I'm Elenora's brother. I'm in town to help out. She has her hands full with the police and reporters. All the kids are back from school. Marsh's students call non-stop with condolences. It's nice that they call, but my sister is a nervous wreck at this point."

"I can well imagine," Jeff said. "By the way, do you know that someone has confessed?"

"Oh, yes. Some Jujitsu lunatic who says he got his inspiration from Kurasawa movies."

A large, muscular black man appeared on the screen. Although dressed in street clothes, he held up what looked like a samurai costume for reporters to photograph. The black man had a soft, round face. He smiled a great, wide Zen smile.

"That's sad," Jeff said.

"Imagine dying like that," said the voice on the other end. "Suddenly, unexpectedly, at the hands of some Crazy whose brain has been fried by Asian action films."

"Poor Marsh. I feel so badly for Elenora. And the children. Listen, I don't want to bother her at such a stressful time. I wonder if you could give her a message for me?"

"What's the message?" The brother's tone softened a bit, eased by the well intentions of Jeff's lies.

Dear Reader, so sorry to interrupt, but it's time I told a little truth about our eager detective Mr. Redwing. He is a chronic liar. That is to say, he lies easily with seldom a concern for the consequences of his actions. For the most part he gets away with it. Sorry. I love him to pieces, but there it is. Here is another lie...

"I'd like to write an article about Marsh for the Carnegie Mellon Alumnae Magazine. A tribute. I'm planning on visiting the funeral home this evening. Perhaps if you mention my name I could speak with her briefly about it."

"What is your name again?"

"Jeff. Jeff Redwing. Comp-Sci."

"Jeff Redwing," echoed the voice on the other end of the line. There was a pause while Elenora's brother wrote Jeff's name down on a piece of paper. "I'll tell her, Mr. Redwing."

"Jeff. Just Jeff. May I ask your name?"

"Jeremy. Richer. Jeremy." It sounded like Jeremy giggled.

"Thank you, Jeremy." There was a swell of noise at the Chester end of the line as if a large group of people had just entered the house. "Will I see you there tonight?"

Thinking the conversation over, Jeremy hung up. 'Well,' Jeff reasoned, 'Jeremy would most certainly be at the funeral home. How could he not attend?' Jeff suspected that Jeremy might be his ticket into the realm of Elenora's trust.

———

Jeff and Xander studied the video of the CNN confession for nuances.

Franklin Baum, a level four brown belt karate enthusiast, owned an impressive collection of VHS tapes and DVDs of Kung Fu/samurai/martial arts movies. Hundreds of them. Baum claimed to represent the ancient spirit of a samurai warrior who returned century after century on a mission from God to rid the world of criminals and mediocrities.

This was not his first beheading. For at least three years he had been severing heads throughout Western Pennsylvania and the Ohio Valley. Remarkably enough, FBI reports verified the discovery of more than twenty decapitated bodies in a five state area that included Michigan, Ohio, New York, Pennsylvania and West Virginia. Several of the bodies were as yet unidentified.

Apparently, Franklin Baum had interrupted a completely unrelated early morning press conference to make his confession and present the samurai costume as proof. The sword, he said, had been tossed off the Sixteenth Street Bridge into the Allegheny River.

Why the confession?

God wanted the human race to know that war had been declared on criminals and mediocrities. Franklin Baum's personal surrender made no difference in God's long-range plans. Armies coming up behind him would continue to execute God's will.

CNN footnote: the decapitated bodies thus far identified belonged to a number of seemingly unrelated businessmen.

Xander squirmed uneasily in his chair.

Jeff said, "Give me your analysis."

"First thing, he's muscular but also a little chubby. He might hold a level four brown belt, but I'm guessing he got it a while ago. If he still practiced, he'd be in better shape."

"You don't think he has the strength to decapitate someone?"

"I don't think he has the speed to vanish afterward as if by magic."

"Remember, only one person witnessed the samurai's escape," reminded

Jeff. "The nun. Who has disappeared herself. Maybe we could track down the nun. The diocese must have computer records somewhere."

Xander dismissed the nun. He continued with his line of thought.

"Here's something else I noticed. There are no wrinkles in his face. No permanently etched scowl. Franklin Baum looks happy, like he never suffered a day in his life."

"So?"

"Didn't you tell me people wear their lives on their face like a mask? We studied faces one day, remember? You showed me how sad people, angry people, frightened people, worried people—their faces freeze after so many years. You can tell what people's private lives are like even if you've never met them."

"What does that have to do with Baum?" asked Jeff.

"The FBI thinks he decapitated over twenty people. Could he kill that many people over a period of three years and still look like he just got laid?"

"Young man, how do you know what people look like after they've just gotten laid?"

"Movies. Television."

"I'm worried about your generation," Jeff said. "But let's look at this from another perspective. God talks to Franklin Baum. Orders him to execute criminals and mediocrities. In time, only Madonna and Stephen Sondheim will be left."

"I don't know," said Xander. "Didn't you say that Madonna's last CD was a criminal act?"

"So just Sondheim will be left. What does that tell us about Franklin Baum?"

"He's nuts."

"What kind of nuts?"

Xander loved the topic of mental illness. Psychology, aberrant behavior, dysfunction. Schizophrenia.

"He's schizophrenic," Xander replied confidently. "He lives in a different world with a uniquely created reality, similar to ours but fundamentally his own."

"In his world, beheading people might be a joyful event," suggested Jeff. "Violence against imagined offenders might actually produce that beatific look on his face. And there's something else. On the surface he confesses to the murders of Chester and Roman. I suspect that subconsciously he is confessing to something else. Think about that for a moment."

Jeff had taught Xander to listen to the subconscious truth hidden behind the statements people say out loud.

"You hate what you fear in yourself," Xander remembered. "He's confessing that he's a criminal or a mediocrity. Or both."

"Probably both, since the two words are his invention. Here's the problem. He might consider himself to be a criminal because five years ago he secretly wished his mother would die and then she died. In his mind that might make him a murderer, a criminal."

"What do you see in the confession?" Xander asked.

Jeff played the confession again in his mind.

"Something bothers me. Baum confessed to killing people in Pennsylvania and the Ohio Valley. The FBI report names a five state area that includes Michigan and New York. Beheadings are unusual. There is probably a serial killer at work here. Franklin Baum likes to brag—after all, God talks to him. I think if he had killed people in a five state area he would have bragged about it on television."

"So there are crimes he did not include in his confession. Did he murder Roman and Chester?"

"It's possible," Jeff started. "But, the other killings, so far as we know, are all beheadings. In the Roman/Chester case one person is beheaded, but the other person takes a sword to the heart. That breaks the pattern. Why?"

"Because Baum killed our people but not the others," Xander asserted.

"Imagine this. Baum is a nut case who talks directly with God. His head is filled with samurai and Kung Fu movies. He hears a radio report of the samurai attack. He thinks about it and thinks about it. What other samurai are there in Pittsburgh? Just him. It must be him. The more he thinks about it, the more real it seems. He concocts a story in his head. He tells this story to himself so many times it becomes the truth in his psychotic world.'

"He imagines he's been committing these murders for years. On direct orders from God he has been beheading criminals and mediocrities in the Tri State area, his home area. He's a member of a vast and righteous army, sent to kill all the people who share the traits he fears are his personal shortcomings. He confesses on television. He confesses to all the crimes he has invented in his head. His subconscious mind knows the police can't verify the existence of the other victims. Their bodies have not been found.

"Except. There is an FBI report. You and I know about the report because the CNN reporter told us about it. Franklin Baum does not know about the report when he interrupts the police conference."

"So you don't think Baum murdered Roman and Chester."

"No, I don't," answered Jeff. "I think he already owned a samurai costume. That's what he's given to the police. They're testing it right now for bloodstains, so we'll probably know before too long. If the blood matches Roman and Chester, the police will file charges against Baum, probably by the end of the day. I'm guessing he didn't own a sword, so he told them he threw it in the river. In any case, Baum did us a big favor."

"How do you figure?"

"He distracted the police so we can go about our business undetected. Quietly, in the background, as I said we would. And he's done something else even more wonderful. He flushed out the existence of that FBI report. If Baum is not our killer, and I don't think he is, then Roman and Chester might just be the latest victims in a gruesome series of killings. If that's true, then we have a whole new set of questions. Why are these businessmen being killed? Why are they being beheaded? And especially, what do Roman and Chester have in common with the other victims?"

"Roman and Chester are not businessmen," Xander noted.

"Not in the traditional sense. Roman, on the surface of things is a loser, maybe involved with drugs, something like that. Chester is a successful but undistinguished school teacher."

"A criminal and a mediocrity."

"That's true," said Jeff. "But it takes an almost Shakespearian overview to conceive of Marshall Chester as a mediocrity. The average person would consider him a role model."

Jeff turned off the video center. Jeff and Xander looked at each other across the grey shadows of a room free of video light.

"Let's not forget," said Jeff. "Marshall Chester was not beheaded. The break in the pattern."

19.

THE FUNERAL HOME OF HORACE MILLER IV, LOCATED IN THE PREDOMINANTLY African American neighborhood of Manchester, stood amidst numerous grand Victorian homes recently restored to strict National Trust codes. Each street conveyed the tidy, tasteful, somewhat unreal charm of 1890s New York. Movie companies often filmed on location in Manchester for precisely that reason.

Four sandstone steps led to the brightly lacquered apple red entrance to Mr. Miller's establishment. The red door was not quite up to National Trust guidelines, but it had been the trademark of the Horace Miller funeral business for over seventy years. It had itself become a part of history.

Jeff and Xander located the building easily by its famous door. Four African American women dressed in high mourning regalia exited the building just as Jeff and Xander approached. Each woman wore black gloves, black high heel shoes, and a black hat with a veil. Two of the women wore completely black outfits. One wore a two-piece plum ensemble with a tiger lily blouse; another a soft yellow dress and jacket with a white blouse. They seemed angry about something.

One of the women in black said, "I'm tired of this city dumping its poor white trash in our community."

Another added, "They send us their diseased people, their worst criminals. We're supposed to stand by and watch this."

"Now we've got this welfare bum had his head chopped off," said the woman in plum.

The fourth woman, the one in yellow, spoke with the clear, articulated speech patterns of a native of the West Indies. "It is disrespectful of our own dead. I intend to speak with Horace Miller about it. I know that money is scarce, but surely there are times when decency requires that Horace Miller put his hand up and say, 'No. That one I will not take.'"

The women at first frowned at Jeff and Xander as the two groups passed each other, then they decided to be gracious. An exchange of 'good afternoons' quietly hit the air. The women shushed until they were out of earshot of Jeff and Xander, then quickly resumed their earlier conversation.

Black and silver flocked wallpaper covered the walls of the inside corridor. The ceiling was made of darkly stained wood. The only light came from an Art Deco-style urn lamp that cast its light up toward the ceiling.

"I can't see," whispered Xander.

A cry that sounded like a shriek and a wail came from one of the rooms off of the dark corridor. Xander tightly grasped Jeff's arm. A tall African American man with short silver hair approached them.

"I am Horace Miller the Fourth," the man pronounced, extending his hand to Jeff. "This business has been in my family for three generations. How may I serve you?"

Jeff said a little uneasily, "We're here for the Roman party." He could not understand why it was so dark.

"Ah, the Roman party. Just follow me, please."

Horace Miller led them to the end of the hall where they encountered a door made of the same dark wood as the ceiling. Mr. Miller opened the door with a degree of ceremony.

"Just down those steps," he said.

"You mean he's in the basement?" Jeff asked incredulously.

"Just down those steps, sir," Mr. Miller repeated.

Jeff and Xander proceeded cautiously down the steps. Jeff thought he might ask for a miner's helmet, the kind with a light facing forward, but thought better of it.

Horace Miller said after them, "If I may be of further service to you at this or any other time, I can usually be found somewhere on the premises." And with that Horace Miller closed the door on them. (Thankfully, Jeff did not hear the door's latch slide into place.)

"I'm scared," said Xander, continuing to hold onto Jeff's arm. "I've never been to a funeral parlor. This is kind of spooky."

"Usually the viewing rooms are on the ground floor," Jeff said. "Usually you feel like you are in someone's well appointed living room. Someone who likes to decorate with flowers."

Another series of shrieks and wails emanated from the lower level. Jeff and Xander followed the sound of these, proceeding cautiously through a dark passageway. They rounded a corner, then found themselves at yet another closed door. An easel to the left of this door held a stenciled sign that read "Roman."

Jeff opened the door.

He expected to find Roman in a small room, a cubbyhole. This room must have run the length of the building. Two columns of pews faced an elevated stage upon which rested a simple wooden casket. A carpeted center aisle led to a set of steps that led to the stage. Bright spotlights illuminated the simple coffin. A few dimly lit Deco wall sconces provided the only other light in the room.

"This is where the vampires sleep," Xander whispered.

Leaning into Xander's ear, Jeff said quietly, "No, this is where the poor white trash get their final viewing. This is what is called a pauper's service. Mr. Miller is one of a handful of funeral directors who accept the dead of limited financial means. The city pays a small fee and Mr. Miller provides the least amenities allowed by law. That's why Roman is in the basement."

"Who are those people seated up front?"

"Let's find out," said Jeff. "Let's pay our respects."

Jeff and Xander proceeded with quiet dignity to the front of the room. Roman's visitors, a group of four women and one man, sat in the front left pew. Jeff looked straight ahead at the casket as if not noticing the group. Xander took in as many details as he could fathom in the dark.

To no one's surprise the casket was closed. Jeff felt an enormous temptation to open the simple wooden lid. How would Horace Miller IV have dressed the neck stump?

Would he even have bothered?

A pair of theatrical spotlights focused an intense beam on the casket area, casting Jeff and Xander's shadows behind them.

Xander whispered, "What are we supposed to do?"

"If it were an open casket we would compliment his make up and remark on how natural he looks."

"But his head is gone and his coffin is closed."

"Look solemn. Bow your head for a moment of silent meditation."

"Like in school."

"Yes, exactly," Jeff replied. "Moments of silent meditation often come in handy for secular people."

The group in the pews shuffled about. One could hear their clothes rustle. Every so often someone snapped a load of bubblegum. After a time Jeff heard the soft patter of footsteps coming up behind him. Fingers tapped him lightly on the shoulder.

"Did you know my son?" came a woman's voice.

Jeff turned and glanced into the pained, expectant face of Rose Roman. "Yes, I did."

Rose shrieked and then wailed. She threw her arms around him.

"Thank God, thank God, thank God for bringing you." She clasped Jeff tightly to her with remarkable strength for an old woman. It actually hurt.

Rose cried into Jeff's chest. "They killed my baby. They killed my only boy."

The man spoke with a deep, craggy voice, "Christ, Rose, you don't even know this guy. Give him a break."

Rose turned sharply on the man.

"He knew my son. That makes us friends. We're friends of the deep, deep soul."

Rose's man friend, Eddie, moaned but let it drop.

Shading his eyes from the spotlights, Jeff looked into the pews and made out the man, Eddie, and three women who looked to be somewhere in their thirties. All three chewed gum and popped it at different times. They bore the tired, impatient look of people kept too long waiting for a floorshow.

"What's your name sweetie?" Rose asked, leading him toward the pews.

"Jeffrey. Jeff."

"And what's your little boy's name?"

Xander spoke for himself. "I'm Xander, ma'am. Pleased to make your acquaintance."

"He's so polite," Rose observed. "So well brought up. You should be proud."

"I am," said Jeff.

"That's my boy in the coffin," said the woman. "I'm Rose Roman. I haven't met you before, have I?"

"No. We've never met."

"Vernon brought so many people to the house. I'm sure I've forgotten a face here and there." Rose looked Jeff up and down. "Although I think I'd remember you." A concerned look darkened her features. Without thinking, she fingered the lapel of Jeff's navy blue blazer. She didn't have to say it. Jeff didn't look like Vernon's other friends.

"I haven't seen Vernon since high school," Jeff said quickly. "I read what happened in the paper. Very sad. He never got to meet my boy, Xander. I thought I should pay my respects."

Rose moved to introduce her party, then suddenly stopped to ask, "Did you also know Vernon's friend Marshall?"

"Yes, I knew them both."

"My baby was a brain," Rose commented sadly. "Straight A's right up to his senior year. Isn't that right, Suzie?"

One of the gum-snapping women answered, "He was a brain, Ma."

"Something happened his senior year," Rose continued. "He wouldn't talk about it. He lost interest in school. Changed his program from academic to general studies. Bought himself a leather jacket. Started hanging out with people he looked down on before. Worst thing was, he ended his friendship with Marshall. They had been best friends since first grade. Just ended it.

No discussion. Then all this time goes by. A year or so ago he picks up with Marshall again." Rose drifted off on a wave of thought.

Eddie stood and introduced himself. "I'm Eddie Mantego. These are Rose's girls, Vernon's sisters."

The girls nodded to Jeff, looking him over. Eddie introduced Rose's oldest girl as Ronnie. She was exceptionally tall; she exaggerated her height with a two foot high beehive hair-do. The second daughter, Suzie, was as short as Ronnie was tall. She wore her hair in a sixties flip. The youngest daughter, Darlene, was skinny and put one in mind of Twiggy.

Rose herself cut an odd figure. She wore a pair of black slacks and a simple floral patterned top. She tied her reddish hair back in a ponytail. To Jeff's eye she looked as if she had gotten dressed to clean the house.

"I didn't realize that Vernon dropped out of the academic program," Jeff said. "My family moved away during my junior year."

Rose broke out of her reverie. She noticed in Jeff something of the man in him: big, solid, darkly handsome, here with his boy but not with his wife. There was an undercurrent of sexual energy in him. Nothing he tried to put over, but it was there.

"I always liked Marshall," she said, continuing to finger Jeff's lapel. "He wasn't much to look at as a little boy. Not cute like your Xander here."

"Thank you, ma'am," Xander replied.

"But he blossomed. After he reached puberty his jaw squared and his hair grew out in chestnut waves. We all used to run after him and run our fingers through his hair, didn't we girls? But when Vernon started bringing him around this last time, I noticed he had lost his looks. He looked tired. Beaten by life already. When people live too hard it drains the beauty right out of them."

"Rose," Eddie interjected, hoping to stop an indiscretion.

Rose continued, "Sometimes gangly boys grow into handsome men. I bet you were one of those, Jeff." For just a second Rose looked over at her daughters. "Then sometimes handsome boys go to seed in adulthood. Not my Eddie here. He started out as seed, didn't you babe?"

"That's right, Rose. I'm still waiting to send up my first shoot."

"Wait till you're in your seventies, baby. You wouldn't want to rush it."

Just then, the door banged opened. Dramatically. Bang. The door hit the wall, producing an echo that reverberated throughout the room. A striking woman stood in the doorway. Tall, blonde hair swept back, perky yet distinctive breasts, expensive frock (colorful yet appropriate for mourning). An indigo scarf draped her throat and danced behind her as she power walked in stiletto heels down the aisle between the pews to the front of the room.

The woman screamed. It was a full-throated, glass cracking, horror movie scream.

The Roman women screamed as if in answer.

Rose threw her hands up in the air.

"Dottie!" she cried. "They killed my baby! They killed my boy!"

Dottie, transfixed by the sight of the coffin, let out another horror movie scream.

"I have to see him, Rose," she pronounced. Dottie approached the coffin.

Dottie cried for quite some time. She cried quietly, then loudly. She trembled as she cried. She spastically shook as she cried. Dottie poured tears into her indigo scarf. Then she stepped back, staring at the coffin as if for the first time. She walked entirely around it.

"Take the lid off of this coffin," she demanded. Then loudly, to the hall, "Somebody take the lid off of this coffin."

Before anyone could respond, Dottie screamed another horror movie scream and threw back the lid of the coffin herself. Everyone, including Eddie, let out a horror movie scream.

Without so much as a second thought, Dottie lifted up the body of her dead lover and held the cadaver in her arms. "Vernon, my Vernon," she whimpered, caressing his sleeves.

Rose and daughters could not contain themselves. They rushed up to join Dottie. Eddie watched for a moment, then covered his eyes as the five women fingered and stroked the black suited corpse. Xander overcame his fear and led Jeff up to the body to see what they could see.

Horace Miller IV had covered Vernon's neck stump with a white sock. It was an all cotton, ankle length, white athletic sock with a green deodorizing toe.

Eddie approached the women and tried to get them to stop. "This is undignified," he said softly. "Let the boy be. Let the boy have his rest." Eddie's admonishments only inspired deeper, more passionate touching of Vernon's body. In the middle of it all, Dottie reached over and pulled off the sock.

Another round of screams filled the basement chapel (this time Jeff couldn't swear his wasn't one of them). Horace Miller IV appeared to investigate all this screaming. It was disturbing his better paying guests upstairs. He was greatly distressed to discover that the coffin lid had been opened, the body pulled up and over the side, and the white sock removed.

"Please, please," came his thunderous voice. "This is a closed coffin viewing. Closed coffin only."

Horace pulled Ronnie away from the body. This was the excuse the rest of them needed to retreat. Except Dottie.

"Take your hands off of this body," Horace Miller demanded.

Dottie looked deep into his eyes. She probed deep inside him with an unrelenting stare until he had no choice but to stop and look right back.

Once she had his full attention, she said, "This is the body of my husband and I intend to touch him."

Dottie reached down with her right hand and rubbed Vernon's genitals through the fabric of his burial trousers. She did this slowly and for a while without once disengaging her eyes from those of the funeral director.

"This is blasphemous," he hissed at her.

"You're lucky I don't take it out and kiss it," Dottie replied. "After all, his head is gone and his dick is my second favorite part." Horace Miller closed his eyes and shuddered. "I'd do it, too, but I don't want to give the little boy nightmares."

"Do what you have to do," Xander spoke up. Jeff glared at him, having no desire to see Vernon Roman's rigor mortisized stiffy.

Dottie held Horace Miller's gaze a few seconds longer. It had become very quiet in the room.

"Now we can put him back and close the coffin," she said, metering out each word. Dottie lowered the body back into a reclining position. Rose returned the sock to the neck stump. Jeff moved behind the coffin, lifted the lid, and laid it gently back into place. Dottie stared into Horace Miller's face throughout the whole procedure. She let Horace Miller know that it was she, Dottie, who controlled her husband's body and not the funeral director.

Mr. Horace Miller calmed down after a time, seemed to fit comfortably once more into his suit, and returned to less troublesome grievers upstairs.

Dottie turned away from the casket.

Shading her eyes from the harsh overhead lights, she took in the room—the church pews, the dim red wall sconces, the vaguely impenetrable darkness, the five friends, the two strangers. Well.

"They need to throw these spotlights into the seats," she declared. "I feel like I should burst into song up here. Life is a cabaret old chum. That's what I should sing." Dottie sat down on the edge of the platform that held the casket. To Rose she said, "Don't you remember Liza Minnelli singing that song about her roommate the whore. Cut down in the prime of life, yet she lived it all to the hilt. No regrets. She made a happy corpse. That's our Vernon. Life was a cabaret old chum. No one needs to feel sorry for him. It's me who needs the pity." She took out a compact and looked at her face in several angles. "Oh, dear," she said. "I just don't look good."

"You look lovely, Dottie," Rose assured her.

"Oh, Rose," Dottie said in a tone that suggested Rose could always be counted on to say something nice, however inane.

Dottie was the ideal daughter to Rose, the daughter Ronnie, Suzy and Darlene aspired to be. Rose's birth daughters admired Dottie but with a tinge of resentment. They felt like the Supremes after Diana Ross left for a solo career.

"You know," Dottie continued, freshening her make-up. "Vernon was just so gorgeous. So gorgeous. But we can't appreciate that today."

Rose touched Dottie's knee. With solemn earnestness she said, "We have to find his head, Dottie. We can't let him be buried like this."

"I'm afraid someone took it as a souvenir, Rose." Dottie glanced at Jeff. "But we just might be able to get it back. I'll tell you what, Rose. We'll hold out for the return of the head. We won't bury Vernon for a while."

"Oh, Christ," Eddie moaned. He imagined Dottie and Rose stealing the corpse and storing it in the basement. This was not at all beyond the pale of possibility.

"Mr. Eddie is such a bear," Dottie teased. "I hope he's good in bed, Rose. We must have our little compensations. What I simply meant, Mr. Eddie, is that we will put our Vernon's body in a mausoleum until such time as his head turns up. Then we can take him off the shelf, dust him off, and put him in the ground."

Rose shook her head. "We don't have the money for a mausoleum."

"I have money, Rose. I've told you this. You've seen my place in Shadyside. Well, Vernon lived there, too. He only kept that hole to collect welfare. It was a couple of nights out a month."

"I don't like taking money from you, Dottie."

"Nonsense. It's Vernon's money, too," she said. " If I had known in time I would never have allowed him to be brought here. Rose, how on earth did you choose this place?"

"The man at the morgue said it was clean and reasonable."

"Rose, listen to yourself. You took advice from the man at the morgue. I mean, this is Manchester, honey. There's nothing wrong with Manchester, but it's not our part of town. This funeral home is for black people, Rose. Didn't you notice? The mortician beautician probably only has black people make-up. What if our handsome Vernon had come in with his head intact? How would he look?"

"Give her a break," Eddie said. "She's half out of her mind."

"I'm sorry, Rose honey," Dottie said. "I don't mean to come down on you. I just want you to know we have money. In fact, after I pay for the mausoleum I'm going to give you the rest of Vernon's money."

"You don't have to do that."

"But I want to. I want to! Now. That discussion is over." Dottie stopped for a moment. She appeared to relax somewhere on the edge of her next thought. She glanced over at Jeff and Xander. Her eyes moved first to Jeff, then to Xander, then back to Jeff, then back to Xander. She settled on Jeff. She looked him over quite thoroughly, as if regarding his value for purchase. "Rose," she said at last, "who is this man?"

"This is Jeff and his little boy Xander," Rose chimed innocently. "Jeff and my Vernon went to school together."

"What school is that, Rose?"

"High school. They were real close right up to eleventh grade when Jeff's family moved to another city."

Dottie laughed.

"Oh, Rose. You'll believe anything." To Jeff she said, "Mr. Jeff, do you have a last name?"

"Redwing," he said, not bothering to corroborate his story.

"Redwing? Are you of Indian ancestry?"

"My father was Cherokee and Irish."

"Black Irish I'm guessing."

"Don't know. The Irish part was not important to him."

"And your mother was?"

"Greek and Welsh."

Dottie signaled to Xander. "Come here, little boy. Come to Dottie for just one moment."

Xander approached her slowly. She looked him up and down. He looked her over just as thoroughly.

"How do you do, ma'am?" Xander asked.

"So polite. So sweet," she said. "Dottie isn't fooled, though. That's all right. We all get along in different ways. You're a clever young man, aren't you? More clever than our Jeff at times I'd wager." She flashed the stink eye to Jeff. "Xander." Dottie ran her well-manicured fingers through Xander's soft brown hair. "Is that a nickname?"

"It's short for Alexander, ma'am," Xander replied. "When I was little it was the only part of my name I could pronounce. Aunts and uncles and cousins called me that. As I grew up I just kept it."

"It's a good handle, honey," Dottie assured him. "I'd keep it, too. This Redwing guy isn't your biological father, that much is certain. What is your last name, Xander?"

"Pooka, ma'am."

"Pooka. That's Greek, isn't it? Or is it some shortened Eastern European thing?"

Xander didn't much think about his father. On a small scale he got even with his father by not caring about his paternal ancestry.

When he didn't answer, Dottie continued: "Do you know something, Xander? Dottie loves the movies. She loves plays, musicals, dance reviews. Anything that has to do with entertainment. And I have a very good memory, just like you do. Do you know who Harvey is? In the movies I mean."

"Yes, ma'am. Harvey is a big white rabbit with magical qualities. He was James Stewart's best friend, although no one else could see him."

"That's right. Harvey was more than a big white rabbit, though. Do you remember what he was?"

"He was a Pooka."

"That's right. A creature from Celtic mythology that could assume different forms. He added magic to people's lives. He also played tricks on them."

"Yes, ma'am."

"Are you Mr. Redwing's big white rabbit, honey?"

"Sometimes. His little white rabbit maybe."

"I thought so. Well, aren't I lucky to get to meet you today, Xander? You have quite a future ahead of you. I wish I were one of those aunts of yours so I could watch you grow up. Vernon and I were together for eighteen years, my Vernon up there in the box. We could not conceive. But I dreamt about it. I dreamt about having a little boy exactly like you."

Dottie pulled Xander to her. She smelled his hair, fingered his body, drank him in, then pushed him away.

"You," she said, pointing to Jeff, "did not go to school with my Vernon. You are a handsome man. I have not seen your handsome face or any proximity of it in a yearbook. He never mentioned you. If my Vernon had been friends with someone as handsome as you, I would have heard about it. There would be stories. Often repeated ones."

"We never met, that's true."

Various members of the Roman family gasped.

"So." Dottie paused. "Are you police?"

"Not really," Jeff said as enigmatically as possible.

"Not at all," Dottie said authoritatively. "Mr. Redwing, I need to see you in the back." Dottie walked, tilting her head toward the exit. "Little Xander, you stay here with Rose. I'm going to have a little talk with your friend and then we'll be right back."

Dottie power steered Jeff out of the chapel. She closed the door behind them.

The hallway outside of the basement chapel was dark, as before. They could barely see each other.

Dottie looked up at the ceiling and yelled at the top of her lungs, "Turn on some fucking lights!" She banged her fist against the wall. "Or hand out miner's helmets at the door." To Jeff she said, "I can't believe she chose this place. I just can't believe it. So. Mr. Jeff."

"I'm not police or anyone like the police," he quickly said.

In an intimate, toying way she said, "And this charade. Aren't you ashamed of yourself? Deceiving a dead stranger's mother and bringing a child in on it. Did you rehearse him?"

"No," he said nervously. "Of course not."

"Hmm. I almost believe you. There is something innocent about you. But you lie too easily." She fingered the lapel of his blazer. Like spider legs over polished stone her long fingers walked over his white shirt, stopped to touch the brass buttons, took measure of the space between his collar and his neck. Close to his face she said, "All cotton. You wash it yourself, I can tell." Moving in closer still she ran her nose along the flesh of his neck to his strong, prominent jaw. "You use Coast soap. I like to smell men when they are naked. I know all the soaps and all the odors. There is another scent, an unusual cologne. I think it's Eau Savage."

"Very good," he said.

"Can you tell what I'm wearing?

"I'm afraid I don't have a very good sniffer."

"Chanel No. 5," she said. "Always Chanel No. 5."

Jeff smiled a goofy sort of smile, not knowing what else to do.

"So what are you, Mr. Redwing?"

"I'm a private investigator," Jeff said resignedly, hoping she'd buy it.

"For whom do you work?"

"I'm afraid that's confidential." And convenient. "I can tell you that the people who have engaged my services have nothing to do with the police. In fact, they would prefer to have nothing to do with the police."

Dottie peered so directly, so deeply, into his eyes that fear shot through Jeff. He could hear the sound of his own heart beating. He was fairly certain she could hear it as well.

"Is it the St. Patricks?" she asked. She was so close he could smell her breath. It smelled sweet from something, sweet from candy.

Jeff didn't answer the question. He tilted his head as if to say Good Guess, but I couldn't tell you if I wanted to. "I can tell you they want me to uncover the identity of the murderer. They don't want me to reveal that identity to the police."

"So your people don't think it was the jujitsu lunatic who confessed."

"No."

"Neither do I. My Vernon didn't need an anonymous lunatic to finish him off, Mr. Jeff. My Vernon had plenty of enemies. Real enemies. The kind who kill people every day. Let me ask you this. Do you think I killed him?"

"Actually, no. I don't think that. But I had to meet you. I had to meet the family."

"Very good. I'll believe you for the moment. I will check you out, you can count on that."

"Fair enough."

"So where does this leave us?" Dottie asked. An undertone of sexuality crept into her tone. Jeff felted trapped in such close proximity in the dark with her.

"I would like to meet with you," he said, trying not to let his voice crack. "Not now, but later, under more relaxed circumstances. I'm sure there is a lot you could tell me about your late husband. Things that might link up with other things I know."

"There certainly are things I could tell you, Mr. Jeff. But what do I get for divulging family secrets?"

"Don't you want justice for your husband?"

Dottie laughed.

"Vernon lived dangerously. So do I. We both expected to die young. Does that shock you?"

"Should it?"

She gauged his reply.

"I'll tell you what." She leaned directly into his ear. He was afraid at first she was going to kiss him. "I will meet with you. I will tell you everything. Well. Most everything. But no one must know. If you find yourself in contact with the police, you don't know me, you never spoke with me, you're not aware of my existence."

"That's it?" Jeff asked. "That's all you want? Discretion?"

"Oh, honey," she whispered salaciously. "I want a great deal more." She ran her tongue along the outer ridge of his ear. She paused. A wave of sensation passed through him. He felt his penis stiffen. When at last she spoke, she said, "I want you to bring me his head."

———

Jeff and Xander felt their way through the dark labyrinth of hallways and stairs, past the black and silver flocked wallpaper, finally out the door of Horace Miller IV's funeral parlor. They covered their eyes for a second, adjusting to the light outside.

"It's like Plato's cave in there," Jeff observed. "Creepy. And unreal. As if the whole thing had been staged for us."

"They didn't know we were coming," Xander noted.

"But they might have been expecting someone. They might have at first mistaken us for that someone. The Roman family is odd. The three sisters, the melodramatic mother. That guy with them."

"Eddie."

"He didn't seem comfortable with the rest of them. He acted like Rose and the rest of them were left to him in a will he couldn't contest. And

Dottie! Jesus H. Christ!"

"What did she do to you in the hall?"

"We talked, that's all. She wanted to know my true identity and what I was doing at her husband's funeral."

"Did you tell her?" Xander asked.

"I told her I was a P.I. That stalled her for a minute. She's going to check up on me though. I'm sure she knows how to do it. Who knows how long my story will hold up."

"We don't have to see her again."

"I do. I shouldn't. But she let something slip."

"She's dangerous," Xander said. "This is a game, a puzzle. Remember? We're supposed to dovetail out at the first sign of danger and I say this is it."

Jeff considered Xander's point for just a moment. He remembered the painful process of extracting himself from the last adventure. The jail time. The damage done to his professional reputation. Even so.

"She asked me if I represented someone called the St. Patricks."

"Sounds like a gang of some kind. That's really dangerous." Xander mimed with his hands the motion of dovetailing out.

"I got the impression from the way she spoke of them that the St. Patricks are people. A husband and wife, a family, a group of cousins."

"Please don't see Dottie again," Xander pleaded.

"Have to. I'm hooked now. I'm a third of the way into the dark mansion. I have to open the next door. I'll be careful. And discreet. I'm always careful and discreet."

Xander reminded him, "Careful and discreet is not always enough."

20.

In the car en route to the Upper St. Clair campus Xander took in the view of the Ohio River from the Fort Pitt Bridge. "It's dirty and gloomy," he said. "Why do people live in the city? All the houses so close together."

"Some people prefer the closeness," Jeff replied, maneuvering across the tricky access lanes that led into the Fort Pitt tunnels. "Other people don't like the city but don't make enough money to escape. They're trapped in all that closeness."

The noise level inside the tunnel prohibited conversation. Once on the other side, in the presence of hillsides and trees, Xander relaxed a bit. He looked casually out the window away from Jeff.

"I think that Dottie has the hots for you," Xander said.

"No kidding." Jeff laughed. "She did everything but feel me up in the hall."

"You're not going to do anything with her, are you?"

Jeff grinned. "Gay. Remember? I put my time in with the opposite sex. I know better now. I might flirt a little if it gets me some answers. Other than that, I intend to keep my vow of chastity to computer science."

"Don't make jokes. When was the last time a guy stayed over at your place? It's been a while."

"In between lovers I always take a vow of chastity. That way I always operate my sex life out of a sense of purpose. You should take a vow of chastity yourself. At least until you're twenty-one."

"Twenty-one! No way. I hit my prime at fourteen. By twenty-one I will experience fewer erections and those will be less stiff. My capacity to perform will already be on the wane."

Jeff gave him a long, sarcastic look. "Don't believe everything you read. Peaking is a frame of mind. I personally haven't peaked yet. And I'm well beyond twenty-one. A vow of chastity until adulthood—that would be the best thing for you."

"Just don't sleep with Dottie," insisted Xander. "Gay or no gay, I know how obsessed you get once you start digging for answers. Don't get me wrong. She's interesting. I'd love to pick her brain or even just hang around while she talks. But I think she'd stab you in the back if you crossed her. She's already caught you in a lie."

A little sidebar, Dear Reader. Even though Jeff is a chronic liar, as earlier noted, he himself is only vaguely aware of it. He likes to think of himself as more of a storyteller. He is one quarter Irish, after all. Just enough to have a bit of the Blarney in him. And the Cherokee have certainly told a story of two in their time. As for the Greeks. Homer. Virgil. Aristophanes. Storytellers, all. I can't say I know much about the Welsh, but they can't be entirely innocent. In Jeff's case it might not be lying so much as honoring one's ancestors. In any case, Xander's last remark hit no target at all. It ppffftzed off of Jeff's force field and landed wistfully in one of the drink cup holders where it shriveled and died to eventually be vacuumed on car wash day.

"All she'll get out of me is talk," Jeff assured Xander. "Actually, I'm the one who requested a second meeting. I want to see that apartment of hers."

"The one she said is in Shadyside?"

"Yes. And we were right about the money, weren't we? The welfare stuff was all a ruse for tax purposes. Vernon made lots of money. Dottie makes lots of money. And it's all out of the tax chain, nice and illegal. There might be something in that apartment, something that talks to me. I don't know what. I'll just have to go and snoop."

"Watch her, that's all."

"No one's ever gotten my pants off with mere glances and words. I'll have a glass of wine if she offers. I'll find out what she knows about the St. Patricks. She promised to tell me everything."

"Why would she do that?"

"I kind of promised her something."

Xander, eyebrows raised, looked at his sometimes crazy friend. "What did you promise?"

"I promised we'd bring her Vernon's head."

"Eeeuwww, gross."

"My sentiments exactly."

21.

IN THE UPPER ST. CLAIR SCHOOL SYSTEM STUDENTS LEARNED TO USE computers in the first grade. The High School Academy rivaled the best prep schools in the country. Jeff had spoken at several computer science fairs sponsored by the school over the years. Beautifully landscaped grounds covered a thirty-acre campus of aluminum and glass buildings, rolling hills, and trees hundreds of years old.

The buildings were closed for the weekend. Jeff lifted Xander up on his shoulders so he could see inside some of the classrooms. Xander's own suburban school, impressive in its own right, was nothing like this.

"These people must all be millionaires," he said.

"They're proud of their school," said Jeff. "The community is the school. It's what everyone lives for. It's the reason people move to this area."

"And Marshall Chester was a prominent teacher here. How much money do you think he made?"

"About as much as a good college professor. A salary worth protecting. Not easy to get a comparable position in a different school district."

They walked down a gravel path to the football arena. Since the grounds were open to the community, many adults used the track and other athletic fields for weekend and evening exercising. Jeff and Xander walked onto the track field where they adopted a walking pace alongside twenty or so students and adults. A group of seniors, led by a middle-aged female coach, power walked past our boys.

Jeff continued a train of thought. "Chester took a post here at exactly the right time. The move to turn suburban schools into small universities had only just begun. The rise in property value that made all this development possible happened at the same time. He was young, he was bright, he was starting a family of his own."

"So he fit in."

"As the school grew, Chester assumed more responsibility. He coached athletic teams, organized extra-curricular activities. His fellow teachers elected him as their representative. He maneuvered himself into position to take over as principal or vice principal should the opportunity arise."

"Do you think he planned all that?" Xander asked.

"Sure. It's what ambitious people do."

They passed two teenage girls on the next lane walking in the opposite direction. One of them wore a letterman's jacket with a large "StC" patch over the left breast. The other wore a cream colored fisherman's sweater. The two girls stared blatantly at Jeff. Jacket girl tried to hide her head in her friend's sweater.

"If he did all this extra-curricular stuff," Xander wondered, "where did he find the time to raise seven kids? My mom says it takes more than half her time to raise me and I'm just one kid. I think I'm an easy kid to raise. I'm smart, I don't give her a hard time, and I'm off with you on weekends."

Jeff thought about it.

"I suspect the kids were part of his plan. You see, some people plan their whole lives like a strategy. Every detail counts. Their education, who they marry, how many kids they have, where they live, how much money they make at each stage of their life, reaching their ultimate goal, retirement. All the details along the way, too, like the handing down of traditions, what each child learns to do at which age."

"Do you do that?"

"God, no," Jeff laughed. "I think my whole life is an accident. And I like it that way. I fell into just about everything, including my relationship with you. Never intended to be a Big Brother. It just happened."

"I'm certain my life with my mom is an accident. I wish she'd planned better about the dad part."

"If she had, you wouldn't be here. You're the special creation of that one in a million sperm breaking through at just the right moment to your mother's egg. Different man, different sperm, no Xander."

"Hmm."

They walked in silence for a moment.

"So," Xander continued. "How do the seven kids fit into the strategically planned life?"

"I don't know why this is, but when I was in school the most respected teachers were the ones with big families. It's a safe bet all his kids went to school here. Chester would have lived and breathed the school and its goals. With the kids he integrated himself into the brick and fabric of the school."

Xander glanced over his shoulder. The two girls had switched directions and were following just within earshot. To Jeff he said, "In this strategically designed life, what happens if one part of it fails? Divorce or a car accident or one of the kids becomes a drug dealer or a child molester."

"Or a Big Fat Queen?" Jeff smiled. "Something like that did happen. The school hired an outside consultant. Her name was Greta Fields. Targeted our man Chester within the first month. In the reports I read she accused him of incompetence. There were even suggestions of improper behavior with female students. That can drive a stake through your strategic plan."

"How come no one noticed the incompetence or the sexist behavior in the twenty years he worked at the school?"

"I don't know," Jeff said. "Some people are good illusionists. They snooker people with their charm. Other times a business, or in this case a school district, is in financial trouble. A Board member brings in someone from the outside to 'get something' on the highest paid individuals. The stuff they get is fabricated. Doesn't matter. The non-targeted employees act like members of a wildebeest herd. It's unfortunate that one of their fellows is going down in the jaws of a tiger, but at least it's not them. Usually they clear out of the way and let it happen."

"That sucks. Imagine doing that for a living."

"Being the tiger?"

"Yeah. Being paid to assassinate the character of a complete stranger. Cost them their livelihood, possibly ruin their lives, to shave a couple of bucks off of a budget."

"Sometimes it's done to win an election, sometimes to get rid of competition. Those people are called sociopaths. They commit action without conscience or concern for consequences. In one walk of life they're called criminals. In other walks of life they are part of the business or political world. They're usually called consultants. Just a Big Brother word to the wise: it's good to keep your gun handy around consultants."

"Aren't you a consultant?"

Jeff sighed.

"Yes. But I'm not of the sociopath variety. I'm suggesting—just suggesting—that Greta Fields might have been someone brought in to make up bad stuff about good people to get them fired. We won't be able to ask her directly because she died. This year. On the Fourth of July."

"Symbolic."

"Might be."

Xander asked, "Do you think Chester aimed a Roman candle at her?"

Jeff laughed.

"Maybe so. I might be able to find out something about this Greta Fields business from Elenora Chester, Marshall's wife. I'll talk with her at the funeral home tonight. I'll probably get a look at the kids, too."

"If he didn't raise the kids, then she did all the work," said Xander. "She'll probably look like a worn out troll."

"Excuse me?"

"I'm basing this on how my mother looks just raising me."

"You'd better be nice to your mother."

"I'm just kidding."

Jeff got tired of walking in an ellipse. He led Xander off of the track field onto a gravel path. The two girls followed closely behind. It was obvious to Xander that he and Jeff were being stalked. The girls were not even quiet about it. They sloughed about on the gravel like inebriated horses, breaking the serenity of the wooded setting with eruptions of uncontrolled giggling. Jeff seemed so deep in thought he didn't notice the girls.

Then, abruptly, Jeff turned around.

"Are you following us?" he asked.

The girls giggled madly. Jacket girl tried to hide her face in her friend's bulky sweater once again. In the process of hiding and giggling, she fell down. This brought on outright laughter on both their parts.

Finally the one with the sweater said, "I'm not following you, she is. I'm just tagging along so she doesn't do anything stupid."

The two girls saddled up to Jeff and Xander. They didn't speak at first, just stared at Jeff. The one with the sweater sported two enormous hoop earrings in her left earlobe.

She introduced herself, "I'm Helen. I know it's a dorky name, but until someone, like, gives me a nickname —" Helen elbowed her friend, "it's the only name I've got. This crazy person is Jackie and she thinks she's in love with you."

'Oh no,' thought Xander, 'it's the Jeff worship thing again.'

"What grade are you girls in?" Jeff asked.

"We're in the eleventh grade," Helen answered, obviously the spokesperson for the duo. "Jackie's not wearing her boyfriend's jacket, in case you were wondering."

"I don't have a boyfriend," Jackie managed.

"That's her brother's jacket," Helen continued. "He used to go to school here. He lettered in tennis, which is so lame. Her brother was a dork and, like, the least athletic person in the school. He didn't even want the jacket. Jackie's dad made him buy it and put the letter on."

"Don't dump on my brother, all right?" Jackie said. "He's an okay guy. He's just complete Geek Squad material. He'll go far in this world."

"Yeah, right, and we won't?"

"We can't. We're too demented."

The girls calmed down for a moment. They stopped giggling but continued to stare. At Jeff. Just stare.

"He's not Elvis," Xander finally said.

They didn't blink. They didn't even hear him.

"I'm Jeff Redwing," Jeff announced, trying to sound as adult as possible. "This is my son, Xander."

"Cool name," Helen said to Jeff. "Are you, like, Native American? Can you track things?"

Xander waved at them. "I'm another person in the world," he said. "I have an I.Q. of 168."

Nothing. He might as well have been a fly on Jeff's shoe. This had happened before. Women and girls, mostly, but occasionally men. Not that it mattered. Jeff was completely oblivious to his looks and the effect it had on people. One time Xander hounded Jeff until he confessed how long it had been since he dated. It had been a long time. "I think you've made that tricky u-turn back to virginity," Xander said at the time. No response.

"So," Jeff said to the girls. "You were following us. I think that's where we started."

"She wants to get to know you better," Helen replied. She turned Jackie's head away from her sweater and toward the object of her obsession. "She thinks you're hot."

"Well. That's nice actually," Jeff said. "Always nice to be thought of as hot. I'd disappoint you, though. I'm kind of a geek, like your brother. You girls go to school here?"

Jackie stood up straight. "Yeah. We heard you talking about Mr. Chester," Jackie said. "Did you know Mr. C?"

"We went to college together. We were close friends back then. I'm going to write an article about his life and accomplishments for our alumnae magazine."

"You went to Carnegie Mellon," said Helen.

"Carnegie Mellon," chimed Jackie. "He was always telling us stories about Carnegie Mellon. We used to tease him. 'Mr. C, you're not going to tell us that story again!'"

"Right," said Helen. "And he'd say, 'You mean I've told you this story before?' Like he didn't tell us every couple of weeks. He was real proud of the school."

"Mr. C was a real nice guy," Jackie added. "It's too bad that thing happened to him."

"Mr. C was murdered, Jackie," Helen chastised her friend. "That thing that happened to him was murder."

"I know, I know. It's a shame that Mr. C was murdered, all right? Because Mr. C was a great teacher. There are a lot of shit teachers in this school we wouldn't mind getting rid of, but no, it's Mr. C who gets the ax at some Wendy's in, like, fucking Shadyside. Really depraved. What was he doing in the city, anyway? Don't we have any Wendy's in the burbs?"

Jackie feigned a look of disgust, as if the act of traveling into the city killed her teacher.

Jeff asked, "So you had him for class?"

"Oh, yeah," Helen said. "He taught tenth grade English. We both had him. At the same time."

"He was a great teacher," Jackie reiterated. "You know, some of them —the teachers, I mean—can't wait for the bell to ring. Can't wait for the end of each class, can't wait for the end of each school day. Some of them want to get out of here as fast as we do. They want to get the hell away from us."

"Not Mr. C," said Helen. "He really took an interest in his students. If you had a problem he'd stay after class with you. His time was your time."

"He followed our progress," said Jackie. "Like, the next year he'd ask your teachers how you were doing. That kind of stuff. All the kids liked him. He was probably the most popular teacher in the school."

"There's Mrs. Rimondi," Helen pointed out.

"Mrs. Rimondi is nice, but I think people liked Mr. C best. You should put this in your article. Kids used to come back years later, kids that Mr. C helped out. These guys came back to school and stopped in Mr. C's class to thank him personally for the difference he made in their lives. This stuff happened all the time. Who was that one loser, Helen?"

"Rodney Cruise. Oh, God."

"El Supremo Asshole. Rodney Cruise was, I swear, the illegitimate child of a rock slug. He came into Mr. C's class one day in a suit."

"A suit, swear to Christ." Helen crossed herself.

"He came in and shook Mr. Chester's hand. In front of everybody. It was huge. Rodney Cruise, corny as Orville Redenbacher. 'Thank you, sir, for all the good advice you gave me and for staying after class. Thank you for the difference you made in my life.'"

Helen added, "He was holding on to Mr. C's hand, tears welling up in his eyes. Do you remember that?"

"I remember it," said Jackie. "I don't know what this school is going to do without Mr. Chester."

"There's Mrs. Rimondi," said Helen.

"Okay, so there's Mrs. Rimondi."

The girls were quiet for a moment.

Jackie refocused on Jeff. Xander sensed this talk had bolstered her confidence. Jeff suggested they continue walking together along the path.

"I'd like to talk with some of the teachers or administrators who worked with Mr. Chester," Jeff said. "Is there anyone who seemed particularly close with him?"

Helen and Jackie giggled again.

"What?" asked Jeff.

"You should talk to Miss English," Helen told him.

"Yeah," added Jackie, "Miss English and Mr. Chester were, like, real close."

"What do you mean by that?" Jeff asked. "You don't have to worry. I'm not going to print anything salacious. This is an alumnae magazine."

"Well," Helen started, "there were rumors."

"Rumors?"

Jackie pursed her lips suggestively. "Rumors that Miss English and Mr. C were f-u-c-k-i-n-g. Sorry little boy."

"No problem," said Xander. "I've had sex ed class. I've seen *Sex in the City*. I know all about fucking."

Jeff sighed. "I do not let him watch *Sex in the City*. His mother does that."

"And yet," quipped Xander, "at least once a week my father reminds me of things that John Lennon said, like 'there's nothing you can see that isn't shown, there's nothing you can know that isn't known.'"

"Please," said Jeff. "I have an article to write here. So Helen, you're telling me that Miss English and Mr. Chester were having an affair."

"Well, if they weren't having an affair they were at least having it off," said Helen.

"How would you know? Were they indiscreet?"

"They were together all the time," Helen continued. "Between classes, after school, during lunch break. All the time, talking."

"They talked real low," Jackie added. "So you couldn't tell what they were saying."

"Yeah, and they smiled a lot while they talked like they shared a secret. They worked on school projects late at night, all alone in the school building."

"He coached boys volleyball," said Jackie. "She coached girls volleyball. I mean, really."

"But none of this is proof," said Jeff.

"They were in love," said Helen. "You could tell. It had been going on for years. My sister, who graduated, like, five years ago, said it was going on when she went to St. Clair."

"But Marshall was happily married," said Jeff. "That's what everyone said."

"Oh, marriage, right," intoned Jackie sarcastically. "Like that's a consideration."

Xander asked, "Did anyone ever see them kissing?"

Helen and Jackie looked at each other.

Helen said, "We don't know of anyone who ever saw them kissing. But we think we know someone who caught them at something."

"Eeeuwww!" hissed Jackie. "Lesbo Fields. Yes, she definitely had it out for Mr. C. She had it out for him from the moment she left her island and docked her boat at this school."

"Who was Lesbo Fields?" Jeff asked innocently.

Helen explained, "She was this—I don't know what she was. Maybe she was a teacher, maybe she was, like, an assistant to the principal."

"Her job was nebulous," Jackie added. "She taught classes, but not like a regular teacher. Sometimes she filled in, like a substitute. She taught a special credit class once on business administration."

"Yeah," said Helen, "and she coached girls Lacrosse."

"Figures," said Jackie sarcastically.

Helen punched her lightly on the elbow. "Cut it out. I told you about that stuff. It's ignorant."

"What's ignorant?" Jeff asked.

"This stuff about Miss Fields being a lesbian and all. I mean, she was a lesbian. Everyone knew that. But Jackie makes this big deal about it, like the reason she was an evil witch was because she was a lesbian. And that has nothing to do with it. I hope it's okay to use the word lesbian in front of your little boy."

"I'm sure he's seen a television show with lesbians on it," said Jeff, meaning it as a tease.

"*The L Word,*" chimed Xander. "There are also lesbians as regular characters on *Queer as Folk.* And I've read the complete works of Freud. And I'm familiar with the island of Lesbos, so I got the reference you made earlier. And I personally know an adult gay man who is a very close family member. I've been able to observe him up close."

"All right now," said Jeff.

"That's cool, little boy," said Helen. "Because I have an uncle who's gay. He's my favorite uncle and I love him. I'm tired of hearing all this ignorant shit about gay people."

Jackie moaned. "I didn't mean to dump on your uncle, all right? I like him, too. But Miss Fields was an evil witch. And if you ask me she hated men. She sure had it out for Mr. C. And what did Mr. C ever do to anybody? He was a great teacher and he was there for us."

"He never fooled around with any of his female students?" Jeff asked.

"Hell, no," said Jackie. "Who told you that? If anyone told you that, you tell them to come see me and I'll set them straight. Mr. C never hit on a student in his life. If he had, it would have been all over this school. You can't keep something like that quiet. Mr. C was a fine teacher, the best teacher, and he was a gentleman. He might have popped Miss English, but, really, these teachers pop each other all the time when their wives or husbands aren't around to see. Big deal. You should know better anyway. He was your friend."

"He confided something to me," Jeff said. "He said someone was spreading rumors that he was having sex with his students."

"That was probably Lesbo Fields," said Jackie. "Sorry, Helen. That was probably the evil witch, vampire blood-sucking Miss Greta Fields. I'm telling you Jeff, she had it out for him from the first day. She insulted him in public —in front of his class, in the hallways, in front of the principal, in front of other teachers."

"Insulted how?" Jeff asked.

Helen answered. "This one time Mr. C was standing around outside of his room waiting for the bell to ring, talking with students. You know. All the teachers do that between classes. Miss Fields was all the way at the other end of the hall, but she charged right up to him like she had a bayonet in her hands. When she gets to within about ten feet she yells so everyone in the hall can hear, 'Mr. Chester, we do not pay you to loaf around in the halls. These students might have a break between classes, but you are being paid to do a job. You should be in your room preparing for your next lesson.' Really, just like that."

"All the teachers hated her," Jackie added. "Except Modani."

"The principal," Jeff confirmed. "Why do you think Modani liked her?"

"We figured she had something on him," Helen answered. "He was a decent guy before Miss Fields came here. Wasn't he, Jackie?"

"Decent. For a principal. But when Miss Fields was around he changed. They both smiled at each other in this really fake way. Like two arch hypocrites. I figured she smiled like that because she really hated people, but she needed to get what she wanted. He smiled that way because he was really a decent guy and she had him by the balls."

Helen said, "She used to smile at me like that when she passed me in the hall. I don't even know how she knew my name. She'd see me coming and she'd flash me this big grin full of big shark's teeth. 'Hello, Helen, you're looking pretty today.'"

Jackie made a face. "Eeeuwww! Make me retch. She used to do that to me, too. She did that to a lot of girls. She never said a word to the boys, except maybe, 'Get out of my way.' If you ask me, that woman had skeletons in her closet."

"Yeah," said Helen, "and maybe a few in the backyard."

"I knew if that witch ever asked me out or something I was going to tell her, 'Hey, I've got a cross and a necklace of garlic waiting at home for you.'"

Jeff laughed uncomfortably. "Aren't you exaggerating just a little?"

"Let me put it to you this way," said Helen. "Miss Fields would be the number one suspect in Mr. Chester's murder if she wasn't dead already."

"Yeah," said Jackie. "And someone should check her casket to make sure she's still there."

22.

Marshall Kennedy Chester was laid out in the Darryl S. Monroe Funeral Home just off Highway 19 in the suburb of Mt. Lebanon. The Monroe Company offered a nationwide chain of funeral homes with an interesting business model. They took over an aging Cineplex, cleaned and renovated each theater, leveled each floor, thereby transforming the facility into a funeral home with eight or more viewing rooms of various sizes. Designers redecorated the entrance and lobby, but otherwise left that area intact. The food island served espresso and scones instead of popcorn and candy. Small tables and comfy swivel chairs replaced the old theater's vinyl clad benches. People from different funerals could intermingle. The exterior and interior marquees advertised the name of the dearly departed.

This design particularly suited people who liked to get away from the viewing area for a respite. People with fidgety children considered it a godsend. Each cheerfully lighted Monroe facility looked comfortably modern. The appearance of so many people in the lobby, so many names on the marquee, made death less threatening, more a part of the ebb and flow of things. Childhood immunization, high school graduation, marriage, social security and then, finally, one's name up in lights.

A middle-aged couple parked beside Jeff in the parking lot. The woman, wrapped in a heavy grey coat and a muted scarf, rolled down the passenger window.

"Are you going to the Chester viewing?" she asked.

"Yes, I am."

"Why don't we walk together?"

The woman introduced herself as Madeleine, an art instructor at Upper St. Clair Academy.

"I worked with Marsh," she said in a friendly way. Her pleasant roundness reminded Jeff of his own high school art teacher. "This is my husband, Jeremiah." Jeremiah grunted. Without the slightest provocation he launched into the subject of his recent job termination.

"I used to be a chemical engineer with Alcoa," he said. "I worked for them for twenty-eight years. Developed over 300 patents for them. Without warning they called me in and told me I was fired. Just like that. No reason, no explanation."

"I'm sorry to hear that," said Jeff.

"A security guard escorted me to my desk and stood over me while I cleared out my things, like I was an industrial spy. I couldn't even say goodbye to the people I worked with all those years. They didn't thank me for all the excellent work I did. We're done with you old man, we don't want to pay your salary anymore, so get the fuck out."

"Jeremiah!" his wife exclaimed. She took his arm. "You'll have to forgive him. He's a little self absorbed at the moment."

"It's understandable."

"They treated him badly," Madeleine said, shaking her head. "How do you know the Chesters?"

Jeff introduced himself and explained his imaginary relationship with Marshall Chester.

"I have lost a career," Jeremiah said.

"You have lost a job," Madeleine reminded her husband. "Whether or not you have lost a career remains to be seen. Even so, there is a woman in there who has lost a husband, a lifetime companion. There are seven children who have lost a father."

"I know, I know." To Jeff he said, "I'm sorry, young man. It just happened. I'm still burning with it."

"That's all right," Jeff assured him.

They walked into the lobby. Madeleine asked Jeff, "Did you say you went to college with Marsh?"

"Yes, that's right."

"You look a little young."

"Native American, some Greek. We look really good right up until the end when we collapse into a giant puffy wrinkle."

"Good for you. Wish I had genes like that. You must have been close to Marsh to maintain a relationship after all those years."

"Actually, no. We were close once. But then he got married, we lost touch. I've come to pay my respects."

"I see."

"I feel a little guilty about it," Jeff continued, loving his part. "I meant to stay in touch. But you know how it is."

"Oh, yes," said Madeleine, "we think to write or call those people we loved in our youth. As time goes on those people mean more and more to us. Still, we don't reach for the phone. What do you think stops us?"

"Fear of incredulity on the other end of the line."

Madeleine laughed. "Are we so timid?"

"Sometimes I find it hard to step out of my customary life," Jeff observed. "I thought I might write an article for the alumnae magazine about Marsh. His accomplishments, his highlights."

"Oh, to have highlights," laughed Madeleine. "I'm sure the family would appreciate something kind in the alumnae magazine."

"That's what I thought," said Jeff enthusiastically. "I owe Marsh something for the time we spent together in college. Can you think of anyone I should interview for this article?"

"Penny English knew him the best, I think. I'm sure she'll be here tonight."

"The math teacher."

"That's right."

They looked up at the marquee. Cecilia Mae Toth, Andrew Parcifal, George "Red" McLaughlin, Evelyn Scofield, Jennifer Stedman-Weiss, Lawrence Mathew Tolliver and, in the 120mm room, Marshall Kennedy Chester. They followed arrows down a long hall to the widescreen, super Dolby room: the one time haunt of *Raiders of the Lost Ark* and *Star Wars*. Jeremiah grunted. Every bit of space was needed to accommodate teachers, administrators, friends of the family, at least half the student body and, of course, funeral crashers like our friend Jeff.

People crowded each other, chatting avidly. It looked more like a Friday night mixer than a viewing.

A tall good-looking man with dark brown hair and cherry wood eyes greeted Madeleine and Jeremiah at the door. The couple passed into the room and merged with the crowd. The handsome man turned his attention to Jeff. He gave Jeff a crotch shot so palpable it felt like a handshake.

"Hello," he said, "I'm Jeremy Richer. Elenora Chester is my sister."

"Then I've spoken with you on the phone. I'm Jeff Redwing. I went to school with Marsh. I mentioned that I'd like to write an article about Marsh."

"For the alumnae magazine. I mentioned that to El. She was touched. She said she'd be happy to sit down with you and talk after all this is over. She didn't recognize your name, though, sorry to say."

"I didn't really know Elenora. I had classes with Marsh."

"Perhaps she'll recognize your face," said Jeremy. "I thought I recognized you myself a moment ago. But that doesn't make any sense. I'm not from here. I'm from Cincinnati. Just in for the funeral."

"I have to say, you look familiar to me as well," Jeff said. "But as you say, how can that be?"

More people lined up to enter the room. It wasn't time for a protracted conversation.

"Why don't you introduce yourself," Jeremy suggested. "That's Elenora up there."

Jeremy pointed to a tall woman standing near the casket. She looked wan, pale white, drained of blood. She mechanically took the hand of approaching sympathizers as they came to pay their respects. Two young boys stood at her side. One looked to be about sixteen, the other maybe Xander's age or a bit younger. They also greeted the mourners.

"Just introduce yourself tonight so she knows who you are," Jeremy said. "These last few days have been traumatic for her. I'm afraid I had to give her a small cache of tranquilizers, poor thing. Her body is here, but her mind is taking a respite."

"I won't add to her troubles," Jeff promised. "I'll be brief."

Jeff took a few steps into the crowd. Several times he got stuck behind a group of people who themselves couldn't move. Helen and Jackie spotted him. They elbowed people out of the way.

"Some funeral, huh?" said Helen. "It's like a Jimmy Buffet concert."

Jackie rolled her eyes. "It's not that big."

"Well, maybe not that big, but look at these people. I think every kid Mr. C ever taught is in this room. I told you Mr. C was popular."

"I don't know anyone," said Jeff. "Point people out to me."

"Okay, okay." Helen clearly enjoyed having a mission. "See that tall guy over there with the shiny black hair next to the old lady with the grey hair?"

"You mean the guy with the black curly hair, short cropped?"

"Yeah," said Helen, "And greasy. He puts a small can of mouse on it every day. That's Mr. Modani, the principal."

Jackie added, "And that old lady with him works in the office. She arrived with the very first brick when they built the school. She's one of those people who go through life without anyone ever remembering her name."

"Jackie, that's cruel," chastised Helen.

"It's not cruel if it's true. Anyway, what do you care? It's not like she's your mother or something."

Helen grimaced, but let it slide in favor of scanning the room for more faces.

"See that guy with the wrinkled suit, looks like Mickey Rourke? That's Rodney Cruise, the guy we told you about this afternoon."

"The student who followed Marshall's advice and turned his life around."

"Yeah. You might want to talk to him for your article. I mean, if you want to write something mushy."

Jackie added, "He cried and cried when he came in here. He looked like he was going to throw himself on the body or something. Mrs. Chester, like, freaked. I thought there was going to be screaming.

"Then it was like Mrs. C understood. One minute she looked at him like he was a wild monkey or something, then she walked over and hugged him. She held him and stroked his hair like he was one of her sons. It was touching."

"We all think Mrs. C is on drugs," said Jackie. "We went up and got a good look. Her pupils are dilated. That's Mrs. C standing next to the coffin."

"Her I know," Jeff said. "Her brother pointed her out to me."

"Oh, yeah," said Helen. "Mrs. C's brother. He's a pig."

New people entered the room and a swell of noise overwhelmed their conversation.

"I'm sorry," Jeff said, leaning closer to Helen in order to hear. "Did you just call Mrs. Chester's brother a pig?"

Helen and Jackie looked at each other and laughed.

"No, of course not," said Helen.

The girls didn't elaborate. Jeff questioned his senses. It was so loud in the room maybe they hadn't said anything at all.

"How are Mrs. Chester's children taking it?" he asked.

Jackie answered. "The two youngest ones are standing beside her. The older one is Scott. He's one grade above us. The younger one is eight or ten or something like that. Don't know his name."

"Jason," Helen remembered. "The others are in their twenties. They're all here somewhere. One of them is married."

"I understand he had seven children."

"Seven," confirmed Helen. "All boys. Can you imagine it?"

"They hold it together pretty well," Jackie noted. "Then you'll see tears in the corner of their eyes. Well, it figures. The way Mr. C talked about his family, they must have been pretty close."

Three teenagers pressed in on Helen and Jackie. They talked together for a while, ignoring Jeff. He couldn't hear their conversation. It looked like Helen and Jackie might drift back into the crowd. Before they drifted too far away Jeff took Helen's arm and gently drew her toward him.

"Is Miss English here?" he asked. "You suggested this afternoon that I speak with her."

"Oh, yes. Wait, wait." Helen scanned the room.

While her friend looked for Miss English, Jackie leaned into Jeff's right ear and whispered, "Jeff, I think you are so hot. I'd like to lick you from top to bottom like a Popsicle." She reached around and gave his nearest cheek a little squeeze.

"There she is," Helen said, pointing discreetly. "In the corner. Next to the weird lamp that looks like a barcode."

"Red hair?" Jeff verified. "Talking with the man in the leather jacket?"

"Lots of freckles. That's her."

Jackie added, skeptically, "That old-timey greaser is supposed to be her boyfriend."

Helen offered her opinion. "God he's a halibut."

"Trust me," Jackie winked. "Her real boyfriend was Mr. C. The only way this toxic waste in cow skin dates Miss English is if he has her parents locked up in a basement somewhere."

"Eeeuwww. Like *Blue Velvet*."

"*Blue Velvet*. Eeeuwww."

Helen and Jackie excused themselves, blending into the sea of high school students around them. Jackie kissed the tip of her baby finger and wriggled it at Jeff as she faded away.

Jeff approached the area with the barcode lamp, slyly taking in details. Miss English radiated a classic Irish beauty, the kind that gives male students irrepressible erections in class. Long Erin-red hair broke into perfectly formed waves at her neckline then cascaded over her shoulders like a shawl. Every so often she tossed her hair, now to the left, now to the right, as if aeration preserved its form and color. Erotic green eyes warmed a fine-lined, angular face splashed with freckles. A moss green dress accentuated the eyes, followed the contour of her gracefully supple body and drew just enough attention to an ample milk-and-freckles bosom. As Jeff drew closer he noticed that Miss English was quite tall, taller than he, with long model-esque legs.

Jeff imagined for a moment Marshall Chester, a presumably heterosexual male, married to the same woman since college, working day after day, often in private, with this lovely woman.

Jeff continued to draw closer. He looked without looking. From a distance she had seemed like a natural beauty who would not deign to wear make-up, nail polish or nylons. At closer range he observed a subtle use of beauty aids. Her make-up accentuated her porcelain skin. Her nail polish, a soft-gloss pink, suggested an artist's rendering of naturally colored fingernails. Her nylons shaded her legs so slightly they appeared to be airbrushed on.

'Indeed,' Jeff thought, 'what saint could work with this woman day after day and not want to touch her? And if not a touch then why not a taste? Of course a woman like this would wear a subtle, distinctive perfume. It suited her.' It made Jeff want to come in closer.

The companion, by contrast, was sharply drawn, even stark. Straight, thick black hair gathered in clumps. He bore the unhealthy white skin of someone who sleeps during the day and works at night. A classic, Elvis Presley black leather jacket looked vintage—heavy, coarse, torn in a few places, worn at the edges of the sleeves. It was a favorite garment kept in service long after its natural lifespan, perhaps for comfort, perhaps for luck.

Penny English turned to face her companion. He grimaced as if they had been having an argument. Rather than introduce himself at that moment, Jeff thought he might gain more information by eavesdropping. Fortunately the sheer number of people in the room made it possible for Jeff to stand quite close without appearing to intrude.

He heard her say, "I just don't think you should be here, that's all."

The man countered, "Mrs. Chester didn't object. She shook my hand. She accepted my condolences."

"She's in shock. And she's too gracious to throw you out."

"I'm your boyfriend. So I don't dress like your teacher friends. People can't be civil to me?"

"I just don't think it's wise," she said curtly.

The man folded his arms across his chest. "These people met me at the Fourth of July party. Wouldn't it seem strange if I wasn't here?"

"I imagine they'd think I had the good sense to move on."

"Whoa. You're a bitch, you know that?"

She pushed him. He pushed back, but just a little.

"Hey," he said. "I'm not getting rough with you in public. I know how you hate that quality in a man. So I'm going to tell you this nice and calm. Dear."

The man dropped his voice. Jeff tilted his head ever so slightly so that he could hear better. The man spoke under his breath in a salacious tone. Jeff couldn't make out all of the words, but it sounded something like this:

"You can decide not to answer the call of the wild when it drifts past your ears. You can decide not to lick my chaps if that's gotten a little boring for you lately. But make no mistake about it—you and I are together, inseparable. We're business partners now."

Jeff stole a look at Penny English. She looked drained of blood, as drained of blood as Chester's wife. The man leaned in to speak in Penny's ear. Jeff was afraid he might whisper, but he spoke in a soft but full voice.

"I don't have to sleep with you. I've never forced myself on any woman. Never had to. But terminating the acquaintance is out of the question." The man pulled back, let this settle in on her. "Now, since you seem to be ashamed of me, I'm going outside for a smoke."

"Larry—" she started.

"Too late," he stopped her. "I'll be outside when you're ready to leave."

The man forced his way out through the crowd. Jeff turned to face Penny English. At just that moment Penny lifted her hand to call back her departing boyfriend. Her hand and Jeff's face collided in a sharp quick blow. A ring on her finger punctured Jeff's cheek and drew blood.

"Oh dear God," she cried.

Blood dripped onto Jeff's white shirt.

"I didn't realize you were there," she said.

"There are so many people crowded together here I feel like it's last call at the dance club."

Penny frowned at his analogy. Nonetheless, she managed to withdraw a tissue from her purse and press it against the wound. A shriek was heard from across the room. Jackie rushed up to the scene.

"Miss English, how could you puncture that gorgeous face?"

"I didn't do it on purpose. He turned and my hand was there."

"Actually, you turned and my face was there," Jeff corrected.

"You better not hurt him," Jackie play pouted. "He's leaving his wife for me and I want him in mint condition."

Miss English ignored the girl's romantic exaggerations.

"Jackie, go see if you can find some ice, will you?"

"Yes, Miss English." Jackie kissed Jeff on his uninjured cheek and dashed off in the direction of the lobby, Helen in tow.

"We won't see her again," said Miss English, dabbing at the tiny puncture. "She'll run into friends in the lobby and she'll forget all about the ice."

"That's all right," Jeff said. "I think she has a crush on me and it's a little embarrassing."

Penny stopped for just a moment. She tilted her head back and took him in, seeing him in his totality for the first time. She looked up, then down, considered the crotch, then quickly reapplied the tissue to the wound.

"A crush," she said. "That's an old expression. You must be an old fashioned boy."

"Not that old or old fashioned."

"Really? Because the last time someone had a crush was back in 1965."

"Is that so?" Jeff laughed.

"Yes. Kids don't have crushes. They get hot. You don't have to worry about Jackie. Being overtly forward and sexually suggestive is what they do. It's a game and most of them recognize the parameters. I think today's kids break through their social fears by being the opposite of shy."

"That's a relief," Jeff said.

She pulled away the tissue.

"There. All better. And it is a handsome face."

"Thanks," Jeff said, indicating the tissue. "I'm Jeff Redwing. I went to CMU with Marsh."

"A college buddy. Imagine that."

"We weren't close. But I liked him. We hung out a few times. When I heard of his death I contacted the alumnae office about writing an article about his life, his accomplishments."

"Ah." Penny folded her arms. Jeff became concerned that she wasn't buying his story.

"Actually, I was on my way over to introduce myself. Helen and Jackie suggested I interview you. They said you were close to Marshall."

"Yes," was all she said. She regarded him a bit longer, a skeptical look on her face. Was his story that transparent?

Penny English opened her purse and withdrew a card.

"I'll speak with you," she said, businesslike. "This has both my work and home phone as well as e-mail. Call me at home. I don't always check my e-mail."

"Thank you. I'll call. Probably soon."

"I presume you intend to speak with Elenora," she said, a strictness in her voice as if she were about to chastise one of her students. "Do you know her?"

"I know of her."

"That's her over there," English said, indicting Elenora and the boys. "She's been through hell. I would like to comfort her, but I'm afraid she doesn't like me very much. You'll be in an interesting position to say something nice to her, make her feel a little better about herself. You understand?"

"I think so."

"She doesn't have any friends, at least none that I know of. Just her family. And the boys are too young to understand about death. They won't know what to say."

"I'll do what I can."

She looked him over again, grimacing. "Look, I've got to meet someone." She pressed the hand that held her card. "Call me. We'll talk."

23.

"Hello," Jeff said, extending his hand to Elenora Chester. "I'm so sorry for your loss."

"I'm sorry, too," she said. A look of distress came over Elenora's face. "I'm sorry I can't cry anymore. I'm all cried out."

Jeff realized it was the drugs talking.

"That's all right. Mrs. Chester, I'm Jeffrey Redwing. I spoke with your brother earlier today."

"Too much time," she said, impatiently. "Who are you? What do you want from me?"

"I'm sorry."

"There's too much being sorry. Don't be sorry. Just talk." Elenora sighed.

"I was a good friend of your husband. From school."

"Not high school," Elenora said apprehensively. "Not from Vernon Roman days."

"No. College. Undergraduate studies."

"I don't remember you. And I should. You're very good looking."

"I was kind of nerdy back then. Coke glasses, a little chubby."

"You look too young to have gone to school with us."

"Good genes. Native American and Greek. We age well. My mother tells me I will always look ten years younger than I really am."

"Lucky for you. I'm tired," she said. "Very tired. I've been standing here accepting regrets from people I don't know for several hours now. My husband's world filing by one person at a time. They shake my hand, they look sadly into my face. I'm so very tired. What did you say your name was?"

"Jeffrey Redwing. Computer Science. What was your major?"

"I was a Dramat!" she said with exaggerated pride. She actually stomped her right foot, like a toreador. The drugs. "Back then we were the number one school for drama in the country. Better than Yale."

"I remember that. Listen. Mrs. Chester. Elenora. I won't lie to you." Jeff paused for dramatic effect, since they were being dramatic. "Your husband and I weren't close friends."

"Aha!"

The older son touched his mother's sleeve and muttered, "Mom. Don't get carried away. Calm yourself down."

"We knew each other freshman year," Jeff continued. "Then we drifted apart."

"Oh," she said, as if disappointed.

"But he gave me some advice, some excellent advice. It had a profound effect upon my life."

"I have read this script before," she said vacantly.

"I'm a successful man today largely because of the advice your husband gave me."

"Advice and direction," she said imperiously, as if beginning a Shakespeare monologue. "It was his specialty. The world is full of people who are standing someplace because my husband told them to stand there. People are always grateful for a place to stand in the world."

It occurred to Jeff that Elenora's brother should really be here at her side, helping her through this ordeal, circumventing the effects of her sedation. One of the sons could better handle greeting people at the door.

"I won't take up any more of your time," Jeff said.

"Ah," she sighed. "And I was just beginning to like you. You're awfully good looking."

"Thank you. I would like to write an article about your husband for the alumnae magazine."

"You're a writer!"

"Well, I—"

"That's really sweet. Really touching." She looked at her husband in the coffin. Tears swelled her eyes. "My husband would like that. My husband should be remembered by his peers." A wave of joy crossed her face. Tears streamed down freely over her cheeks. "It seems I do have tears for you after all."

Mrs. Chester spread out her arms and gave Jeff a great big bear hug. She cried into his shoulder. For the first time in this murder affair he found himself taking sides. He fervently wished that Marshall Chester had not been in love with Penny English.

Very gently he asked, "May I call you in a few days?"

——

Jeff took a moment to pay his respects to the man himself. He looked down into Marshall Chester's once handsome face. Marshall died just at the age when the health starts to fail. Little failings. Warts in odd places, floaters in the eyes, shortness of breath after minor exertion, tiny gallstones. He knew from his experience with his mother that it was the age when mortality starts dropping hints. Little whispers. Your time is coming to an end. Perhaps Marshall Chester had needed louder hints.

"What secrets did you keep?" Jeff muttered under his breath.

He remembered the scene at Vernon Roman's viewing earlier that day, Dottie Hatfield rubbing the groin of her fallen lover. Jeff looked down at Chester's smallish mound. He wondered if Chester and his wife still had sexual relations toward the end of their marriage. How long before his death had it been? Who was the last person to bring him to orgasm? He imagined Chester's body alive, intertwined with Penny English, meshed together with Vernon Roman. When was the last time this face smiled? Who made you happy for an innocent moment? He looked at the mound again and thought, Genitals have so much to do with murder, don't they? The connecting up of genitals.

Or was it money? What arrangement or displacement of dollar bills brought you to this place? It appeared that Vernon Roman was involved in a lot of money. Dottie had a lot of money. Dirty, untraceable money. Couldn't be a coincidence, all that dirty untraceable money. Penny English and her boyfriend/business partner. There's money in that relationship, he thought. Can't be clean money if she can't get away from him.

And Greta Fields. Who the hell is Greta Fields in all of this? Her harassment of Chester, her supposed problems with men, her melodramatically (or was it ironically) timed death at an Independence Day barbeque. Was sex involved? More dirty money? Did Greta Fields cause Marshall Chester's death or did she presage his death? Sex or money? Sex and money? Or was Chester the innocent victim of an un-medicated schizophrenic?

Upon his retreat, Jeff stopped to say goodbye to Jeremy Richer. Elenora's brother clasped Jeff's proffered hand in both of his. The men locked eyes. Jeff felt at once a pang of recognition.

"I talked with your sister," Jeff said.

"I saw you talking with her."

"I'm going to call in a few days."

"Then possibly we'll see you again. At the house."

"Yes." Jeff looked over toward Elenora. "I hope she remembers our conversation."

"I'll remind her," Jeremy offered. "I'm sorry if she seems incoherent. You just can't imagine how awful it's been. The police practically live at the house and when they're not there they call. Then the reporters. Then neighbors and well-wishers. I don't think Elenora was expecting to see all these teenagers here tonight. Without the drugs I'm afraid she wouldn't have made it."

"I understand." Jeff withdrew his hand. Jeremy let it go, but reluctantly. Of course Jeremy was gay. Of course he was. "I just wonder why you aren't over there with her. To steady her a bit."

Jeremy laughed at the suggestion. "Then we'd have a real scene on our hands. You see, Elenora and I remember our childhood differently. I don't actually think we were in the same childhood together. I remember, well, struggles with my sexual orientation for instance. Elenora remembers every tiny affront, every practical joke I played."

"Like what?"

"Oh. One time she had a favorite doll. While she was out of the room I rigged it so that when she opened her door the doll's head flew off. She tells this story—and many others—with a certain regularity. I must have been six or seven years old. I thought it was hilarious. She still hasn't forgotten it. Every detail of every injustice lives in its own special shrine. When she is medicated she sometimes forgets to be appropriate. I didn't want that to be a problem this evening."

"I guess I can understand about the doll," Jeff said. "My mother tried to wean me from my Teddy bear with similar results. To this day I can vividly see Teddy mixed in the garbage with coffee grounds and food scraps."

"Don't get me wrong," Jeremy said. "My sister and I have a wonderful relationship. I'm the one she called to get her through this tragedy. And I will get her through it. It's just that when she feels the need for chemical adjustment."

"I understand."

"Were you an only child?" Jeremy asked.

"I was."

"Then you were spared the dynamics of sibling rivalry. I don't know if I'm happy for you or sad."

Jeremy smiled. Jeff looked into the swarthy dark face of Jeremy Richer and he knew—he just knew—

"I'm sure I know you from somewhere."

Jeremy laughed. "I thought the same thing about you when you came in. But then, it doesn't seem possible, does it? Perhaps there will be a moment in the future when it comes to us."

"Perhaps it will," Jeff said, still puzzled. "I have a good memory."

"Of course, you remind me of a famous actor."

"Really?"

"Alec Baldwin. In his *Beetlejuice* days. He was quite extraordinarily handsome."

"Are you flirting with me?" Jeff teased.

"Maybe just a little. But that might explain why you seem familiar to me. Alec Baldwin is a favorite of mine. I've seen just about everything he's done. Love the *Saturday Night Live* stuff."

"I see."

Jeremy laughed. "That doesn't explain why I look familiar to you, now, does it?"

No, it did not.

24.

You might have noticed, Dear Reader, that Jeff has long forgotten his agreement with Xander to solve this mystery in front of a computer keyboard. Well, it's exactly what happened the last time. It all started out so innocent and hands off. When he couldn't get the answers he wanted by invading people's computer records, he concocted a plausible story, knocked on their doors and got involved in their lives. And when it all got settled out, the police didn't like Jeff's interference one bit. He just managed to avoid jail time and was warned by a rather mean-looking judge never to get involved with police business again.

During that last scene as Jeff looked into the casket at Marshall Chester, asking by what happenstance of sex and dollar bills poor Chester found himself horizontal in front of his students, I found myself looking over Mr. Redwing's shoulders asking, And just what brings you here? Aren't you getting a little too involved with these strangers? I still remember the look on the face of that mean judge as he shook his finger at you. Why don't you remember it?

But before anything happens, he leaves the funeral complex. Other guests, those that can, saunter out into a night of dropping temperatures. They bundle up against the wind and scurry to their cars. Jeff leans against an iron railing and looks up into the sky. He misses the stars.

Jeff notices another person leaning against the railing. She looks thin and rather frail. Every so often a great heave shakes her body as she attempts to suppress tears. People give her a wide berth. Some of them seem to recognize her, but don't want to get involved with her.

Dressed in classic black (including a veil—not many people wear a veil these days), she clutches a black patent leather purse close to her side. She slowly brings the purse around so that she can see to unfasten the clasp. Her hands shake. A sob rises up through her body and she tries to suppress it. It's too much for someone so frail. She looses control of the purse.

The contents scatter across the walkway. Lipstick, compact, cigarettes, two lighters, a breath spray, followed by a delicate black lace handkerchief that gently sways this way and that as it descends to the ground like a fallen maple leaf.

People step over and around the woman's things but will not help her pick them up. The woman bends down very slowly. She picks up the lipstick, puts it in her purse. She picks up the compact, puts it in her purse. All very slowly. A sob erupts through her shaken and bent body. This time she can't suppress the tears. She cries. Silently. Slowly picking up one of the lighters.

Jeff can't stand it any longer. Who is he? Margaret Mead in the jungle? He approaches the woman and helps her retrieve her things. He holds them collected in his large hands. The woman selects one item at a time and returns it to her purse. She looks at its place in the purse, then selects another item. It all takes a terribly long time. They both stand.

"I desperately needed a cigarette," the woman explains, looking down at the ground rather than into his eyes. "Do you smoke? I guess you don't. If you don't smoke you couldn't possibly understand."

Jeff doesn't reply. The woman's face pulls tightly together; she starts to cry again. Silently. Jeff doesn't know what to do. Should he comfort her? After all, she is a complete stranger. Maybe she has a husband who won't appreciate his solicitations. He thinks, "Surely someone knows this woman. Surely someone will stop and take care of her." But not one person stops.'

After a time, the woman summons enough strength to speak.

"I shouldn't have driven here. I don't drive very well at night. I forgot how quickly it gets dark in December. I don't know what I was thinking coming here on my own."

"Why don't you have a cigarette?" Jeff suggested. "It might relax you a little."

"You're right, you're right. Of course, you're right."

The woman methodically removed the pack of cigarettes from her purse. She looked into the pack and gingerly removed one cigarette as if that cigarette had a name. She felt around inside her purse for one of the two lighters. She didn't like the first lighter, so she put it back and felt around for the other one. She performed these tasks as if they were complex steps she had only practiced for the first time that morning.

Once the cigarette was finally lit, she took a long, deep drag. A wave of relief traversed the length of her body. Within seconds she regained at least a functional portion of her composure. She blew a jet stream of smoke into the air.

"It's very kind of you to stop and help," she said. A small tremor shook her body like an aftershock. "People have been so rude to me tonight. These tears are not for the loss of someone I loved. I hardly knew the man. I knew about him from stories. I met him at a party once."

She stopped and considered this.

"Then why did you come?" Jeff asked.

"His wife. I came for his wife. Elenora Chester. When my companion died, Mrs. Chester was so sweet to me. Really, so very kind. I thought to myself at the time, 'If ever I get the chance to do something nice for her.'" She took a deep breath. "Well. I came for her tonight."

She looked away, tears building once again. A drag on her cigarette and then another brought her back. She released the smoke up into the air, seeming to forget that Jeff was even there.

"I think I saw you inside," Jeff said.

"Really? At the Chester viewing?"

"Yes."

"Were you at the Fourth of July barbecue?" she asked.

"No," he said. "I missed that one, though I wish I hadn't. Everyone keeps talking about it."

"Small wonder. My lover died of a massive coronary at that barbecue."

"Oh my God, you're ... "

"Jane Lund, the bastard lover of Greta Fields." She hissed at two women who went out of their way not to cross Jane's path. "That's right. Keep your distance." Jane took another long drag. This time she let the smoke puff out with each word that she spoke. "They hate me. Not one person would talk with me tonight. Not one person would shake my hand or say hello. I knew I shouldn't have come. I debated it. I said to myself, 'You won't be welcome.' But I wouldn't listen to my own best advice." She tilted her head down and started crying. A long cigarette ash fell across her patent leather pumps.

"I have an idea," Jeff said. "Why don't I drive you home. Your car will be safe in this lot until tomorrow. You can call a friend or take a cab back in the morning."

She nodded vigorously. She had hoped he would make just that suggestion.

————

Jeff tucked Jane into the passenger seat and respectfully asked her not to smoke.

"That's all right," Jane replied. "We're only fifteen minutes away from Virginia Manor. Do you know where that is?"

He knew. Acres of multi-million dollar homes. Land of sunken tubs and marble foyers. More money surrounding Marshall Chester. Jeff turned out onto Highway 19.

"I'm sorry you had such a difficult evening," he said. "You seem like a lovely person to me. Why do you think so many people went out of their way to be rude to you?"

"It's not me they hate," Jane said. "It's Greta. They hate her so much they're getting at her through me even though she's dead. Just in case her ghost is around watching."

"I didn't know Greta," said Jeff.

"It's just as well. She wouldn't have liked you."

"Really? I'm a swell guy."

"Doesn't matter. You're a man," Jane said flatly. "Greta hated all men. I don't mean on principle or in general. She hated men like Hitler hated Jews. She thought womankind would be better off if all of the men were exterminated."

"You're not serious."

"I'm quite serious."

"Well, didn't she work for men? The principal of the school is a man."

"Greta could be devious. She sucked up to men, manipulated men, to get at other men. She planned it like battle strategy. Later when she was in a position to topple the men who helped her, she got them too. It's not admirable. It's not how I would choose to earn a living. On the other hand, I'm not Greta. I don't hate men. I deserve to be treated as if I have my own identity."

"She earned her living destroying men's careers?"

"Well, no. Not exactly."

Jane looked dreamily out the window. She held up her right hand as if holding a phantom cigarette. Jeff thought he'd lost her for the duration of the trip, then she came back.

"I expected to be treated rudely by that Upper St. Clair crowd, but I was hurt by Elenora's reaction. She was so nice to me at Greta's funeral. She was the only one who comforted me, the only one who understood my loss. It's not easy for someone like me to find companionship, much less love. Greta might have been evil to everyone else, but she treated me like I was a rare jewel. She called me that. She called me her rare jewel. I don't expect to be loved like that again."

"What did Elenora do exactly?"

"Well. I went early in the evening. Even then there were hundreds of people in the viewing room. All those teenagers. They make me nervous." Jane turned to Jeff. "I need a cigarette. Couldn't you make an exception and allow me just one cigarette?"

"I'm sorry. I drive someone in this car who is asthmatic." Xander is not asthmatic. But how many of us have told this little lie to our smoker friends? Just a little lie. Just a little one.

"I understand," Jane said resignedly. "I'd quit if I could. But I can't see that happening. Not in this lifetime."

"So you went up to pay your respects to Mrs. Chester?"

"That's right. I approached her, arms out wide. 'Elenora,' I said, 'I'm so sorry.' She stared at me for the longest time like she couldn't place me. Then her eyes got real wide and her lips stretched across her teeth in this hideous way. She looked at me as if I had killed her husband myself. She started screaming. Screaming and screaming out of control. Then that Penny English—do you know her?"

Jeff nodded.

"She grabbed me by the arm and dragged me away. 'How dare you show up here,' she said to me. Everyone stared as she pushed me into the lobby. I was mortified. Imagine being treated like that. I stood right where she left me and cried. I've suffered from severe mental anguish, Jeff. I have spent more than a month or two at Western Psych. That is not the way to treat a sensitive human being. I can't defend myself."

Jane tilted her head down. She cried again.

"I wouldn't take it too seriously," Jeff said, trying to comfort her. "Elenora's brother told me she is on some pretty powerful medication. She said strange things to me, too. I'd never met the lady."

"Really?" Jane looked at him hopefully.

"Really."

"That makes me feel better. I'm very fond of her."

Jeff turned into Virginia Manor. Jane directed him along the curved drives into an exclusive wooded area. She pointed out the house. Quite an impressive house. Jeff stopped in the driveway.

"I need a cigarette," said Jane.

———

Jane's house, designed to look like a Gothic cottage, featured pointed arched windows, massive blocks of dark gray stone, and an iron lantern suspended swag style from a chain over the doorway. Jane begged Jeff to keep her company. Just for a little while. Just until she calmed down.

"Do you like Scotch?" she asked.

"If it's very good."

"Well, I'm no Scotch connoisseur, but Greta loved a good belt now and then. She paid a couple of hundred dollars a bottle. I don't drink alcoholic beverages myself. If you stay with me for a while I'll give you all the Scotch that's left in the house. I think there are three or four bottles."

"Sounds like a deal," Jeff said.

Jane walked him through the first floor of the house. She gingerly proceeded from one room to the next turning on lights. She looked surprised by the appearance of each room as if she was a house sitter rather than the homeowner. The rooms were expertly furnished with a deft blend of antiques, modern furniture and art. Interiors created by decorators sometimes felt cold to Jeff. These interiors felt cold.

"Everything's so clean and organized," Jeff commented.

"We have a maid service. There are rooms in this house I have never seen. I do most of my living down in the basement. This floor and the second floor I could do without. If I think of it, I sleep in my bedroom upstairs. Most of the time I fall asleep on the couch in the basement. I've never been in the attic. I have no idea what's up there."

"Why don't you get a smaller place?"

"Oh, I will eventually. But this house was Greta's pride and joy. She bought it for me. It seems disrespectful to just clear out."

Jane took Jeff's coat and hung it in a closet near one of the first floor bathrooms. She left for a moment, then returned with a fresh pack of cigarettes and a lighter.

"There used to be cats," Jane said with a certain amusement. "Can't you just imagine cats in this place? Five of them. Greta loved cats. I gave them away, though. I'm afraid I'm not very good with living things. I was afraid I would forget to feed them and they would starve or something." Jane laughed a strange hiccupping kind of a laugh. "It's all I can do to keep myself alive."

Jane led him down a short set of carpeted stairs into a basement suite of rooms. The largest room featured a gas fireplace, a large screen TV, and a cabinet that contained stereo and home theater equipment. Overstuffed recliners faced the TV in rows, movie theater fashion. Against the back wall stood a professional popcorn machine, a juke box from the fifties, and an elaborate wet bar with leather barstools.

"Take off your shoes," she said.

The extra thick carpet felt good on his aching feet. From the wet bar Jane procured a crystal glass, some ice and a bottle of Scotch unfamiliar to Jeff. McGlaughlain. Aged twenty-four years. While he poured, Jane walked into a pantry-sized room next to the bar.

"There are two bottles and a full case," Jane pronounced, re-emerging. "I forgot Greta bought her Scotch by the case. She smuggled it in because of our state store system."

"Did she like to drink?"

"She did." Jane seemed confused for a moment, then she realized she had spoken rashly. "Greta wasn't an alcoholic. She didn't have a drinking problem. But I would say she drank a little every day. Mostly the Scotch.

Very expensive brand she brought over from Scotland every year."

Jeff sipped it. Smokey, peaty, rich, dark, potent. The first sip sent a shiver through his body, which he cast off with a shake of his head. "Whew!"

Jane laughed. "That first taste is a banger. It hit Greta like that, too. I think she used it as a signpost to mark the end of her work day."

"I have a million questions about Greta," Jeff said.

"She was a strange woman. An individual. Well, I don't mind talking about her. I just hope she doesn't mind. Her spirit is in the house, you know." Jane walked off in the direction of the next room, indicating to Jeff that he should follow and bring the bottle. "I won't tell you anything too personal."

"No, of course not."

"Then again I hardly ever think anything is too personal. It's a character flaw of mine. Nothing seems too personal to me."

The next room turned out to be an elaborate kitchen, complete with a Viking stove, professional microwave, wall ovens and a sub-zero refrigerator freezer. Jane withdrew an oversized mug from a cabinet, poured full fat milk up to the top, and microwaved it. She added two tablespoons of Ghirardelli cocoa. This was done slowly, methodically, with the utmost concentration, as if she had just learned to do it. Then she added another tablespoon of cocoa, then another. She laughed her odd, staccato laugh. It pierced the silence of the room.

"I don't know why I worry about how much chocolate I put in here," she said, amused.

"You don't look like you have to worry about your figure," Jeff remarked. "You have a very trim figure."

"Oh, I worry Mister," she said. "I worry about every calorie." She blew across the top of her cocoa, then took a sip. "After all, what does a girl have except her figure. Follow me."

Jane led Jeff into yet another room. Here a floor to ceiling plate glass wall provided a view into the woods. Opposite this wall was a ceramic hot tub that looked large enough to hold twelve people. Jane pushed a button on the side of the tub. Lights came on inside the water, then bubbles erupted. Soon steam came off of the water and filled the room. Condensation fogged the plate glass wall.

"Do you like music?" she asked, testing the water temperature with her fingers.

"Very much. I write music. In fact, I have a recording studio in my home."

"I, myself, like Diana Ross and the Supremes. For years I wanted to be Diana Ross. I used to fantasize about it all day."

Jane set her cocoa and her cigarettes on a ceramic ledge that surrounded the tub. As if completely unaware that Jeff was in the room, Jane started to undress.

"When I was a hooker at the Descending Angel Massage parlor—did you ever go there, Jeff?"

"No, I never did."

"Wouldn't that be ironic," she said hiccup laughing, "if you turned out to be someone I gave a BJ to back in my parlor days. Hmm. Well." She cleared her throat. "Anyway. One of my jobs at the massage parlor was to stand in this glass booth. Men would come in, sit down in a little chair. Then I would slowly undress and, you know, tease them while they did their business. All day long I'd take off my clothes, listen to the perverted things they said, wait until they came all over the glass, then put my clothes back on so I could take them off for the next guy. I'll tell you, you acquire an interesting perspective on humanity when you're the naked woman in the glass booth."

"I can imagine."

Jane stripped to her bra and panties. The bra gave her a moment's difficulty. She looked back at Jeff as if to say, 'Would you?' He gallantly unhooked her bra. Without a hint of hesitation she dropped the panties, kicking them off to the side.

Jeff sucked in his breath at the sight of her—so skinny the color of her ribs showed through her flesh. Her ass looked like little more than skin-clad pelvic bones. She looked like a famine refugee.

"I used to get through the tedium of the day by imagining I was Diana Ross." She laughed, looking back at him with an innocent smile. "Yes, it's true. I'd do my *Stop In the Name of Love* routine. *Ain't No Mountain High Enough.* Then I'd do my costume change, you know, and come back out and do *Touch Me In the Morning.*" Hiccup laugh. "I thought of writing Diana Ross. I thought she might get a kick out of it. But then I thought, no, what if she writes a horrible letter back to me. I'm so sensitive. I'd be crushed. I'd never be able to listen to the Supremes again. And they give me so much happiness."

Jane sat on the edge of the hot tub, looking forlornly into the water as if pondering the bleak, meaningless void of a life with no Supremes.

"What did the men think?" Jeff asked. "The men who watched you."

She laughed. "Perverts don't care what you do as long as you are naked. Perverts have remarkably few standards."

With that she swung her legs over and nestled down into the bubbling steam. Once adjusted to the heat, she took her mug and her cigarettes and drifted over to the far side of the tub so that she could look through the glass wall into the woods.

"You can come in," she said. "But no funny stuff. I'm a lesbian."

———

Jeff took his glass and his bottle of Scotch and stepped into the tub. He settled near Jane, not too close but not too far away, facing the same direction, looking out through the plate glass wall.

"So how did you become a hooker?" Jeff asked. "I don't actually know any hookers, but you don't match up with any of the ideas I have about them."

"Oh, you'd be surprised. The massage parlors were filled with girls who just wanted to earn a better wage than they could get out in the minimum wage world. I fell into it, really. I have difficulty focusing or concentrating for long stretches of time. I kept getting fired from my Kelly Girl jobs." Staccato laugh. "So I answered this add for a receptionist. Light duties, the ad said. I'll never forget that."

She sipped her cocoa, dragged on her cigarette, and drifted off for a while.

"So what happened?" Jeff asked.

"Well, this Mafia guy who owned the place told me the receptionist position had been filled, but he had something else available if I was interested. This is how they got all their girls. He told me they needed a girl who could give good BJs. I know this is hard to understand, but he was very persuasive. He told me how easy it would be, how much money I'd be raking in. He offered to teach me everything I needed to know.'

"Of course, I learned on him first. He taught me exactly how to do it, how men really liked it. Then he had me give all his Mafia friends BJs, you know, to refine my technique. It wasn't difficult. And, you know, the work wasn't so bad. We had time to rest up between clients. The girls could sit around and talk. There was a microwave and a refrigerator, so we could fix lunch. There was a television so we could watch our soaps.

"It was the perfect job for me because it wasn't the same thing, constantly, over and over again for eight hours. And I could smoke cigarettes. You don't know how difficult it is out in the working world when you smoke like I do. Of course, you're never allowed to smoke in a business office, never. So, it was a job with certain perks. And he was right about the money, at least at first. On paper I was making, like, like forty bucks a BJ. Some days I'd do as many as fifteen. Of course, you had your slow days, too. But, if the bastards had given me my money I would have been pulling maybe as much as fifty grand a year.

"But they never let the girls have their money. At first they give you fists full so you think you're heading toward easy street. Then they start fining you for this and that, buying you clothes you don't need, taking money out of your pay for things they call supplies. If the customers like you and you make a lot of money they actually charge you rent. Yes, rent for the little room you give the BJs in. And it's strictly downtown prices, I can assure you. No, the girls end up with just enough money to survive.

"But it's worse than that. After you're there for a while and you catch on to the game—I mean, really, you're giving BJs the live long day for what amounts to the minimum wage so that these Mafia characters can live in castles in Sewickley Heights—then they make it clear you can't leave, you can't quit. If you're a good moneymaker, you're in until they kick you out. Or they kill you. One way or the other. These people mean business. They beat me up, locked me in a basement room once for several days, made me eat feces. I'm dead serious. You wouldn't believe the stuff they did to the girls."

At that point Jeff wondered if he wouldn't be better off back at home, safe in a comfortable data stream instead of Jane Lund's bubbling tub. It was strange and dangerous out here with these people who keep up appearances, these people who live in stone cottages with landscaped grounds, these people who pretend to get along with each other.

In reality they don't get along at all. Inside their properly quaffed shells they carry around thousands of unrelated, self-created standards. Sometimes something as unacceptable as murder creeps within the range of what can and cannot be done. And there he was in Jane Lund's tub. Naked. Buzzed from really, really good Scotch.

Then he remembered Penny English and her leather-clad friend. What had he said? She could end the sex but she could not end the relationship.

"So how did you get out?" Jeff asked.

"Greta. She found me at this woman's bar on the South Side called Bloomers." She looked at him as if to ask, 'Ever heard of it?' He hadn't. "A variety of support groups met there on certain nights. Some were lesbian groups. I happened to join an eating disorder group. Greta was part of that same group. She took a liking to me. I don't know why. I was the exact opposite of her. She was pushy, I was quiet. She was over confident, I lacked confidence. She couldn't stop eating, I couldn't eat at all—at least I couldn't keep anything down. But she liked me.

"When she found out about the abuse, how the Mafia family that owned the massage parlor wouldn't let me go, she marched me right over to Johnny D's place. Johnny D was the owner of Descending Angels. He lived in this palace in Sewickley Heights. Palace. Castle. Whatever. If you think this place is nice, it's nothing compared to Johnny D's place. It's eight times the size of this. He has horses and stables, the whole bit."

"She marched you over there?" Jeff asked. "Wasn't that dangerous?"

"Very. At least I thought so. But I couldn't stop her. Greta was bull headed. No man ever ran her or denied her and Johnny D wasn't going to be the first. I have to say, she got away with it. Johnny D's wife ushered us to his private study. Big joke, this pussy hustler with his study full of dark wood and leather books in enclosed bookcases. Well," Jane blew a cloud of smoke into the air, "Greta paid him ten thousand dollars to train a new girl. She wrote out a check, slapped it on his desk, and pointed a finger at him. 'You bother her again, I'll shoot you dead,' she said. She actually said that to Johnny D. Yes, yes."

"So what happened?"

"He never bothered me again."

———

"I really wanted intimacy," Jane said. "I think when I met Greta I was just inches away from chronic, irreversible mental illness. She pulled me back from the brink."

"Really." Jeff took another sip of the wondrous Scotch. It was so easy to take a sip and then another. He found himself drifting into that realm where everything is peaceful and profound. God knows just what He is doing and the entire universe is exactly the way it should be. Oh, and wasn't it lovely of Him to share with humankind the recipe for this mysterious, magical golden elixir. Sip. Sip. "How did she do that?"

"She sat with me, took an interest in me. She was such a successful woman, so strong, I couldn't help but stammer in front of her. But that was okay. Everything about me was okay. Even my bulimia. When I moved in here she said, 'I know you throw up. You don't have to hide it from me. If you're going to do it, just go ahead and do it.' She took better care of me than my parents."

Jeff couldn't stand the hot water another second. He pulled himself out of the tub and sat on the outer edge.

"There's something I don't understand," he said. "The person you're describing sounds empathetic, kind, nurturing. Why did the teachers and students from Upper St. Clair hate her so much?"

"Um, well," Jane blew out another stream of smoke, "there was a difference between her social self and her work self. Socially people loved Greta. She was very popular at Bloomers. She was generous, she made everybody laugh."

"What was the difference at work?"

"She despised many of the people at work, especially the people who worked under her. She told me once that organizations are filled with Old Ivy People."

"Old Ivy People?" Jeff found a towel and started to dry off.

"People who have been with an organization so long that ivy grows up their backs. It was Greta's philosophy that Old Ivy People caused organizations to stagnate. Career people, loyal people, the kind of people who stay with one company all of their lives, the people who consider themselves to be part of a family instead of part of a workplace—she considered it her duty to rid the organizations that hired her of such people."

"That was her official job? She was hired to fire people?"

"I think so. I mean, she always had other duties. The employees couldn't suspect or they'd band together to undermine her work."

"I see. So how did she go about getting rid of these Old Ivy People?"

"She claimed Old Ivy People were always lax and inefficient. They felt so secure about their place in the family that they didn't have to be careful. They took their jobs for granted the way children take their place at the table for granted. All she had to do was watch and report lax attitudes and inefficient performance to the higher ups. Soon the Old Ivy People found themselves falling out of favor. She usually got them fired. She said she liked her job. She liked scraping the ivy off of the walls."

Jeff wrapped the towel around his middle and put the cap back on the top of the Scotch bottle. He offered to fix another cup of cocoa for Jane; she readily accepted. From the kitchen he asked, "Was Marshall Chester one of her targets?"

"I'm afraid so," she replied. "Of course, I thought he was a perfectly nice man. His students seemed to like him. But Greta saw him as a wimp who, through sheer likeability, was on his way to becoming principal of the school. The school could not compete with other suburban school districts with a mediocre principal. Greta said for the good of the future of the school she had to scrape him off the wall out to the bottom of someone else's organization."

Jeff returned with her cocoa, six heaping tablespoons.

"Thank you," Jane said, taking the cup. "Of course, people catch on after a while. You can see why she wasn't popular."

"Indeed."

"At the Fourth of July barbecue only the principal and the board of supervisors—the people who hired her—would talk to us. Everyone else excused themselves or outright turned their backs on us. Except for Mrs. Chester. She didn't have anything to say to Greta, but she took a liking to me. She went out of her way to engage me in conversation.

"Greta just thought she was sucking up to me so I would use my influence to get Greta off of her husband's back. You see, they didn't fully understand what was going on. They thought Greta was doing these things out of spite, or because her life was miserable, or for some other personal, pathological reason. They didn't understand that Greta had been hired by the boys—or the girls—upstairs."

"Are you telling me that Marshall Chester was the reason the Board hired your companion?"

"He wasn't the only target, but he was certainly the most important one."

"I don't understand something. Why didn't the Board just fire him?"

"Well, the way Greta explained it, you can't just fire someone who has been around long enough to be an institution. You have to get stuff on him. You have to be able to demonstrate incompetence in a court of law. If you want to keep staff loyalty, you have to diminish your target in the eyes of his coworkers. They have to get the idea that they were wrong to think so highly of him. They have to think in retrospect that he deserved to get the ax."

"But if the people at the barbecue shunned Greta, she must have failed at her job. Don't you think?"

"Greta had problems at Upper St. Clair," Jane said. "Penny English confronted her directly any number of times. She knew exactly what was going on. She told Greta in no uncertain terms to lay off Chester or she'd pay a stiff price."

"Sounds like a threat."

"Greta took it that way. She thought Chester and English were lovers. She was trying her damnedest to catch them at something when she died."

"She died at that barbecue, didn't she?" Jeff asked. "Someone told me that. You told me that."

"Yes. Massive coronary. She was rushed to the hospital, but she was dead before she got there."

"What caused the coronary, did they tell you?"

"Clogged arteries, probably. We all assumed. Too much cheesecake. Greta never stopped eating. She had a heart condition. The doctor told her it was inevitable."

Jeff mulled it all over. He looked around for his clothes.

"What hospital?" he asked.

25.

Old Mrs. Ornish waddled slowly down the wooden steps to her basement, one step at a time. She carried too much weight. She knew that. Carried too much weight ever since she was a little girl. But if Father didn't mind, then she didn't mind.

In the second basement, adjacent to the root cellar, Father had built several walls of enclosed shelving for Mrs. Ornish's preserves. Father liked to tinker with wood, had a natural talent for it. Most people thought Father would have made a good carpenter. The preserves cupboards, constructed of maple, fitted tongue and groove style, looked and felt like substantial furniture.

Mrs. Ornish preserved everything that came up out of the earth. Pears, cherries, apples and even peaches grew on the Ornish property in addition to raspberries and blackberries. Mrs. Ornish also pickled watermelon rind, baby cucumbers, beets and even Scotch Bonnet peppers.

Of course, when she and Father were young they didn't have much money. Putting up food was a necessity. Now that the Ornish children had grown and were out of the house, Mrs. Ornish put up food to give as gifts to neighbors or to distribute at church. Some jars went to the food bank. One of the neighbor boys offered to create interesting labels on the computer for Mrs. Ornish's preserves so they could be sold in the local markets, but, well, they didn't need the money and the whole thing seemed like a lot of bother.

Into a large wicker basket Mrs. Ornish collected jars of apple butter, tomato butter, piccalilli, and raspberry preserves along with a few small jars of her Scotch Bonnet relish. These were destined for an assortment of gift boxes upstairs, colored boxes lined with straw and colored tissue paper. Food made such a nice gift at Christmastime.

It was her custom to prepare three boxes each day starting just after Halloween. That way she had all the gifts she needed by December 24th.

A handmade cloth item went into each box on top of the preserves. This year, Mrs. Ornish had prepared colorful cotton aprons from a bolt of fabric featuring flowers native to the Virgin Islands. Last year she had made oven mitts. Next year she thought she might make tea cozies. More people drank tea these days. Her neighbors might just appreciate a handmade tea cozy.

Mrs. Ornish waddled back upstairs, one step at a time. It was a slower process going up than going down. She was getting old now, but she thought it was a good idea to tackle the steps every day. Exercise was very important. Mrs. Ornish walked as often as possible, always took the stairs, did her own cooking and housework. Of course, she did her own eating, too. That was the problem.

At the kitchen table she assembled her boxes, straw around the edges, tissue between the jars. Very beautiful. Just the kind of gift she enjoyed getting herself. Wouldn't everyone be so pleased. The aprons went on top, then another sheet of tissue, then she fitted the lid over the box. Father would have to help her with the bows. She thought for a moment of the three families who would receive these particular boxes, each family needy in some way. She said prayers over the boxes, asking the Lord to watch out over her neighbors and bring them better fortune in the years ahead.

Just then Mr. Ornish came in from outside. He had been working in the shed where he kept his carpentry tools and his supply of wood. He was always working on something these days. This time it was a new Star of Bethlehem for the Christmas tree on the church lawn. A pair of goggles rested on his head.

"I need a beer," he said.

"I don't want you drinking when you're operating that buzz saw," said Mrs. Ornish.

"Mother, I've got a hundred saws. Not all of them buzz."

"But they all cut off fingers. And we know what else."

"Never mind. Whose boxes are those?"

Mr. Ornish withdrew a bottle from the refrigerator. Bottle, always had to be a bottle. Canned beer didn't taste natural.

"One is for Ethel and her two boys."

"Ethel Childs."

"Yes," she said. "You know which one she is. She sits in the middle pew with her two boys. Always sits in the middle of the middle. Even on the bus, she told me."

"No kidding." Father took a long drink of his cold beer, downing almost half the bottle in the first gulp.

"This middle one is for Mr. Lubinski on Meadville Street. You know, the widower."

"Two years now, isn't it?"

"Going on three. I saw him in the supermarket the other day. The man doesn't know how to buy an apple for himself. I took him around and showed him. This is how you buy a cantaloupe, this is how you buy broccoli. I'll bet that man forgot everything I told him."

"Probably."

"He doesn't want to learn to shop for himself. He wants his wife to come back from her grave to do the shopping for him. You men," she pointed a finger, "you believe what you hear on television. You all think you're going to die before we do. But let me tell you something, many times the woman goes first. I could go first, easily."

"Mother," said Mr. Ornish. "It doesn't matter. When they lower you into the ground I'm jumping in with you."

"When I die you'll be living off of the preserves in the basement."

"Ah, well, go pound salt."

Father helped his wife tie the bows on top of the boxes. She could smell the beer on his breath already. She didn't like the smell. She wished he wouldn't drink just now. She had something on her mind. This thing, she couldn't stop thinking about it. It made her sullen and gave her doubts."

"Jacob," she said, looking down. "I want to talk to you about something."

"What is it, Mother?"

"It's about Pittsburgh."

He knew, but anyway—

"What about Pittsburgh?"

"They buried that boy without his head."

"What else could they do?" Father shrugged. "They didn't have his head."

Mother nodded. She had something bigger in mind, something she had put off asking for several days, ever since she heard the news.

"Jacob."

"Yes, dear."

Almost in a whisper. "We don't have it. Do we?"

"No, Mother. I don't know who has that boy's head, but it isn't us."

"I looked for it," she said.

"You didn't find it."

"No, I didn't."

"That's because we don't have it."

She was going to let it go—clearly he wanted her to. But she had to say it, just to be complete. "I thought you might have done something, something I don't know about. Business that you thought you should keep from me."

Mr. Ornish embraced his wife. "Now, Mother, you know I don't hide things from you. Never."

She started to cry. "I liked that boy."

"I liked him to. It was a dirty rotten shame what happened to him."

"He was bad," she said. "But he was good, too."

"Yes, he was," Mr. Ornish agreed. "Did his job well. I had no complaints."

Mrs. Ornish broke away. Walking to the window, she pulled a hanky out of her dress pocket and wiped her eyes.

"What about the money?" she asked.

"We got most of it, long before this happened. He was very dependable that way. I shouldn't have agreed to installments, though, Mother. We violated our own solid business practices there."

"It's a shame about that boy."

Still Mrs. Ornish wondered. She wondered who killed that boy. She wondered why someone would take his head of all things. That was odd.

She didn't doubt her husband. In all their years together he had never given her reason to doubt his word.

"We'd better make sure the rifle's handy," she said.

26.

Jeff shared sensitive, proprietary information with a few well-chosen Internet friends around the globe. He, quid pro quo, tapped into their resources from time to time.

Jeff never passed up an opportunity to talk with the Eggman. For that reason he rigged his Mac to play a certain Beatles song when the Eggman dialed in. Monday morning, still groggy from Scotch, *I Am the Eggman* played clearly over the Bose speakers. The computer screen jumped to life with dancing blue walruses. A caption underneath read: Walrus, are you there? Walrus, Walrus answer do. Walrus, Walrus, Goo-goo-ga-choo.

Jeff typed:

I'm here. Rough evening. Too much good Scotch.

EGGMAN
Oh-oh. 10,000 brain cells gone, never to return.

WALRUS
A drop in the bucket. I've got plenty left.

EGGMAN
Hold that thought. It will give you comfort
in your silver years. How is Xander?

WALRUS
Brilliant, gifted, and white middle class. He is
too sharp for his school, too sharp for his grade,
too sharp for his mother. He already outsmarts

me on the odd occasion. Will eclipse me entirely
by age fourteen. Another Eggman in the making.

A giant, pale white egg, wearing a graduation cap, appeared on Jeff's
screen. It turned a subtle crimson color.

EGGMAN
I blush, but then you always know what to say.
Got the info you requested on the Fields woman.
Why didn't you just come to me directly? Anyway.
Whoa on the Fields info.

WALRUS
Is it hot?

A Vargas-drawn rear end appeared on Jeff's screen. A finger touched
it, then pulled quickly away. The sound of sizzling steam played over Jeff's
speakers.

EGGMAN
Greta Fields is lava hot. Maybe New Jersey
mob hot. Not a nice person. Want specifics?

WALRUS
Please.

EGGMAN
Am sending the written details over fax. Born
in Waterbury, Vermont. Attended Catholic schools
K-12. Parents some money, not rich. Sarah
Lawrence College, double major: history and
economics. Mostly Bs. MA from Duke
University, business administration. Mediocre
grades at Duke. Thesis: Our Aging Workforce.
Subtitle: The Evolving Work Ethic in the Post Nuclear Age.

WALRUS
What was the gist?

EGGMAN
Thesis not on electronic file. Review Committee

comments available. Tweny-page doc. Accepted thesis
with reservations: failed to take worker morale
into account.

WALRUS
Mediocre grades in graduate school.

EGGMAN
Yep. Here's an interesting stat, my watery
friend: nine jobs in seventeen years. Hired most
places as consultant. I picked up a couple of resumes
along the way. Called herself a Workforce
Evaluator. Got 60+ per annum. She basically
targeted lifetime employees and fired them.

WALRUS
She did the firing?

EGGMAN
No. She collected evidence, built cases for
firings.

WALRUS
Anything interesting about list of employers?

EGGMAN
Two Jersey companies, Amalgamated Resources
and Garden State Construction, suspected mob fronts.
Laundered money specialists. Went from one straight
to the other. Did she know? Can't find that info in
her files. Did her usual targeting and firing, then
moved on.

WALRUS
How recent?

EGGMAN
Jobs 7 and 8. Just before Pittsburgh.

WALRUS
Jesus. What else did you find?

EGGMAN
Four husbands, four divorces, four big
settlements. Soaked them all for cash
upfront. No alimony. No court fights.

WALRUS
Blackmail maybe. Exact figures by any chance?

EGGMAN
What do you think I am? A miracle worker?
Okay, okay. You forced it out of me. About
three million in cash and investments. Some
property.

WALRUS
Anything strange on divorce records?

EGGMAN
Money looks kosher. Strange, perhaps, that
she marries and divorces four husbands while
maintaining memberships in numerous gay and
lesbian organizations.

WALRUS
Do you know which ones?

EGGMAN
Friends of Stonewall. National Gay Task Force.
National AIDS Task Force. Joined at least
one organization in every city she worked.
Dropped big bucks. $200,000 for AIDS
research. Maximum for political candidates.

WALRUS
How did you get this stuff?

EGGMAN
Government files, of course. Naive boy.

WALRUS
Must be the Freedom of Information Act.

The government's freedom to collect our
information. So what brought her to
Pittsburgh?

EGGMAN
Last in a line of spinster aunts died and
left her real estate and mucho bucks. The
woman was good at having money handed to
her. Graduated top in her class in that field.
Looks like she decided to settle down at
last. Considered several Pittsburgh jobs.
Alcoa courted her.

WALRUS
Go on.

EGGMAN
Isn't much else. She took the Upper St. Clair job.
Enter the Grim Reaper.

WALRUS
I understand she died of a massive coronary
on the Fourth of July.

EGGMAN
That's what the records show. St. Clair
Hospital. Heart failure. History of heart
disease. 160 pounds overweight. Sky-high
blood pressure. Boom! Looks like she ate
one mint too many. That's a Monty
Python joke.

WALRUS
I know it well. Every sperm is sacred.
Can you fax me the autopsy report?

EGGMAN
I'd rather not.

WALRUS
Can't you copy the hospital files?

EGGMAN
Don't be impertinent. I've copied FBI for you;
I've copied Homeland Security for you, which
is a little harder. Autopsy report was boring.
I didn't choose to copy it. Sorry.

A happy face formed on Jeff's screen. The ends of the smile line turned
down, making a sad face.

WALRUS
Can you remember what it said? It's important.

EGGMAN
One artery completely clogged, two partially
clogged. Severe heart tissue damage.
They probably didn't look at this one too
closely. Fourth of July. Busiest day of the year
at most ERs. Do you suspect foul play?

WALRUS
I'm investigating two murders. Lots of people
got something they wanted when she died,
including one of the murder victims.

EGGMAN
I don't see lots, but I see one glaring
beneficiary.

WALRUS
Who?

EGGMAN
Jane Lund. Picked up about 2 million in
real estate, half a million in cash, another
mill in stocks, an entire row of apartment
buildings in a place called Mount Lebanon.

WALRUS
Wow!

EGGMAN
You know this Jane Lund?

WALRUS
Shared a hot tub with her last night.

EGGMAN
Hope you had your rubbers on. So
tell me, what do the stinking rich look
like with their clothes off?

WALRUS
This one looked undernourished. She's
anorexic and bulimic.

EGGMAN
She's also just a little nuts, padre. Lots of
medical bills to a place called Western
Psychiatric.

WALRUS
I think she's better now.

EGGMAN
Walrus, baby, they're never better. Just
releasable. Watch yourself. These are
dangerous people.

WALRUS
I know it. Look, I owe you for this.

EGGMAN
You bet your ass you owe me. You owe
me big, Mr. Inventor, Mr. Three-Hundred-
Patents.

WALRUS
What can I invent for you?

EGGMAN
A virtual reality machine that gives good
head.

WALRUS
I'll work on it.

EGGMAN
Hey, we can't have these breakthroughs
fast enough.

WALRUS
You're a juvenile.

EGGMAN
I'm horny, I'm lonely, and I'm ugly—
the fatal trinity.

WALRUS
You're beautiful to me, Eggman. Keep
in touch.

EGGMAN
Goo-goo-ga-choo.

27.

Jeff called the coroner's office and asked for Ellen Coffey.

The previous year Mrs. Coffey had provided a number of important insights that led to the solution of the mystery that got Jeff into so much trouble with dangerous criminals and then, ultimately, the law. Mrs. Coffey, being quite fond of Jeff, warned him to keep his investigation within the realm of intellectual exercise. Like many of us, Jeff patiently listens to good advice, nods his head vigorously, then doesn't take it.

It had all started very innocently, with a simple crime reported in the *Post Gazette*. Jeff asserted, based perhaps on the occasional work he did with the computers used in FBI forensic labs, that entire crimes could be solved at the keyboard itself. No need to interview suspects, no need to risk undercover work with bloodthirsty killers. Xander challenged him to prove it. Solve the crime reported in the *Post Gazette* using only the tools available through his impressive array of computers.

Jeff thought, 'Ah ha! This would be a good Big Brother/Little Brother exercise for Xander.' The library, the Science Center, even the penguins at the zoo had gotten just a bit tedious lately. A little forensic investigation, conducted from the safety of the Cloisters, might excite things a bit. He and Xander could puzzle out the tricky little murder reported in the paper. Purely an intellectual exercise.

Evidence, investigation, deduction, theory. Investigation led to more evidence, further deductions, additional theories, all leading inevitably to more investigation. How simple it would be to pretend to be someone else, introduce himself to the suspect in question, and unearth the missing link. He had lied so successfully so many times before and gotten away with it. He was certain he could sneak into reality incognito, get his clue, then sneak back to the safety of the Cloisters. Finish up there.

Xander, the little lawyer, agreed whole-heartedly that a little hard reality would give them both a fresh perspective.

And it did.

Mrs. Coffey's secretary, Lionel P. Mansweater, answered Jeff's call.

"I'm sorry Mr. Redwing. She's really busy right now. They brought in four bodies this morning. Like to leave a message?"

"Ask her to call me at home, will you Lionel?"

"I'll do that. As soon as she pops upstairs."

Jeff's computer work required maniacal concentration. He sat down at his iMac and tried to work, he really did. But the puzzle of the Wendy's murders intruded on his concentration.

He kept thinking about the strangeness of the people involved. Dottie Hatfield and Jane Lund, for instance, both from a darker, more illicit side of life. They threatened the sanitary safety of Jeff's lab coated universe. Beautiful Penny English and her greaser boyfriend. Greaser was such an old word. From Jeff's mother's time. But it described Penny's boyfriend so well. He looked like a leftover from *West Side Story*.

Then there was Vernon Roman's family. Such odd people. Rose and Eddie and the Shirelles. Elenora Chester, the stressed out, drugged up widow, half mad, receiving hundreds of sympathy gestures from people she didn't know. It reminded Jeff of the film of Jackie Kennedy reaching back for pieces of her husband's head. That image reminded him of the Andy Warhol silk screens of Jackie. There was something Andy Warhol about this whole scenario. These people could have hung out with Andy in New York.

Greta Fields. The central enigma. At least at the moment. A fat, unattractive lesbian with four ex-husbands. Character assassinates loyal, decent lifetime employees for a living. Has a pathological hatred of men. Shrewd, calculating and cunning. Involved somehow with organized crime. Jeff mistrusted Jane Lund's interpretation of the story of Greta Fields marching into the lair of the crime boss, freeing Jane with a payment of ten thousand dollars. The reaction of the crime boss struck a false note.

Someone murdered Greta Fields. He just knew it. She was the first murder. And the key.

The phone rang.

"I understand you want me," Mrs. Coffey teased.

"I'm desirous of your considerable expertise. And your company, of course."

"Oh," Mrs. Coffey laughed, "if only my husband talked to me like that. Will you bring Xander?"

"I'll rescue him from his afternoon chores. He'll appreciate that. He's in love with you, you know. He's told me he intends to marry you when he grows up."

"Did you tell him how old and shriveled I'll be by then?"

"In a kind way I alerted him to the potential age difference. He doesn't care. He doesn't want you for your body. He wants you for your mind."

"Forensic science does warm the heart. Completely understandable. So when can I see my two favorite men?"

"Xander races home right after the final school bell rings. If there's no problem with his mother we'll head straight into town. About four, I guess."

"Someone will bring you down or I'll come up and get you. If Lionel brings you down he'll treat you to his favorite joke. He looks around at the corpses and says, 'I see dead people.'"

"That Lionel's a riot," said Jeff. "We'll see you at four."

————

As predicted, Xander raced to Jeff's house on his twelve-speed bike in ten minutes. He found Jeff upstairs reading a graphic novel that featured lots of well-built men in tights, which was as close as Jeff got to reading porn.

"How was school today?" Jeff asked.

"Boring mostly," Xander replied, peering over Jeff's shoulder. "We watched videos in English class. Nouns and verbs and adjectives and modifiers drove around in little Honda Civics, arranging themselves in this thing called a Linguistics Parking Lot. So lame. The sad thing is, it was over their heads."

"Don't condescend. They're not slow, you're exceptional."

"The school administrators should move me ahead then. If it weren't for you I'd have fungus growing on the unused portions of my brain by now."

"Do you want me to talk to your mother about advancing you?"

"Yes! She says she doesn't want me in a class with older boys. Maybe she thinks they'll pick on me or something. I'd rather take up martial arts and fight off the older boys than languish with my current crop of dimwitted classmates—no condescension intended."

Jeff withheld comment.

"Are you sure you could live without your entourage? Those kids follow you everywhere."

"Oh, please."

"All right," Jeff said. "I'll talk with your mother. Do you have any homework?"

"Did it in study hall."

"In that case I have an adventure planned for us. How would you like to ride downtown and see your future wife?"

———

Mrs. Coffey possessed a crisp, tidy, intuitive mind, clear as a perfect tone. She saw with a snap of the fingers a field of possibilities and likelihoods it took Jeff hours to envision. Xander, not one for fantasy, dreamed of his visits with Ellen Coffey, imagined elaborate romantic scenarios, played back her conversations in his head, even pictured her naked.

Xander worships her as the paragon of womanhood.

He secretly hates Mr. Coffey, who stays at home to raise the four Coffey children. How could she love the chubby, balding man in the photographs on her desk? She deserved a handsome, athletic man with career ambitions. She deserved the best man imaginable. Himself in a few years.

Jeff and Xander passed through the metal detectors at the entrance to the City County Building. They proceeded to the Coroner's Office. Mrs. Coffey was not the official Coroner, the elected official and national celebrity often seen on television. Mrs. Coffey was a Deputy Coroner, happy to work in the background. Her office contained its original Edwardian woodwork (the original walnut desks as well). Ellen's secretary, Lionel P. Mansweater, possessed one of the two PCs in the room. It was a Zenith that ran one of the very first versions of Windows ever produced. Lionel struck just the right balance of irony and cynicism when using his computer.

The man himself rose to greet Mrs. Coffey's guests.

"I saw you in the corridor," Lionel announced. "I buzzed her straight away." (Lionel wasn't British but he watched a lot of British television and used the occasional odd Brit word.)

"Neat fish tie," Xander commented.

"Fish ties are old," Lionel mused, "but it's silk and expensive. I haven't gotten my money's worth yet. I was drunk when I bought it. Let that be a lesson to you young man: never drink and shop."

"Or drive," added Jeff. "Or have sex. It's best not to talk because you'll say things that will embarrass you later. You can't drink alone because that's a sure sign of alcoholism."

Xander knew a set up when he heard one.

"So when am I supposed to drink?"

"Only as a sort of Zen challenge," chimed Lionel. "And, need I add, only as an adult."

Mrs. Coffey popped in behind Jeff and Xander. She wore a white lab coat spotted with blood and smeared with some kind of purple mess. A wisp of hair fell straight away (as Lionel might say) into her face. She teetered on the edge of compulsive action.

"You pulled me up out of the depths," she said, nearly breathless. "And for that momentary salvation I am grateful. But I'm afraid we have to talk downstairs. I've just finished Miss Haigy and the boys are due to take her away. I should be there. Instructions and all. Xander, if you think the sight of a dead body might make you ill you can stay up here with Lionel."

She knew damn well Xander wanted more than anything to go downstairs. She wished just one of her children showed such avid interest in her work.

"I've seen dead bodies before," Xander boasted.

"All right then."

Jeff and Xander followed Mrs. Coffey out into the corridor. At the elevator Mrs. Coffey produced a special key that instructed the old Otis to descend an extra level into a subbasement. This particular subbasement ran beneath Grant Street, connecting with a number of satellite municipal buildings. Jeff encountered many such subterranean walkways in his work, but for Xander this was a magic realm.

No windows, of course. Just ventilation ducts. White tile walls and polished cement floors amplified and reverberated their voices. City and County employees walked stiffly in this space and looked away from each other. Jeff and Ellen spoke in hushed tones about Ellen's husband and children, idle chitchat about home life. A bus passed by on the street above. It produced a monstrous roar as if dragons lurked in the urban woods overhead.

A man in a grey uniform drove by in what looked to Xander like a go-cart. From the opposite direction two men in lab coats wheeled a body on a stretcher past them. Xander strained to catch a discreet glimpse, but the unfortunate individual on the stretcher had been body bagged. Xander wondered if just two days ago these same lab coated men had wheeled Roman and Chester through this hall. It was all so cool.

They turned into Ellen's suite of rooms which included a small office, a cold storage unit for storing samples and perishables (and sometimes lunch) and a large rectangular room in which Ellen examined the sad unfortunates who required her expertise. Stark florescent lighting cast a glow over several stainless steel tables and a surgeon's palate of scalpels, knives, scissors, tweezers and an assortment of scary objects of mysterious utility.

To brighten the place Ellen's husband, Benjamin, had painted *trompe l'oeil* windows on the walls. These windows looked out on a tropical paradise of sand and palm trees and ocean and near naked people, some of whom enjoyed fruited cocktails. Beside one of the windows Benjamin had painted a fichus tree and a chubby calico cat that looked very real indeed. Jeff tried to pet him once, much to Xander's amusement.

These painted delights contrasted sharply with the cold reality of the naked body of the woman on one of the stainless steel tables.

"Who is she?" Xander asked.

"Gentlemen, meet Matilda Haigy." Ellen gestured toward her current interest, a middle-aged white woman, a redhead (a real one, with freckles and orange pubic hair). "A Jane Doe until a couple of hours ago."

"She looks familiar," Jeff said.

"You might have seen her a hundred times on the North Side. She spent most of her day in West Park, slept at night in the cement caves left over from the demolition of the old Fort Wayne Station."

"Can I touch her?" Xander asked excitedly.

Jeff moved to reprimand Xander, but Ellen stopped him with a light touch on his arm.

"I don't see what harm it can do," Ellen said. "We've washed her now. I'm pretty much done with her."

This surprised Jeff. "You wash the bodies?"

"Sometimes we have to. Matilda here came in wearing six layers of clothing. She probably hadn't bathed in several years. The homicide boys took a series of photos where they found her. We took more photos after we undressed her. Without bathing her we couldn't get a proper look at what actually happened."

Xander walked around the corpse slowly. He prodded her midriff, pinched the skin on her forelegs. She felt cold and rubbery.

"Would she be this cold if we found her outside?" Xander asked.

"At first she'd take on the temperature of her environment. In time she'd heat up a tiny bit as the micro-organisms in her body metabolized her body tissue."

"Cool."

Jeff asked, "What happened to her?"

"Strangled. Probably for kicks. Bruise marks on her neck suggest roughly four hands the size of Xander's."

"Oh God," Jeff shuddered.

"Yes. The sad part is that her relatives knew she was out there on the streets. They even knew where she slept and hid her few possessions. That's how we found out about the Fort Wayne caves."

"She wasn't killed there?" Xander asked.

"They found her in West Park near the Aviary. We do everything we can to identify the homeless. Relatives have sometimes been looking for their loved ones in earnest. We like to give each person an opportunity to have a service and a decent burial."

"I'm surprised, what with the tax cuts and all," Jeff said.

"It's not as heartless as everyone thinks. These people might be dead, but they're very real to me. I can almost hear them talking sometimes. As it turned out, Mayview had matching dental records for Matilda. She was mentally incompetent but not violent. They turned her out on the streets during the first wave of the Reagan budget cuts. She was only in her early twenties then. Her brother, Nathan Haigy, a Jew like myself I'm ashamed to say, refused to pay to keep her institutionalized."

"Perhaps he didn't have the money," Jeff suggested. "It's quite expensive, I understand."

"No, he had the money. Successful lawyer with a minor Gothic manse in Monroeville. He didn't want to be bothered with her. He told me that, in so many words. No shame at all. He and his wife used to visit Matilda in West Park and even once in the cement caves. Took her cookies. It's amazing she lived as long as she did. All those years scrounging for food, surviving Pittsburgh winters."

Xander, fascinated with Matilda's tiny breasts, cupped one of them in his hand. He wanted to know if they had hardened: flesh breasts or stone breasts. The one cupped in his hand felt like an impersonal lump of something.

"Xander," Jeff cautioned.

"I'm not feeling her up," Xander explained. "I want to know the effects of rigor mortis on the female breast."

Jeff wondered himself for a moment if this woman had ever been touched by a lover, if her breasts had ever been fondled when she was warm and alive. He imagined himself dying of mysterious circumstances, naked on this slab, his large balls, his Black Irish licorice colored penis, stripped of its L.L. Bean protective covering, laid bare to satisfy idle scientific curiosity. Would Mrs. Coffey touch his body in fondness? Would she, in the privacy of this room, stroke the thick black chest hair of her friend before cutting into the flesh? He shook his head vigorously, chasing such notions out through his ears.

"So," Mrs. Coffey interrupted the private thoughts of both of her men, "why the urgent visit?"

Jeff described the Roman/Chester murders and his purely academic interest in sussing out the killer. 'Academic interest indeed,' thought Mrs. Coffey.

"I didn't get to work on them," Mrs. Coffey admitted. "High profile homicides go to the Big Cheese."

Jeff asked, surprised, "This is considered high profile?"

"The samurai for one thing. Lots of publicity. The Big Cheese likes publicity. It might mean another television appearance, for which he gets paid. Mostly it's high profile because of one of the victims. High school teacher with seven children. Good Catholic family man. The citizenry don't like it when good, decent folks, such as they imagine themselves to be, get run through with a sword in a fast food parking lot."

"Did you get a look at the bodies?"

"Took a peak. We don't get decapitations every day. It was important to identify the type of weapon used. Some witnesses saw an Elizabethan sword, some a curved Arabian weapon. One person swears it was just a long knife."

"Do you know which it was?"

"Samurai sword. The real thing. We had to consult a Japanese forensic specialist."

"You flew in someone from Japan?"

"Heavens no. We consulted him via satellite conference. We broadcast the wounds to him using a handheld camera—not unlike the handhelds used in Hollywood, I'm told. Talked with him live. That's what happens when your Coroner is world famous. Trust me, we have the latest of everything here. Turns out our samurai could have cut through a tree trunk with the sword he used. Professionally honed."

"No kidding." Jeff whistled. "Does it look like a professional hit to you?"

"It does and it doesn't. I can't see one of our Italian friends donning a samurai get up. It's not their style."

"What about drugs? Could this be a gang killing of some kind?"

"Could be. Our gangs get their inspiration from bad movies. Drive-by shooting, automatic weapons. This samurai thing looks like a bad movie."

Jeff detected reservation in Ellen's voice. "But you don't think it's gang related."

"I don't. I'll tell you why. This murder tells a story."

"That's what I told Jeff," chimed Xander. "The samurai showed compassion to the second victim."

"Perhaps." Ellen put up a cautionary finger. "But I wouldn't read too much into that. The first kill reflects anger. That's clear. The second man —what was his name?"

"Marshall Chester," answered Jeff. "The suburban school teacher."

"Chester might have been killed because he was along for the ride. Or because of his association with the victim. If you're friends with this guy, you deserve to die, too. That kind of thing. Remember, to kill Chester our samurai broke his knee then reached around and cut the hamstrings so the victim couldn't escape. That took cold calculation. I wouldn't say the killer felt compassion for Chester. That's going too far. My best guess is this. Our samurai was personally acquainted with Chester. Regrettably, it was necessary to kill Chester also."

Jeff thought this over. "Why do you think they were acquainted?"

"Chester was wearing a heavy winter coat. The blade of the sword went straight through the coat into the solar plexus. By doing this, one avoids the rib cage. One shot in, one shot out."

"I'm sorry, " said Jeff. "I don't understand why that means they were acquainted."

"It is difficult to distinguish the location of the solar plexus vis-à-vis the waist line or the rib cage when someone is wearing a long coat. The samurai had seen Chester at least once without his coat."

Xander looked longingly at Mrs. Coffey, as longingly as an eleven year old can look. He wanted to say, 'I love you, I love you, I love you. I want to be your little boy, I want to be your husband. Your lover, even. Whatever I can get.' What he really wanted, more than anything, was to be Mrs. Coffey's assistant: 24/7, gleaning information, receiving wisdom.

"Xander and I are perplexed by the style of the murders," said Jeff. "It looks on the surface like Chester chose the wrong time to renew an old friendship."

"Or maybe it's the other way around," suggested Ellen. "Maybe Roman chose the wrong time to get involved with an innocent. Professional criminals and honest schoolteachers don't walk comfortably down the street together. You know what I mean? It's curious how often race car drivers die in simple every day car accidents."

"You should be a detective, Mrs. Coffey," said Xander, the shine still in his eyes.

Ellen laughed. "Oh, no thank you. I prefer my hardened criminals dead on a slab. Detectives deal with criminals when they are desperate to escape detection. Real live criminals are very dangerous indeed, which is why you two," here she looked directly at Xander, knowing he is the main instigator, "need to keep your puzzle solving on a purely academic level. No personal contact with suspects like the last time."

'Too late for that,' thought Jeff.

———

Mrs. Coffey called for two assistants to wheel Miss Haigy away. Jeff knew this was their cue to leave, but he hadn't yet asked the most important question.

"Mrs. Coffey, I do have a forensic biology type question I'd like to ask," he said.

"Shoot."

"There is a woman involved in all of this—on the Chester side of the murders as it turns out. Her name keeps coming up in conversation."

"You think she might be your samurai?"

"No. Actually, she died this past year at a Fourth of July picnic."

"Was she beheaded?" Ellen asked (only half jokingly).

"No, but her death seems awfully suspicious."

Jeff described Greta Fields, her position at Chester's school and her apparent interest in separating Chester from his job.

"Interesting," Ellen nodded thoughtfully.

"Vernon Roman attended this party," Jeff added.

"More interesting. How did she die?"

"Heart attack. She was a high-risk candidate. Obese. High blood pressure. No exercise. Even so—"

"You think she was poisoned," Mrs. Coffey finished for him.

"I don't have anything to go on," Jeff added quickly, a little under his breath. "It's just that her death solved a lot of problems."

"For Chester."

"And others. When you consider what later happened to Roman and Chester."

"I see your point. Yet, as you say, she was a high-risk candidate."

"But I'm curious," Jeff pursued. "What can be done to trigger a heart attack in a high-risk candidate?"

"Overexertion," suggested Mrs. Coffey. "If you want to kill off a middle aged husband, make him shovel snow. Was she playing volleyball or softball when it happened?"

"No," answered Xander, "she was eating cheesecake."

"Hmm." Mrs. Coffey turned from her guests, pondering something. She took up a magazine from a nearby table and flipped through it. "Hmm," she said again.

"What is it?" Jeff asked.

"I have an idea," she said finally. "It's a long shot, but I have to check a few things first. You mentioned cheesecake. That made me think of something I read recently. I thought it was in this magazine, but it might be in the *New England Journal of Medicine*. I'll have a look when I get home. The substance is called Hydroprotosilicate."

Jeff and Xander repeated the new word, stammering over its multi-syllables.

"Hydro-proto-silicate," Mrs. Coffey pronounced. "You won't find it in a book of poisons. It's not toxic per se. It's actually a food additive. It can be quite deadly, however. If you can tell me which hospital performed the autopsy, I'll look for symptoms."

The assistants arrived with a stretcher for Miss Haigy. As they wheeled the poor woman off, Xander asked, "What happens to Matilda now?"

"Incineration. No ceremony. Her bastard brother forbade me—forbade me—to call a Rabbi. He took cookies to her in her cave. I wish it were the old days so we could banish him from the tribe."

"Sounds like he's banished himself," Jeff said.

"He can't forbid me to say a prayer for her with my family tonight. Now go. I have work."

Outside in the corridor a dragon thundered past overhead. Mrs. Coffey yelled after them, "I'll call, I'll call. Stay out of trouble. I mean it!"

28.

Mrs. Pooka arrived home late.

She hung her sad winter coat on the cheap wooden rack near the door, shuffled into the kitchen and draped her weary body across a kitchen chair, arms to her side, nailed to the cross. Her grooming was not all it could be. A nail that started the day cracked ended the day broken, deformed, and representative of a life in shambles. Her lovely eggshell white blouse betrayed the professional image she wished to project with ink smears from the copier cartridge she changed that afternoon. Her coiffure, styled in the manner of The Serious Business Woman, hung about her head like a collapsed soufflé.

"Poor baby," Jeff chimed, shaking his inspired, soccer player ass as he transferred Chinese food from carton to plate. "We've prepared a Chinese banquet just for you. Xander has already set the table with the wonderful, scalloped Asian style plates we bought for you today from Bed, Bath & Beyond. I'm warming the Moo-Shoo. You don't have to lift a finger. If you can't move from your chair we'll even feed it to you a chopstick full at a time."

"I think I could handle a pair of chopsticks," she managed weakly (some might say pathetically), "if only someone would rub my feet for just a while."

She desired Jeffrey's strong soccer player hands (everything about Jeff would remind you of a soccer player, a really hot soccer player, except for his brain) set loose on her aching plantars, but she knew she wouldn't get them. He never knowingly stepped over the imagined line of propriety. Xander, dutiful son, assumed the lotus position at her feet. He removed the horrible, hard, high-heeled shoes forced on her by a sexist culture. Xander's hands, still small and soft and supple, felt like pure heaven as they scattered across her skin, plying and manipulating and digging at just the right spots.

Sally Pooka moaned. "I've had many bad days. This was a bad day. No one wants to buy advertising anymore. Not even at Christmas. Assholes."

Jeff, ever so good at multi-tasking, stirred the Moo-Shoo and at the same time poured a Scotch for Sally, over ice with lime as she liked it.

"There, there," he murmured in a musical tone.

Xander's mother seldom drank. In fact, she kept the Scotch in the house for Jeff. But she sometimes found it took the edge off of a bad tasting day.

"You could make money at this," she said to Xander, then quickly, "That is not a suggestion. Don't listen to me. I'm beleaguered."

"Beleaguered?" Jeffrey smiled.

Mrs. Pooka took a deep drink of her Scotch and thought, 'Oh my God that man is yummy.' She watched him arrange Asian style bowls. His five o'clock shadow, now a seven o'clock shadow, set off the brilliant white of his teeth when he smiled. It lit her up. And stirred her nether regions. 'It's just not fair, she thought. There is a beautiful, black haired, swarthily handsome man in my kitchen, wearing a barbeque apron, cooking Moo-Shoo for me, flashing reassuring smiles at just the right moments, and he's not going to fuck me tonight. And I need a fuck. Dear God, I need a fuck. It's been over six years.

I shouldn't have these thoughts while my son is massaging my feet.'

The first drink disappeared. A second took its place. A wave of releasing, gratifying heat passed through Sally's body. She took in the length and breadth of the beautiful cooking man in her kitchen, her child's friend. She closed her eyes and savored a thought. After the Scotch (and she'd have another) couldn't the man tuck her boy into bed and then fuck her really hard in her bed? I mean, aren't we really all supposed to be bisexual?

She felt his powerful hand on her arm, she smelled his scent. She opened her eyes. He was just as close as she wanted him to be.

"There's that smile," he said. "Why don't you go upstairs and change for dinner."

He'd never do it. Never.

———

He didn't do it that evening. I'm not suggesting he ever did it, Dear Reader. I am suggesting that never is a long time. And doesn't really exist on the human scale. Not really. Until that giant asteroid hits Manhattan and resets the world order. Might be a never on the human scale then. Just a thought.

Sally drifted in a Scotch filled haze toward the television after supper, but Xander stopped her mid-remote, suggesting a nice game of Scrabble. Sally excelled at Scrabble, having a talent for word composition. She often beat her son at the game. Jeff begged off, citing mounds and mounds of work waiting for him at home.

The idea of a second round of work starting at 9 p.m. horrified Mrs. Pooka. Punishment for living. On sleepless nights she sometimes looked out her window in the direction of Jeff's house. Past the ridges of intervening suburban dwellings she discerned the glow from the lights of his glass attic, as the neighbors called it. She pictured him, still fully dressed, staring into a monitor, his long Horowitz fingers alighting over the keys of his instrument of mastery.

When she wasn't feeling sorry for herself, she felt sorry for him. When she felt sorry for herself, she envied him. Sally had mastered nothing in this world. No great talents or interests. She gave birth to a brilliant child—that was her accomplishment. She had no idea how to raise him, how to contribute to the development of his genius. She needed Jeff for that.

He cut such a solitary figure. Sally took a photo once of Jeff and Xander posing in front of the historic carousel at Kennywood Park. He looked like a man alone with a child by his side. Not connected, awkward in company. She wondered if he was lonely. On those restless nights Sally sometimes considered just walking over to Jeff's house. She'd take a bottle of something and just knock on the door. They'd sit and talk, just the two of them. They'd develop a friendship. Don't gay men like to have a best woman friend? She could be his Grace. What would they talk about? Perhaps over a glass or two of wine she might unravel the truth to him, confess that she doesn't know how her life ended up like this. Absent husband, no friends, sucky job. *I live for my son*, she'd say.

———

A sip or two of Scotch lubricates the rusty hinges of ancient sentiment. Jeff turned on the lights in his glass attic, looked about at the stacks of magazines, the plants, the light film of dust that had settled on everything in his absence. He considered getting a rag and wiping off the dust, even at that hour, because dust, is not permitted to settle on Jeff's world.

Another sip of Scotch, a scorching hot ounce of alcohol, slid down his classic Adam's appled throat. Jeff had sensed Sally's mood, of course. He's not insensate. Nothing he could do about it.

Like Mr. Pooka, Jeff's father abandoned his family. Jeff's mother suffered horrible bouts of loneliness. She cried in her room at night when she thought Jeff was asleep. It went on for years, the crying. At school the other children neither liked nor disliked Jeff. He got used to walking to school alone, sitting in the cafeteria beside people but not with them, creating after school projects with an assigned partner who couldn't care less and ducked out early. In high school he shot up to his current six-foot plus height, blossomed into a stunningly beautiful boy. He developed his body by engaging in sports he could do alone: swimming, mountain biking, hiking, climbing, weight training. Girls admired him but he already knew his nature. He formed a few convenient acquaintances with fellow geeks, but no abiding friendships.

At Carnegie Mellon he received a great deal of personal interest, much of it of a sexual nature, all from women. Once under the influence of alcohol he had sex with a friend from his dorm. The sex was so extraordinary, so beautiful that he imagined himself in love with the boy. They kissed good-bye in the morning. From that point on the boy gave him the cold shoulder, then avoided him altogether. He was engaged to be married, you see. And was in love with his girlfriend. They could have continued to have sex if Jeff had been cool about it, but Jeff couldn't be cool about it. For the first time in his life Jeff allowed himself to fantasize. He invented scenarios in which the boy made love to him again and again, endlessly. The boy married him. They created a life together, an extraordinary partnership of love and business. At last. Finally.

The boy was quite good in bed,. He laughed, he had fun. Engaging, intelligent, artistic. Nice swimmer's body. Tight. Leanly muscular. So yummy. It was Jeff's first time. He didn't know.

After college, Jeff, avoiding the "bar scene," ventured into a gay coffee house or two. Two exactly. The first coffee house, located near a large inner city high school, served primarily high school students, otherwise known as jail bate. The second, located in the basement of an Episcopalian church (a children's Bible study room, tiny tables and tiny chairs), hosted a scary assortment of people who, at least at first glance, appeared to be losing rather badly at the game of life.

On that occasion, Jeff prepared his cup of Nescafe with a bit of non-dairy creamer in a Styrofoam cup, then gingerly sat down in a tiny chair at a tiny unoccupied table. He took a sip, gathered his courage, lifted his eyes and took in the room. It was the circus, people. I won't go into details. That would be unkind. They stared at him, wondering no doubt what brought him to their desperate outpost. Jeff smiled, then looked down, not wishing to encourage interest. How best to tactfully withdraw?

A young man on crutches with a serious speech impediment entered the room. He spotted Jeff, the handsomest man in the world, the man of his wildest dreams, and started to scream. He flailed his crutches madly about in the air like a crab defending itself from a hungry attacker. Since he needed the crutches to stand, the young man fell to the ground, screaming a heart stopping, spittle sparked stream of vehement, incomprehensible exclamations. Friends rushed to his aid.

Jeff stood up, muttered something like, "So sorry to have caused a disturbance," and slinked past the disaster toward the door. The young man on the floor twitched violently as Jeff passed. He squealed something at such an earsplitting pitch that he just might have cracked one of the stained glass windows. Jeff shut down his ears and his soul and forgot to breathe until he was outside in the fresh air. The young man was saying, "Don't let him go! Don't let him go!" He said it for some time, over and over again, more softly toward the end, whimpering it finally. His friends got him situated in a tiny chair and sat with him while he sobbed.

Jeff drove as fast and as far away from the church as possible. A mile or so out, he stopped in a Boston Market parking lot and cried, pounding the steering wheel. Why did it have to be this hard? That poor man. Paraplegic and gay on top of it. Here he was a healthy, intelligent, articulate, physically fit, reasonably attractive man feeling sorry for himself and slinking about cowardly in basement coffee houses. Two weeks later Jeff went to his first gay bar. It wasn't so bad. He soon discovered that men as handsome as himself were seldom alone at the bar for long.

A number of one-night stands satisfied his sexual curiosity. He entered into two relationships: one lasting four months, one lasting three years. As you read this, Dear Reader, Jeff stands at a crossroads. I have had sex, he says to himself, I want more now. He has become, in a word, wary. In another word, picky. Wary and picky. Xander might consider this a celibate phase, but for Jeff it is merely a time of waiting.

Is he lonely, as Sally surmises?

Yes.

However, on that particular evening of Sally Pooka, the Chinese and the Scrabble, Jeff neither ruminated about loneliness nor worked into the wee hours. He picked up a magazine, paged through it without reading, considered poor Miss Haigy on her slab. He ran an image through his mind of Xander cupping one of her boobs and winced at the thought of it. Why didn't he stop Xander from doing that? Surely it wasn't appropriate. Why didn't Ellen stop him?

Out of the corner of his eye Jeff noticed the red light blinking on his answering machine. He played the message. A familiar, groggy voice spoke.

"Hello, Mr. Redwing. This is Rose Roman, Vernon's mother. I hope you remember me."

Jeff heard Dottie in the background. "Of course he remembers you, Rose. Get on with it."

"Yes," Rose sputtered. "Anyway. Dottie and me were, you know, just sitting around shooting the breeze. We thought, Wouldn't we like to see that handsome young man again? Wouldn't that be nice? Didn't we say that, Dottie?"

"Oh for Christ's sake, Rose. Give me the phone." The phone changed hands. "It's just drinks, hon. Nothing special. I thought we should chat. I peeked into your background, just a teensy peek. You might be a big dick but you're not a P.I. All those connections to sensitive government agencies. Who are you really, Mr. Jeffrey Piedmont Redwing? Please stop by this evening, doesn't matter how late. We'll wait up. Rose wants to marry you off to one of her daughters and I, well, I wish to share information. I understand you're something of an information specialist. Am I right? I have some information for you I'm sure you will find illuminating. We're in the Winchester Arms in Shadyside just across the street from where my poor Vernon met his demise. I'm listed under my maiden name, dear. Dottie Hatfield, 411."

———

Jeff reached Shadyside in about an hour. The twelve story Winchester Arms indeed overlooked the Wendy's parking lot. Jeff parked alongside St. Stephen's Church where he had made a fool of himself in front of a priest. Now he understood why Chester and Roman chose Wendy's for their assignation. Convenient for Roman, the one without a car. Jeff wondered who else might have known the two men were meeting there. Dottie almost certainly. Probably Rose.

He pressed the button for 411. Rose answered.

"It's Jeff Redwing."

"I'm so glad you came!" Rose gushed through the intercom.

A buzzer sounded, unlocking the security door. Jeff entered a lobby richly decorated with chintz loveseats, suede wallpaper, Edwardian wainscoting and oversized tropical ferns in shiny brass planters. Well-to-do elderly women moved here after selling off their large homes. He pushed aside the iron filigree doors of an old fashioned self-serve elevator and pushed an ivory button inlaid with the number "4". The elegant cage graciously ascended.

Mrs. Roman greeted him at the elevator, a broad smile on her face. Dottie stood less enthusiastically behind her.

"Here you are!" exclaimed Rose, as if now all of their problems were solved.

Jeff entered into an awkward embrace with this woman he hardly knew. She kissed him on the cheek. A whiff of gin blew past his nostrils. He glanced at Dottie and realized in an instant Rose still thought he was Vernon's old friend from high school.

"Rose was afraid you weren't bright enough to find 411 on your own. She pictured you in an eternally perplexed state, wandering about the halls. Plus she's drunk. And you're such a happy drunk, aren't you Rose dear?"

Mrs. Roman slipped a hand through Jeff's arm and led him in the direction of their apartment. "I'm just a little drunk," Rose giggled. "We decided to start early. Besides, I've been through hell and alcohol is the only thing that makes me feel better. I can't help it, I'm always happy when I drink. How does liquor effect you, Jeff honey?"

"Hardly at all," he confessed. "People can't really tell I'm drunk."

Dottie said slyly, "I bet I could tell."

Jeff grunted. It couldn't have been easy getting the information she leaked over the phone. He would remember not to underestimate her resourcefulness.

"My poor Vernon didn't take after me," Rose said, slurring her words just a bit. "He was a nasty drunk. Foul tempered. He threw things around. Broke things."

"But," Dottie added pointedly, "that boy fucked like an angel with a couple of shots in him. Why not be frank, Rose? Mr. Redwing is such a good friend from high school days. Vernon drank in high school. Nobody knows that better than you, Rose. And he was a switch hitter. You knew that, didn't you Jeffrey?" Dottie winked behind Rose's back.

"I didn't know him that well."

"Betcha did. Quite exciting reading, your little dossier. Ooo, I've got names, dates, orgasm counts."

A white haired lady with a pink sweater draped across her shoulders exited her apartment, locked the door behind her and walked gingerly down the hall with the aide of a silver-knobbed cane. The woman looked at Dottie, looked at Rose, looked at Jeff. A pained expression crossed her face. Dottie and Rose nodded "Good evening," in passing. The woman lifted her body upright and rigid as if the severity of her judgment protected her from evil.

At the door to 411 Dottie lowered her voice. "I don't now what that woman's problem is. I have never, absolutely never, brought a trick back to this apartment."

"She's just a tight assed broad," Rose slurred.

The woman clearly bothered Dottie.

"I go to so much trouble to look good," she said, turning the key. "No one could ever tell. That witch can't tell."

"No one can tell," said Rose. "She's absolutely lovely, don't you think Jeffrey?"

In fact she did look lovely. Chanel jacket and dress, pearls, sensible shoes. Not at all theatrical like at the funeral parlor. The apartment, decorated primarily in shades of white, also surprised Jeff. Thick white wool carpet, white draperies with white linings, white wicker chairs with plump white cushions and pillows. A large, white paper sculpture-type artwork filled an eight by six spot along one wall. In the corner stood a white wire mannequin dressed in a Victorian lace wedding gown. White, of course.

"Is that an antique?" Jeff asked.

"Oh yes," said Rose, rushing to the dress to ruffle the edges of the finery. "Isn't this the most elegant wedding gown you've ever seen? Dottie wanted to marry my Vernon in this gown."

"Get married in it!" Dottie exclaimed, tossing her head. "I'd wear the thing around the house if it fit. Women must have been so much smaller a hundred years ago."

"We're all bigger now because of the milk we drink," Rose pronounced, crossing to the bar. "I heard that on NPR."

"Is that what you're having, Rose?" Dottie teased. "Milk?"

"No. I'm having gin, as you damn well know."

From behind a white patent leather bar Rose procured a gallon gin bottle. She mixed herself a generous gin and tonic, using slightly less tonic than the classic recipe requires.

"Jeff will have Glenfiddich, neat," Dottie instructed. To Jeff she said, "I'm sorry, but I couldn't get Macallan on such short notice."

"Your research is thorough."

"It's not my research. Your taste in Scotch is recorded in several confidential government documents. One of them expressed a concern for your drinking."

"So you want me to know you have some power over me," suggested Jeff.

"Now, now, Mr. Redwing. You have chosen to work for the government. I detest government organizations, myself. Their information gathering skills have proven useful over time. But I loathe the information gatherers. They're the real enemy, aren't they. Or don't you agree?"

Rose knew her way around a bar. She produced a nice double in a lovely crystal glass with professional expediency. Jeff needed a drink at that moment to calm his nerves. He wondered if the government report hadn't been right about his drinking. Rose mixed a colorful cocktail for Dottie in a sizeable tulip shaped glass. Jeff recognized the drink. A sloe gin fizz.

Dottie continued, "I won't say which government branch produced the most interesting details, but one of them described your sexual proclivities in great detail."

Jeff grunted. "That must have been boring reading."

"On the contrary. It included one-night stands, people you dated, favorite brand of lube. Number of times a day you masturbate. Favorite rooms to do it in. Whether or not you take off all your clothes or just drop your drawers and have at it."

"All right."

"They must have lived in your closet for months. The things we do to earn a living in the land of the free and the home of the brave." Dottie chuckled, but not meanly.

"Did you bring me here to humiliate me?" Jeff regarded Rose out of the corner of his eye.

"Certainly not. I thought it was something you should know. About your employers. About choices you made. I get the impression you don't think much of my lifestyle or the choices I've made. Perhaps I associate with a stratum of life you find abhorrent. But with whom do you associate? Men in suits who invaded the privacy of your home, put cameras and microphones in your bedroom, in your shower, in your car. They know you're gay but not likely to betray your country for sex. You have not run afoul of the law. Except for that teeny incident last year. They don't understand why you did it. You left your safe, customary mold. You bear watching."

"Jeff's not gay," Rose announced incredulously.

"Yes he is, Rose. Gay as last year's Christmas tree, aren't you honey?"

"Perhaps not that gay."

"Perhaps so," said Dottie. "I could show you your files."

"I've seen them."

"That's right. Not very bright of them to let an information specialist work on the computer that holds his own files."

"Not very bright, no," Jeff said quietly. "Unless they meant for me to see them."

Dottie took a deep drink of her tropical cocktail and regarded Jeff. "They certainly helped themselves to your files, didn't they. Stuck a camera and a microphone up the ass of your life. How do you feel about that?"

"I don't like it, of course," Jeff answered, annoyed with this line of questioning. Not a person in his universe knew about the surveillance conducted during his security check. This woman was not really a part of his universe, except now, perhaps, that he had stupidly annexed her. It occurred to him for just a moment that Dorothy Hatfield might be an agent. Maybe that's how she got access.

"Don't like it? C'mon Jeff, you're a human being. You have feelings. What was it really like?"

"I felt violated, ok? Is that what you want to hear?"

"Boys," interjected Rose. "Girls."

"I want to hear the truth, that's all," continued Dottie. "I'm just curious. Trying to see through your eyes. How would I actually feel if someone stole my dignity in that manner? You know they had a good laugh at your expense. They sat around in a room, a bunch of straight guys in suits, and watched video shot through an open window, listen to you fuck your boyfriend. I'm sure they went into hysterics when you said, 'I love you, Denny.' Boyfriend number two, right? The one with the tattoos."

Jeff flushed crimson. He slammed his drink down on a table.

"Fuck this shit." Jeff marched toward the door.

"Don't leave," cried Dottie. "Don't leave. I didn't mean to insult you. I just want to know. I honestly want to know."

Jeff turned. "Know what? What exactly?"

"Did you hate them? I just want to know."

"I didn't hate them," he said. "Hate is a strong word."

"You lie, you lie, you lie!"

"All right, I hated them. For a moment I hated them."

"For a moment my ass. You hate them still. You'd murder them if you could. The ones who actually did it. Invaded your house. Laughed at your most intimate moments. In the name of patriotism."

Jeff shook his head vigorously. "I am not a murderer."

"Don't you bet on it, pretty man. We're all murderers." Dottie found her glass empty. She crossed the room to fix another drink. "Aren't we, Rose? Aren't we all murderers?"

"I am," Rose muttered, glancing out the window to the Wendy's parking lot below. She discerned a faint chalk outline, the ghost of her fallen son. "I murdered my baby."

"So did I, Rose. So did I."

"Are you confessing to Vernon Roman's murder?"

"We're not that drunk, honey," Dottie laughed. She took a sip of her fourth or fifth or who's counting sloe gin fizz. "I'm talking about the little murders we commit throughout the course of a lifetime."

"Gossip," hissed Rose. "Forgotten birthdays. The truth said in anger. Picking on a defenseless child."

"We've all died a hundred tiny murders by the time we become adults," said Dottie. "We've committed hundreds more. But every once in a while, Jeff, a little murder hits a vital organ. Someone snaps. A big murder occurs. A big murder with a samurai sword. Isn't that right, Rose?"

"Little murders and big murders." Rose downed her gin. "We've been talking about it all day."

"I don't commit little murders," Jeff asserted.

"Oh no?" Dorothy got up in his face. "Doesn't little Xander ever want something you won't give him? Doesn't he want you to marry his mother?"

"Well—"

"It doesn't have to make sense to hurt," said Dottie. "Human beings aren't about sense and logic. He loves you. Every day he goes home to a house you don't live in he suffers a little murder. Every day another one. Every unfulfilled wish. Think about it, Jeff. We're so vulnerable. Little murders are so easy to commit."

"It's not something I can help," Jeff said.

"That's right. It can't always be helped."

Rose ran the business about Xander's mother through her gin soaked brain. Wasn't his mother dead? Or in another state? Or what? She couldn't remember.

"Is this why you brought me here?" Jeff asked. "To discuss your philosophy about the little murders of day to day life?"

Dottie sighed. Such a thick man for someone with such a high IQ.

"We brought you here to give you information. Since my husband's death seems to be of interest to you. I don't know who you are exactly. I don't trust you entirely. But frankly, there isn't anybody else. I'm alone. I'm resourceful, but there are limits to what I can do in this situation. You can do so much more."

"Can I?"

"Yes. But we want you to keep our discussion in mind as you follow the leads we give you. We want you to follow the trail of the little murders."

————

Rose inhaled an impressive succession of gin and tonics. She lost focus, drifting in and out of the tide of conversation. At one point she screamed out, "I buried my baby this morning!" Her drink dropped to the floor as her hands shot up to cover her face. Tears rolled through the openings between her fingers. "My Vernon," she whimpered. "My only boy."

Dottie put her arms around Rose's shoulders. To Jeff she said, "You see, she's not always a happy drunk. There, there Rose. Jeff is here to make things right. You'll see. He has important government connections."

"I've never buried a child," Rose cried, unable to take her hands from her face.

"He hasn't been buried, Rose darling. He's been entombed. If we decide sometime in the future we want to go stand beside him we don't have to dig him up first. We can just walk into his little cement house and open the door of his little bronze coffin."

'How macabre,' Jeff thought. After her performance at the funeral home he could easily imagine her doing it.

Dottie said to Jeff, "We did get a new coffin. We are not paupers, as you can see." Dottie tossed her head at the grand sweep of what she clearly considered to be a scrumptious suite of rooms. "Of course we will be visiting our dear Vernon sometime soon, won't we Jeff? Our dear Vernon is missing something in his little bronze box."

Rose dropped her hands from her red and veined face. Desperately she pleaded, "You will help us, Jeffrey, won't you? You will help us."

Dottie made a face at him as if to say, 'Get over here and comfort her you big lump.' Jeff approached Rose and embraced her gently. In an instant she collapsed in his arms. Her weight surprised him. She looked so thin, so Laura Petrie, and yet she felt heavy. She must have gone to great lengths to tuck herself in. She cried and cried until she cried herself out. Then she went limp. She passed out there in his arms.

"Thank God," said Dottie. "I've been trying to get her to pass out all night."

Dottie took Rose's legs while Jeff gripped her under her arms. They carried her into Dottie's bedroom and laid her out on the bed.

"She's staying with me until she lives out some of the pain. Eddie doesn't know what to do with her. At home she wanders from room to room, talking to herself, crying out loud, shrieking. She scares the neighbors. And those daughters of hers! They don't have enough sense between them to calculate change for the bus. It's a sin, really. They were born the best possible sex and what have they done with it? No imagination."

They settled back in the living room.

"Did Vernon live here with you?" Jeff asked.

"Most of the time. I've had this place since, well, since I found my true calling. That was about twenty-two years ago."

"Was Vernon your, uh—"

"No. Oh, heavens no. Vernon was in another line of work entirely. He and I met and fell in love about fourteen years ago. He came to live with me about a year into it. He didn't always stay here, though. Some nights he actually slept in that horrible shack he kept in Polish Hill."

"I've seen it."

Jeff tilted his empty glass, wondering again if he didn't have a drinking problem. Dottie gave him full reign over the bar. He poured himself another double.

"The women's clothes, the costumes," he said. "Those were yours?"

"Some of them," she replied. "Some were his. Some were for other people."

"Other people?"

"Don't ask me to explain," she said flatly.

"You know, when the landlady told me about the costumes, I couldn't help but wonder—"

"If the samurai costume came from that collection. I'm afraid so. I take it the police haven't found it."

"Not to my knowledge. That guy on television held up a costume. I don't think that was the real one."

"Nor do I. I'm sure the costume has been ditched somewhere." Dottie added quickly. "We did not own a samurai sword. Just the costume. We didn't go in for props. You see, we needed everyday costumes. Police uniforms, nurse's uniforms, hospital scrubs, clerical outfits, gas company shirts. That kind of thing. It so happens two crates of theatrical costumes fell off of a truck. The samurai outfit came in one of the trunks. It wasn't something we could use. There were a lot of costumes we couldn't use among the ones that we could."

"You can't tell me how you used the costumes?"

Dottie shook her head.

"I don't really know you," she said. "And God knows who else might be listening."

Jeff took a deep drink of the Glenfiddich and sighed. She wasn't simply going to tell him the truth. She offered up puzzles within puzzles.

He drifted into a Scotch haze for several minutes, then, "I'm curious about something. Vernon and Marshall were best buddies in school, right?"

"Their whole childhood. They met when they were three years old."

"Rose said Vernon was an A student up to a point. Was that an exaggeration?"

"No." Dottie sighed, sipping more of her fancy drink. "They were both A students. Two eggheads joined at the hip. Until eleventh grade."

"What happened then?"

"Vernon left the academic program for general ed. It was a little murder, you see, directed at Marshall."

"Ah. One of those little murders you want me to follow."

"Exactly. You see, they had been so close. Played together every day, ate at each other's houses. Went through puberty together. Back when they were thirteen or so they even indulged in a little mutual oral gratification. Nothing serious, just teenage experimentation. The point is they were as close as two people could be. Almost twins. Did you ever have a relationship like that, Jeff?"

"No, I'm afraid not."

"It's something special. I'm sure Marshall expected they would double date at the prom, go to the same college, enter into similar careers, marry girls from college, live in the same neighborhood. Their kids would be best friends just like they were best friends. A lovely scenario. Marshall presumed they'd be friends forever. Then one day, without warning, Vernon changed."

"That's what makes me curious," said Jeff, suddenly sitting up. "The nature of this sudden change. Did Vernon ever confide in you?"

"Marshall wanted the traditional American Dream. Career, two story Colonial in the suburbs, the wife, and a brood of children. Vernon didn't share that dream. Truth was he hated school, hated studying. He kept up his grades for Marshall's sake, to continue their friendship. But when he got to be sixteen, closer to manhood, it dawned on him he was living another man's life. Vernon didn't want a career or children. He hated the suburbs. He craved sex with men as well as women. Everything Marshall held in high esteem, Vernon held in contempt. I'm sure Marshall considered it a betrayal."

Jeff considered this while lounging on the comfy white sofa in the endlessly white room. He noticed Dottie Hatfield's legs. Classic legs. Long, tapered, strong Tina Turner legs. The bottom half of her Chanel two piece was a dress. Of course it would be. The dress allowed him a view of the legs. Which she was showing off, he realized. To him.

She followed his eyes and read his mind.

"Would you like another touch of Scotch?" she asked.

"God no," he replied, shaking her off. "Your husband—and his friend."

"Vernon and Marshall."

"Yes. They parted company and didn't see each other for, what. Some twenty years?"

"That's correct," said Dottie. "Until—"

"Until?"

Dottie crossed the room to a wicker lamp table. She opened a small drawer located just under the ledge of the table and withdrew a pocket-sized address book. Moleskin. A sadness crept into her expression as she gazed at the worn, black object. She stared at the thing for such a length of time that Jeff wondered if perhaps she intended to keep it from him after all. Then she brought it over to him. It felt warm and a little moist from perspiration.

"Vernon's?" he asked.

She nodded.

"You are on your own with this book," she said. "If certain people knew that you had it, I'd be murdered within the day. Here's a bit of history you might find useful. Vernon started out as a hustler. That's what he did for a living. That's how we met. He worked one side of the street and I worked the other." She looked to see if he knew what she meant. A gay man should certainly be familiar with the term hustler, yet this man did not seem to fit a mold. "He sold his body to men for cash."

"I know—about it—."

"He was very beautiful, my Vernon. Ruggedly handsome, tight and muscular. Flawless body. Even Rose noticed that about her own son. Dark chestnut hair that fell slightly over his forehead. You just wanted to touch it and run your fingers through it. And a big dick. Really big. Scary big. You understand? Do you like big dicks?"

"It's not my favorite thing."

"Well, many do. They pay a lot of money for a man who looks that good with a big dick. Vernon did quite well for himself. And he didn't do drugs. He lived in that shack in Polish Hill. He stashed his money away with the intention of investing and retiring early. I did the same thing. Except I won't live in a shack."

This had all the earmarks of a long story. Jeff stared into the empty well of his glass. 'I really do have a drinking problem,' he thought. He looked down at the floor while at the same time holding his glass up in the air. Dottie poured him a fresh one.

"Shall I continue?" she asked.

"Please do."

"When AIDS came along, Vernon's work got a little too dangerous. A man named Larry Cone offered him a position with a new company, a sort of family run enterprise headquartered in Cleveland."

"Cleveland," Jeff echoed, trying to make sense of it.

"Larry Cone is one of the people listed in Vernon's book. Larry Cone also knew Franklin Baum, the black man who confessed to Vernon's murder."

"I don't understand."

"It's all subterfuge. Franklin Baum did not kill my husband. But his name is in the book as well and might prove useful. How much do you know about Marshall Chester? His family? His associates?"

"A little," Jeff said. "I met some of them at the viewing last night."

"There's another name in the book that might surprise you. Larry Cone's girlfriend. She's a teacher at Chester's school. She was his best ally during his recent siege there. He also fucked her from time to time, Marshall did. Meant more to her than it did to him apparently."

Flipping through the tattered book, Jeff located her entry. "Penny English." 4267 Silverbird Lane. A 724 exchange.

"Penny introduced Chester to Larry Cone. Is it falling into place yet?"

It's falling about my ears, he thought.

Dottie continued. "One day Larry Cone gives Vernon a lead on a job. The lead comes through Cone's girlfriend. The lead turns out to be a teacher. Chester is his name. Marshall Chester. His old buddy from high school."

"Oh my God," Jeff said, shivering despite the heat from the Scotch.

"There's one more name in that book," she said.

He knew. He instinctively knew.

He turned the pages to the next tab in the book and there she was: Greta Fields.

29.

JEFF REACHED HOME AROUND 4:30 A.M. HE WANTED TO SLEEP. AT THE SAME time he wanted to study the address book. He opted for leafing through the address book while reclining on his bed.

He found no listing for a business in Cleveland. Likewise no listings, business or personal, in the state of Ohio. Larry Cone's entry included a phone number but no address. Logical. Roman no doubt already knew where Cone lived. He wondered if people like Roman and Hatfield ever sent Christmas cards.

He recognized only five names in the book: Marshall Chester, Penny English, Greta Fields, his Polish Hill landlady Bertha Moore and Dottie Hatfield. Here and there Roman had written the names of significant others off to the side. Elenore, rather than Elenora, beside Chester's name (7 kids! in parenthesis). Jane Lund earned a mention next to Greta Fields' entry. Four women's names followed Larry Cone's name. A line had been drawn through the first three. "Penny" remained at the bottom of the list, his active duty woman.

Within each alphabetical tab the first two or three names had been written in light blue pencil. Perhaps Roman had originally stored a light blue pencil within the book's wire spiral. The blue names were mostly men, perhaps repeat customers from Roman's rent boy days. Dottie Hatfield appeared in blue, the name Bart beside it. Bart must have been Hatfield's significant other during the blue pencil period.

More recent entries recorded out of town folk. Four listings for people from Virginia, two from Washington D.C., one from Philadelphia, one from Lancaster. One from Baltimore. Two in the state of Michigan. Where else? Vestal, New York. Where the hell was that? And then someone named Griselda Steiff all the way down in Kitty Hawk, North Carolina. Kitty Hawk is just down the road from Duck in the Outer Banks, Jeff's favorite retreat from the world's madness. He did not recognize the name, but then again he didn't live in the Outer Banks. He merely vacationed there.

Maybe he'd call this Griselda Steiff tomorrow, poke around in her brain a bit.

Jeff reflected for just a moment, Dear Reader, on the devious turn his life had taken in recent days. But wasn't it exciting!

At that point his eyes closed, his arm fell to the side of the bed, and the address book dropped soundlessly to the soft carpeted floor. Jeff, at last, fell asleep.

———

Put to bed two nights in a row by good Scotch, Jeff thought as his eyes popped open at 9:30 a.m. Blinking, he had a further thought: *The Chester funeral starts at 10!*

He'd never make the final goodbyes at the coffin, probably wouldn't make the eulogy, but if he hurried he might make the tossing of the dirt by the weary widow at the gravesite.

The beard stubble on his embattled face resembled an abstract arrangement of iron filings. Jeff hated shaving without showering, but there was no time for proper grooming. He used a fresh blade but still cut himself numerous times. While inspecting the damage he noticed his teeth weren't as white as they could be.

All of his dress shirts needed laundering. He pulled the least offensive one out of the hamper. It smelled—well, it smelled. He doused himself with a generous portion of Eau Savage (a hint of citrus for that illusion of freshness). A dark blue suit, a vest and a wide rep tie hid most of the shirt wrinkles. A damp rag over dusty black wingtips brought his shoes to near respectability.

Fully dressed, he checked himself in front of the bedroom's full-length mirror. It was just as he feared: a mighty fall from once high standards.

Well, it couldn't be helped. And it was almost certainly true that he needed to drink less. Almost certainly true.

———

Elm Hills Cemetery occupied twenty-eight acres of prime South Hills real estate. The Dutch Elms of decades past had long ago succumbed to Dutch Elm disease. Serviceable, if less magnificent, maples stood in their place.

Jeff drove about slowly, looking for other cars, some sign of the gravesite. He spotted no cars, no people, not even a bird. The place seemed eerily empty. Then, rounding a bend, he spotted a young man in a green uniform, probably a grounds keeper. Jeff pulled over beside the young man.

"Excuse me. Have I missed the Chester burial?"

"Haven't arrived yet," answered the young man, beaming a big smile with lots of blindingly white teeth. "They say it's big. A couple hundred people coming. But it looks like you're the first."

"No kidding."

"I was helping one of the family members set up chairs. He sent me away, though. Says he's got it handled. I think he just wanted to be alone."

This young man was really quite handsome, Jeff noticed. And cut a nice figure in his tight green uniform. Muscled. Not gym muscles, but healthy outdoor living muscles. He continued to beam that big smile into Jeff's face. At one point Jeff felt the need to avert his eyes.

The cheerful young man added, "You could go up, though. They're all be here in twenty minutes and he'll never finish those chairs by himself."

"How do I get there?"

"Continue along this road. He's around the next hill, to the left."

"Thank you."

"You're welcome. I'm Gregory," the young man said enthusiastically, thrusting his hand into Jeff's car. Jeff shook the paw-like hand, crusty with dirt. Still, nice and warm and inviting. It stirred Jeff up a bit. "I'm always around if you need anything."

Gregory winked, then went on his way.

As Jeff slowly drove off he checked Gregory out in the rear view mirror. Nice butt. Gregory turned around for just a moment and smiled, as if knowing all along that Jeff would be looking. Jeff shook it off. That's what he needed after all, a romantic entanglement with a gravedigger.

Around a bend in the labyrinthine drive Jeff spotted a grouping of chairs and a man methodically unfolding and placing chairs, one at a time, from a generous stack. It was Jeremy Richer. Gregory was right; he'd never finish them all himself.

"I see the press has arrived," Richer intoned as Jeff drew near.

"An article in an alumnae magazine hardly makes me a member of the press. May I help?"

Jeremy looked at the remaining stack of chairs and sighed.

"Yes, please."

The two men unfolded and placed chairs in silence for a moment, then Richer said in a more intimate voice, "You know what really bothers me about the press? They could be helping to solve these murders. Instead they're hanging around waiting for us to cry on camera. I know, for instance, that Vernon Roman was a member of organized crime. Did you know that?"

"No, I didn't," Jeff lied (again).

"The police know this. They've known about Roman for years."

"How do you know that?"

"I know, that's all. No one in their right mind could think these murders were random acts of violence."

Jeremy looked down the road, then at the remaining stack of chairs.

Jeff said, "I'd like to help but alumnae never do bad things in alumnae magazines. It's a rule."

"Yes, well." Jeremy snapped a few more chairs in place. "So you went to CMU with my sister."

"We were there at the same time. I didn't know your sister. I knew Marsh. By the time he and Elenora started dating we had drifted apart. You know how that is."

Jeremy stopped as if to consider it.

"I wish you'd known her then," he added. "She was a gifted artist. She graduated with Holly Hunter. Took a class with her."

"Hmm. Not sure I know who Holly Hunter is."

"You're not serious."

"I don't follow actors."

"That's right," Jeremy remembered. "I compared you to Alec Baldwin and you didn't know who he was. Did you rush right out and rent one of his movies?"

"I'm embarrassed to say no." Truth to tell, Jeff couldn't care less.

"I compared you to one of the handsomest men in motion picture history and you forgot about it? Oh well. I shouldn't expect everyone to be as enthusiastic about movies as I am. Entertainment is my thing. It's what I live for. I really, really wanted to be the brother of a famous actress. People say I look like Montgomery Clift. What do you think?"

Jeremy turned his profile for Jeff to admire. Jeff shook his head.

"Montgomery Clift?"

"Oh my God," said Richer, a smile sneaking across his lips. "We'll have to tear up your American Culture membership card."

"I do see some movies," Jeff added quickly in his own defense. "I saw *Jurassic Park*."

"Oh, well. *Jurassic Park*," Jeremy teased.

"I wanted to observe the computer graphics. I've worked on animation software."

"You're a computer geek!"

Jeff shuffled his feet and took a modest bow.

"You're forgiven then," Jeremy laughed. "Although I don't know why computer geeks should be exempt from cultural awareness. By the way, I appreciate you helping like this."

Jeff shrugged it off. "I'm surprised I'm early. I was sure I'd be late."

"It's all the people, " Richer remarked, annoyed. "There hasn't been a funeral this size since Valentino died. I think every student who ever heard him utter a word showed up this morning. Really, he might have been a good teacher but he wasn't Annie Sullivan. God, I wish my sister hadn't married that man."

More chairs snapped into place. Richer looked down the road again. Jeff became aware of the hole in the ground. For just a moment Jeff felt a tiny bit of shame for intruding into these people's lives, using Xander's education as a justification for what amounted to morbid voyeurism. But it was just a tiny bit of shame, quickly overwhelmed by his next question.

"You disliked your brother-in-law?"

"Don't get me started."

"We drifted apart so long ago" said Jeff. "You won't hurt my feelings. And I'd be interested in your perspective."

Interested in his perspective.

"I shouldn't judge him so harshly," Jeremy started.

But we know, Dear Reader, that by the end of things Marshall Chester will be judged quite harshly. It's coming.

"Elenora had a good life with him, at least by most people's standards. Their union produced seven glorious children, etcetera, etcetera. And I'm fond of my nephews. They're strong, self-assured kids. No geniuses in the bunch but they will certainly fulfill their father's dreams for them. Professional careers and a family of their own."

"And yet?"

"Look what she could have had," Richer continued, regret in his voice. "If she hadn't married Marsh she would have moved to New York after college. She could have taken a loft in Soho, hobnobbed with Andy Warhol, lived a life of theater and art and dance. Parties. Restaurants. Liaisons and adventures. She could have pursued her acting career—her dream since she was a small child."

"So you think she sold out on her dreams by marrying Marshall."

"It's this damned city," Richer said. "Pittsburghers have an innate drive to achieve stability. Stability. It's attractive, it's seductive. For a person with dreams, it's deadly."

"Strong words."

"You should have known her, Jeff. As a teenager Elenora was inventive, wild, fiercely original. She entered college a bright, burning ingénue with purpose and vision. She left college a schoolteacher's hausfrau. I know people think so highly of poor Marshall Chester. Such a compassionate man, such a committed teacher. In my eyes he's a killer of orchids. He found a beautiful, one-of-a-kind orchid growing wild in the forest. Instead of stopping for a moment to admire its beauty, allowing it to propagate in its natural habitat, he cut it and took it home."

"Wow," said Jeff. "It sounds like you hated the man."

"I didn't hate him exactly," Richer pondered for a moment. "I resented him. He was a mediocrity."

"I sometimes think that's the cruelest thing you can say about someone," said Jeff. "What about his accomplishments as a teacher? He made quite a name for himself at that school."

"He climbed a rung or two in a suburban high school in Pittsburgh. Do I applaud now or later? Forgive me. I know I'm a snob. I can't help it. I am."

Jeff considered out of meanness asking Jeremy for a list of his own accomplishments. He rather liked Pittsburgh and didn't consider rivers and beautiful green hillsides a hindrance to the accomplishment of dreams.

"At least he provided well for her," said Jeremy. A black Cadillac, bearing the body of the recently slandered deceased, rounded the bend in the drive. "Ah, they're here."

Not willing to let this part of the conversation go, Jeff asked quickly, "So Marsh put some money aside? Elenora won't have to work?"

"Better than that. Didn't you know?" Jeremy looked Jeff slyly in the eye. "A Prudential agent stopped by the house yesterday morning with some rather amazing news."

More cars pulled up behind the hearse. People got out of their cars and headed for the gravesite.

"What news was that?" Jeff asked.

"Six weeks before his murder good old Marsh took out an additional life insurance policy on himself. Three million dollars. I saw the policy. My sister's signature is forged. Tell me he didn't know his life was in danger."

At that moment Elenora emerged from the limousine just behind the hearse. Several of her children escorted her across the grassy knoll. The priest followed the family. Other cars arrived, additional mourners joined the fray. Penny English, as beautiful in mostly black as she was in mostly green, held back, wanting to be inconspicuous.

Jeremy Richer finished his thought darkly out of the side of his mouth.

"He was into some kind of dirty business," he said. "That much is certain."

———

Before greeting her brother, Elenora drifted toward Jeff.

"Thank you for coming," she said gently. She lifted her veil and kissed him ever so softly on the cheek. "I want to apologize for Sunday evening."

"No need," he assured her, clasping her hands.

"They had me on drugs."

"I know."

"I would like it if you wrote something nice about my husband. It's important to me." For a moment Jeff saw the beautiful woman in her, the woman she must have been all those years ago in college. Classic cheekbones, auburn hair. Off of the drugs her personality hinted at magic and a certain originality of style. The orchid in the woods. Jeff perceived a kindness in her, part real, part theatrical. "Do you have my address? My brother can give it to you."

"I have it."

"Tomorrow if it's convenient. I'm all right now. I can see people. I'll make us a lunch."

"Lunch isn't necessary."

"It will give me something to do. Just sitting around thinking is painful. One o'clock is good."

"One o'clock."

The priest signaled to Elenora. The seven Chester boys wore dark suits and conservative ties, even the one with the nose ring. They gathered about their mother. Additional mourners took seats.

Penny English saddled up to Jeff.

"Miss English," he said.

"My students call me Miss English. Why don't you call me Penny."

"All right, Penny. I'm Jeff."

"Oh, I know. I poked your face with my vicious female claws, remember? I drew blood."

"A minor wound. I cut myself more seriously this morning shaving. I'm embarrassed to say I almost forgot the service and had to dash out of the house."

"Such a rough beard," she said, play pouting. Her eyes flashed as she thought of what she might do with that manly sandpaper face. Just as quickly, she let that thought go and turned her attention to the burial. "Such a circus. I think I'm reaching my limit. Do you need to see this?"

"Actually," Jeff whispered in her ear, "I came to see you."

"Really?" She regarded him. "Let's take a walk then."

———

With a certain deftness they withdrew from the crowd and disappeared behind one of the grassy hills. Jeff didn't want Elenora to see him go. Not long into their walk Penny English removed her patent leather shoes. The ground was a bit damp but that didn't seem to bother her.

Penny clearly defined herself by a sophisticated, daring sense of dress. The black wool suit, exquisitely tailored, might have cost several thousand dollars. Under the jacket she wore a lily-white blouse, silk Jeff imagined, that sported small gleaming gold buttons set with emeralds so tiny they were almost dust. Below this, around her waist, she wore a tartan plaid cummerbund/vest sort of a thing, the dominant color of which was dark Erin green interwoven with strands of red and black and gold. The green set off the emeralds and her eyes; the red highlighted her long copper hair (which she tossed back every couple of minutes), the gold brought out the buttons on her blouse, and the black tied in with the suit and ultimately the occasion. And she wore perfume. Subtle but there. To the funeral. *Thank God I'm gay,* Jeff thought. *This woman must drive straight men crazy.*

"Elenora was horrible this morning," Penny said after a period of agitated silence.

"Horrible in what way?"

"This morning of all mornings she went off the drugs."

"I noticed that. She seemed more settled, more in control."

"Oh yes. She claims now that she's on her own she needs a clear head. Cogent mental faculties."

"Good for her," Jeff asserted. "Brave move, really."

English glowered at him like an offended dominatrix.

"I didn't ask you to walk with me so you could take her side."

"Sorry."

"I need to vent. Of all the stupid, fucking men on this planet you at least look a little empathetic. You're gay, aren't you."

Jeff nodded.

"Figures." Penny trudged ahead intently. Jeff just barely kept pace, regretting once again the Scotch haze. Hadn't eaten anything either. Penny continued sharply, "Students, teachers, men, my family. They give nothing to me. They steal my energy, they steal my time, they steal my sex. This one sweet man loved me with all of his heart. Not a romantic love. Not like that. Real love. He was much more to me than any stupid, worthless husband could be." She screamed, "That bitch! That bitch!"

"What on earth did she do?"

"Oh, she did plenty, Mister. See, I know I'm a bitch. I'm good at it. I've turned it into a craft." Jeff saw no reason to doubt this. "Elenora is a sneaky bitch. She pretends to be this meek, ineffective little housewife from the burbs when in reality she's a mammoth, first class, big city sneaky bitch."

"Elenora is a bitch. I got that. So tell me what she actually did to make you so angry."

Penny turned away.

"I shouldn't tell you."

"You should most definitely tell me," Jeff said, exasperated. "Gay men make good, dedicated listeners."

"Good gossips, too."

"I should tell you I'm not a typical gay man. I'm a computer geek. I don't have anyone to gossip to. I don't have any friends."

"I hope you're joking."

"Only a little. Actually, my best friend is an eleven-year-old boy who is pretending to be my son. It's sad, really."

"You're not diddling him, are you?"

"God no. It's an unofficial big brother, little brother thing. He likes me for some reason."

"You probably have qualities you don't suspect."

"Probably. Now tell me about Elenora and the sneaky bitch thing she did this morning."

"It's so personal," Penny protested.

"Give me a break. I just told you my only friend in the world is an eleven-year-old boy. I've never said that out loud to anybody. You know why? Because I don't have any friends. Very personal. Embarrassing. So what happened?"

"All right, all right. I'll tell you. Wait, I'm walking too damn fast. I have to stop and breathe." She put her arm out to his chest and stopped him, for which he was very grateful.

"If we could walk a little slower in general that would be great," he said. "I drank way too much Scotch last night and I'm really hung over."

"Are you an alcoholic?" she asked.

"Maybe. That's another embarrassing confession never before uttered out loud. So, about Elenora."

They continued walking.

"These past few days," Penny started, "I have been consoling Elenora. I'll be honest with you. Elenora and I have never been friends."

"No kidding."

"I don't really like her. I think Marshall married beneath him. Be that as it may, I was Marshall's dearest friend, closest colleague."

"You felt obliged to look after his widow," Jeff helped.

"Yes. I didn't see anyone else stepping up to the plate. That brother of hers is a complete flake. Her sons are emotionally immature. Well, what do you expect? She raised them. Our principal is a gutless shit eater. His main concern is staying as far away from this murder business as he can get. So the job fell to me."

"I take it Elenora didn't appreciate your efforts."

"She was fine when she was doped up. Erratic, schizzy. But she let me take care of her. I took her to lunch. I made the hundreds of arrangements that funerals require. I kept reporters out of her hair. Hell, I even took the poor girl to the potty. So. First two days, so far so good. I'm on my way up the aisle to accept my Mother Teresa award when, boom, Elenora goes drug free. On the third day she brought her real self—someone we haven't seen for years—to the funeral service."

Jeff suggested, "She must have done some soul searching."

"Maybe she did," said Penny. "Who cares. This story is about me."

"Sorry. Forgot."

"I sauntered up to her this morning, naively expecting a little hug. Mind you, we were about to bury the only human being I have truly loved. I was fighting back tears of my own, drawing on reserves of strength I didn't know I had, in order to do the decent thing by Elenora.

"She turned to look at me. Her face was so severe I instinctively withdrew the hug I was about to offer. In this prim, bitchy voice she says, 'I don't need your help. Don't hold me, don't sit beside me, don't even talk to me. I have nothing to say to you. I want nothing to do with you.'"

"Damn."

"That's right. There were a hundred people standing around us. Her brother, her children, my colleagues, my students. God knows my supervisors."

"You didn't see it coming at all?" Jeff asked.

"No. I was shocked. Before I could think of a response, she blurts out, 'I know you were sleeping with my husband. Don't pretend that you like me. Don't try to give people the impression that we're in this together. And please don't have the gall to think you're riding with me behind the body to the cemetery. That place is reserved for family.'"

"What did you say?"

"I didn't do anything. There was a buzz in my head. I couldn't think. Then—here's the clincher—she reaches into her purse and says, 'Here's a memento from my late husband.' And she hands me a rubber."

"A rubber?"

"A prophylactic. In it's plastic enclosure. 'It was in his wallet when they found him,' she says. 'I'm sure he meant for you to have it.' Do you believe that?"

"What did you do?"

"I took it from her! I wasn't thinking. My face was flushed, my pulse was racing. I stood there like a dummy and took it. I stared at it as if it were a mystical fetish or something. That bitch!"

Penny screamed, then threw one of her shoes across the green. It hit a grave marker, knocking the heel off cleanly.

"What have I done," she yelled chasing after her shoe. "These shoes are fucking Prada."

———

Penny tossed her expensive shoes on a pile of used flowers behind the cemetery's work shed. She flaunted this brazen act of waste, laughing.

Two dubious looking lawn chairs, circa 1962, reposed ten feet or so from the shed's door.

"Let's sit for a while," she said.

"I think these chairs are for the workmen," Jeff replied.

"Oh, so what. What can they say? We're paying customers."

Penny dismissed the concerns of workmen everywhere by dramatically lounging across the nearest chair. Snapping her fingers in the air, she cried, "Waiter! Waiter! Drinks all around. Drinks for my friends." She gestured to the headstones scattered across the hillside. More quietly to Jeff she said, "You don't happen to have a flask on you?"

"I'm afraid not."

She sighed. "Too bad."

Jeff eased into the other chair, wincing. A hand broom and wishful thinking would not save his suit from the dry cleaners this time. Jeff started, cautiously, "I'm curious about something that's none of my business."

She stole the question from the edge of his lips. "Yes, we were lovers once. For a couple of weeks. Eight or nine years ago."

Jeff was surprised. He figured they had been lovers eight or nine years, not eight or nine years ago.

"It was one of those things," Penny continued. "We worked together all the time. We came to love each other. It was a friendship kind of love. In the beginning friendship love can be confused for romantic love."

"I see," Jeff said, trying to sound experienced in such matters.

"It was wonderful the first time," she confided. "Marshall was a gentle lover, a considerate lover. Lots of small tastes, like a Japanese buffet. But as you might have guessed, that's not my style, really. I like things a little rough, a little edgy. And he felt guilty about his wife. Lots of Catholic guilt. We fucked about six times before we admitted the whole thing was a mistake." Like a teacher Penny checked out Jeff's reaction to make certain he had absorbed the material. "I know everyone thinks we've been bonking each other for years. That's because we loved each other so much. People presumed."

Jeff shifted in his dirty chair and asked, professorially, "Why was there a condom in his wallet?"

"That's a good question," English replied, closing her eyes for just a moment. "The nurse keeps a bowl of them in the waiting room of her office. The kids take them like mints. They throw them at each other in class. One or two of them have been left on my desk with a suggestive note."

"So you think he picked one up in his classroom. Maybe off of the floor."

"It's possible. I'm sure he's done it numerous times."

"Not likely, though," said Jeff. "A teenager might keep a condom in his wallet for years because a teenager doesn't have much to put in his wallet. An adult man has credit cards, ID cards, business cards, photographs. No room for a condom. An adult man would have put it in his trouser pocket."

Penny sighed impatiently. "There was no condom in his wallet. Elenora invented that story to cause a scene and humiliate me."

"Or," said Jeff, "there's another explanation."

Jeff knew so little about Elenora Chester, even less about her history of drug taking. Still, the idea of staging this confrontation on the morning of her husband's funeral strained credulity. There probably was a condom in his wallet. This would have been included in the parcel of personal belongings returned to the widow. The police might have placed the condom deliberately in the parcel to gage her reaction. That would be cruel, of course, but in Jeff's experience the scarring of psyches was all in a day's work for the police.

"He wasn't having an affair," Penny declared flatly. "We were as close as twins. He would have told me."

———

Jeff retreated from the subject of murder for just a moment. For appearances' sake he asked Penny a series of questions pertinent to the imaginary article he was writing for the alumnae magazine. Penny chronicled a tedious but impressive list of achievements. Chester volunteered for a mind-boggling amount of after school work: coaching, administration, career counseling, student charity projects. Sounded like he gave more time to his students than to his children.

"You said earlier you wished Marshall had never married Elenora," Jeff threw in off handedly.

"He chose badly, that's all I meant," Penny replied. "I don't mean to dump on Elenora. In her own right she's perfectly fine. Their marriage might have worked better if she had gone into teaching. She could have taught theater. Some theater teachers only work half days. Then too, she could have had two children instead of seven."

"Didn't Marshall want a large family?"

"Yes," Penny answered, annoyed. "But a woman is not a dog dependent upon a master. A modern woman can take a stand about how many children she will have. A modern woman can take a stand on how much time will be devoted to children and how much time to a career."

"You are clearly a modern woman," Jeff observed in a rational tone. "But is Elenora? Was she a modern woman twenty-plus years ago when she married Marshall?"

"Well," English said, tossing back her hair, "I can't answer for that."

"You mentioned teaching. Not everyone is cut out to be a teacher. What if she deliberately chose to be a housewife and a mother?"

"Then she had no business marrying a teacher. I'm certain, I'm absolutely certain, Marsh would have lived a richer, more fulfilling life if he had married a teacher. By the time he realized his mistake his life was over."

"Did he think his marriage was a mistake?" Jeff asked as casually as possible.

"I thought it was a mistake. I. Me. I thought it. I'll tell you one thing. If she had been a good teacher's wife, if she had hung out with the other teacher's wives, put on dinners, helped with charity functions, she would have been in a position to nip the Greta Fields thing the moment it started. I will not apologize for my position. She was a jellyfish of a wife. I gossamer nobody with a fertile womb."

Penny surprised herself with the ferocity of her own opinion. She laughed at herself. "That's what I should have said when she handed me the rubber. 'You jellyfish! You gossamer nobody with a fertile womb! I was a better wife to him than you. And I was just a friend.'" Penny laughed so hard that tears formed at the corners of her eyes. "Oh!" she cried, stomping her foot. "I'm so damn mad! Marshall would still be alive today if he hadn't married that woman. I'm sure of it."

Just then Gregory drove up to the shed in a motorized cart. The cart hauled a wheelbarrow that contained more flowers as well as expired wreathes and tree branches. Getting out of the cart, Gregory pointed a friendly finger at Jeff.

"I remember you," he said cheerfully. "This beautiful lady wasn't with you."

"Aren't you nice," said Penny.

"I hope we're not sitting in your chairs," said Jeff.

"Oh, that's all right. I put them out for company. I don't get much company, but they're there just in case I do."

Gregory disconnected the wheelbarrow and dumped its contents onto the flower pile. Penny followed the young man with her eyes. Gregory sported an athletic physique and looked more nattily attired in his clean, pressed work clothes than Jeff looked in his suit. Handsome, too. Nice square jaw.

Gregory picked out a perfect white lily from among the dying flowers and presented it to Penny. She accepted the gift graciously.

"I don't ever waste the good flowers," Gregory said. "I pick them out and put them in water. There are always fresh flowers in my shed."

"Where should I wear it?" Penny asked, looking for a spot on her jacket.

Gregory took the flower and very gently placed it behind her left ear.

"You make the flower look beautiful," he said.

Penny feigned shock. "Someone taught you that line."

"Yes," Gregory confessed easily. "My friend Paul. Did it work?"

"Almost."

Gregory beamed a big wide smile, then returned to the business of sorting flower refuse. Penny enjoyed watching him work. So, for that matter, did Jeff. Finally Jeff came back to business. "You mentioned the Greta Fields thing."

"You heard about that?"

"Bit and pieces. I heard she was an unpleasant woman."

"Our dickless principal, Modani, brought her to the school almost two years ago. Like most school districts ours has been losing money. People are moving away, taking lower paying jobs. The Amazing Shrinking Tax Base. Greta Fields was brought in to oversee the operations of the school. Her purpose was to root out waste, identify unnecessary programs, that kind of thing. She was also supposed to weed out the uninspired teachers and perhaps induce a few of the older ones to early retirement."

"Did you know that was why the principal brought her into the school?" Jeff asked.

"Oh, yes. It sounded good on the surface. Necessary. And she taught business administration, coached the girls Lacrosse team. Made herself useful."

"So what happened?"

"Instead of eliminating unnecessary waste, she targeted perfectly good teachers. She operated out of some kind of personal agenda. First she targeted the gay teachers—only the men, mind you, she didn't target the lesbians. They were all fired at once. There were rumors, which I'm sure she started, that they had formed a student molestation ring."

"Do you think the rumors were true?"

"Absolutely not. They were excellent teachers. I think Fields found out they were gay, targeted them, planted rumors, worked on Modani and the Board until she got them fired."

"Why do you think she targeted gay men? Was she a right wing fanatic or something?"

"I don't know. Greta Fields was gay herself. I just know those teachers were excellent teachers and they were not fired for the good of the school. They were fired for purely personal reasons known only the Greta Fields."

Gregory turned around and looked at Penny. "I know where she is," he said, trying to be helpful.

"Where who is, dear?" returned Penny.

"Greta Fields. I know where she's buried. Well, she's not really buried. She lives in one of the little stone houses. A ma- ma-"

"Mausoleum," Penny finished. "She's in this cemetery?"

"They put her in her house in July. I remember that. I remember when every dead person came here. I know all their names and I know exactly where they are. Marshall Chester came here today. See, Paul tells me the name when we dig the hole. Then I memorize it. Then I look at the letters on the marker and see how they go. Do you know what I mean?"

"I think I do," said Penny. "Like—" she looked for a word he might understand.

"Like tattoos."

Gregory thought about it. "Yes, like tattoos," he said, pleased with the analogy. "I know every person buried since I started working here. I started working here when I was fourteen."

Jeff finally understood. Being a teacher, Penny knew much earlier. In fact, while admiring his nice, tight workman's body she allowed herself a fantasy along the line of Colleen McCullough's *Tim*. Life might be so much easier with a Tim than with a Larry.

Gregory continued, "There's a woman who comes to see Miss Fields. Her name's Jane Lund. She dresses all in black and brings lots of flowers. We go inside the little house together and arrange the flowers. Jane sings to Miss Fields."

"She sings?" asked Jeff, surprised.

"Music plays in the little house twenty-four hours a day. It's a CD that repeats. Jane sings along to the music on the CD. She puts on little shows, too. The music is very important, she says. She pays me extra to check on the CD every day to make sure that it's working."

"I'm surprised there's room in the mausoleum for both of you," noted Penny.

"Oh, sure. There's a bench in there. There's a bed. Well, not really a bed. It's the place right across from Miss Fields where Jane is supposed to go when she dies. Jane laid down in it once to see what it was like."

Penny laughed. She made a disparaging remark about Jane Lund, perhaps more cruel than accurate. Gregory blushed and jumped to Jane's defense. He let it be known he considered Jane his friend. 'Well, 'thought Penny, 'more than one of us has looked you over. Maybe there is more to this Jane Lund than any of us guessed.' Then Penny had a morbid thought. She wondered if they had ever opened the coffin and looked inside. After all, it was right there on the shelf.

Jeff found himself staring at the bulge in Gregory's pants. 'Enough of this,' he thought.

"I didn't get a chance to eat this morning," he said to Penny. "Can I take you somewhere and buy you breakfast?"

"I'm sorry," Penny protested. "I've got to get out of these clothes. And I need shoes. I'll tell you what. Come back to my place for breakfast. We'll have a nice long chat for your article. Gregory, I'm so sorry I can't invite you, but I know you have to work."

"That's right," Gregory replied. "I have to compost the flowers. Then we fill the dirt in on Mr. Chester. Then it's time for lunch."

Penny and Jeff walked back in the direction of their respective cars. Gregory called after them, "If you ever want to visit your friend just come see me at the shed. I'll take you right to him. I'll know exactly where he is."

30.

Penny lived on a winding, isolated country road called Silverbird Lane. Her quaint red brick house, more of a cottage really, overlooked the river valley.

"It's small, I know," she said. "I'm single. I'll probably always be single. It suits me. I could die here. That's my criteria." Penny headed upstairs. "Make yourself at home. Take off your shoes by all means. Men have such uncomfortable looking shoes." From upstairs she called down, "There's some champagne in the fridge. Open it, will you? I need something with alcohol in it. There are glasses in the cupboard in the dining room."

Despite his considerable hangover, Jeff needed something with alcohol in it, too. This fueled the debate about alcoholism going on in his head. Didn't stop him from locating the champagne and the glasses. Booze to the top. He sipped from his own glass as he poked around Penny's cottage. Warm, quality furnishings. She decorated it herself, he was certain. It had a small Irish cottage feel to it. He could almost smell the peat.

Jeff especially admired Penny's collection of art. He recognized many of the artists as being regional. Jeff knew little about contemporary television or film, but art and artists fascinated him.

Most Pittsburgh art galleries included Jeffrey Redwing and Guests on their mailing list. He often took Xander and Sally to openings. He made a point of chatting with the artist or artists. If he found their approach or philosophy interesting, he introduced Xander to the artist. If Jeff felt a particular artist needed financial support, he bought a piece or two. He lived with the art for a little while, then gave it to friends or donated it to charity auctions. He felt that for himself, personally, it was inappropriate to own art.

He admired the moral courage required to live with art, the same art, every day. He admired Penny's tasteful if eclectic collection of artists. Two large Ben Klaas geometric cityscapes. There was a rural scene by Jim Nelson. Along a hallway he noticed two paper Braille sculptures by Emile Sauer. A couple of smallish Philip Rostek paintings on the subject of Saint Francis. These were the artists he recognized.

Jeff called upstairs, "Do you think Gregory lives in that shed?"

"I think he might," Penny called back. "Maybe it's cozy in there. His clothes were nice and neat. He'd be the only person in Mount Lebanon with forty acres of land outside his door."

"I realized he was listening in on our conversation."

"Was he?" she asked.

"Yes. I thought it might be good to have some privacy."

Penny returned to the first floor wearing black exercise tights and a white cotton top. Very plain, yet like all of her clothing, this simple ensemble accentuated her exotic beauty.

"Is there something private you wanted to say?" she asked.

"It's about Greta Fields. It seems there are people like her everywhere in business these days. Something similar to what you described is going on at one of the companies where I work."

"What's going on exactly?" she asked, taking up her glass of champagne.

"A new person came into the organization about a year ago. This person appears to have access to everyone's computer passwords. E-mails are being erased. False e-mails are being sent. Good employees of long-standing and considerable reputation are being set up, it seems, to be fired. These people seem to be targeted. They are consistently given more work than they can do, then being written up as incompetent. The atmosphere has gotten tense at this organization. Two people have been fired already. One employee said to me privately that he wouldn't be surprised if someone came into the office one day with an automatic weapon to kill this career assassin and the management personnel who allow him to operate."

Penny went into the kitchen and withdrew a couple of skillets from a drawer under the stove.

"That's the atmosphere at the school. At least it was before Greta Fields died."

"From where I stand, the management team knows what's going on, don't agree with it, but are helpless to stop it. This career assassin has been brought in from someone higher up. The management team must cooperate or risk losing their own jobs. I'm sure your Principal Modani is in the same position."

"I'm so glad you understand," said Penny, withdrawing milk, eggs and cheese from the refrigerator. "Sometimes when I look back on what has happened, I doubt my own judgment. I think I must have imagined it all. It's too horrible, too cruel. I think I must be exaggerating the events." In a glass bowl Penny cracked six eggs, added milk and vigorously stirred. "Because what I imagine she did was blatantly evil. I'm not a religious person and I'm not superstitious, but Greta Fields, to me, represented something close to pure evil."

Jeff let her words stand for a moment.

Then he said, "I think your instincts were right about Greta Fields. Most of us operate out of a sense of morality. We might not all have the same moral standards, but we basically care about each other, get along with one another. We act as if things like justice and truth and what we call decency are important. We honor them and do our best to be guided by them. But then someone like Fields shows up. She stirs up a little gossip with the right people, places a few damning lies. It costs people their jobs, their reputations, their marriage, custody of their children, their standing in the community. Good decent people make excuses for people like Fields, try to spin them in a positive light. 'Fields is only doing her job,' they'll say. 'Where there's smoke, there's fire.' Until it's their turn."

On a chopping board Penny sliced enough cheddar cheese for two omelets. Then she chopped a bit of onion, a bit of parsley.

"I guess I'm not one of the decent people then," she said. "I saw right through that snake bitch the first day she showed up for work. She started in on Marshall, you know."

"That's what I heard," Jeff replied.

"He thought I was exaggerating. That first year while she sabotaged the gay men she was also laying land mines around his career. God knows why. The man was sensitive, concerned, committed. Exemplary teacher. The second year she went after a second wave of teachers and Marsh was singled out for special humiliation."

"How did he respond?"

She instructed Jeff to prepare bread for toast. A little olive oil slid into each heated skillet and Penny started the omelets.

"He defended himself, of course, but to no avail. Modani backed off. Other teachers, many his friends, drifted away so they wouldn't be targeted next by association. They knew they'd be next if they interfered. Only I stood up to her and wouldn't back down."

"But Greta Fields died before Marshall got fired."

"That's right. Oh, I forgot plates. Get some plates out from the cupboard to the left of the sink, would you?"

They took their breakfast into the dining room. Penny put the champagne on ice. There was more champagne, she promised, should they want it. It was a rough day for her, she said. She might as well get drunk. He was free to do what he liked. Crash on her sofa if necessary.

―――――

Spreading jam on his toast, Jeff said, "I understand Fields died of a heart attack."

"At the Fourth of July picnic," Penny affirmed. "The fat pig choked on a piece of cheesecake. She died before the ambulance arrived. Marshall called it 'an epiphany of Joycean proportions.' I called it poetic justice. The witch was dead. A great sigh of relief was heard throughout Munchkin Land."

Jeff thought he understood the background events leading up to the Roman/Chester murders. One lone piece of the puzzle didn't fit. Casually, he brought the subject around to this odd issue.

"You know, Elenora's brother told me something this morning that perked up my ears."

"What was that?"

"I brought up the subject of money. All those children. A wife with no profession. How was Elenora situated financially? Was she going to be able to survive without her husband's income?"

"Good question," Penny said pensively.

Jeff leaned toward the pretty woman, speaking in hushed tones.

"Jeremy Richer told me Marshall took out a life insurance policy six weeks before he died. Elenora and the kids are due to collect several million dollars."

"That's right," Penny said matter-of-factly.

"You knew about it?"

"I introduced Marshall to my insurance agent—who I'm sure will never speak to me again. But in any case. Marsh didn't feel he could go through his own agent."

"Because?"

"Because he didn't want Elenora to know about the policy. She would have jumped to the wrong conclusions."

"Jeremy told me Elenora knew nothing about the policy. I just presumed he was lying. Or she was lying."

Penny shook her head. "No. He was correct. Marshall went to a lot of trouble to keep it from her. You see, Elenora worried everything to death. And she hadn't been well. All those drugs, those stabilizers or tranquilizers or whatever they were. Elenora would have jumped to the conclusion that Marshall suffered from cancer or some other fatal disease."

"Elenora told Jeremy her signature on the policy was forged."

Penny raised her right hand as if to say I confess.

"You forged her signature?" Jeff asked.

"If you repeat that I'll deny it. And then I'll come after you."

"Hey, I'm just an old friend from college," Jeff said, backing off. "But it looks odd. Don't you think? Six weeks before his death. Did he have a premonition? Was someone stalking him or sending him threatening letters?"

"Nothing like that," Penny said. "He just wanted to protect the one thing that mattered most in his life: his family."

Penny poured Jeff a cup of coffee from an ornate sterling silver pot. The coffee itself was Maxwell House brewed in a Mr. Coffee, the ripple of the Java world. There was a certain amount of veneer to Penny English. Rosewood over pine.

On his way out Jeff commented on the many local artists represented in Penny's collection.

"I noticed: no women artists," he said. "Do you prefer the male perspective?"

The question took Penny by surprise.

"I've not considered the gender orientation of my artwork. Wait a minute. The ceramic pieces are by Juanita Miller. And in my bedroom I have a glass top made by Kathleen Mulcahy. I bought it at the Art for AIDS auction. It meant something to me because I used to play with Duncan tops when I was a little girl."

"I saw that piece," Jeff said. "I attended the auction. I go every year. They've changed the name of the auction now to something so complicated I can't remember it."

"I go most years," Penny said. "Now that I think of it, I've seen you there. At the funeral home the other night I thought that I had seen you before, but I just couldn't think where. So that's it. You were with a little boy."

"That's right."

"And a woman. Brownish blond hair. Lady Clairol perm. You looked like a family."

"We are a family in an odd way. I'm gay, so I'm not dating the woman. I'm kind of a Big Brother for the boy. Nothing official. He's from my neighborhood. I told you a little about that already."

"Where is his birth father? Or is that too personal to ask?"

"Not personal to me. The father abandoned his family when Xander, the boy, was four. Disappeared. No letter. No nothing."

"Maybe something untoward happened to him."

"His clothes were gone."

"Oh."

"You know," Jeff said. "I'd love to acquire a Juanita Miller for my own collection. I wonder if you have the phone number of the gallery."

"I might," Penny said. "Let me check."

Penny crossed the room and took up a hardbound address book, quite attractive. A reproduction of Mary Cassatt's *The Letter* graced the cover. Penny found the number and copied it for him.

"That's a beautiful address book," Jeff said, making sure to inflect his voice with a note of envy.

"It's from the Metropolitan Museum," Penny said proudly. "Each divider features a work of art that relates to the subject of letter writing. I think they still have it for sale."

"Really?" Jeff said. "May I see it?"

She handed over her address book. Jeff flipped through the pages.

"I love this Walker Evans," Jeff said, showing it to her. "Oh, and look at this Japanese wood block. *A Girl Thinking How She Will Write a Letter.* How often I've struck that exact pose." Turning a few more pages Jeff found a reproduction of an old Greek piece, circa 480 B.C.—*Hermes Speeding on an Errand.* "Isn't this wonderful? I've always admired the clean lines of Greek art."

"And the clean lines of Greek men, I imagine."

"Well." Jeff smiled the smile of a conspirator. Hunters of men, he and Penny. At least in the conspiracy. "I've seen this on sale in the catalogue. I just didn't realize how beautiful it was inside." He handed it back to her.

At the door she gave him a soft kiss on the cheek.

"Since Marsh died I haven't had anyone who could listen," she said. "Thank you for listening."

He acknowledged her gratitude with an embarrassed nod. If she knew how well he had listened, she might not have thanked him for it.

31.

"Honey, I'm home," Jeff called up the stairs.

His trusty mainframe hummed happily away. He really needs to get a dog.

The too-dirty-to-wear-even-to-a-garage-sale jacket landed in the dry cleaning basket. Everything else he tossed into the hamper. He desperately needed a shower. Naked, he glanced at the bathroom door. Well, it's not like he had any appointments. He could check his e-mail first. And his calls.

He trudged up to the attic. Nothing in e-mail. Aha. A call from Ellen Coffey.

"Hello Jeff. Have something for you. Maybe. Call after three." It was only 2:47. The shower could wait another fifteen minutes. What could he do that would only take fifteen minutes? He could call one of the numbers from Roman's address book. The Kitty Hawk lady. What was her name? Where was that address book?

He scoured the house for it, then remembered he had been reading it when he fell asleep. He located the address book on the floor next to his bed where it had dropped. Teddy bears. Her name had something to do with Teddy bears. Steiff. That's it. He found her entry. Griselda Steiff.

Jeff pondered for a moment the coincidence or perhaps irony of Vernon Roman knowing someone so close to his favorite hideaway in the Outer Banks. How many times a week did Jeff drive into Kitty Hawk? Three or four. He might have passed Roman on the highway, might have picked over shrimp beside him at a fresh seafood stand, might even have sat at a nearby table at a restaurant.

And what about in Pittsburgh? Jeff sometimes ate at the Wendy's in Shadyside where Roman met his death. Roman lived right across the street the whole time with Dottie Hatfield. Jeff probably stood beside Roman at the ketchup pump, exchanging excuse me's and pardon me's. How often had he stood beside a dangerous criminal or a future murder victim just in the course of everyday life?

While thus pondering the subtle shades of synchronicity, his next-door neighbor, Sharon Beineke, caught a glimpse of Jeff's firm, fleshy buttocks from her second floor window. She took up the pair of high-powered German binoculars she kept on a nightstand facing Jeff's house and zoomed in on a few pertinent details. Without missing a beat she picked up her cell and called her friend and neighbor, Sheila Romney.

"Sheila," she said, "he's naked again. Left bedroom, second floor." There was a pause while Sheila retrieved her own set of binoculars. "Lord have mercy," Sharon continued. "Look at that ass. I tell you I'm going to write a soap opera with this man. *Splendor In The Afternoon*. Wait! Wait! He's turning." Sharon gasped. "Steal my breath away. Look at that magnificent chest. All that hair, like a carpet. My God. Don't talk dirty, Sheila, you're not supposed to be looking down there. Think of your husband. My husband and I are fighting. I can look. Can you imagine this man in your bed every night? Can you just imagine? Sheila, honey, if this man was in my bed he'd get no rest. I do! Every time we have a party I invite him. He just won't come. Oh, look, he's stretching. I'm going to faint!" Sharon and Sheila screamed into their phones at each other. "Who's fucking this man, Sheila, that's what I want to know. I want details. Don't talk to me about Sally Pooka. She's not getting anything. Oh, no, he's starting to move. Don't go, Jeff! Don't go!"

Jeff, oblivious to uncurtained windows, took his fuzzy bumpers back upstairs to his desk. He dialed Griselda Steiff's number. The usual clacks and static-filled pauses marked the passage of his station-to-station landline call. At Kitty Hawk a recorded message broke in. Disconnected number.

Jeff called Kitty Hawk information.

"Operator, I'm trying to reach an old friend of mine, Griselda Steiff. I just called the number I've been calling for years and got a disconnect notice." Jeff conveyed a sense of distress in his voice. "Would you check it for me?"

In a soft Southern voice the operator replied, "I'm sorry, sir, it appears that number has been disconnected. Would you like me to check for another number?"

"Would you please? It's not like her to change numbers without telling me. I'm a little worried."

"Sorry, sir. I find no listing for a Griselda Steiff in Kitty Hawk. In fact, no listing in the greater Outer Banks. I show a listing for an R. Steiff in Kitty Hawk."

"That might be her mother. Why don't you give it to me?"

Jeff dialed the number for R. Steiff. By this time the LED on his desk clock read 3:09. Must call Ellen soon. 'Pick up, R. Steiff. Pick up. You're not at work, you're not out shopping. You're at home. Pick up.'

After the fourth ring an answering machine clicked on. A woman's voice, young sounding and a little husky, verified the number without verifying the name. It was a noncommittal message scripted by the answering machine company for people who wished to remain unidentifiable to strangers. After the beep, Jeff started:

"Hello. This is Jeffrey Redwing calling from Pittsburgh, Pennsylvania. I vacation several times a year in Corolla (close enough). I'm trying to reach a Griselda Steiff. The number she gave me has been disconnected."

Someone on the other end picked up.

The husky voice from the answering machine asked accusingly, "Who is this?"

"I'm an acquaintance of Griselda Steiff's," Jeff said, trying to sound self-assured. "I met her while on vacation—not this last time but the time before that." She waited for him to continue. "Griselda suggested I call if I was coming down for any length of time. Are you a relative by any chance?"

A pause.

"I'm her sister."

The voice sounded hard, maybe a little angry, maybe a little suspicious.

"I think she mentioned you briefly," Jeff added. "Robyn? Roberta?"

"Ramona."

"I'm sorry. She mentioned you, but didn't tell me much about you."

"That sounds like my sister," said Ramona. "Not one to waste words."

"Yes, well. Ramona, I'm coming down to the Outer Banks in a couple of months. I wanted to get in touch with your sister but the number she gave me has been disconnected."

Jeff waited, the ball in her court. Wait. Wait. He could feel Ramona thinking, weighing considerations. Palpable. Heavy. Ramona sighed.

"I'm afraid you're a little late for a date," she said. "I hate to tell you this, but my sister is dead."

Another bead of the abacus slid into place. Jeff felt lightheaded.

"Are you still there?" came Ramona's voice.

"I'm sorry," Jeff said, gasping. Some of it was acting, some of it not. "I'm shocked. She seemed fine when I saw her last. What happened?"

"Highway accident."

"Oh, God."

"It was horrible. I can't tell you."

"I'll have nightmares now," Jeff said. "I always do."

"No reason for you to have nightmares. You didn't see it. I saw it. I'm the one who has nightmares."

"You don't know how I am. I can face it," Jeff said, "if you tell me exactly what happened."

"I can't do that," Ramona said quickly.

"You must," Jeff returned just as quickly. "I'm an artist. I make up horrible scenarios in my head. What I invent is always worse than the truth. That dear woman. I only knew her for a short while, but Griselda touched my heart. I'll be haunted by my imaginings. If you just tell me what happened, I'll be upset at first but then I'll be all right."

For a tense moment Jeff thought Ramona was going to hang up on him. For her part, Ramona had no good reason to tell this man anything. And yet there was something in his voice. He sounded like a nice man. Ramona pictured her sister with this man. (Griselda had been fifty-three years old; she pictured Jeff as middle-aged and pudgy.)

"Please," Jeff pleaded.

Ramona sighed. "It happened at night," she started.

"At night?"

"Yes. She had been out on a date." She waited. Jeff remained silent. Let her think he is jealous. "I didn't know the guy. Met him once, briefly. He wasn't from around here."

"Tourist?"

"No. He worked construction. You know, the boom out Corolla way. I'm sure I don't have to tell you."

"Know it only too well," he said disapprovingly.

"Griselda and this man—can't remember his name—went out drinking. At some point he left her. The police think they had a fight, although I have my doubts."

Exactly, thought Jeff.

"Then what happened?"

"She took out on the highway toward Virginia with enough liquor in her bloodstream to be certified legally blind. The police think she drove to clear her head. They think it's a miracle she got as far as she did."

"Sounds like you think the boyfriend played a role in her accident."

"Not necessarily," she said cautiously. "It doesn't make sense to me that Griselda headed out on the highway toward Virginia to clear her head. If she wanted to clear her head she'd drive back here and take a walk on the beach. We live at the beach. And for fuck's sake, pardon my French, Griselda never cleared her head in her life. Her job involved restructuring companies. Demoting people, firing people. She snapped her fingers and made decisions, right or wrong. She wasn't one to agonize."

"Where did Griselda work? She told me once, but—"

"She was a territorial director for New South Banking. When real estate bottomed out they brought her in to trim and cut. Property values fell as much as thirty percent in some areas. Then there was the hurricane. They had a lot of good, decent people they needed to fire. Longtime employees. Salt of the earth types. Griselda could do that kind of thing because she didn't have much of a conscience. Don't get me wrong. My sister could be real sweet if you were her friend. I'm sure she was real sweet to you. But she didn't stay up nights worrying about what people thought about her."

"I see."

"You're probably disillusioned, aren't you, hon? I'm sorry. I'm just telling you the truth. If you're as sensitive as you say, it's just as well. She thought men were dicks without batteries, excuse my language. That's really why I couldn't see her getting all worked up over this sleazeball she took out drinking. She wanted some laughs. She wanted a fuck. Not much to clear your head about. Truthfully, if she'd had a fight with this guy she would have gone out and gotten herself another dick without batteries."

Jeff wondered if the particular dick in question resembled Vernon Roman or Larry Cone. Or was it a third party? Someone from Ohio or that African American guy who confessed on CNN. Franklin Baum. Jeff couldn't think of a tactful way to ask for a physical description of the sleazeball. For that matter, he wouldn't recognize a description of Roman. Jeff hadn't yet seen a photograph.

"So she drove her car in an intoxicated state," Jeff urged her on.

"It was horrible," recounted Ramona. "They took me to her car. The police, they wanted me to identify the vehicle and to—to show me what happened. I wish they hadn't. I wish I didn't have those imagines in my head. They told me she was driving one hundred and ten miles per hour. That's how fast the car would have been speeding to do what it did. I imagine poor Griselda screaming, putting her hands up to her face. She missed an electrical pole, but then drove straight into the back of a truck."

"Where was this?" Jeff asked.

"It was one of those small produce farms about forty miles up the highway. Pickup truck parked in a drive just off of the road. The farmer used it to haul baskets of corn and squash and beans and whatever else he offered at his stand. Normally it would have been loaded with empty baskets. On this particular day the farmer had picked up a set of advertising signs."

"What kind of advertising signs?" Jeff asked.

"Flat tin signs with pictures of corn and squash and beans painted on them. The farmer intended to post these every so many miles along the highway leading up to his stand. You know the kind of thing. Ten Miles to Fresh Corn. Five Miles to Ripe Peaches. When Griselda hit the back of the truck the signs went flying."

"Oh, no."

"They were brand new. Sharp as razors. They broke through her windshield."

Ramona stopped, momentarily unable to continue her narrative. She took a few breaths, stifling tears.

"The plates killed your sister," Jeff finished.

"It was horrible," Ramona started crying. "Just like Jayne Mansfield, they said."

"I'm sorry. Jayne Mansfield?"

"A movie star who died in a car crash in the sixties. Her head—"

"Her head was severed," Jeff mouthed the words.

"The police said it was an extremely sharp cut."

"Don't tell me they made you look at that."

"I had to identify her body without her head," said Ramona. "At the morgue."

"You poor kid," said Jeff.

"Nothing can prepare you for it," she said. "I threw up. I couldn't help it."

"Of course you couldn't."

"This is what I see in my nightmares," Ramona sobbed. "The cut across the neck. Gashes on her body where the tin sliced into her skin. Deep gashes on her breasts, her stomach."

"But you knew it was your sister," Jeff asked. "Even without a face."

"It was my sister all right. She had a tattoo, you see."

"But they found her head later, right?"

"No," said Ramona. "They never found it. The police think it flew out of the car and maybe raccoons took it away. Can you believe it? Maybe buried it somewhere. They searched and searched."

"Never found it," Jeff muttered.

"I told you it was horrible!" she screamed. "Why did you make me tell you that story?"

"I'm sorry," Jeff said softly. "I had to know."

———

Jeff quickly called the other out-of-town numbers in Roman's address book. Most calls met with a disconnect notice. A Baltimore number still in service brought a Mrs. G. Armistice Black to the phone. Jeff gave her a spiel about a class reunion. Jeff could almost see Mrs. G. Armistice Black smile as she said, "You'll have to strike his name from your list. George drowned while boating in the Chesapeake Bay." She then added, wryly, "By the time they recovered his body most of it had been eaten by fish. So you see, he won't be attending his high school reunion this year. And I won't be attending on his behalf." Jeff got the impression that Mrs. G. Armistice Black regretted widowhood a little less than she might.

"You're naked," came a nonplussed eleven years-old voice from the doorway. "Haven't you put on any clothes at all today?"

"Don't be impertinent," Jeff said defensively, standing. (They'd had the naked talk before.) "I went to the Chester funeral today. Well, not the funeral really. The burial. I left before the blessings and the internment. I've learned a hell of a lot in the last eighteen hours."

"Didn't you get any sleep?" Xander enjoyed playing the exasperated parent with his so-called Big Brother.

"Of course I slept. I'll have you know I got plenty of sleep. Well, a little sleep."

"A couple of hours by the look of you."

"I don't much care to be interrogated," Jeff said. "I'm reminding myself at this very moment that I am the adult here. And you know what they say, Xander. Plenty of time to sleep when you're dead."

Xander folded his arms. Jeff, despite himself, felt just a tad guilty.

Jeff added in his defense, "This is all new nakedness. I was on my way to the shower when I decided to check my messages." He gasped. "Ellen Coffey! I was supposed to call Ellen at three o'clock."

"It's past four now."

"I absolutely have to call her. If you get me a robe, I promise I will wear it."

Jeff dialed Ellen Coffey's number while Xander left in search of a robe. Lionel P. Mansweater put Jeff on hold. Xander returned with a bright blue silk robe made especially for him by a Vietnamese seamstress. An elaborately stitched dragon roared fire across Jeff's back.

"I don't know what the big deal is," Jeff said. "You've seen me naked before."

"The women in this neighborhood look at you through binoculars."

Jeff laughed incredulously. "They do not!"

"They try to pump my mother for information about you. Don't act surprised. Their husbands are out of shape dullards who talk about work, football and their lawns. These women lead lives of quiet desperation."

"Thank you T.S. Eliot."

"To them you look like a tasty piece of male flesh."

"And thank you Jacqueline Suzanne. It's a part of your charm, Xander, that you combine two such diverse influences in the same reference. But I wonder if your teachers would admire it as much as I do. I'm sure they'd be thrilled that you take your Eliot lessons to heart—"

Xander interrupted, "My Eliot lessons! I'm in sixth grade. We're reading *Swiss Family Robinson*. Those who can read."

"Surely it's not that bad."

"Surely it is." Xander lowered his voice as if imparting a secret. "I'm reading Eliot in study hall."

Jeff took this in while slyly looking out the window. Not a single soul peeped at him with binoculars from behind curtains. No sign of discontented housewives. Where did Xander get these ideas? The boy was going to reach puberty in another year. How was he going to guide this precocious young man through such a traumatic awakening? Especially since he, Jeff, felt barely awake himself.

"My DNA stretched end to end would reach the sun and back ten times," Jeff announced. "I deserve to be considered as more than a tasty piece of male flesh, as you put it."

"Tom Beineke's DNA stretches just as far as yours," Xander replied. "He's still a dullard. And his wife looks at you through her windows with binoculars."

Jeff raised his index finger. Before he could make a clever retort, Ellen Coffey came on the line.

"I spoke with Dr. Amarato, the resident who performed the autopsy on Greta Fields," Ellen started. "He's one of the better ones in terms of conscientiousness and efficiency. Turns out Dr. Amarato checked for a number of poisons, including potassium chloride, curare, and the usual household poisons."

"Curare?" Jeff asked, surprised.

"Yes, I know. But he checked for it. This is not standard procedure. Fields' ex-husband, a Frank Fields, called from Michigan when he heard about the death. He claimed that Greta had taken up with a suspicious person, possibly a grifter. He wanted her body checked for poisons. Apparently Greta Fields left a considerable fortune to this woman. Do you know anything about this?"

"I spent an hour or so with the beneficiary of that will." Jeff thought it best not to mention the hot tub. "She had been a prostitute at one time. In and out of Western Psych. I wouldn't describe her as a hardened criminal."

"Do you have any idea how much money she inherited?"

"It wasn't a DuPont fortune," Jeff replied. "But it was a substantial amount of money. Mostly income-producing real estate."

"Well, this Frank Fields was convinced his ex-wife had been poisoned for her money. All the tests came back negative."

Jeff pondered this.

"So it was just a routine heart attack that just happened to result in a death that was convenient and desired by a lot of people."

"Looks that way."

A skeptical note in Ellen's voice betrayed her suspicions. She had spent a considerable time the previous evening pouring through old research documents and issues of the *New England Journal of Medicine*. Her readings cast a dim but perceptible light on Greta's convenient demise. Her regard for Jeff's safety, however, gave her pause.

Jeff, impatient with the whole Greta Fields thing, blurted out his true thoughts.

"That woman was murdered," he said. "I know it like I know this is December—whatever the date is today."

Mrs. Coffey edged in, "There is a possibility."

"I knew it!" Jeff was elated. "I knew you had a theory."

"It's not a theory," Mrs. Coffey cautioned. "It's more of a possibility. Not a very likely one. I don't know how we'd test it."

"But."

"But. Over the course of the last twenty years or so many food companies and some research firms have, as you know, been working on a variety of low fat substitutes. Olestra is one. There have been others. Something with the mouth feel of fat that passes through the body. The ideal is to replace the fat in cheese or ice cream or chocolate."

"These haven't taken off yet," Jeff noted.

"The primary compounds are known as hydrosilicates. They tend to become unstable when exposed to heat. That's why you find them primarily in frozen dessert products. Silicone is indigestible and passes through the body like roughage. Are you with me so far?"

Jeff put on the speakerphone so that Xander could hear.

"I'm with you so far. Xander is here, by the way."

"Hello Xander!" called Mrs. Coffey. "Jeff, I hope you didn't take Xander with you to meet this grifter person."

"I don't think she's a grifter," answered Jeff. "But no, of course not. He was safely tucked away in bed when I met Jane Lund. That's her name. But go on. You were saying about hydro something or other."

"Hydrosilicates. Here's the interesting part. Some forms pass from the small intestine into the bloodstream like simple fat particles called chylomicrons."

"Chylomicrons," Jeff repeated. Xander shrugged. Not part of his biology studies in school.

"Yes. Under normal circumstances these chylomicron-type hydrosilicates run their course through the body and are processed by the liver as waste. They are microscopic, of course. They would have to be."

"Of course," said Jeff, although he had no idea.

A note of warning came in Mrs. Coffey's voice.

"Here's the problem. When heated, hydrosilicates expand. If there is water nearby, they take on water. Marketed versions break down in the baking process. That's why they can't, so far, be used in cakes or pastries or cheesecake, for instance." Mrs. Coffey paused for effect. "Some unmarketed versions do not break down."

She let it sink in.

Jeff was unsure of the point. "So you can bake with those."

"No, no, no," said Mrs. Coffey. "When they heat up they take on water. They swell, then clump together until they take on a form that is no longer microscopic. Do you see?"

Jeff was still not getting it. Xander was beginning to get an idea.

"Imagine this product," Mrs. Coffey continued, "in the bloodstream. As it heats to body temperature it takes on water, it swells, it clumps together."

Xander jumped in, "The arteries leading to the heart would clog."

"Worse than that. By the time the molecules assume enough heat to take on water they have dispersed throughout the blood supply. It happens all at once. They reach 87.6 degrees, then boom, all at once, they swell, they clump, they clog. It's instantaneous. One minute you're smiling, the next minute every blood passage in your body clogs shut. Even a team of cardiac specialists right there on the spot at that Fourth of July party couldn't have helped her. Blood flow would only ease as her body dropped in temperature."

"Amazing," said Jeff, a devious smile crossing his lips. "If this version of hydrosilicate remains stable at high temperatures it could be baked into cheesecake."

"Or cookies or pie crust. Here's the insidious part. Within ten or so minutes body temperature drops. The hydrosilicate molecules give up their water and break down into their microscopic form. Massive heart tissue damage leads to a diagnosis of heart failure. If the victim had been raised on the Pritikin Diet such a death might look suspicious. Someone with a history of clogged arteries and heart disease, like your Greta Fields, and the conclusion is inevitable."

Jeff remembered his simple omelet prepared by Penny English that morning.

"It must be pretty difficult to get this stuff," Jeff suggested. "If I understand you correctly, the substance you're talking about is a failed formula."

"Yes, exactly. But here's the thing, Jeff. It has, in fact, been used. Let me look at my notes here—yes, a Michael Tompkins of Akron, Ohio. Died from a massive heart attack at the age of twenty-six. It turned out his best friend happened to be a medical student. He claimed Tompkins was a strict vegetarian with a cholesterol level in the low seventies. He swam every day, had the heart of a lion. Sure enough his autopsy revealed his arteries to be completely free of plaque. The coroner, baffled of course, checked the heart and the blood for whatever he might find. He found something called Formula 417, a hydrosilicate developed by Cleveland Pharmaceuticals of Cleveland, Ohio."

"Cleveland," Jeff whispered.

"Does someone from Cleveland figure into this, Jeff?"

"I'm afraid so. I don't have an identification. I don't have an address or anything."

"Do you have enough evidence to go to the police?" asked Mrs. Coffey in a stern voice.

"No concrete evidence," Jeff replied. "Just things I've learned panning for gold in sedimentary conversation. I've come by a few things with the aid of a hacker friend. Can't reveal his name or his information."

Mrs. Coffey audibly sighed.

"The police," said Jeff, "say they appreciate cooperation from the public but it has been my personal experience that they resent it. Xander and I, we work on the puzzle behind the scenes, put the pieces together. If we actually solve the puzzle we submit what we know anonymously. That's presuming we solve the puzzle, excuse me, murder, before the police."

"You probably will," said Mrs. Coffey. A sadness crept into her voice, a sadness born of her long relationship with the detective branch of the police department. "I suppose you know they let Franklin Baum go. It took the police two days to figure out he was a madman who knew nothing."

"Ah, but they're wrong about that. He knows plenty. Franklin Baum knew Vernon Roman personally. His name and phone number are in Roman's address book. They might all be mob related. I don't know yet."

"Do you think Franklin Baum committed the murders after all?"

"I don't think he killed Chester and Roman, but I think he knows who did. This charade with the press conference, the sword in the river, pretending religious lunacy, it's all meant to distract the police while the real culprits erase their tracks. All this ties up to a person or an organization in Cleveland. St. Patrick or the St. Patricks. Might be a secret society. Might be a family name or a code."

"I'm worried about you, Jeff," said Mrs. Coffey. "I know you have enough sense to keep Xander out of danger, but do you have enough sense to keep yourself out of it?"

"Not to worry. It's all computer research. Isn't it Xander?"

"Yes. All behind the scenes research," Xander answered. It was the truth, after all.

"I went to the Chester funeral. That's all I did," said Jeff.

"Just so you remember," said Mrs. Coffey, "that these people aren't as easily fooled as you think. And though I hate to say it, you might not be as clever as you think. My advice to you is to turn over what you know to the police. Anonymity is fine. Just push it their way and let them deal with the secret societies and the mob. Put as much distance between yourselves and these events as possible."

'But what fun would that be?' wondered Jeff. 'We'd have abandoned the puzzle just as the pieces were coming together.'

32.

Jeff shouted above the coral reef shower curtain, "The world opened up since I left you last night. First there was a message on my machine from Dottie Hatfield and Rose Roman. I actually went over there for drinks."

The water sput-sputtered, then thundered into "Power Shower." Jeff let out a cry of delight. Once thoroughly drenched, a happy face peeped over the edge of the curtain.

"Hand me the oatmeal soap," he said. "I'm so dirty I'm going to have to scrape off my whole epidermis to get clean."

"Wasn't it a little dangerous going over there?" Xander objected. He instinctively feared Dottie Hatfield above the others. "You could have been walking into a trap."

"She has amazing connections," Jeff said, spitting out water. "She knew everything about me. And I mean everything. No point in pretending with her. Although she hasn't pieced it all together. She knows that I work for important government agencies. She knows enough people, or at least one important person."

"Who do you think she knows?"

"Hard to say. She's a call girl or something like that. Probably knows someone in the government. These days all she needs is someone with access to computer codes. Maybe she knows an Eggman who works at the Federal Building. Someone she keeps happy."

"Or blackmails," said Xander.

"She tried to get me riled about it. Pressed me over and over about the invasion of my privacy."

Soap flew in sheets against the coral reef shower curtain.

Xander asked, "What does she want with you? If she knows all about you, she knows you're a systems analyst software trouble shooter."

"Ah, but see, my association with clandestine government agencies suggests I myself might be a clandestine operator. After all, I appear to be investigating the death of her husband. These murders worry her beyond, say, the level of justice or revenge."

"Why is she worried?"

"I'm not sure. She made the expected fuss about putting her husband's killer behind bars. I'm sure that's one motive. She seems to have loved him very much. But here's a lesson for your eleven-year-old brain." Jeff pulled the curtain aside and stared at Xander with a soap-streaked face. "Human beings are not noble creatures. They are at the spiritual level, of course. But we don't live at the spiritual level. We live at the day-to-day level. Day to day, human beings are about survival. Survival from the first breath to the last. Whenever someone spouts off about justice and virtue and the rest of it, listen for the truth lurking behind the altruism and the high ideals. The truth will be very personal and tied directly to survival."

With a flourish the curtain slid back into place.

"She probably thinks she's very clever," Xander asserted, "catching you at your lies."

"She is clever," Jeff said. "But I'll tell you this. She's also scared. She's worried that whoever killed her husband will be coming after her next. I think she knows who killed her husband. She's knows the samurai. She implied the existence of a network of people involved with this crime and presumably many others. She gave me Roman's address book. She hinted it contains all the answers to the puzzle."

"So she's decided to trust you," Xander said.

"That's how it looks. She can't trust the police because they have always been her natural enemy. I also suspect she is involved in whatever got Roman murdered. She can't risk exposing herself as a member of this network. She can't trust Roman's former business associates because she suspects they are responsible for Roman's murder."

"So you're at least a fed."

"Right. Maybe just a notch above the local circle of corruption."

"She's wagering you'll ferret out her enemies and put them behind bars."

"Reward her," Jeff finished, "by keeping her pretty neck out of prison."

"Do you think she's pretty?" Xander asked.

"I suppose so. She has a certain pizzazz . By the looks of her apartment she's been fetching a good price out on the streets. What do I know about womanly beauty?"

"You're gay, not blind. Where is this address book? Can I see it?"

Jeff directed Xander to the computer room and the address book. Xander returned, leafing through its tattered pages. His mind worked quickly. Greta Fields, Penny English, Larry Cone.

"Franklin Baum," he said incredulously.

"That's right," said Jeff. "We thought he was a nut case. It turns out he is a clever manipulator. He handed the police, on camera, a samurai costume with no blood on it. A copy. Not the one used in the murders. He directs them to some phony sword, which I'm sure by now they've dug up from the river. Not the murder weapon. They'll conclude he's a nut case and won't look in his direction again. Meanwhile, he's guilty. He's at least guilty of something. Even if he didn't commit the murders, he is in on it. He knows who did. He knows why they did it."

Xander asked, "Is this why Dottie Hatfield gave you this address book? So you could see Franklin Baum's name in it?"

"Possibly. There's more though. She suggested that Roman's book would lead to a trail of what she called little murders."

"Little murders?" asked Xander.

"Murders of the heart. Murders of the psyche." Jeff stuck a hand outside the curtain. "Hand me the scrubber, would you?"

Xander retrieved the loofa scrubber from its wall hook and handed it to Jeff. The hand disappeared once more behind the steamy waterfall.

"An address book is like a diary in code," Xander surmised.

"That," said Jeff, "is almost wise. I had a similar thought last night." Xander made a face which Jeff, fortunately, could not see. "At Chester's burial service this morning I ran into Penny English. She had a lot on her mind. She invited me back to her place for breakfast."

"Boy. You have been hob knobbing with the criminal types."

"Lots of money, Xander. Cute little cottage overlooking the river valley. Some Mission antiques. Nice ones, too. Investment quality art. Too much money for a teacher. The Roman address book gave me an idea. As I was leaving I noticed Penny's address book and admired it. It's one of those artsy things from a museum—the Met, I think. Each tab featured a different work of art related to the subject of writing. This gave me an excuse to leaf through her tabs. I discovered something important."

"What was that?"

"I discovered a listing for Roman's Polish Hill apartment."

"But he didn't have a phone," Xander noted.

"Must have. But we didn't see one and the police hadn't removed anything."

Xander turned down the lid on the commode and sat. Someone had obviously stolen Roman's phone. But then—

"What if it was a cell phone?" Xander asked.

"Wasn't. I scanned her phone listings. She put a "c" before her cell phone listings. It was a land line and she didn't have a cell for Roman."

"Then someone stole it."

"A good guess," said Jeff. "Someone stole it immediately after the murders or immediately before the murders."

"It was a business phone," Xander deduced.

"Yes. We thought Roman used the apartment as a ruse to collect a government check. But let's face it, the government doesn't give out very big checks these days. Not to poor people. He'd have to subtract the rent from the check. Not worth it really."

"He used the apartment for business," Xander said.

"I think so. The landline was for business. You know, it's easier to tap a cell phone. You can intercept a broadcast from a satellite. Lots of hacker types can do that without a court order. A landline has to be mechanically tapped, most efficiently at the source. Requires a court order or requires breaking and entering."

"It was a digital answering machine," Xander guessed. "That's why it had to be stolen."

"God, you're good," said Jeff. "He used that Polish Hill apartment as his office. He received messages there. Messages from Larry Cone, Penny English, Franklin Baum. Maybe this St. Patrick guy. Those costumes were props of some kind. Look at the facts. Roman and Chester were murdered by a man wearing a samurai costume. What do you think those costumes were used for?"

"Whoa," said Xander.

"Exactly. There's a trail. I've been tracking it all day. From Pittsburgh to Cleveland to Detroit to Washington D.C. to as far away as Kitty Hawk, North Carolina. The trail may be more extensive than that. But it's not a trail of little murders, as Hatfield suggests. It's a trail of full out, cold-blooded murders. Most of the victims are business people, corporate executives. This whole thing is a lot bigger than two murders in a Wendy's parking lot. Everything comes down to Cone. I'd like to get my hands on his little address book. He is the hub that leads to Roman and English and Baum and, I'm sure, St. Patrick. It's St. Patrick's address that I need."

Jeff turned off the water and let out a great sigh.

"So nice to be clean again," he said. "I was beginning to look like Pigpen. Not the *Peanuts* character with whom I most identify."

Jeff toweled off his face. Through the thick steam in the room he caught Xander's expression. Xander was looking down at the address book in his hands as if it symbolized all of the loss he had experienced thus far in his young life. Jeff thought, I know why. I've been doing all the neat things without him.

"I bet you identify with Lucy," Xander quipped in a tone of voice more bitter than he intended.

"How could you say that?" Jeff smiled broadly. "Lucy's a terrorist. I identify with Snoopy, of course. Snoopy is cunning, Snoopy is wise. Just like me. Don't you think?"

"I don't know," Xander countered. "It's not my generation."

"Ouch. He's getting nasty now," teased Jeff. "I hope you intend to lighten up by this evening because I have something planned, Sherlock, and I need your help."

Xander lightened up immediately. "Oh yeah?"

"Be here at 6:30 tonight. Wear grungy clothes. We're getting dirty."

"Cool. What are we going to do?"

"Can't tell you. Got to keep it a secret until tonight," Jeff whispered clandestinely for effect. "I'll tell you this much. We're going on an adventure."

33.

As arranged, Xander appeared just after twilight at Jeff's door. He brought with him a pair of threadbare corduroys —throwaways that had just barely survived one too many bike skids.

Jeff described their mission in a conspiratorial whisper.

"Change quickly into your grungy clothes," Jeff urged. "We have much to do."

Jeff packed a picnic sized Igloo thermal chest with dry ice, then carefully locked the lid in place. Next he opened an old wooden box that at one time contained three bottles of Italian wine (yes, he had saved this box for many, many years knowing that one day it would come in handy). He lined it with red checked Williams Sonoma dishtowels; on top of the towels he laid a series of tools, each neatly wrapped in similar towels of a green checked design. Very Christmassy. If Williams Sonoma only knew where their cute Christmas tea towels were going tonight.

Among the tools Jeff counted a scalpel (a matte knife, really), a pair of clamps (pliers), and a suction tube (turkey baster), in addition to such pedestrian items as scissors, a large sewing needle, a reel of fishing line, and twenty Ziploc Baggies in a range of sizes (one never knew). Lastly he included a package of cotton balls and four latex surgical-quality gloves. Once fitted snugly for travel, Jeff closed and clasped the box.

Xander returned suitably dressed for a hoedown.

"Load this in the back of the Subaru," Jeff instructed, handing the box to Xander. "The garage door is closed, so load from inside the house. I don't want Mrs. Wightman to spy us while out walking her kitty."

Xander nodded vigorously. He could be trusted to carry out his all-important mission.

Jeff paused to consider. What else would he need? He had his watch, his flashlight, an extra bulb for the flashlight. There was a blanket in the car he wouldn't mind burning later. Paper towels, steel wool, degreasing solution, Goo Be Gone, Lysol, hydrogen peroxide. What else? Think, think. A crow bar. There should be a crow bar under the floor of the wagon with the car's emergency tools. Make sure to check, though!

Xander reappeared.

"What next?" he asked.

Jeff handed over the ice chest. Before proceeding downstairs, Xander rummaged through the other supplies.

"Where's the book on human anatomy?"

"Oh, shit," said Jeff. "I don't have one. How could I be so stupid? What did I think I was going to do out there?"

"Don't panic," said Xander. "You have the interactive Columbia University Medical Library on CD-ROM."

"That will take too long. I should have thought of that earlier."

"It won't take too long," Xander asserted. No way was he giving up this evening's adventure. "Cut to internal organs and print out a couple of screens. Go do that. Hurry! I'll load the rest of the stuff."

Jeff ran two steps at a time up to the Cloisters, cursing himself as he went. Excuse me, doctor, but where did you go to medical school? Oh, medical school. I forgot.

He fumbled around frantically through his CD-ROM collection. Where could it be? His clothes are so well organized, Dear Reader, and yet his CD-ROMs —such a mess!

"Here it is."

He loaded the first disc. The table of contents directed him to the second disc. Internal Organs. He pulled down the file, clicked on Illustrations. So many illustrations. Click, click, click. Next. Click, click. So many fibula, so little time. Cross-sections and muscle tissues and tubes by the zillions. Tubes going everywhere doing God knows what. Each of these tubes had a long, complicated name. What made him think he could do this?

Wait. There's a nice cross section of the chest cavity. Let's print that. Click. Here's a nice big illustration of the heart nestled among its neighbor organs. Click. I wonder, he thought, if men and women have everything in the same place. Click, click.

It didn't take Xander long to load the rest of the supplies in the back of Jeff's wagon. He pulled the flap across to hide it all.

Outside the first snowflakes of winter fell. It occurred to Xander that things would move along faster if he warmed up the car. Retrieving Jeff's keys from a hook on the kitchen wall, Xander turned over the ignition. Piece of cake, really. He often warmed up his mother's car in the winter months. There wasn't much to this driving business anyway. Adults made such a fuss. He had logged as many as forty hours in the Race Car Motion Simulator at the mall and hardly ever crashed, even at speeds of 160 miles per hour. Xander believed in his heart and soul he could drive a car in a pinch. Two tiny problems: his feet didn't reach the pedals and he couldn't see over the dashboard. But hey, these were solvable problems.

Jeff appeared breathless, color illustrations in hand.

"Do you want me to drive?" Xander asked optimistically.

"I don't think so." Wry, nasty grin. His mother's customary response. Oh, well. One day they would learn.

———

Within a remarkably short space of time, the temperature dropped from chilly to frigid. Giant flakes of snow wafted down on the evening drivers. These flakes turned to brisk, whirling eddies. Jeff kicked in the four-wheel drive.

"So," Jeff started. "With which cartoon character do you identify?"

"What?"

"Earlier at the house. We were talking about cartoon characters. I said I identify with Snoopy. You rudely pointed out that *Peanuts* is the domain of an earlier generation. So I want to know with which cartoon character you identify."

"I'm not big on cartoons," Xander said, hoping to snuff the issue.

"Such a snob," Jeff teased. "C'mon, you live in this culture, too."

"I don't live in this culture of my own free will. I am a prisoner here."

"Oh, please. Spare me."

"Let's examine the options," said Xander. "*South Park* is mean spirited, features a talking turd as a character, and espouses a dumbed-down right wing political philosophy. *Manga* and its offshoots are about girls in mini skirts who brutally kick people while fulfilling some implausible destiny. The animation consists of drawings that don't move. *The Simpsons* is for fat older men who belong to bowling leagues."

"Ouch. I happen to like *The Simpsons*. Marge alone is one of the great cartoon characters of all time. I agree with you about *South Park*. The first year was inspired. The whole Kenny's dead thing. Somewhere along the line it turned into right wing propaganda for kids. What about *Beavis and Butthead?*"

Xander sighed but did not reply.

"It's a conversation here," said Jeff. "Talk to me. Say it in words."

"The heroes are shiftless, brain dead, do nothings. I'm supposed to find this amusing? I hate the kids in school who act like that. Why would I like a cartoon about them? Besides. Domain of an earlier generation."

"Oh, man. Knife through the heart." Jeff pretended to be wounded. "Your opinions are just a little severe, kid. We're talking about cartoons here. Do you know how many people like *Manga*? A lot. One day you are going to want to date and you'll be very lonely because none of the other people in the world live up to your standards."

"I'll take pointers from you about dating," said Xander, "when I see you actually date someone."

"Oh. Such a smart ass. I told you, I dated people before I met you. I have been to the woodshed. I am on a sabbatical, that's all."

"An enforced sabbatical. Because the other people in the world don't meet your standards."

"Well," said Jeff, "you got me there."

They drove in quiet for a short while.

Jeff remembered two men from his dorm who reminded him of Beavis and Butthead. Neither of them wanted to be in school or were even qualified to be there. They had rich daddies with influence who paid full tuition and made a substantial alumnae contribution. The school admitted them and looked the other way. These guys played pinball all day. They took their meals (with beer) at The Original Hotdog in Oakland.

Thoughts of Carnegie Mellon and its sometimes odd admissions policies reminded him of Elenora Chester. At one time CMU had the number one rated drama school in the country. It was tough to get into. The discipline was rigorous. So much pressure. He planned to talk with her about it tomorrow.

"Xander, would you get a pencil and a scrap of paper out of the glove compartment? Scratch paper, not a piece of one of my manuals."

"Give me a break."

"Write this down. CMU drama department number one. Elenora Chester."

"That's it?"

"That's it."

"You got it."

Jeff put the note in his shirt pocket.

"Hit the breaks!" Xander screamed.

Jeff hit the breaks just in time to avoid being the fourth car in a pile up accident. Near the entrance to the Fort Pitt Tunnels one of those old American cars from the seventies, the size of a boat, stalled. Drivers attempting to avoid the stalled vehicle managed instead to ram into each other.

"We won't get through the tunnels anytime today," Jeff said, annoyed. "Click on the GPS. Let's use the Land Track feature."

Jeff's GPS system tied in with Google to show satellite pictures of discreet locations. Xander played with the Land Track whenever he was in the car. He especially enjoyed zooming in on streets in England. This particular evening he focused on the South Hills of Pittsburgh. Of course, the blizzard blocked the clear view they really needed.

"I think," said Xander, "we could head over to the West End Bridge and reach South Hills from there. Traffic is slow but not stopped."

Jeff knew the way from the West End Bridge but used the Trip-Tic feature to map a route to Dutch Elm Cemetery. Many of the roads wound up and around through residential portions of the county where the increasingly severe snow storm kept most people off of the streets. Jeff's four-wheel drive maneuvered admirably as long as they drove slowly. Driving slowly set Jeff on edge. His mind raced at a heady pace and he liked to drive at a comparable speed. To distract himself, he explored his "Leakey Link" theory with Xander.

"We have two distinct groups of people involved in these murders," Jeff started.

"The first group is honest, hard working and responsible. This group includes Marshall and Elenora Chester, Elenora's brother Jeremy, Penny English and maybe, if we stretch our definition of honest and hard working, Greta Fields.

"The second group features criminally inclined, opportunistic, irresponsible outcasts. Vernon Roman, Dottie Hatfield, Franklin Baum, Larry Cone and, if we stretch our definition of opportunistic, Jane Lund.'

"Now. You remember from school the story of Dr. Richard Leakey."

"From the Science Channel," Xander interrupted, "not from school. You way overestimate what they teach us in school."

"In any case. He's the anthropologist who searched in Africa for the connecting link between man and ape. If we view this case in an evolutionary context, what do we have? We have two diverse groups of people living alongside each other."

"Like the Cro-Magnons and the Neanderthals," Xander exclaimed.

"Let's not mix up our analogies. That happened in Europe, not in Africa. But the point is well taken. Two diverse groups of people living side by side. One is civilized and progressive; one is uneducated and destructive. Imagine you and I are Dr. Leakey. Where do we find the link between these two groups?"

Xander considered the question. "Roman and Chester, obviously. They were buddies in high school. They're the link."

"Possible. But they hadn't seen each other in many years. Someone brought them together. See, I think the link that binds these two groups together consists of Penny English and Larry Cone. Penny English is a civilized woman with an interest in the rough element. Larry Cone is uncivilized with aspirations. Penny is looking for someone a little rough, a little criminal, to fulfill her kinky needs. Cone is looking for someone above his station to elevate his status—if only in his own mind.'

"I saw it at the Chester viewing. Cone wanted to be part of her world, wanted her to show him off. But he looked out of place. He embarrassed her. At one point he realized it and he left angry.

"All along," continued Jeff, "the odd thing about this case is the coexistence of incompatible worlds. These people have connections to each other, connections across class lines. It's odd. I think it's tellingly odd."

Xander considered the Leakey Link theory. It didn't make as much sense to him as it did to Jeff. To Xander, class distinctions amounted to a big so what. But he knew this was the way Jeff examined problems. He laid out his facts and viewed them through a variety of prisms to see how the light shined. The Leakey Link theory would yield results or not. It might just yield an interesting detail.

Playing devil's advocate, Xander asked, "What if it doesn't have anything to do with class lines? If your suspicions are correct, we have a crime syndicate killing off corporate executives. If we find this hydroprotosilicate stuff in Greta Fields' heart tissue, we will know she was murdered."

"That's right," said Jeff enthusiastically. "Then we know Chester hired someone to kill Greta Fields. This St. Patrick character or Cone or maybe Roman. Maybe Cone and Roman as a team. Maybe Franklin Baum. Maybe Franklin Baum is St. Patrick."

"Maybe they're all St. Patrick," said Xander. "But why do we know Chester did the hiring?"

"Because we know Fields was after his job."

"In that case, it could also have been Penny English. From your description she sounds more cold-blooded than Chester. And why not Jane Lund? She was heir to millions of dollars. Could be one of the gay teachers Fields fired. Or an overlooked gay teacher."

"There has to be a reason why Chester and Roman were murdered," said Jeff. "The gay teachers have no motivation to kill Chester. They don't know Roman. Jane Lund doesn't connect with Roman and just barely connects with Chester. You haven't seen her yet, but it's ludicrous to think of poor frail anorexic Jane Lund dressing in a samurai outfit and yielding a heavy metal sword. Besides, I think she genuinely loved Greta."

"You're no expert on love." A little dig.

"I know it when I see it, Mr. Lawyer." Jeff stuck out his tongue.

"So adult."

They approached the entrance to Dutch Elm Cemetery. Rolling hills of serenely virginal snow, accented by neat rows of granite markers, crosses and statues of Mary. It heightened Xander's expectations of the macabre. Restless ghosts and tortured spirits. Never mind that these particular dead, in their time, lived in an uppity suburb with nothing to be restless or tortured about.

Off in the distance Xander spotted a stone replica of the Parthenon, scaled to the size of a single car garage, a dusting of snow gracing its triangular cap. Was this the resting place of Greta Fields? He could hardly wait to get his hands on her cold cadaver. Would she be rotted and filled with bugs? Would she stink?

"I think Gregory's shed is up this way," Jeff said, driving along the same serpentine drive he had traversed that morning.

"I see smoke up there."

Jeff steered in the direction of the smoke. Sure enough, they came upon Gregory's tool shed. With snow on the roof and smoke trailing out from a crooked chimney it looked picturesque and cozy.

"Penny English thought maybe he lived here," Jeff said. "I think maybe she's right."

"Can you live in a tool shed?"

"Many people live in cardboard boxes along the rivers. Remember the colonies of homeless people we saw from our excursion on the Gateway Clipper? That poor woman we saw in Ellen Coffey's lab lived in caves. I think our Gregory here doesn't make enough money digging graves to afford an apartment or transportation to work. I imagine the cemetery owners let him live here for free."

"Are you telling me that people own this cemetery?" Xander asked, perplexed. "Like a business?"

"Certainly. What did you think?"

"I thought the government owned all the cemeteries."

Jeff laughed. "The government doesn't even own the gas company. Everything is private enterprise in America."

"That means that even when you're dead you have a landlord."

"That's right. And if you don't pay up, out you go."

Jeff knocked on Gregory's door.

"Gregory? Are you in there? This is Jeff Redwing. We met this morning."

The door opened. Gregory appeared shirtless and without shoes or socks. Jeff noticed a hairless torso, six pack abs, brilliant white teeth, silken smooth skin glistening from the light of the fire in his fireplace. He might have been a cliff diver. In the midst of all this snow, there was sweat on his brow.

Gregory was excited to see Jeff.

"The Chester funeral!" he exclaimed. "I always remember. Always."

Gregory vigorously shook Jeff's hand.

"Welcome to my home." He shook Xander's hand just as vigorously. "And you, too. Welcome to my home. Come in. It's very cold outside."

Jeff introduced Xander as his "sort of" son.

"No need to explain," Gregory said, smiling. "I know all about that 'sort of' stuff."

Gregory walked his guests past the foyer, which also functioned as the tool repository, into the back room, which functioned as the living room. The fireplace took up most of the north wall. Its fire filled the room with a toasty warmth. Not a bad little place, thought Jeff. A small sofa, a stuffed chair, a coffee table, a mattress off to one side, a hotplate in the corner. Bookshelves covered every inch of wall space. Scanning the titles, Xander found mostly paperback fiction titles by authors such as Leon Uris, Alex Hailey, Harold Robbins, Ian Fleming, James Patterson.

"You must work out every day," Xander said, admiring Gregory's physique.

"I do!" replied Gregory. "Mr. Wolitzer—he owns the cemetery—has a universal gym in his basement. I do a full routine, then I shower and come upstairs. Mrs. Wolitzer makes dinner for me. I just came back from dinner a little while ago."

"Ah," said Jeff, peering around restlessly, taking in random book titles. He decided it might work best to engage in a little casual conversation before launching into the subject of disturbing quiet graves. "I see you have a lot of books. Do you like to read?"

"Um. Well. I read a little, but mostly Mrs. Wolitzer reads to me. She brings me these books. They make great insulation. And then afterward, you know—she reads to me."

"Afterward?" Jeff asked.

"Mrs. Wolitzer is one of my babes," Gregory announced without the slightest hesitation. Then he remembered, "That's my secret, though. Mr. Wolitzer isn't supposed to know."

In an unconscious gesture, Gregory ran his hand over his chest, then down over his rippled stomach.

"You have babes?" Xander asked.

"Sure. The babes love me."

"How many do you have?" Jeff asked.

"Hundreds."

"Hundreds?"

"Oh, yeah. All kinds, all ages. Old babes, fat babes, ugly babes, horny babes. Married babes—lots of married babes. You know, their husbands don't like to tumble anymore. Mr. Wolitzer doesn't like to tumble anymore. That's why Mrs. Wolitzer is one of my babes. Women must tumble. They like it."

"I see," said Jeff, astonished. He wondered for a moment if this was really the truth. But then, it didn't seem to him that Gregory was the kind of person who would need to invent such a story. Surely it wasn't hundreds.

"High school babes are my favorites," Gregory continued. "They're insatiable. They want it a couple of times a night, then they want it the next night and the next night. I've had babes from all the schools around here. I've had some from schools I've never heard of. I've had lots of babes from your friend Chester's school."

"You have?"

"Oh, yeah. They told me all about him. And they told me about that Greta Fields woman you was talking about this morning. I don't forget. I remember."

"How do you get girls here?" Xander asked with a note of incredulity. "I mean, do you hit on them when they're here burying relatives?"

Gregory laughed. "No, no. My friend Paul brings them."

"The guy you mentioned this morning," suggested Jeff.

"Yeah. Paul. First he brings them. Then they come on their own. Then they bring friends. See, it's a game. After the first time, I tell them it's my birthday. The next time they bring me a present. That's how I get all my stuff. Babes bring me clothes, bottles of wine, watches. I got a lot of watches."

"How long have the babes been coming here?" Xander asked.

"Nine years," he said proudly. "Yeah. Ever since I came here and that was when I was fourteen. I'm twenty-three now."

Part of Jeff wanted to chastise Gregory or at least warn him of the dangers of sleeping with hundreds of babes: STDs, paternity suits, murderous husbands, statutory rape. Another part of him thought he should play the role of Margaret Mead in the bush—strictly hands off observation of an alien culture. He decided to venture a tiny comment. He broached the topic delicately, not wishing to antagonize someone whose cooperation he required.

"Has your friend talked with you about the law at all?"

"You mean statutory rape? I know all about that. The law doesn't apply to me, Paul says. I'm mentally incompetent." Gregory beamed a great, wide smile full of gleaming teeth. "So. Tell me why you're here."

———

Gregory of Babeland, Special Agent Redwing and his "almost son" Xander Pooka trekked across the cemetery grounds through ever deepening snow.

Xander carried the Igloo chest of dry ice, Jeff the wooden wine box of surgical instruments.

A silvery luminescence infiltrated their coats and seeped into their skin. They were walking on graves. 'Hundreds of dead people lie under my feet,' thought Jeff. And I'm about to commit the ultimate invasion of privacy. I'm about to open her coffin and cut into her rotting guts to prove or disprove a theory that even Mrs. Coffey thinks is farfetched. And I have chosen very cold weather in which to do this.

It actually dawned on our friend Jeff that he was perhaps going too far. This is not library research, he reasoned. And this going too far business is exactly what happened last year. He couldn't resist the temptation of taking one step too many. And just like last year he was dragging Xander into trouble with him.

'I'm probably guilty of child abuse,' Jeff thought. 'I have no moral standards, none. Of course, Michelangelo did it. That's right. Drag Michelangelo into it. I'm probably a certifiable sociopath. Who am I to admonish Gregory here on the fine points of the law? Look at him. He's having a wonderful time. I'm filled with dread.'

"There it is!" Gregory cried, pointing in the direction of a free standing Doric structure.

"Why do all these things look Greek?" Xander asked.

Gregory took a set of keys from his coat pocket. He knew exactly which one opened the heavy metal door to Greta Fields' final resting place. The door croaked open, aided by a brisk wind that snuck in from behind and pushed.

Looking into the dark chamber, Jeff asked, "Is there a light?"

"She doesn't do much reading," answered Gregory. "Give me your flashlight."

Gregory installed Jeff's flashlight on a high ledge just inside the mausoleum door. It cast a dim pall over the bare, stone room.

"I thought it was going to be like the inside of a pyramid," Xander remarked.

Jeff laughed uneasily. "You were expecting hieroglyphics?"

"I was expecting something. Wall paintings, artificial flowers."

Gregory laughed comfortably and easily. "You guys are too much. This place is for dead people. She can't look at paintings. She can't even see the lid of her casket." As if they needed final convincing, he added, "Her eyes are glued shut, you know."

On the west side of the mausoleum, on a stone shelf, rested a bronze coffin with silver handles. Jeff noted an identical stone shelf on the other side, probably the future resting place of Jane Lund. A stone bench positioned between the two shelves invited the visitor to sit and contemplate the coffin.

Jeff and Xander cautiously entered the room, half expecting a confrontation with Greta's ghost. A sudden blast of sound shook Jeff and Xander out of their shoes. Jeff screamed, "Fuck!" They both jumped back out the door. Within seconds a familiar pattern of base notes created a fast, snappy beat. Diana Ross sang, "You know love, love, don't come easy." It was the opening to *You Can't Hurry Love.*

"I know she doesn't read," quipped Xander, "but does she do much dancing?"

"This is Jane Lund's idea," explained Gregory. "She describes it as immortal music for her eternal sweetheart. Jane believes that Greta's spirit resides at least part of the time in this temple. If I were a spirit I wouldn't spend any time here at all. I'd go someplace warm and interesting. But Jane says spirits like to be near their former bodies."

"Oh great," said Jeff, letting out the breath he'd been holding. He reentered the mausoleum.

"I see you're not used to the dead," said Gregory. "They can't harm you. They're very quiet. They appear, they stare at you. That's about it."

"You're just trying to spook me," said Jeff.

Jeff didn't believe in ghosts but was deathly afraid of them. Xander, curious if a little wary, asked, "Are you saying you've seen ghosts of people buried in this cemetery get up and walk around?"

"Never seen them walk," Gregory answered matter-of-factly. "Never seen them move at all. Never seen them outdoors, either. Usually I'm asleep in my bed. I wake up and they're there in the room watching me."

A deeper chill crept over Jeff in the already cold stone room. He told himself, 'There are no ghosts, there are no ghosts. It's all bullshit.'

"What about Greta Fields?" asked Xander. "She ever come watch you?"

"I don't know," answered Gregory, curious about the question himself. "Don't know who any of them are. I don't get to see the bodies before they are buried."

"Okay," said Jeff. "That's enough. We've got work to do. And I, for one, would like to get the hell out of here as soon as possible. Let's put our tools down. I guess we'll have to move the coffin onto the stone bench." He looked at Gregory. "How heavy is a coffin? I've never been a pallbearer."

Gregory rubbed his chin as if estimating. "Depends on how big she was and how much of her is left."

"Eeeuwww gross," said Xander.

Gregory and Jeff each took an end and eased the thing out of its shelf. An organ swell filled the room. The Supremes thrust their hands out in front of their bodies like English Bobbies and demanded, *Stop In The Name of Love!*

The casket came down rather easily, being lighter than Jeff expected.

As they set it gently onto the bench, Gregory chatted away, "You should see the routine Jane does to this song. I bring her in here, you know, so she can visit. I usually stay with her. We talk. She loves Diana Ross and the Supremes. She has Diana Ross wigs and Diana Ross gowns. One time she did a whole nightclub routine for me right here in the cement house. She said she learned it from a drag queen that used to work Liberty Avenue."

They stared at the casket for a moment, none too eager to start.

"Guess I can unlatch it for you," Gregory offered.

He did so. They stared at the casket once again. Diana launched into a refrain of *My World is Empty Without You Babe.*

"Do you want the matte knife?" Xander asked.

"Let's see what we've got first," said Jeff.

Xander focused his flashlight on the left end of the lid. He was ready for surgery.

Jeff slowly lifted the lid; Gregory helped a little. It went cleanly back. They all got a good look at the corpse.

"My God," said Gregory. "How did this woman die?"

Most of the embalming fluids must have settled in her buttocks, her calves, her shoulders. Just enough had leaked out of her neck to stain the satin pillow that once held her head.

They wouldn't be needing the matte knife, or the Ziploc bags or the dry ice. There could be no doubt now that Greta Fields had been murdered. Someone had gotten here before them, someone with an instrument much bigger than a matte knife. A cleaver, maybe. Or a very sharp sword. Someone had severed her head at the base of the neck.

Someone had taken her head away.

34.

"I CAN'T ENCOURAGE YOU TO ENGAGE IN ILLEGAL ACTIVITIES," PREFACED Mrs. Coffey, secretly thrilled, "but a tissue sample might have answered a few questions. Since you were already there, scalpel and Ziploc in hand."

"I'm not going back," Jeff flatly declared. "In the space of five days I have looked into two coffins at two headless corpses. No more headless bodies for me, thank you."

Mrs. Coffey switched ears, dangled a loosened shoe on the tip of her toes. She glanced around her workspace. Ninety percent of her work these days involved drug related crimes. How exciting it would have been to find hydroprotosilicate in that woman's heart tissue. She could have helped Jeff unravel a series of devious middle management execution style murders that have been taking place up and down the eastern seaboard. That would have perked up her holiday season. The Fat Substitute Killings. One could only dream.

"You have enough to go to the police," she reminded him. "You could make your anonymous call."

"Not without getting Gregory in trouble," Jeff quickly added. He didn't want to hand his information over to the police. He was having too much fun. He wanted to solve the puzzle himself. "I'd get myself in trouble as well. I impersonated an FBI agent."

"How did you do that?"

"I showed Gregory the special photo ID that gets me in FBI headquarters to work on the computers. He jumped to a convenient conclusion. That and I identified myself as Special Agent Redwing."

Mrs. Coffey laughed. "I hope no one is listening in on my line."

"It gets worse. I introduced Xander as my Special Assistant."

"You took Xander!"

"Just to carry the ice chest. It was all very innocent."

"Innocent! You illegally exhumed a cadaver for the purpose of cutting into the heart to collect tissue samples. To conduct private research. What part of that involves innocence?"

"The part where Xander averts his eyes," said Jeff. "Besides, Michelangelo did it. There's a precedent here."

"I want to be in the room at your trial when you cite Michelangelo as a precedent to a Pittsburgh judge."

"Well, in any case, you can see why I can't contact the police about Greta Fields' missing head. At the very least the FBI would put me through the process once again of obtaining security clearance. I might not pass this time. I've acquired a few moral blemishes with age."

"That you have." Mrs. Coffey clucked her tongue. She knew she had a moral obligation to call the police herself. If it came back later that she knew about this and did nothing, it would end her career. They'd put Jeff in jail. And what if something happened to Xander? He's just an eleven-year-old boy. He shouldn't be involved in these activities. "So what will you do?"

"Tie it all together myself. I'm pretty close already. This St. Patrick character is the key to these murders. He's in Ohio somewhere, probably Cleveland. You told me the drug company that manufactures hydroprotosilicate is in Cleveland."

"That's right."

"It all fits very nicely."

'Nice and dangerous,' thought Mrs. Coffey. 'If Xander were killed or hurt, how could she face Xander's mother?'

Jeff added, "I have a plan for acquiring his address."

"Do you?"

Mrs. Coffey's mind drifted. So much snow outside and more on the way. The mayor would no doubt close government offices sometime this afternoon. She'd have to stay, of course. Murder victims don't wait for the snow to clear. What could Jeff be planning to do in all this snow?

"Penny English," Jeff broke into her thoughts. "The Upper St. Clair teacher so closely tied to Marshall Chester. I think her boyfriend might be the Pittsburgh connection. He hired Vernon Roman or at least introduced him to St. Patrick. I'll be paying him a visit today."

"Do you know him personally?"

"I know of him. I know him to see him."

"For God's sake, Jeff, be careful. If you're right about these people they'll cut off your head next."

"They all think I'm an old college buddy of Chester's. I'm supposed to be writing a piece about him for the alumnae magazine. I don't think they've given me a second thought."

"I hope you're right about that. I can't see how all this risk is worth it to you."

"Well," said Jeff, "I guess it's the irrational enjoyment of these things. Duplicity, complicity, murder. The study of evil."

"We're both scientists, Jeff. The notion of evil belongs to the study of mysticism," argued Mrs. Coffey. "In any case, I've learned in my line of work that it's wise to give dangerous people a wide berth."

"I'll be honest with you," Jeff said quietly. "What appeals to me most about these people is their use of theatrics and slight of hand. Rich people, poor people. Straight people, gay people. Suburban people, city people. Civilians, criminals. It's not us, it's them. Look, we're in Pittsburgh. No, we're in Cleveland. Guess again, we're in Michigan, in Baltimore, in Kitty Hawk. It's a marvelous shell game. The shells have come to rest and I feel like I'm about to tap one. What do you think I'll find?"

A disembodied head, thought Mrs. Coffey.

"Jeffrey. I want you to promise me something. If you're bound and determined to do this, promise me you will leave Xander out of it. He's an eleven-year-old boy. What you're doing has gone way beyond library research. It's too dangerous for him. You know that."

"Believe me, Mrs. Coffey," Jeff said. "Xander is safely in school where he belongs."

————

Xander caught up with the Subaru just as Jeff was pulling out of the driveway.

"No school today," he shouted, rapping on the passenger window. "Too much snow. Let me in."

Well, Jeff didn't plan to do all that much on this particular expedition. And Xander could stay in the car. He flipped the door lock. Xander jumped in.

"You eat lunch yet?" Jeff asked.

"I haven't even had breakfast."

"We'll pick up lunch along the way. I'm driving to Larry Cone's place. According to Penny English's address book he lives on Kentucky Avenue in Shadyside."

"What are we going to do there?"

Jeff started carefully down the snow-laden street.

"I don't know yet. I want to see where he lives, check out his house. I think Larry Cone just might have St. Patrick's phone number in his address book. Of course, that means I'll have to get inside the house somehow. I haven't figured that out yet. After that, I can either drop you off at home or you can come with me to visit the widow Chester. I have an appointment to interview her for the article I'm supposedly writing."

"I'm going, of course."

"I thought so."

"Where's lunch?"

———

Berba's Deli in Squirrel Hill was alive with people despite the bad weather. The wait for a seat was prohibitive; they ordered take out. Jeff looked over the menu. "Hmm...Hmm..." he pondered. Xander waited. There was a final "Hmm" before Jeff launched into the story that inevitably accompanied any gastronomic adventure.

"I came here all the time in my Carnegie Mellon days," Jeff said. "Best hot pastrami in town. Of course, this place was called Iz Cohen's then. I wonder if Marshall Chester ever came here. Could be a nice detail."

"What do you mean a nice detail?" asked Xander.

"When I talk with Mrs. Chester this afternoon. I could tell her stories about her husband and I hiking here after class for pastrami and blintzes."

Xander folded his arms over his chest. First of all, the food was not sounding either healthy or tempting. Whatever pastrami turned out to be, he was quite certain he wasn't going to like it. And secondly, "Doesn't it ever bother you? All these lies you tell?"

Jeff considered for a moment There might be another pathology or two racing through his brilliant, black haired brain. "No," he said. "It's fun, really. It's acting, in a way. Acting for justice."

"Good grief."

Xander scanned the simple take out menu. He flipped the pages back and forth as if looking for a missing page. The sandwich maker, a plump butterball of a woman everyone knew as Diva, waited impatiently for Jeff's order. Well, really, to be precise, she waited sarcastically, as if knowing in advance that he couldn't possibly place an order that would please a seasoned Jewish deli sandwich maker. Diva was an institution. She had been preparing deli sandwiches to go since Iz Cohen days. She had out lived Iz Cohen. She was not an easy woman to impress.

"Diva," Jeff started, "I think my friend here will have a pastrami sandwich."

She shrugged as if to say "how original." She started loading the hot greasy slivers of meat onto thick dark bread. Xander's eyeballs widened alarmingly.

"Is that pastrami? That's gross. I'm not eating that."

Diva stopped, hand in mid-air, wriggly meat dangling through latex gloved fingers.

"It's delicious," Jeff argued. "And it's something you should try if only once."

"Spare my arteries please," Xander complained. "Food like that constitutes child abuse."

"Little boy," Diva said, leaning over the deli cooler, "you're gonna die like everybody else. So have a little fat."

Xander didn't trust food prepared by chubby chefs. He was on the verge of saying something unkind when he caught a forbidding look from Jeff.

"Diva, for the sake of keeping peace, I will take the pastrami sandwich. Make my friend here a lean Reuben."

"Gladly," she said. "But it's not as good without the fat." She cast a stern look in Xander's direction. To compensate for the dry meat she added a little extra sauce to his Reuben and grilled it in lakes of sizzling butter. She simply did not make a bad tasting sandwich—and that was that.

———

Jeff parked across the street and down about half a block from Larry Cone's Kentucky Avenue residence. It was not an apartment. It was a three-story, single family, wood frame with grey-blue clapboards and dark blue shutters. Heavy, ornate oak double doors fronted an elaborate wood and glass foyer. Large grapevine wreaths, one for each door, featured tastefully placed sprays of yellow orchids. A small railroad tie porch led to a railroad tie walkway that culminated in a Japanese garden that incorporated railroad ties as dividers and borders. The sidewalk, walkway, steps and porch had all been cleared of snow that was still falling. Most of Cone's neighbors had not even started on their sidewalks.

"What did you call this guy?" Xander asked, staring at the house through the car windshield. "A greaser?"

"That's what he looked like at the funeral," Jeff replied. "Crude. The kind of person who drops out of school. Greasers always wore leather jackets. It was their emblem."

"Nice house for a drop out."

"Maybe he doesn't actually live here. Maybe he's staying with someone. Or maybe it's part of the money trail. All of these people have more money than their station in life warrants."

"So what are we going to do now that we're here?" Xander asked.

"I don't know. Sit here, look things over, wait for inspiration. At the very least we can have lunch."

Jeff broke open the take-out bag from Berba's. They each ordered latkes (well, Jeff ordered latkes on Xander's behalf). Jeff stuffed his latkes into his face with his fingers, like sausage into a tube. Xander ate his with a plastic fork, dabbing each bite into a container of applesauce first. Guttural primate sounds resonated up out of the tiny part of Jeff's throat not occupied by latkes. Nothing like a good Jewish delicatessen. Jewish deli food, Chinese stir-fry, Lebanese and Southern Italian, these were the foods of his childhood. His mother often worked late into the evening. She brought home take-out or they went to a cheap neighborhood restaurant. Baked kibbe, pirogies, fried rice with vegetables, latkes with sour cream and applesauce, beef/chicken/shrimp/pasta in marinara. Pittsburgh's ethnic treasures.

Xander examined his Reuben.

"Corned beef, Swiss cheese, sauerkraut (he made them sound like dirty words) with some weird pink no-doubt mayonnaise-based dressing, all on rye bread that's been cooked in half a cup of grease. This can't possibly taste good."

"Trust me, it does." Jeff nudged him. "Go ahead and take a bite. Don't be a food coward."

"It's a big sandwich and I have a small mouth," Xander quipped. "Don't rush me."

Jeff's hot pastrami sandwich glided into the vortex of his gaping mouth. A particularly long strip of fat laden meat dangled out of the corner of his lips. Jeff sucked it in like a spaghetti noodle.

"Gross and disgusting," Xander shivered. "After all those lectures you've given me about nutrition and percentage of calories derived from fat. This is who you really are. Where are the vegetables in this meal?"

"Latkes are made from potatoes. There are tiny pickles in your pink dressing. And sauerkraut is fermented cabbage. Cabbage is good for you on some level I'm sure."

"Latkes are French fries in the shape of a pancake. Who are you kidding?"

"Hey, give me a break here," Jeff said, swallowing more pastrami. "I eat responsibly most of the time. You know that. Nobody likes a food spoiler. I pay my taxes promptly and I never have sex. Once a year I'm entitled to a hot pastrami sandwich."

Suddenly Xander grabbed tightly onto Jeff's arm.

"Someone just came out of the house," Xander whispered.

Larry Cone stood at the end of the porch. He looked up and down the street, clearly anxious about something. True to greaser form, he wore jeans, black boots, a loud polyester shirt and his vintage black leather jacket. Black hair, slicked straight back, overdue at the barber's by a couple of weeks, revealed a perhaps too broad temple. The jacket was open. No scarf, no gloves.

Cone turned back, locked the door, and headed off on foot in the direction of the business district.

"Looks like a man with a problem," Jeff said.

"He acted like somebody's after him," said Xander. "What is it you want from this guy?"

"Dottie Hatfield suggested that Cone is the contact for the organization that operates out of Ohio. If that's true, then he'll have at least one Ohio listing in his address book." Savoring the last bite of his pastrami sandwich, Jeff added, "But I'm not willing to break and enter to get it."

Xander gave this a quick thought.

"You don't have to."

Xander opened the passenger door and got out of the car.

"What are you doing?"

Xander threw his coat onto his now empty seat.

"Just watch."

"I don't want to watch. I want to know what you're doing," Jeff said in a panic. He threw the empty, greasy deli bag into the back seat. "Shit," he said, greasy fingers slipping off of the door lock.

"Trust me," Xander said.

"Not a good idea. Wait."

Before Jeff could stop him, Xander ran coatless in the direction Larry Cone had just taken. He ran one block, checking for Cone, then doubled back to Kentucky Avenue.

Disregarding Jeff's admonitions to get back into the car, Xander dashed onto Larry Cone's porch.

Xander rang the doorbell, then pounded on the door.

"Elaine! Elaine!" he cried. "Let me in."

He banged harder on the door.

"Let me in. It's cold out here."

Xander wrapped himself in his own arms, shivering. Repeatedly he called for the mysterious Elaine to open the door.

What the fuck is he doing? Jeff wondered. I better go get him.

Just then Cone's next-door neighbor peeped out of his door. He was a well-fed, gray haired gentleman dressed comfortably for the cold in gray Dockers and a flannel shirt. He viewed the situation while pretending to check his mail.

"Oh, hello." said Xander. "My Uncle Larry just ran up the street and my sister Elaine has locked me out. I'm freezing."

The neighbor didn't say anything, but continued to audit the proceedings.

Xander banged on the door again, crying out for admittance.

"She's a music freak," Xander said. "She's probably got her iPod stuck in her ears. It's my fault. I wasn't supposed to leave the house. My uncle says it's not safe for an eleven-year-old boy to wander around loose in the city."

"Your uncle is right about that," the neighbor finally spoke.

"Stupid of me to go outside without my coat. But there's a kid who lives around the corner. He has a cool video game. I was only gone for an hour. I thought I could sneak out and sneak back in without anyone noticing me. Now I'm freezing to death."

Xander banged on the door once more for emphasis.

"I don't suppose my uncle leaves a key with you," Xander said with remarkable deftness.

"No, I'm afraid he doesn't."

"Wait. I have an idea."

Uncle Larry's mail slot looked just wide enough for a skinny eleven-year-old arm to slip through.

"Let's hope it works," Xander said to the neighbor.

Xander knelt down and lifted the mail slot's brass flap.

"Uncle Larry doesn't usually lock the dead bolt. Especially if he's just going out for cigarettes. He just pushes the button on the doorknob and pulls the door closed behind him. He says the street is well lit and the neighbors watch out for each other. Anyone fiddling with the locks would be noticed and reported to the police."

Xander's hand found the inside doorknob. He turned it. The lock mechanism popped.

"I hope Uncle Larry didn't set the alarm. Well, why would he? Elaine is still inside."

Xander pushed open the door. No alarm—except the one going off in Jeff's head.

"Thank God," Xander sighed, visibly relieved. "I thought I was going to freeze to death."

The neighbor watched as Xander entered Larry Cone's house. Jeff, in a panic, kept thinking, 'He's breaking and entering. His mother is going to kill me. What should I do? Think fast, think fast.'

The neighbor went back indoors, presumably to his roaring fire. Jeff got out of his car and checked for signs of Larry Cone. His first impulse was to get inside the house and collect Xander and escape before Cone returned. On the other hand, Cone had already been gone ten minutes or so. What if he had just gone up the street for a paper? Or cigarettes, as Xander had suggested? He'd be back any minute. Perhaps Jeff should stay out on the street, intercept Cone, and keep him occupied until Xander came back out. Jeff antsied back and forth on the sidewalk in front of Cone's house until he just couldn't stand it another minute. He had to get Xander out of there.

He rang the bell, hoping that alone would be enough warning to force Xander to retreat. The neighbor once again came out to check his mail.

"Do you know if Larry Cone is in?" Jeff asked. "I have an appointment but he doesn't seem to answer."

"It appears Mr. Cone has stepped out," replied the neighbor. "But the nephew—"

Xander opened the door.

"There you are," Xander exclaimed as if redressing a recalcitrant child. "Uncle Larry just called. He's running late. He says I'm to make you at home."

Xander grabbed onto Jeff's wrist and pulled him into the house.

"We can't stay here," Jeff urged under his breath. "He'll be back any minute."

"You don't know that," Xander answered calmly. "He might be gone for hours. I haven't found his address book yet. But I've found a few things. And there's this really interesting room upstairs. Come and see."

Xander pulled his friend into a spacious sunken living room. Second and third room balconies overlooked this airy, beautifully designed center. The house was decorated in a modern Italian style, accented by a few choice antiques. Vernon Roman's armoire would have been at home here.

"This house is amazing," said Xander. "But I have to show you the room upstairs first."

Xander led an astonished Jeff up a carpeted stairway.

"There must be over a million dollars invested in this house," Jeff said. "It's just incredible. I don't understand it."

On the second floor landing they encountered a progression of bedrooms and bathrooms. The doors to these rooms had been left open except for the room at the very end of the landing.

"It feels like it's locked at first," said Xander, "but it isn't. Try it."

Jeff pushed on the door. Although the doorknob disengaged from the doorframe, the door did not budge. Jeff put his shoulder into it. The door opened about a foot or so.

"There's a mattress leaning up against the other side of the door," Xander explained. "It's really heavy, but the door will open just far enough for us to squeeze through."

"This is not a good idea," Jeff said as Xander eased himself inside.

"Get in here."

Seduced, perhaps, by the lure of adventure, Jeff pushed a little harder on the door, thereby gaining entrance to the secret chamber.

Closed curtains made the room nearly pitch dark inside. Xander felt along the wall for the light switch. A single low watt bulb, suspended on a string cord, cast an orange glow over the room's unusual contents.

Two large metal tool chests dominated the back wall. These were open. Inside, Jeff found an assortment of clamps in a variety of sizes. He also found a soldering gun, chains of varying strengths, thicknesses and lengths, and thick wax candles. Also a chef's knife, a paring knife, a fillet knife. Tacks, nails, staples. A box of fireplace matches.

To the left of one of the chests he spotted what looked like a medieval mace. Here and there on the floor he found leather straps, a horsewhip, wooden paddles, a bamboo cane. A box of kosher salt. Cans of beer, many of them empty.

"This looks like an interrogation room in El Salvador," said Jeff.

"Look at this." Xander pointed to smudge marks on one of the walls. "You can make out hand prints. And there's, like, wax on the floor and dark spots on the rug."

Directly across from the hand stained wall Jeff spotted an old Kodak film projector. There was a short 16mm film in the take up reel. Mounds of magazines littered the area around the projector. Xander kneeled down and sorted through some of the magazines.

"Don't look at those," Jeff warned, feeling a little sick.

"I want to know what's in these," Xander said, more challenged by the room's novelty than frightened by it's reality.

"Believe me, you don't want that stuff in your imagination. It's like a car wreck. You want to see it, but then it's stuck in your memory for the rest of your life."

Xander opened one slowly. "There's nothing you can see that isn't shown," he reminded.

Jeff rested his right hand on his chest just beneath his throat. What he wanted to say stuck there. He was afraid he was going to puke.

"Besides, I already looked at a bunch of these while you were outside. Naked people, tied up, beating each other, licking themselves. Weird sex stuff." He let the magazines drop. "It smells in here," he added, as if noticing for the first time.

Jeff stifled his gag reflex long enough to say, "I thought you were going to show me something that had to do with the case."

"This might have to do with the case. Don't you think? I mean, look at this." Xander gestured with a sweep of his arms at the magnitude of Larry Cone's perversity.

"Somehow I can picture Vernon Roman taking his pleasure in this room," said Jeff. "But I can't see Chester here. And I can't see what this would have to do with the murder of middle management executives in Baltimore and Kitty Hawk." Jeff closed his eyes for a moment. His heart beat loudly in the silence of the dimly lit room. He collected himself. "Let's get the hell out of here."

Jeff pulled the mattress back as far as he could without toppling it over. Xander slipped out through the modest opening and waited on the landing for Jeff. Before Jeff could open the door wide enough to fit through they both heard a loud bang. Xander stiffened.

"Shit," he said. "Cone's back."

Xander slipped back into the room. They quickly closed the door and fortified the resistance afforded by the mattress with the weight of their bodies.

Listening at the door crack, Jeff whispered, "God, what if he comes in here?"

"This is his playroom," Xander whispered back. "Why would he come in here by himself?"

Jeff cast him a look. "Maybe he wants a stale beer."

They hushed as Larry Cone pounced up the carpeted stairs, apparently two at a time. He sounded restless. He walked quickly from room to room as if looking for something. They heard a thud—maybe a drawer slamming shut, maybe a book dropping onto a wooden surface. Cone cussed, walked again from room to room. Things were quiet for a while, then Cone came out onto the landing. He stopped in front of his playroom door. Jeff heard the staccato sounds of plastic phone buttons being pushed.

"Son of a bitch," Cone swore.

Cone leaned against the wall and dialed again. This time he was close enough for Jeff to make out the musical notes that sounded with each pressing of the buttons. Ten numbers. Long distance. He tried to follow it. A...C...A flat...F...F...A...G...something....B....something.

"It's Larry in Pittsburgh," Cone announced. "I need to know what to do."

Jeff strained to hear the voice on the other line. It sounded like a man's voice. Before he could make out any words, however, Cone pulled away from the wall and started pacing. He seemed to go into one of the bedrooms, return to the landing, go into a different bedroom, back to the landing.

"I've been straight with you," Cone continued. "I've been nothing but straight with you. I'm telling you something went wrong and it's not on my end. I looked all over that bitch's apartment. Not a fucking thing. Nothing."

The party at the other end talked for a while. Definitely a man's voice. Cone cut in aggressively. "Let me ask you something. No, let me ask you something. Are you happy with me? Because if you're not, it doesn't have to be such a big deal. You know what I'm saying."

Pause. The other man talked. Then Larry, "Okay...okay. I'll keep lookin'." You could almost hear the word Dad at the end of Cone's sentence. The man at the other end represented an authority figure of some kind. Jeff detected an edge of fear in Cone's voice. He looked around at the S& M accoutrement spread throughout the room and wondered what it would take to frighten a man like Larry Cone.

"I'll keep in touch," Cone finished.

He hurled the phone into the wall and yelled something unintelligible at the top of his lungs.

Jeff and Xander tightened up. Jeff felt like the man in *The Tell-Tale Heart*. He thought surely Cone could hear the drumming of his heart, even through the mattress and the door.

They didn't hear anything for what seemed like minutes. Jeff felt certain Cone was still on the landing. Cone was not the type to step lightly. Jeff strained to hear, leaning as close as possible to the crack of the door. Footsteps. He heard footsteps. Slow and deliberate footsteps. Creep, creep. One step closer. The footsteps stopped right outside the door. 'No,' Jeff thought. 'It must be my paranoid imagination. There is no reason for him to be suspicious about this room.'

Then it hit him. It came to Xander at the same time. The light. They had forgotten to turn off the dingy twenty-five watt light bulb that hung in the center of the room. It's dim luminescence seemed so negligible, so harmless. Could Cone see this tiny bit of light at the bottom of the door? In a movement so fast it hardly seemed to happen, Xander flipped off the switch.

The door handle turned.

'Shit,' thought Jeff. He and Xander instinctively stepped back and to the left, away from the door. Cone slowly, slowly pressed against the door. It moved in painfully slow segments of time. The mattress lifted up and up. Jeff and Xander plastered themselves against the wall. Cone slipped into the room, letting the door close.

He did not flip on the light. He walked slowly in front of the mattress. He looked directly at the wall with the curtained window. He turned to the right and looked at the wall with the hand print smudges. He turned to look at the wall upon which Jeff and Xander had plastered themselves.

In that moment something clicked in Jeff. A shot of adrenalin. He grabbed the edge of the mattress. With astonishing strength he forced it down on Larry Cone, knocking Cone to the floor. Jeff screamed at Xander, "Run! Run!"

Cone struggled to get out from under the mattress. Jeff jumped on top of it, beating with his fists at the area securing Cone's head. Jeff screamed again for Xander to run.

Xander didn't run, however. He jumped onto the mattress and jumped again, up and down, again and again, near Olympic leaps. Jeff continued to beat the mattress with his fists.

Cone struggled with extraordinary strength, lifting the mattress higher. Jeff and Xander assaulted the mattress with more ferocity. Eventually the strength of the man beneath the mattress waned.

Xander pulled on the door. The mattress, now horizontal, blocked their escape. While beating on the thing, Jeff and Xander moved the mattress an inch at a time away from the door until there was enough space for Xander to slide through.

"Get to the car," Jeff yelled. "Hurry!"

Xander ran as fast as he could. Jeff grabbed the medieval mace. With all the strength he had left he slammed it into the mattress. Again. Again.

"You bastard!" he screamed. "You bastard!"

The spikes on the ball tore into the skin of the mattress. Padding flew everywhere. Cone stopped moving.

Jeff stood, waving the mace.

"Don't you dare fucking move!"

He counted to two. One, two. Larry Cone did not move. Jeff tossed the mace and ran like hell for the front door. Cone's next-door neighbor watched as Jeff, mattress stuffing flying in his wake, dashed sprinter speed to his car.

"Get inside," Jeff yelled, adrenalin still pumping.

"I can't. The door's locked."

Jeff struggled with pants too tight with pastrami to liberate his keys from his pocket. "Fuck, fuck, fuck, fuck," he exclaimed, jumping up and down as if that might help. Finally the keys came free.

Jeff popped himself into the car and flipped the lock for the passenger side. Xander jumped in. The ignition turned over immediately. Jeff kicked in the four-wheel drive, put the pedal to the floor, and they were out of there, flying. Even in the snow. For once Xander thanked his lucky stars for Jeff's anal obsession with auto maintenance.

Jeff raced through Shadyside toward downtown Pittsburgh. Xander stared out the back window for at least ten minutes. No sign of Larry Cone. No sign of the Pittsburgh police either.

"I'm going to wake up tomorrow with gray hair," Jeff declared. "Shit!" He banged his fist on the steering wheel. "We didn't even get his address book. I tried to follow the musical notes when he dialed the phone, but I couldn't hear them all. He was talking to St. Patrick. I just know it. Shit!" He pounded the steering wheel one more time. "How could we go through all that and get nothing?"

"We don't need his address book," Xander said calmly.

"What do you mean?" Xander pulled five crumpled 5" x 3" sheets from his pocket.

"I couldn't find his address book," Xander said. "But I did find his telephone bill."

35.

AFTER SO MUCH INTRIGUE JEFF EXPECTED SOMETHING MORE GLAMOROUS from the Chester abode. As it turned out the Chesters lived in a modest suburban plan made up chiefly of ranches and split levels clad in pastel aluminum siding. The Chester residence, a two-story structure with powder blue siding, fit unobtrusively into the plan. Three bedrooms, Jeff estimated, maybe four. Jeff tried to imagine seven boys and two adults sharing such a small space.

A young boy, dressed formally in black trousers and a white shirt, answered the door. Jeff remembered this boy from the Chester viewing. He was the youngest of the seven boys.

"Glad to make your acquaintance," the boy pronounced with studied politeness. "You must be Mr. Redwing. I'm Jason Chester. I'm to show you in."

Jason opened the door wide, admitting Jeff and Xander into a tiny foyer that doubled as a staircase landing. Elenora Chester chose just that moment to descend the carpeted powder blue stairs to greet her guests. Jeff noticed something different about her. Something fresh.

Elenora had put on make up and lipstick for this interview. A soft, silk top of gold, accented with bright red, lifted and billowed with each step she took. Tight black Laura Petrie slacks showed off an astonishingly good figure for a woman with seven children. This Elenora Chester bore no resemblance to the pathetic, stricken woman Jeff encountered at the funeral.

"Jeff," she said, extending her hand, "I see my little gentleman has greeted you."

"Yes, indeed."

They clasped hands. Jeff felt the impulse to lean in and kiss her cheek and he wondered why. He introduced Xander as his son, which surprised her.

"Did he travel with you?" she asked.

"No," Jeff answered, feigning embarrassment. "He lives here."

"Ah." One knew instantly she considered it tactless to pursue the issue further. "Let's go into the front room. I think we'll be most comfortable there. Jason, why don't you make a spot of tea for us? Perhaps Xander can help." To Jeff she said, "Is tea all right?"

"Tea is fine."

"What's your favorite?"

"Oh, well, my favorite is Formosa Oolong. I don't suppose you have it."

Jason rolled his eyes, but only just slightly to amuse himself.

"Of course we have it," said Mrs. Chester with a flourish. "We collect teas. Don't we Jason?"

Jason nodded without enthusiasm. It would be difficult to gage his true feelings about tea. Without saying a word, he turned and proceeded into the kitchen. Xander shrugged and followed closely behind him.

Mrs. Chester gestured toward the front room.

"Did Marshall have a thing about tea?"

Elenora cracked a smile. "No, I'm the tea fancier. Whenever we travel I add local varieties to my collection. Whenever our friends travel they bring tea back for us as gifts. My brother Jeremy, whom I think you've met, travels extensively and sends me whole crates of tea from his exotic adventures. I have quite a collection at this point."

"I imagine you must," said Jeff. "Is your brother around today?"

"He's off at the movies," Elenora chimed. "I insisted. Jeremy got me through these last few days. I thought he deserved an afternoon of indulgence. Movies are his obsession. He'll go to a Cineplex, often alone, and just see one movie after another."

"Do you share your brother's enthusiasm?"

"I'm afraid I don't see many movies," Elenora replied. "My passion is The Theatre." The next part she pronounced with special emphasis, as if by imparting this information she was giving him a glimpse into her being. "I am a graduate of the Carnegie Mellon School of Drama." She let it sink in. "It was the number one school for drama in the country in my day."

"I remember that," said Jeff. "I did a little math before coming over this afternoon and I realized that both you and Marsh entered college right out of high school. That was unusual for a drama major. Carnegie Mellon was a difficult school to get into. Most students worked in summer stock and community theater before they were good enough to pass the audition. You must have been a naturally good actress."

"I was," she blushed. "Am. That's not why I got in right after high school, however. You see, my father was an alumnus."

"Ah."

"He led a small band of influential alumnae who encouraged other alumnae to contribute large sums of money to the engineering school. My father was an engineer. He owned his own firm. Richer and Searing?"

"Oh, I've heard of them," Jeff said, thinking *Here's the money.*

"So you see, they had to admit me. And boy did those professors resent me for it."

The front room functioned as something of a parlor. A hardwood floor polished to a high sheen, covered partially with a thick Chinese patterned throw rug, sported a mahogany tea table and several large plants in polished brass pots. A charming little fireplace crackled with a charming little fire. It was all very crisp and new and lightly scented, like a showroom. The family obviously did not use this room. It was reserved for the (not very often) formal entertaining of guests.

Elenora indicated Jeff take a seat on a thickly padded chintz sofa. Elenora sat close enough to Jeff for quiet conversation but far enough away to suggest good manners. She continued her narrative.

"I remember one particular insult. It was leveled by a Miss Mattingly, Grande Dame of the American Theatre. She had apparently dined with the Eugene O'Neills on a regular basis and had acted some small part in *Mourning Becomes Electra.* Well, she reminded us one afternoon that admission to her class constituted a privilege. She was, after all, Who She Was. Her class was limited to twenty students a semester. After saying this she paused dramatically, turned, and looked directly at me. 'I stand corrected,' she said. 'Twenty-one.'"

Elenora smiled, then shrugged.

"I was one of those students. I had a rich daddy with influence." She laughed.

"I didn't realize you came from money," Jeff remarked.

"Not real money," she replied, looking away as if into dreamy childhood memories. "But we were comfortable."

Jeff waited a moment, watching some of Elenora's memories play upon the phantom screen in front of her eyes. "You must have given up quite a lot to marry a school teacher," he said.

She turned her head to him, giving him a wry look.

"I did, yes. But when you've grown up with comfort I think it's easier to make a sacrifice. You see so clearly that money itself is not a worthwhile goal. Life must be about something. Even by the end of our first conversation, I knew that I loved Marshall. It was a powerful love. I knew with great clarity that I wanted to step into that man's life. I wanted to immerse myself in his dreams, his goals, his purpose. I wanted to have his children. I wanted to create an unexpected life for myself, for us together. Out of nothing.'

"That's what theatre people do," she said. "We create from nothing. Theatre people live created lives."

She waited. Jeff got out his yellow legal pad and jotted down a few notes. Something out of nothing.

———

Jason used a footstool to reach the kitchen spigot. He poured water into an old fashioned Revere kettle. After putting the kettle on a fire, he moved the footstool over to a series of above-the-counter cabinets. He opened the doors to reveal an Ali Baba's treasure of exotic teas.

"Wow," said Xander. "How can you drink so much tea?"

"We don't drink it at all," Jason replied matter-of-factly, going about his business. "Some of these tins are older than I am. My mother collects teas from around the world. Like some people collect wine or antiques."

"Really. How do you know which ones you're allowed to drink?"

Jason mulled it over. Withdrawing a basic tin of Twinings' Formosa Oolong from the shelf, he replied, "We can brew any one we like. There are no rules. But you wouldn't want to drink tea brewed from nineteenth century tea leaves."

"No, I guess not."

With a butler's methodical calm Jason moved about the kitchen. He gathered a sterling silver tea tray, a teapot, two cups with saucers, a miniature pitcher for cream, a matching bowl for sugar, sterling silver spoons, and linen napkins. He adroitly maneuvered the footstool about the room to acquire any object above the reach of his ten-year-old hands.

Scary, thought Xander.

———

"How many children do you have?" Jeff asked, although he knew the answer.

"Seven," Elenora said wide-eyed, as if astonished herself by the number. "All boys." She laughed. "I've surrounded myself with pillars of maleness. Even my one and only sibling is a man. The testosterone in this place is palpable at times."

Elenora threw back her head and laughed. Her exaggerated gestures, her bravura, reminded Jeff of scenes he'd witnessed at CMU in the cafeteria, along the pathways between the buildings. She was behaving like a Dramat. He had often enjoyed watching groups of Dramats talking together, acting out together. So colorful, so self expressive, so physically beautiful. They reminded Jeff of wild horses, magnificent and unconfined. Sometimes silly.

Sitting beside her, Jeff experienced something of an epiphany. He saw her as she must have been seven children ago, back in her college youth.

An achingly beautiful woman. Jeff had imagined Elenora Chester as quiet, reserved, maybe even a little mousey. But of course she wasn't that way. She was a Dramat. She was lovely, fresh, enthusiastic, fascinating, compelling. Her classmates would have liked her, maybe loved her. She had been popular in college, of course she had.

The men on campus would have pointed her out, remarked upon her beauty and her style. What a prize she must have seemed to the likes of Marshall Chester.

"Only two of my boys are with me," she continued, breaking the spell. "Jason you met. He's ten. Scott, sixteen, is out at the moment. They're always out of the house at that age. Jason was unexpected, as you might have guessed. But I'm so glad he came along. In many ways he's my favorite. I know it's terrible for a mother to say she has a favorite, but I can't help it. I love him to pieces. He's my little Buddha boy."

"I think I saw your other sons at the funeral home," Jeff said. "Where are they now?"

"Gone back to school already. End of term, you know. Most of them have finals and papers due. The twins— our first-born—are both in graduate school. David is at Amherst and Daniel is at UCLA. David and Daniel are the kind of twins you don't hear about very often. They go out of their way to be different from one another. They fought all through puberty. I didn't think I was going to survive it."

"Tell me about your other three boys. I'll probably write something about them in the article."

"Well, let's see. Tobias is at Boston College studying museum management. Randolph is at Penn State. And Andy just started at Slippery Rock. He's studying creative arts therapy. My artistic nature has obviously influenced a few of my children."

Jeff said, "I didn't catch what the twins and Randolph are studying."

"Oh, technical things. Computers. Information highway type stuff. I don't understand any of it. I suppose that's how it goes in big families. Some of the children emulate their mother and some emulate their father. Scott just wants to get away from us all. I suspect he'll go to school in China or Africa. Someplace far away, he says. He's a difficult boy but at least he has a mind of his own. I just hope he still talks to me when he's an adult."

"Adolescence is a difficult time," Jeff said, dismissing the Scott issue. He didn't want to spend too much time on the children. "I'm curious about something, though. I noticed out of seven boys there is no Marsh junior."

"There's a story there." Elenora shifted a little closer to Jeff on the sofa as if including him in a confidence. "It was a tradition in my husband's family to name the firstborn boy Marshall. My husband hated his name, absolutely hated it. He was an only child. There were no family members left to offend. So he decided to end the family curse."

Jeff laughed. "Well, in any case, you must be proud of the job you and Marsh did raising your children. So many in college."

Before Elenora could respond, Jason and Xander entered with the tea. Jason shuffled in slowly, holding the rather large tray out in front of him as if it held the Crown of England. He set the tray on the tea table and methodically poured a cup first for Jeff, then for his mother. Jeff dutifully took a sip.

"Excellent," he pronounced.

Jason explained, "Five minutes in hot but not boiling purified water."

"Such a gentleman," Jeff said. "You even know how to brew the perfect cup of tea."

Xander smirked as if to say, 'Don't hold your breath waiting for me to turn into a little butler.'

Mrs. Chester held open her arms; Jason gratefully settled in for a hug. "This is my angel," she said, gently kissing his forehead. "My sweetness." To Jeff she said, "I think he was more comfort to me over the last few days than I was to him."

"I didn't love Dad as much as you did," Jason said matter-of-factly. "He was never here."

'Now that's a telling remark,' thought Jeff.

Elenora sought to redirect the discussion. Before she could utter a word, Jason let these words fly out across the sterling tea service, "Don't write that my Dad was a good father. He didn't love us. He loved other people's children."

"Jason!" Elenora exclaimed. "That was not nice. Mr. Redwing is an old college friend of your father's. He's just writing a little article for our alumnae magazine—just a little something for our old classmates to read. He's not writing stone tablets."

'Well,' thought Jeff. 'Put me in my place.'

Embarrassed by the whole communication, Jeff muttered something unintelligible. Even he couldn't be sure what he said. It managed to bring a satisfactory end to the episode.

Elenora patted Jason's behind. "Why don't you take little Xander up to your room and play for a while," she said. "Let Mr. Redwing and I finish our conversation."

"Yes, Mummy."

Jason perfectly and politely left the room and ascended the stairs. Xander followed. Not a word passed between them.

———

Mrs. Chester talked at length about her husband's career. Jeff recorded every detail on his yellow legal pad. The subject of awards came up. Mrs. Chester crossed the room to a small desk and procured from a drawer a typed list. It was an impressive three-page document describing the name of each award, its significance, along with the date of its bestowal. Jeff wondered for a moment how many pages his own accomplishments would fill. Had he actually won any awards?

"Marshall considered writing his own textbook," proclaimed Mrs. Chester. "He was always complaining about the inadequacies of the textbooks on the market."

"I'm flabbergasted," Jeff said. "I had no idea he had accomplished so much. Makes me wish I hadn't lost touch over the years."

Oh, he's good, Dear Reader. The trick is meaning it, even if you know you're inventing and lying.

"I'd forgotten myself how much Marsh had done until I compiled this list," said Mrs. Chester. "The remarkable thing is how little it mattered."

Jeff looked up from the awards document. "I'm sorry. How little it mattered?"

"All those accomplishments. Best teacher awards from the students, best teacher awards from the teachers, a special commendation from the Allegheny County Commissioners, recognition of outstanding achievement by the National Teachers Association. You would think that so many accolades would shield a man from reckless incrimination. Yet how easily, and in how little time, one mean-spirited individual managed to undermine my husband's career."

Jeff lowered his voice. "The Greta Fields woman. Penny English told me something about accusations, the harassment. I have to tell you, none of it makes sense to me."

"Oh, it certainly doesn't make sense," Elenora said flatly.

"Ms. English didn't tell me much. I'd like to understand." Jeff put his legal pad aside. "Off the record, of course."

Elenora sat up straight. She poured a touch more tea for herself and for Jeff. Then she began.

"A woman named Greta Fields mounted a campaign against my husband. It was a deliberate, orchestrated campaign to separate him from his job and destroy his career."

"This is what I don't understand," said Jeff. "With all of Marshall's accomplishments, how could the school administration allow that to happen? And why would anyone want to do this to him in the first place? What was Greta Fields' motivation?"

Elenora sipped her tea, gathering her thoughts.

"The School Board hired her. She was supposed to be an administrative assistant with part-time teaching duties. No such position was ever advertised. We should have been suspicious right there.

"To tell the truth Jeff, she seemed nice at first. We all liked her. She was charming. Jolly in that way that fat people can be—kind of like Mrs. Claus."

"I'm curious," said Jeff. "In what way was she charming? Did she do anything in particular?"

"Well..." Mrs. Chester sorted through a series of mental pictures, "she blustered about with a kind of cheerful energy. She smiled a lot. Always happy, it seemed."

"Now, that I haven't heard," Jeff said darkly.

"Oh, yes. She was that way. In the beginning. And she told charming little stories. It kind of reminded you of being read to as a child."

"What kind of stories?"

"Um—they were like mythological stories or allegories. Maybe it's just the way she told them. Each story had a moral. I'll give you an example. She told a story about an executive with whom she worked in Detroit. She said he was particularly anxious to impress the board of directors. The members of this particular board liked to go fly-fishing. The executive in question was not a fisherman, but he pretended to know all about it. So fishing day rolls around. The executive arrives at camp with a Mason jar and a lid. They ask him what the jar is for. He tells them, 'To catch the flies.'"

Not being a fisherman, Jeff didn't get it.

"See, you don't go fly fishing with actual flies. A fly is really a fancy lure. Fly fisherman collect them and have special lucky ones and so on. The man made an ass of himself. She told the story with an impish innocence. It put you in mind of Gracie Allen, if you remember Burns and Allen."

"I've seen a few things on TV retrospectives."

"Greta's stories featured important people who were brought down by their own foibles," continued Mrs. Chester. "In the beginning we found these stories amusing. Like children's stories. Modern day Aesop's Fables. We all laughed. Marshall would come home and tell me these stories. He'd say, 'You should have heard the one Greta told today.' I enjoyed hearing them, Jeff. And then suddenly they weren't so funny anymore."

Jeff asked, "Did her stories change over time?"

"Oh, no," she replied. "Her stories didn't change. How we heard them changed."

"How do you mean?"

"Well, I don't know if you've heard anything about this. She started witch hunting some of the gay teachers. Or at least the teachers who were rumored to be gay."

"I heard a little about this," Jeff acknowledged. "Apparently she only targeted gay men, not gay women."

"That's right," Elenora nodded. "Greta Fields was a lesbian herself. That made the whole gay witch hunt thing so bizarre. These were good teachers, Jeff. We just couldn't understand it. Did she just happen to hate gay men? Had some gay man cost her a job in the past? Hurt her in some way? She wasn't a right wing extremist of any sort. What she did was unfair, unjustified and even cruel. Nothing like this had ever happened in our school district before."

"What sort of things did she do?" Jeff asked.

"Oh, she targeted people for firing. Good people, not people who were underperforming or who might in some way be perceived as deserving it. She mounted campaigns against these people, accusing them of negligence or incompetence. This is one way it worked: she'd drum up some slippery accusation against a certain teacher; Principal Modani would write a letter to that teacher; Fields then stole this letter from the teacher's mail slot before he could see it; Modani would then accuse the teacher of ignoring his letter. Modani would then request in writing a formal meeting with the teacher to discuss his performance—a letter that was put on file with the School Board."

"Let me guess," said Jeff. "Modani put the letter in the teacher's mail slot and once again Fields would steal the letter. The teacher would then fail to show up for the meeting."

"Exactly. Then Greta Fields became more vociferous with her complaints. A new round of stolen memos and letters would ensue. Modani at least pretended to be angry with these teachers for months before they even realized there was a problem. They would hear about the problem as gossip from other teachers."

"In order for a campaign like that to work, Modani would have to have been in on it," Jeff noted. "He can't possibly have been that blind or stupid."

"That's what Marsh and I thought," Elenora nodded. "He wasn't a mean spirited person. We figured this charade had been forced on him by the Board. He was a good man, Jeff. He cared about his teachers. On his own he would never have allowed Fields to get away with it. But Modani was eight years away from retirement, eight years away from his pension. If he didn't cooperate, she might target him next. That's what we figured."

"But why didn't the teachers intervene? They have a union, don't they?"

"Indeed they do. But this is where Greta was smart. She had two faces, you see. One was the charming, affable Mrs. Claus. The other was the sinister, sociopathic executioner. Most of the teachers only saw Mrs. Claus. She championed some of the teachers, wrote commendations for their files. Half the teachers thought she was sainted. They thought if Greta had something negative to say about one of their colleagues, it must be justified.

I'm telling you, it was a well-orchestrated campaign. She manipulated the teacher body like a puppet master."

Jeff asked, "What about the teachers who saw the evil face?"

"Most were too shocked to act. Some wanted to wait it out, see what came of it all. A few teachers with backbone talked to Modani on behalf of the targeted teachers. Most were afraid to be targeted next.'

"Think about it Jeff," Elenora continued. "A case of incompetence can be built against anyone. We are none of us flawless executioners of our daily tasks. Take my job as a mother. Even with all the care and devotion I've given my children, if someone wished to do so they could point out a hundred ways I've fallen short. What happens if my neighbor and I have a dispute about the border between our properties? I take the case to court and win. She decides to get revenge by falsely accusing me of abusing my children. Let's say her best friend works with a social services agency. This friend comes in on the scheme. I'm suddenly in jeopardy of losing my children. Even if the courts don't buy into the scheme, I've lost my reputation in the community. The Salem Witch trials started as a border dispute between neighbors."

Elenora took a sip of tea, then continued, "Take a look at your life. Where might the competence police find fault with you? Even if you happen to perform your duties flawlessly, how easy would it be for someone to destroy your reputation with lies?"

———

"This is my room," Jason indicated, leading Xander inside.

Methodical and neat, like Jason himself. Toys arranged for high visibility and easy access. Smithsonian chemistry set, lots of V-tech stuff, an impressive collection of Legos. Off in one corner Xander spotted an erector set, Lincoln logs, a brick construction kit, even Tinker Toys. Along the wall with the window stood a series of cardboard cutout buildings and skyscrapers, each perfectly assembled. There was a three-foot high Sears Tower, a Chrysler Building, and Empire State Building.

"I'm building a city," declared Jason. "As soon as my brother Scott leaves for college, I'll move all of these into his room. I can't build an entire city here." Jason cast a forlorn look around the limited dimensions of his private quarters.

"You like building things," Xander observed, touching the tip of the Chrysler Building.

"I intend to be a famous architect when I grow up. Right now I admire Philip Johnson and Frank Lloyd Wright. Frank Furness is okay, I guess."

"God." Xander admired Jason's handiwork. "I haven't gotten to architecture in my studies yet. Jeff took me to Fallingwater once."

"I go to Fallingwater several times a year," said Jason. "I consider it a pilgrimage."

———

Jeff brought up the subject.

"In her second year at the school, Greta targeted Marsh. Is that correct?"

"Yes, although we suspect she laid the groundwork in the first year." Elenora sat back in the chintz sofa. "We were stunned. It was generally agreed that Marsh was Upper St. Clair's best teacher. You've seen the list of awards. It was all but cast in cement that in eight years time upon Modani's retirement, Marsh would become principal of the school. Then Fields launched her attack."

"I'm sorry if this question seems indelicate, but did Fields think Marsh was gay?"

Elenora considered. "No, I don't think so. He wasn't. I'm sure of that. I know that many loyal wives have been suddenly surprised to discover otherwise, but I am not naive about sexual matters. I'm used to theatre people. If my husband had been homosexual I would have known it. I would have known it in college. No, that second year she had a different agenda —one that didn't follow a recognizable pattern. We never knew why she targeted Marsh."

Jeff suggested, "There must have been speculation."

"Money, perhaps. Marsh was the highest paid teacher in the school. Money might have been the inspiration for all the firings. The teachers union resists attempts to reduce teacher salaries or reductions in the teacher-to-student ratio. The teachers' union can't do anything about incompetence. The school has the right to remove any teacher found to be negligent or incompetent."

"I see."

"Starting salary is twenty-seven. Marsh made over seventy. If they could place a newly hired teacher in his position, they'd save a bundle. Multiply that by the number of teachers run out of their jobs by Greta Fields and it amounts to a two hundred thousand plus reduction in payroll. That's what we surmised."

"This is the first time I've heard this argument," Jeff said.

"Penny English pointed out that each of the gay teachers had been on staff for at least ten years. Since so many of the parents are ignorant or paranoid, gay teachers make easy targets. It was one theory."

"A plausible one," Jeff observed.

"Still, it doesn't excuse what happened. Even if the school was in financial trouble, it doesn't justify the Board bringing in someone like Grate Fields to destroy the reputations, not to mention the well-being, of perfectly good and loyal people. One of the gay teachers fought the attacks levied against him. He committed suicide over the summer. Did you know that?"

"No, I didn't."

"That's murder in my book. Murder committed directly by Greta Fields, Principal Modani and the members of the School Board. It's too bad you can't write about that in your article."

"Well, I'm curious," Jeff started, changing his tact. "Marsh was clearly a model teacher. What could Fields possibly say against him that could stick?"

"Greta Fields asserted in writing that she saw my husband exhibit improper sexual attention to certain female students. This is off the record, of course."

"Of course."

"My husband never, never behaved improperly with his students."

"I would never have believed it of Marsh." Jeff added, "I understand Penny English openly confronted both Modani and Fields."

Elenora hesitated. Then, "I'll give Penny this. She saw right from the beginning what was going on. She threw up the red flag when Fields went after the gay teachers. When Fields went after Marsh, Penny rushed vigorously to his defense."

Mrs. Chester stopped for a moment. The subject of Penny English clearly made her uncomfortable.

"Look," she said. "You probably heard about my outburst at the funeral. I can't pretend that Penny English is my friend. Last year at school she behaved courageously confronting Fields and Modani. Even so, she seduced my husband into betraying his family. You seem to have spoken to a number of people about my husband. I'm sure you've heard the rumors."

Jeff didn't quite nod. He let her go on.

"I know that on the surface Penny English appears to be the adversary of the Greta Fields of the world. I'll tell you something, Jeff. In reality she is Greta Fields in another form."

"That's an outrageous statement," Jeff couldn't stop himself from saying. "How can you justify such an idea?"

"I see she's won you over. I've known her longer than you have. Greta Fields is what happens when an inherently evil being expresses itself in business or politics. Penny English is what happens when an inherently evil being expresses itself in the domain of sexuality. She's a sex addict, you know."

"I don't know her that well," Jeff said warily. "You seem to have given this a lot of thought."

"She brought sadness and ultimately tragedy to my family," Elenora said. She fussed with the teapot. Alas, no more tea. She set the thing down.

"I can't prove it, but I'm certain Penny English brought Vernon Roman back into my husband's life."

"Vernon Roman," Jeff reiterated. "The man with Marshall that day. The one—"

"Who was decapitated. Yes. They were boyhood friends, you see. When Vernon showed up here one day, seemingly out of the blue, my husband couldn't help but breathe new life into those old memories." She leaned closer to Jeff. "Have you ever thought about how many people one truly loves in a lifetime?"

"I beg your pardon?"

"I'm talking about deep, spiritual love. One? Two? I'm not talking about the love you have for your parents or for your children. I'm talking about the people who affect you deeply, spiritually. Have you given it any thought?"

"No," said Jeff, not sure where she was going with this. "I can't say that I have."

"I have," she said firmly. "There are two such people in my life. I have deeply loved my brother Jeremy and I have deeply loved Marshall Chester. I'm getting older now. It's possible these two are the only ones I shall ever deeply, spiritually love. You can see how important these two people are to me."

"Certainly."

"My husband loved me. And he loved Vernon. Of course, he loved us in different ways. He knew Vernon from his childhood. But he knew Vernon intimately, knew him in his soul. Even though Vernon had devolved over the years into something repulsive, even criminal, my Marshall remembered Vernon as he had been in childhood. He remembered Vernon's beauty of spirit. He remembered all that they had shared together. Vernon had been one of Marshall's two people, you see. Once given the opportunity, he couldn't help bringing Vernon back into his life."

"I can see that," Jeff said.

"But it should never have happened," declared Elenora. "Vernon wasn't the same man. There wasn't even a ghost of the old Vernon left, the Vernon from all the old stories. Vernon should have remained in my husband's memory." And then she said, "If Penny English hadn't brought Vernon back into our lives, my husband would still be alive today."

———

Xander liked this kid. Someone close to his own age with genuine intellect. Could lighten up a bit, though.

"I wish you lived in my neighborhood," Xander said out loud.

Jason looked into Xander's face. A barely perceptible smile turned the corners of his mouth.

"Where do you live?" Jason asked.

"Wexford. Way out on the outer fringes of North Hills. About as far north from here as you can get without being in Erie."

"Too bad. I don't have any friends here," Jason said. "Maybe your dad could bring you over sometime."

"Jason, I should probably tell you something. Jeff isn't really my dad." 'There, I've confided in you.' "My real dad is gone. Jeff is just this cool guy from my neighborhood. He's kind of like my Big Brother."

"Big Brother," Jason echoed. "It's a social program, isn't it? I think I've heard of that."

"Yes, buy he's not really my Big Brother either. He didn't come to me through an agency. I sort of picked him. It's difficult to explain, so we just tell people we're father and son. Don't tell your mom, though. She might think it's weird."

"Don't worry. I won't tell." Jason lit up a bit, delighted to share a secret. "Is your real dad dead, too?"

"No. He left us. Mom and me. He ran away. Didn't say goodbye. Didn't leave a note. Didn't even hint to my mom that he was going. He just left for work one day and didn't come back."

"Maybe something happened to him," Jason said excitedly. "Like maybe he was kidnapped or...or..."

"Naw. He sent us a postcard from Wyoming. 'Dear Family, I had to leave. Don't try to find me.' My mom tried to find him anyway. She even hired a private investigator, someone who specializes in tracking down people who disappear. Didn't work. We couldn't find him." Jason shuffled his feet, looking down at the floor. Xander added, "I'm sorry about your dad, getting murdered and all."

Jason shrugged. "He played with me about ten minutes every Christmas. One time I asked him to his face, 'Why did you have me? What was the point?'"

"What did he say?"

"He said, 'Go to your room, Jason. We'll discuss it later.' We never did discuss it later. I hated him. He made my mother miserable."

"How did he do that?"

"He cheated on her. It made her sick on drugs for a long time. More than a year. Valium and stuff like that. I'm glad he's dead."

"You don't mean that."

"I do mean it. I didn't cry at the funeral. My brothers cried, but I didn't cry. And I won't. I can get along without ten minutes at Christmas."

"Well...fathers are over-rated," Xander said with a sigh. "That's what Jeff says. His father ran away too."

———

"They met in kindergarten or even before, that's how far back they went," said Elenora. "Marsh told me they were inseparable. Did everything together, shared everything together. They were both straight A students. I think they even planned to go to the same college."

Jeff said, "And then they had a falling out?"

"Not a falling out exactly. They didn't have words or anything like that. Vernon changed. It was like he made a decision, privately. During their junior year in high school, Vernon dropped out of the AP program. He joined the General Studies program. You know what that is. It's the school's way of providing dimwitted children with a diploma. From General Studies a student goes on to vocational training or simply doesn't go on at all."

"What reason did he give for this change?"

"Marsh says he wouldn't talk about it. Vernon avoided Marsh. Then he started hanging out with the leather jacket crowd. We used to call them greasers."

"I remember."

"Marshall was very upset. He tried to get his friend to talk. All Vernon would say is, 'I just changed.' A couple of years later Marsh ran into Vernon downtown. Marsh was in CMU. Vernon was working as a messenger boy. Very sad. In my heart I think Vernon is the reason Marshall devoted himself so diligently to his students."

Elenora looked at Jeff, then glanced down at his notepad. Jeff dutifully wrote down "devoted diligently to his students."

"He literally pulled kids up from drowning," Elenora continued. "He spent a great deal of time working with troubled students after school. He studied his students, watched for signs of the Vernon Roman syndrome. If he found a kid who was beginning to lose interest, Marshall worked with that kid, gave him attention and strokes he didn't get at home from his parents. You saw how many students came to his funeral."

"Astonishing," Jeff agreed.

"This was all because of Vernon. Vernon came to define my husband's life. I was my husband's lover, the mother of his children, his lifelong companion. But Vernon was the key to his career, his goals. Vernon's failure gave my husband's life purpose."

Jeff stopped writing for a moment and flexed his fingers.

"I have to tell you, I probably won't include much about Vernon in the article. They're only giving me about eight hundred words. Maybe I'll mention him in a passing reference to...the deaths."

"The murders." Mrs. Chester declared an end to her sensitivity on the matter.

"Murders, as you say. I'm wondering, just for my own knowledge, do you think Marsh was reaching maybe subconsciously back into the past to save his old friend? When Vernon showed up again?"

"No," Elenora said with authority. "My husband knew that Vernon could not be saved. When we encountered him a little over a year ago he appeared vulgar, tactless, even stupid. He lived on welfare checks. When I looked at him, I thought, 'You could be an educated man now. Financially secure. You could still be my husband's best friend. You could be Uncle Vernon to our children, living in this neighborhood.'"

They sat in silence for a moment. The life not lived. Jeff imagined himself as a musician, a composer, in his alternate life. The life that got away. Sometimes he pictured himself married, the father of a small brood. One made choices. Some choices imply sacrifice. Jeff wondered if Elenora was thinking at that moment of Vernon's alternate life or if she was thinking of her own. She could, after all, be a famous actress at this moment. Elenora Richer, gifted artist, rare orchid.

He broke their reverie.

"You said Penny English brought Vernon back into Marshall's life?"

"He called out of the blue. It seemed a coincidence at first. Later we found out he ran errands for Penny's current sleazy boyfriend. What's his name? Cone."

"Yes. Larry Cone. I've met him."

He blushed, Dear Reader, thinking of Larry Cone back in Shadyside under a mattress.

Elenora didn't take note of it. Too self absorbed.

"I'm certain Penny English is the connection," she said. "Without her interference, Marshall would be alive today. She is an evil woman. She channels evil. Look what she's done to my family."

———

Jason suggested they play a computer game.

"What do you have?" asked Xander.

"We have Galactic Flight," Jason suggested optimistically. "It's neat. You take off from Earth and guide your capsule past Mars, the asteroid belt, out past the outer planets and their moons. It uses the latest graphics from Voyager."

"Done it," Xander replied.

"We have Jurassic Reality. You go back in time and see life through the eyes of prehistoric creatures. You eat and avoid being eaten."

"No more dinosaurs," said Xander. "I'll puke."

"Well..." Jason wasn't sure how to appeal to the interests of his new friend. "Why don't we pull down the menu and look over our options."

———

"Vernon Roman was my first encounter with what you might call street people," Elenora said. "I grew up middle class, went to private schools, attended a private university, married and then moved straight to the suburbs."

"You say he ran errands for Larry Cone?"

"Vernon had some kind of money making operation on the side. Illegal, I'm sure. It had something to do with Cone. I asked Marsh about it but he told me more or less to mind my own business. I'll tell you this much. Vernon always had ready cash and plenty of it. Rolls of paper money. Much more than public assistance provides. I don't think he sold drugs, though. The man didn't drive a car. Marsh had to pick him up whenever they went anywhere."

"So Marsh and Vernon started seeing a lot of each other?"

"Quite a lot. Marsh met his responsibilities at school and at home. I can't complain about that. But he saw more of Vernon than I wanted him to. Frankly, I thought one visit was plenty. There but for the grace of God. But then he came again. And again. I didn't like having that man in my house."

"That's understandable," said Jeff. "This rekindling of their childhood friendship. Did it take place during the Greta Fields dilemma?"

Elenora thought about it. "Yes. In the second year of Greta Fields. Sounds like a date on the Catholic Calendar, doesn't it."

Jeff smiled. "Marsh must have been under a great deal of stress. Maybe his old friend provided a bit of consolation."

"It was hell for us that year, that's for sure. We all felt the stress. That's when I started taking tranquilizers. I just couldn't cope."

Respectfully and solicitously, Jeff commented, "Greta Fields' death must have been an enormous relief to your family."

"One hates to say it. If you are a compassionate human being and a Christian you hate to feel that you've benefited in some way from the death of a fellow creature. And yet, it was a relief. Her death genuinely surprised me."

"How so?"

"You might think I'm superstitious for saying this."

"That's all right," Jeff assured her. "I indulge in the occasional superstition."

"It's been my observation that bad people, evil people if you will, don't die easily. The woman was pushing fifty, grotesquely fat, history of high blood pressure and heart disease. Circulation problems in her legs, I understand. In the back of our minds some of us thought, 'perhaps she'll die of her debilitating diseases and our problems will go away.' It's a horrible thing to say, but several of us thought it. Some people said it out loud."

"Really?"

"Yes. At faculty dinners, privately in the corner, always with a chuckle afterward. This is where my most unscientific superstition comes in. You see, it's been my observation that when good people are in frail health they drop dead with the first harsh wind. But bad people, no matter how sick they are, go on and on and on. Years beyond their doctor's most optimistic prediction. They seem to live like vampires off the blood of their victims. That's why Greta's death surprised me. We all wished for her to die and she did."

———

The Chesters owned an Apple similar to the one Xander used in school.

"It doesn't have much memory," Jason quipped.

"I know. Computers are out of date so fast," said Xander as he opened a menu. "I think Jeff is getting me an iMac for Christmas."

"Wow. He must really like you."

"Yeah, he does. My mom and I are getting him all kinds of stuff from the L.L. Bean catalogue. It's going to be a big box of goodies. Flannel shirts, moose hide slippers, a camping knife, super-cool sunglasses with leather on the sides, maple syrup from Vermont—all kinds of stuff. Jeff lives out of the Bean catalogue."

"You're kidding."

"Nope. All his clothes. Blankets, shoes. Jeff can be a freaky dude. He raised himself. That's why he's so odd."

They turned their attention back to the screen.

"The games are under the Monopoly man," Jason said.

"I figured that."

Jason headed the cursor over to the Monopoly man, but then hesitated. He slipped it over to the dollar sign and opened that instead."

"Hey, I'm not allowed in there," said Jason.

"You're not in here. I am. Cool. It's Quicken. That's what my mother uses." Click, click.

"I don't think this is a good idea," Jason said anxiously.

"Don't you want to see your family's finances?"

"Actually—" started Jason.

"What?"

"I've already looked through our finances," Jason confessed. "It's pretty boring. Lists of all the written checks, savings records, discounts they got by shopping wisely. That kind of stuff."

"That's called a paper trail," Xander said excitedly. "Paper trails can be a lot more fun than computer games."

"Oh yeah?"

———

"That whole party was strange," Elenora asserted. "We held it in our backyard here. Marsh thought it might be a good political move to host the Fourth of July picnic. He invited the Board members. We made a point of having our children attend."

"What was strange about the party?" Jeff asked.

"It was hot and muggy. We don't have trees or any other kind of shelter in the backyard. It's long and open, so people stood directly in the hot sun all day. There was a great deal of tension in the air because of the attacks on Marsh. We thought Greta Fields might not attend, but she did. She brought her lesbian partner, Jane Lund. I remember it was funny because we all knew Greta was a lesbian but we couldn't imagine what sort of person she'd choose for a lover.

"She was actually very sweet," Elenora continued. "Jane Lund, I mean. She seemed shy. She didn't join conversations easily. I talked with her a bit to bring her out of herself. She stuck with me all afternoon. Greta, on the other hand, took charge of the picnic as if it were her own backyard. As I told you, she could be quite charming. She laid on the charm that particular afternoon. She told wonderful stories and had people laughing, despite the heat."

"What about Penny English?" Jeff asked. "Did she attend?"

"Oh, yes. In fact, she brought that sleazy boyfriend of hers, that Larry person. That was the first time I laid eyes on him. Pure white trash. Leather jacket, straight scuzzy hair. He wore pants that showed off his equipment, if you know what I mean. It was quite incredibly large and you could tell he was circumcised." She laughed. "Modani was scandalized. Imagine dressing like that to a school barbeque!

"Oh, and my husband insisted on invited Vernon," Elenora quipped. "That's when I realized that Vernon and this Larry person knew each other. They spent the entire afternoon together."

"Why do you think he invited Vernon?" Jeff asked. "Considering that he was campaigning for his job."

"I thought he was out of his mind. We tiffed about it, but by that time, I was deep into Valium escape. I took a pill and let him deal with it."

Jeff shifted on the sofa.

"So tell me how Fields died."

"Well," started Elenora. "She'd been eating all day. Plate after plate of burgers and hotdogs and pasta salad and potato salad. There's a picture emblazoned on my memory of Greta eating a corn on the cob that was just dripping with butter. The butter fell to the ground all around her as she walked. She was so obese and her breasts were so large that her jersey top was covered with splotches of food, like a baby's bib.'

"Then she started in on the desserts. It was like a show at the county fair. 'How much food can this disgustingly fat woman shove into her mouth, folks, before she vomits?' I am not exaggerating. She took a sizeable piece of just about every dessert on the table—there must have been twenty—and she forced them into her mouth like someone had a clock on her. Pecan pie and cherry cobbler and sheet cake and fruit torte. Her companion, Jane, and I stood together observing this spectacle. I remember thinking, 'How can anyone eat this much rich food and not drop dead of a heart attack?' And then it happened."

"She dropped dead of a heart attack," Jeff asserted.

"Well, she didn't drop dead, no. She started chocking. She gasped for breath, holding her neck. At first I thought something got stuck in her pipe. Mrs. Hughes, the swimming instructor, hit her on the back to loosen whatever was stuck. That didn't help, so she attempted the Heimlich Maneuver, but she couldn't get her arms all the way around Greta's body."

"Greta wasn't clutching her heart?"

"No. Her throat, as I said. Someone pulled out their cell and called an ambulance. Greta fell to the ground, clawing at the dirt. She shook with spasms while her mouth kept moving. She looked like a fish that had been pulled out of water. It took at least half an hour for the ambulance to arrive. July 4th is the worse day of the year for ambulance service, I've since learned. She had been dead for at least twenty-five minutes by the time the ambulance arrived. Dead in that clawing, mouth gaping pose, her clothes stained with food."

Elenora shuddered. Just when Jeff thought Elenora had described the death scene with more than sufficient gruesomeness, the woman continued.

"There was a ring of dessert residue caked around her mouth. It was a sort of pastiche of whipped cream and chopped nuts and icing and cherry goo. Quite a dramatic advertisement for Weight Watchers."

Despite herself, Elenora started to erupt in a giggle. She cupped her hands over her mouth. She tried desperately to suppress it. Holding her mouth closed simply forced the giggle out through her nose. She snorted. A bit of snot went flying. She broke loose into outright laughter.

"I understand it was the cheesecake that dealt the final blow," Jeff said, erupting himself.

"What are they laughing about?" Xander inquired.

Jason moved close to the door and listened. "I can't tell," he said. "They've been laughing for five minutes."

"Jeff likes to laugh at the silliest things," said Xander. "He has a boxed set of this British comedy group called Monty Python's Flying Circus. Have you ever heard of them?"

Jason shook his head.

"He makes me watch them. There's this one episode where this penguin doll, sitting on top of a television, explodes. This sends him into hysterics."

"Really?" L.L. Bean and now this. Jason listened to the continuing laughter downstairs as if it held a secret meaning for him.

Xander added, "I told him, 'That's not even funny. You're laughing at things that aren't even funny.' He plays that episode a couple of times a month. Every time the penguin explodes he laughs. I don't get it."

Quietly Jason observed, "My mother hasn't laughed in a very long time."

"Oh well." Xander refocused on the Chester family finances. Paper trails could be very interesting indeed, especially if one of them led in the direction of Ohio. "At least you're not broke. There's a decent amount of money in savings and investments. A hundred thousand dollar insurance policy."

"Oh, there's more than that," said Jason. "Six weeks before he died, Father took out a second life insurance policy. Mother gets a million some dollars. Each of his sons gets a one-seventh portion of two million. Mine will be held in trust for me until I come of age."

"Fuck," said Xander. "That's—"

"$285,714.28 plus interest. The insurance agent says my share shall be worth close to half a million by the time I'm twenty-one."

"Not eighteen?"

"No. It's stipulated in Father's trust arrangements. Twenty-one."

"Interesting."

———

"Marsh struck me as being a responsible man," Jeff asserted. "One who plans ahead. I trust he provided for you and the kids?"

"Better than I imagined," Elenora confirmed. "Several months before he died Marsh took out a three and a half million dollar life insurance policy."

Jeff faked surprise. "Three and a half million!"

"One and a half goes to me. The other two gets divided between the boys."

"That's a lot of money. I can't even imagine what the premiums would be like on such a policy. Why such a large policy?"

Elenora sighed. "I shouldn't really be discussing family finances with you. But I haven't had anyone to talk with about this, except my brother. You see, I knew nothing about the insurance policy."

"No?"

Elenora shook her head. "He took out this policy on his own. I would have objected. I mean, really, Jeff. We didn't make the kind of money that allowed for extravagant insurance premiums."

"It was for such a short time," Jeff said. "It's as if he knew."

Mrs. Chester looked away. She didn't answer for some time.

"I thought of that myself," she said at last. "Jeff, let me ask you a question. I would like you to answer honestly—not give me an answer you think I'd like to hear."

"I'll do my best."

"Do you think they will catch my husband's killer? This samurai man?"

"Yes, I think they will."

"What makes you think that?"

"The Pittsburgh Police have a remarkably good record when it comes to homicide."

"Yes. Yes, they do," Elenora muttered. She delicately touched Jeff's hand. There was a tenderness in this gesture that hinted at vulnerability. "You don't think this is the random act of a lunatic?"

"No. To be honest, I think it was planned. I think it was an execution."

Elenora considered Jeff's answer.

"I'll tell you what I think," she said. "Mind you, this is just what I've come up with in my head. I'm not privy to any special information held by the police."

"I understand."

"Like you, I think this was a planned killing. I think the target was Vernon Roman. I think our samurai knew that Vernon stopped from time to time at that particular restaurant. Maybe Vernon had even been set up."

"Who do you think would set him up?"

"I don't know," Elenora said in a low voice. "Maybe that girlfriend of his, that Dottie or Dorothy person. Vernon was involved in illicit criminal activity. I'm certain of it, Jeff. There was a business relationship between Vernon and this Dottie person and Penny English's boyfriend. Maybe even Penny herself was involved. Drugs. Who knows. Everything truly evil seems to be about drugs these days. I don't know enough about street crime to know what Vernon was into, but he was into something. He just had too much money."

"Yes," echoed Jeff pensively, "Too much money."

"I think Vernon crossed someone. I think his murder was a professional hit. My poor Marshall was killed because he happened to be there. It was almost like fate."

"Fate?"

"Greta Fields tried to bring my husband down but failed. Five months after her death his long ago childhood friend gets him killed. The writers of Greek tragedies would say Fate shot first with an arrow and missed, then with a sword and hit its mark."

This particular view of spousal mortality stuck Jeff as bizarre. There was something abstract about Elenora Chester, some part of her that believed in ghosts and spirits guides and Tarot cards and such concepts as Fate. He had expected her to be better grounded in reality, more of an absolutist, but he couldn't say why.

"Do you really believe in Fate?" he asked.

"Dear Jeff," she said. "Here I am a middle aged woman with no job skills. A would-be actress with no husband and seven fatherless boys. As a Christian woman I pray fervently for a reprieve from Fate. But I do believe in it. Yes, I do."

36.

"SHE WAS NOT THE WOMAN I IMAGINED," JEFF SAID IN THE CAR ON THE WAY home. "She was strong, interesting. Even a little flamboyant."

"A little!" said Xander. "She's a phony."

"No, not a phony. An actress. That's what surprised me the most. After seven kids and God knows how many years living in suburbia she still possessed that quality I remember the Dramats having at CMU. A childlike sense of self-possession. 'I'm gifted, I'm rare. Watch while I amaze you.' In her mind the interview was really about her. I kept bringing the subject back to her husband. She kept taking it back to herself. In her mind she never left school. She imagines Holly Hunter reading about her in the alumnae magazine. I imagined her in parts like Isadora Duncan, Amelia Earhart, George Sand. Not housewife, not mother. I see her as an independent woman of will."

"What about Lady Macbeth?"

Jeff laughed, "No, not Lady Macbeth. I believe she is an innocent in all this. I do."

"She's an actress. Perhaps you're the innocent," Xander said.

"Of course, she might have fooled me. It's possible. But I don't think so." Jeff considered the acting angle, however, as he maneuvered streets heavy with snow. "The house, too, was a little ordinary. Like a Ford station wagon. One really nice room set aside for entertaining. The other rooms furnished plainly for the wear and tear of seven children."

"What's strange about that?" asked Xander. "Most of the houses in our plan look exactly like that."

"She comes from money," answered Jeff. "That's what's strange about it. Not millions, but hundreds of thousands. I get the impression she and her brother take money for granted. A necessity of life that's always there, like water in a faucet."

"Then where is all the money? I learned from Jason that his father controlled the family finances. They lived strictly on the money he earned."

"How much did you find out about their money?" Jeff asked.

"Plenty. They have Quicken on the same computer as Jason's games. I didn't even have to use a password to get in."

Jeff glanced over at Xander, who appeared to be taking his role in all this rather casually. 'Sometimes I underestimate this kid,' Jeff thought.

"I take it you surfed through their records. Did you find anything?"

"The bank records have been manipulated," Xander asserted. "He transferred $20,000 over time from a savings account into checking. He did it in $5,000 increments."

"How much time?"

"A couple of months. Then it looks like he siphoned it off a couple thousand at a time. Like, he would write a tuition check for $2,500 but remove a thousand more than that from the ledger. With five kids in college he wrote a lot of tuition checks. There were also a lot of checks for food and clothes and things like that. Lots of money coming and going. He had many opportunities to fudge the books. You wouldn't notice it unless you were looking for it. There were no gaps in the check sequence, so I don't know how he got the money out of the bank. I mean, he would have written two checks, right? The larger one he recorded and the smaller one he wrote for the kids."

"He probably used a counter check," Jeff said. "You don't have to use the checks the bank prints for you. Any piece of paper that uses a check format works for the bank. In fact, Quicken will print checks for you right there on the computer."

"I didn't know that," said Xander. "Wow."

"Don't get any ideas about tapping into your mother's checking account."

"You don't have to worry about that," said Xander. "There's nothing to tap. We're always just a paycheck away from bankruptcy. That's not just a joke my mother makes. I've seen our accounts."

Jeff touched Xander lightly on the arm.

"I don't want you to worry about that. Your family will never go bankrupt while I'm around. And don't worry about college either. I've got that covered. Don't tell your mother I said that. She's very proud. Just like my mother was. But reality is reality."

Xander nodded, unable for the moment to comment. How he hated his father for leaving.

"So," continued Jeff. "Does it look like Chester siphoned off the whole twenty thousand?"

"Close to it. I couldn't add it all up with Jason there. I'll tell you something, though. That Jason could have added it all up in his head on the spot."

"Why do you say that?"

"He knows all about the insurance money. He has calculated down to the penny how rich he is going to be when he turns twenty-one."

Jeff laughed. "Wouldn't it be ironic if Jason turned out to be our murderer. He's the only one still living who claims to have hated Marshall Chester. If our organized crime theory thins out on us, Jason is the only one left with a motive."

"He's too short to be the samurai," Xander said flatly.

"I'm being facetious. Wait a minute—maybe he did it on stilts."

"He's not the athletic type."

"I'm getting punchy," said Jeff.

———

Later that night, Jeff dialed the Ohio exchange listed on Larry Cone's phone bill.

A woman answered.

"To whom am I speaking?" Jeff asked.

"This is Mrs. Hornish. Hector, is that you?"

"No." Jeff hesitated. Here goes. "I am a friend of Vernon Roman's." He cleared his throat.

"You'll have to speak up," the woman spoke loudly into the phone. "I'm having trouble hearing you."

Jeff heard a man in the background yell, "Turn up your hearing aid, Mother. You have your hearing aid turned down."

"Oh. Damn blasted thing." She apparently adjusted her hearing aid. She bellowed into the phone. "Who are you?"

"I'm a friend of Vernon Roman's. I was wondering if I could speak with Mr. Hornish."

She cupped her hand over the phone. Jeff heard muffled voices, back and forth, back and forth. A man came on the phone.

"This is Mr. Hornish," came a gruff voice. "You say you're a friend of Vernon's?"

"Yes," answered Jeff. An insecurity registered in his voice. He was too close now, he realized. Too close. Even so. "A couple of months before he died he gave me your number."

"Oh did he? And why did he do that?"

"I've been having trouble at work," Jeff said with a practiced reticence. "He said you might be able to—advise me." Jeff waited. Mr. Hornish waited along with him. "We talked, Vernon and I. He was very frank with me. I couldn't make up my mind, you see...whether or not to call. I kept hoping things would get better. At work, I mean."

"And did they, son?"

"Things have gotten worse."

There was another long pause in which it seemed to Jeff that Hornish was waiting for something.

"What's your name, son?" Hornish asked.

"Jeff," he said meekly.

"Tell me something, Jeff. Do you work hard?"

"Very hard. Long hours. Sometimes sixty to seventy hours a week. I almost always work on Saturday. Not that I'm complaining. I'm not a complainer or a whiner. My work is exemplary. That's the truth, sir."

"Be honest with me here," said Mr. Hornish. "Do you drink, son? Do you do drugs?"

"No, sir."

"Too many sick days? The truth now."

"I haven't taken a sick day in over two years."

"Are you married or single, son?"

"I'm a widower," Jeff answered. "I have an eleven-year-old boy."

"An eleven-year-old boy," remarked Mr. Hornish. "Isn't that nice. I don't want you to take these questions the wrong way, son, but I've got to ask them."

"I understand."

"Was there anything suspicious about your wife's death?"

"Absolutely not. She died of a brain hemorrhage." 'God will strike me dead for these lies,' Jeff thought wincing.

"You know," said Mr. Hornish, "people are cold these days, Jeff. People don't value the quality of life anymore. There are religious extremists in this country making it their business to get people fired. Divorced people, blacks, Jews, Muslims, homosexuals—even Christians who don't hold to the same extreme view they hold. You can't always recognize these people, Jeff. They lie about who they are and what they are up to. Any reason why one of these people would target you?"

"No, sir. I'm a white, middle class, heterosexual Christian male."

"Mind you," said Hornish, "I'm not talking about my own standards here. I'm discussing what goes on these days in the workplace. You know first hand the almost random cruelty that exists, don't you son?"

"Yes, I do. I...I..." Jeff stopped as if gathering enough air to speak. "I didn't know what to do after Vernon died. I didn't know if it was all right to call."

"Now don't you worry about that," came the voice from the other end. "Mrs. Hornish and myself, we like to help people."

"That's what Vernon told me."

"There's just one thing I need from you, son." Mr. Hornish waited. When Jeff didn't respond, Hornish prompted, "What did Vernon tell you to say?"

Jeff kept quiet for a minute, hoping something logical would come to mind. A clue—something. Nothing came. "It's been a while since I saw Vernon."

"What did he tell you to call me, son? What is my name?"

Well, it was worth a shot. "St. Patrick? He mentioned something about St. Patrick in regard to you. To tell you the truth, I didn't really understand."

That must have been the magic key. Jeff felt Hornish relax on the other end of the phone.

"I'm going to give you directions to my home," Hornish said. The directions led not to Cleveland, interestingly enough, but to a lakeside summer spot in Ohio called Rock Creek. "And bring that son of yours. Mrs. Hornish loves children. She can ply him with fresh rhubarb pie while you and I talk a little business."

37.

The next day the North Allegheny School District cancelled classes due to snow. Xander showed up bright and early on Jeff's doorstep.

"You're not coming with me to Ohio," Jeff asserted. "And that's that."

"You're not leaving me here. Get a grip." Jeff turned away, fiddled with the laces on his snow boots. Xander tried a different approach. "Besides, if these people are dangerous, you're better off if I'm there. They won't kill an innocent child."

"You keep hedging that bet," Jeff said.

"It will be an educational experience for me. I've never been to Ohio. I need to see what all this beautiful snow looks like in a land that's perfectly flat."

"God," Jeff grimaced. "You're pathetic."

"Please!"

Due to slow snow driving on the highways, the trip to Rock Creek took over four hours instead of two and a half.

The resort of beautiful stone summer homes looked isolated, abandoned. Jeff's Subaru cut the first tire marks since the snowfall. No footprints anywhere, not even animal tracks. A large prehistoric bird of some kind —maybe a heron—flew out across the lake.

"I think we're the only ones here," said Xander.

"No shit. Do you see smoke coming out of any of the chimneys?"

"No. Wait—I see some smoke," said Xander. "It's in further, past this block of homes."

Jeff drove on. They looked for house numbers, signs of life, anything that might help them locate the Hornish residence. There seemed to be hundreds of homes, most without address plates. Xander wondered how the mailman managed to deliver the mail.

"Can you still see the smoke?" Jeff asked.

"Yeah. We're getting closer. This place is like a ghost town. Doesn't anybody live here?"

"It's a summer retreat," said Jeff. "These are second homes. Some might be timeshares. You wouldn't expect to see many people here during the winter, but I thought there might be a few people who come here for Christmas. And there are always a few people who live here year round."

"What prevents their houses from being robbed?" Xander asked.

"I imagine the police drive by now and then. At least I hope they do." Jeff looked over at Xander. "We could go back if you're scared. It's not too late."

"No way, forget it. I want to meet this St. Patrick guy."

They encountered a snow drift that even the four wheel drive couldn't maneuver around. They decided to get out and walk to the house with the smoke. The late morning sun, though not warm, reflected off of the seemingly endless flat plain of snow. Xander thought it was like being in the desert.

A somewhat amiable, egg shaped man emerged from the cottage with the smoking chimney. He wore jeans, a thick flannel shirt, boots and suspenders. No coat or hat. He waved a friendly greeting toward them.

"This must be him," Jeff said under his breath. "What's our story?"

"Mother died two years ago of a brain tumor. You work for Digital in Forest Hills. I go to school in the South Hills with Marshall Chester's son Jason, the same school system where Chester taught."

"The name of the school?"

"St. Clair Middle Academy."

"What's your last name?"

"Redwing, not Pooka."

"That's right. But if they don't ask, don't offer. The less we say the less likely we are to trip over our lies."

"Stories," Xander corrected. "We are agents of justice. We don't tell lies, we fabricate stories. These stories act as spider webs to trap perps and conspirators."

Jeff moaned. 'I'm in way too deep,' he thought, as they were approaching the egg shaped man. Way too deep.

Mr. Hornish spread out his arms in a giant welcome, as if Jeff and Xander were family come for Thanksgiving dinner. Jeff fell into a hearty handshake that evolved into a hug. Xander fell into the big man's belly.

"We've been looking forward to your visit," said Mr. Hornish.

"Oh?" Jeff tried to conceal his sense of alarm. "Who is we?"

"Mother and me. And there's Cleo and her brood."

As if on cue a tiny puppy appeared from behind Mr. Hornish. It was a baby basset hound so light he walked on top of the snow without falling in.

"You little devil you," Mr. Hornish laughed at the puppy, scooping him up with his big, paw-like hand. "This here is Topper, one of Cleo's five pups. The other four stay close to their mother. This one's got wanderlust. He's always running off getting into trouble." To Xander he said, "What's your name son?"

"Xander, sir," he replied.

"Polite. That's nice. Always like to see manners in our young ones. Hope you all built up an appetite on your long trip here in the snow. Mother's been cooking all morning."

"She didn't have to go to all that trouble," Jeff protested.

"Nonsense. Don't you fret about it. Mrs. Hornish likes to spoil our guests. It gives her pleasure."

They followed Mr. Hornish and Topper into the stone cottage. The side door entered directly into the kitchen. It was very warm inside. Oven warm. A large, plump woman in a simple print dress set a casserole of scalloped potatoes onto a handcrafted maple table. The potatoes nestled comfortably beside a beautiful baked ham. Steam rose off of the ham, drifting toward the ceiling. Green beans, a basket of biscuits, hot applesauce with a swirl of cinnamon on top and a wilted German salad with hot bacon dressing rounded out the offerings. 'This is the Twilight Zone,' Jeff thought. 'I'm in a Norman Rockwell painting come to life.'

"Mother, this is Jeff Redwing and his boy, Xander."

"Two fine looking men," Mrs. Hornish declared. "And not a moment too soon. We were just about to start without you." She pulled a ceramic pot of baked beans out of the oven and placed them on a rattan trivet. "We've got baked carrots coming and chickens."

"Chickens too?" exclaimed Xander.

"Not everyone likes ham," Mrs. Hornish noted.

"We don't go hungry in this house, do we Mother?" Mr. Hornish presented the puppy for Mrs. Hornish's examination. "Snuck out behind me. We'll have to keep an eye on this one or he'll end up in the stew."

"This is so much food," said Jeff. "I hope you didn't go to all this trouble just for us."

Mrs. Hornish set the carrots on the table. "What we don't eat you can take home," she said. "Father told me you don't have a woman at home cooking for you any longer. I baked an extra cherry pie. You can take that with you, too."

"Really, that's too much," said Jeff.

"Pish posh," said Mr. Hornish. "Mother's packing a whole box of goodies for you to haul on home. Strawberry preserves, apple butter, peaches, hot sauce, mince meat. No one leaves here empty handed, especially two men on the loose."

Mr. Hornish winked.

Twilight Zone for sure. Nice to know they planned to let him go home again. Jeff wondered if he had gotten the wrong idea about St. Patrick. For his part, Xander, at first seduced by so much glorious food, was young enough to remember the story of Hansel and Gretel. He made a mental note to keep his guard up.

Mr. Hornish took Jeff by the arm. "Let me introduce you to the rest of the family."

He led Jeff and Xander into a simple but comfortable living room. In one corner, resting on a generous Doggie comforter Jeff recognized from the Bean catalogue, lay a swollen and sad looking mother basset hound. Four puppies rested up against her side, snuggling in as close as they could get.

"This is Cleo," announced Mr. Hornish. "She's just a little tired of motherhood at this point. Aren't you, baby?"

Cleo begrudged Mr. Hornish an anguished look.

"Now watch this."

Mr. Hornish set Topper down on the floor. Instead of squirming in among his siblings, Topper took the high road. He climbed up onto his mother's back, stopping when his nose came to rest just under her ear flap.

"Ain't that a hoot? Does it every time. Sleeps up there on top of his mama. That's how he got his name. He's a frisky one. Can't sit still. The others stay close to Cleo. He wanders off every chance he gets. Yesterday Mother found him in the laundry basket. Almost got himself thrown in for a rinse and spin." Mr. Hornish laughed a deep, hearty laugh that bounced off of the walls. "That dog has character. He'll make a good companion if he doesn't get himself killed."

Jeff thought for a moment he was going to be offered a puppy to go along with his goodie box. Then Mrs. Hornish called from the kitchen.

"Father. Table's ready."

———

Xander carefully trimmed all the fat from his ham. He placed the tiniest dot of butter on a biscuit, then spread it evenly so that the faintest yellow tinge glistened across the biscuit's steamy white heart. Before he could eat it, Mrs. Hornish snatched the biscuit from his hand, lathered a generous dollop of soft butter across its top, then handed it back to him. Xander stared at the thing as if she had painted it with arsenic.

"Oh, eat it for Christ's sake," Mrs. Hornish laughed. "It's delicious!"

Mr. Hornish narrated the family history. Back in the twenties his grandparents owned a large working farm just outside of Cleveland. During the Depression the farm became unprofitable. The family kept the farmhouse and ten surrounding acres but sold off the rest. Mr. and Mrs. Hornish still owned the land. They grew most of the fruits and vegetables for Mrs. Hornish's preserves on that land.

When a young man, Mr. Hornish took a job with a pharmaceutical company called Cleveland Pharmaceuticals. Being a good bullshitter at heart, Mr. Hornish took naturally to sales. Over time he secured an important managerial position with the firm.

God blessed the Hornish family with five beautiful children, three boys and two girls. When they were old enough to work, all three boys and one of the girls went to work for the pharmaceutical company. Like their father, the Hornish children took naturally to their work and rose up through the ranks to positions of authority. Johnny went into sales with his father, Margaret into publications, Frank into marketing, Leon into research. Even though the company was publicly owned, board members teased Mr. Hornish that it was really a family business. His family.

"What happened to the other girl?" Xander asked.

"She moved out of the area," said Mrs. Hornish.

"Where exactly?" Xander pursued.

Neither rushed to answer the question. After a good chew on a chicken leg, Mr. Hornish cleared his throat and replied, "Our Kaye moved to San Francisco for a couple of years. Now I believe she's up your way in Pittsburgh."

'Well,' thought Jeff. 'Doesn't that have intriguing possibilities?' He considered continuing with the subject of the second daughter when Mr. Hornish ended table chat by pushing back his chair.

"Mother, that was an excellent meal. Now, if you'll excuse us, Jeff and I have some business to discuss."

Mrs. Hornish said, "Xander, why don't you keep me company?"

"That's right," said Mr. Hornish. "Your dad and I are going to take a walk outside. When we come back we'll all sit down and have some of Mother's wonderful cherry pie."

———

"It's beautiful here," Jeff said, watching his breath crystallize in front of his face.

"It's especially nice in the winter," said Mr. Hornish. "I don't know why more people don't come up at this time of the year. The air is so pure. You can sense the presence of God."

'Yes, sir,' Jeff thought. Out loud he asked, "These are summer homes?"

"Mostly southerners. We go down there to escape the cold, they come up here to escape the heat. Mrs. Hornish and I were one of the first to move into this plan. It was just a nice, isolated spot then. Didn't know it was going to turn into a lakeside resort. Mrs. Hornish and I built here to get away from people."

"That's too bad."

"Well, we're alone now." Hornish cast a wry grin in Jeff's direction. "Only Horace Easterbrook lives here during the winter. He's gone to his daughter's place for the Christmas season."

They stopped at the edge of the lake. Jeff admired its frigid, pristine beauty. Docked in front of them was a six-seater pontoon, covered with snow. Next to the pontoon Jeff noticed a small wooden row boat, it's top protected with a canvas cover. Mr. Hornish stepped into the water and unfastened the canvas.

"Those boots waterproof son?"

"Gore-Tex. Why?"

"You're going to have to step into the water to get into the boat."

"Sir? We're going out onto the lake?"

Mr. Hornish moved the oars aside, stepping in. He smiled back at Jeff.

"But why?" Jeff asked incredulously.

"Best place to talk," answered Mr. Hornish. "If we take the pontoon, the motor might die on us in the middle of the lake. Then we'd be in a pickle. You'll have to take the oars, son. I'm not as fit as I used to be."

Reluctantly, Jeff stepped into the cold water and then into the boat. With thickly gloved hands he took up the oars, tried to get the feel of the handles.

"Isn't it a little cold for an outing on the lake?"

"Nonsense," replied Mr. Hornish. "It snows in Ohio in the winter. Can't stop living just because of the snow."

Jeff thought for a moment about the places in the world where people do, in fact, stop for the snow. There are places in Alaska where leaving your house in a snowstorm means certain death.

"How big is this lake?"

"Not big. We're in one of the creek branches now."

"You're kidding. I thought this was it."

"This? This is nothing. But you'll see. It's not the size of Lake Erie. From the center you'll get a full panoramic view of the plan. It will take your breath away, I promise."

Jeff's Gore-Tex boots kept the water off of his feet. Unfortunately, they weren't high boots. Water seeped into the cloth of his pants leg. The water from his pants leaked down to his feet. 'This is not good, he thought as the oars hit the water. I should be toasty warm right now. I should be solving

MENSA puzzles instead of murder mysteries. It's this child, Xander. He manipulates me into positions like this. I have unwittingly become the pawn of a child I am meant to guide and protect.'

"Are you retired?" Jeff asked—anything to occupy his mind. The man murdered people for a living, so really it was a stupid question.

Without missing a beat, Mr. Hornish replied: "I have a small custom milling business. Newel posts, staircase spindles. Carpenter Gothic restorations. I don't need the money at this point in life. It just keeps me busy." He pointed over Jeff's shoulder. "Head out to the right, son."

With considerable effort Jeff rowed out from the creek branch into the lake. As they progressed further through the water, Jeff got an idea of the vast size of the plan. Hundreds and hundreds of expensive, attractive looking homes. Many creek branches lined with even more homes. It distressed him to see so many homes and yet not a single waft of smoke from a fireplace. He longed for witnesses, just one face looking out of a window, just one person to wonder what the hell these two crazy people were doing rowing out into the middle of the lake in the aftermath of a snowstorm.

"I haven't rowed in a long time," Jeff said through strained breaths. "I work out regularly, but rowing..."

"I know," said Mr. Hornish. "It requires special conditioning. Looks simple, but halfway through you wish you hadn't started."

Jeff laughed uneasily. "Then why are we doing this?"

"Privacy." Mr. Hornish let the word settle on the cold crystal water. "I have a story to tell you once we reach the middle of the lake. It's not a story I want overheard. People can listen from behind bushes and house corners and snowdrifts, but they can't hide out in the middle of the water." Hornish looked wonderingly at Jeff. "Young man, are you afraid of me?"

"I'm just uncertain. I am a little afraid, yes."

"If you're afraid of me, Jeff, then you misunderstand the nature of the service I offer. When I look at you and your boy—" Hornish took in the vista of the empty houses as if drawing inspiration from their beauty. "I feel confirmed in my convictions. I doubt myself at times, of course I do. But when I look upon a good Christian man like yourself so clearly in need of help, then I know that God walks with me. God guides me. He leads me by the hand."

Hornish stopped and closed his eyes. It seemed that God was speaking to him at that very moment. "There is an evil in this country, Jeff. A profound and destructive evil. It is something new. When I was a young man this evil did not exist. This evil has a target, Jeff. Do you know what this target is?"

Jeff shook his head.

"The target is you, Jeff. You and your little boy.

"You've felt it yourself, haven't you Jeff?"

Jeff didn't answer. He rowed, methodically, looking away into the water as if powerfully affected by Mr. Hornish's speech.

"People who work hard. People who give freely of such qualities as loyalty and commitment. People who aren't ashamed to apply the Golden Rule throughout life when it comes to dealings with their fellow workers, their supervisors, their clients."

Hornish paused the pause of a professional orator.

"You've felt it yourself, haven't you Jeff?" Hornish repeated. "You are the same honorable, loyal person you have always been. You work hard, put in long hours. You give all that is asked of you and more. Better yet, you are a likeable man. Your fellow workers respect you and enjoy working alongside you. I'd bet they are even personally fond of you. And yet, in the workplace, you find yourself under attack."

"Yes," Jeff said quietly in a tone that conveyed disillusionment.

"There seems to be no reason for it. Someone new has come into your work environment."

"Yes."

"This person has launched a series of unreasonable attacks upon your work. He has even ventured some sly attacks upon your personal character."

Jeff perked up, as if startled by the clairvoyance of his boat partner.

"Yes," he confirmed.

"You find you have no recourse to these attacks. This new person, this snake, has hissed his venomous words into the ears of your supervisors and select peers. Remarkable as this seems to you, some people are enchanted with this snake. Almost as if he has cast a spell, your coworkers have forgotten years and years of personal experience working alongside you. They're tempted to believe the snake."

"That's right," Jeff said numbly.

"Over the course of—what has it been, six months? a year?—you find yourself on the verge of losing not only your job but your reputation as well. You are poised to lose not just your current but any future earning power. You can see on the horizon the end of your career, everything you have worked for. A lifetime of planning and accomplishment. Gone. Dissolved to nothing under the fire of the acid from the snake's tongue."

Jeff nodded slowly, unable to speak, a little sick to his stomach.

"And you're not the only one, are you Jeff?"

"No," Jeff answered. "He has targeted others."

"Good people, just like yourself. Loyal. Committed to their work. Devoted to their company."

"Yes," said Jeff. "That's what makes it so mystifying." Jeff looked up into the direct and powerful gaze of Mr. Hornish. "If this snake, as you call him, if this snake succeeds, the company will be adversely affected. It doesn't make sense."

"It makes perfect sense," replied Mr. Hornish knowingly. "The snake has a plan, an agenda. Very personal. Often selfish and wicked. The snake finds a vulnerable operation, one that has not had to protect itself from snakes in the past. The snake looks over the field. The mediocrities, the lazy people, the weak, the incompetent, and certainly the bad—these people he can manipulate.

"Good people, however, are not so easily corrupted. People with vision, purpose, a built-in commitment to doing the right thing, these people will see through the machinations of the snake. These people will always be a barrier. These people can be counted on to object to the snake's ideas, to point out the snake's illogical ideas. Upon entering a new environment the snake does what it must do. He seeks out and targets his natural enemies."

"Jesus."

"Yes," declared Hornish. "It is an infestation. The American workplace has become slowly, gradually infested with snakes. Not committed to the goals of the firm, the business, the organization, but committed to something else, something private. Financial gain, the amassing of personal power and reputation, glorification of the ego. For some it is the joy of expressing their evil, their madness. They wish to advocate and promote a personal pathology."

"But haven't there always been people like that?" asked Jeff. He listened to the slapping of the water against the side of the boat. He was beginning to shiver from the cold.

"When I was a young man, Jeff, I certainly encountered ambitious people who sometimes disregarded personal feelings to get ahead. What's happening today is different. Today we have a segment of the population that operates without regard to moral values. They haven't the slightest concern for the consequences of their actions. There is no right or wrong for them. No sense of fair play or justice. Their personal wants and goals are the holy shrine at which they worship

"What is best for the nation, what is best for the economy, what is best for their own personal business—none of this matters. History itself doesn't matter to them. They will willingly and knowingly run any organization into bankruptcy for person gain. They don't consider for a moment what is best for their company or the people who work for their company. They strategically destroy careers, ruin reputations, drive people to suicide, even commit murder to accomplish their goals.

"It is something new, Jeff," Hornish summed up. "It is an infestation of snakes." Mr. Hornish let his words roll across the water. "And I have been sent to banish the snakes."

———

Mrs. Hornish handed Xander a giant-sized wicker basket. It was a Red Riding Hood basket with a pair of hinged wooden lids across the top. Xander followed Mrs. Hornish to a doorway that led to the basement.

Due to her enormous girth, Mrs. Hornish took the steps sideways, slowly, one step at a time. At the bottom of the steps she pulled a string light. A bare bulb cast a bright but harsh glow. Xander blinked like a high speed camera shutter, making adjustments.

The basement was divided into three sections, each separated by a doorway. The far left room held stacked split wood for the fireplace. The center room just off of the steps contained several walls of floor to ceiling maple cabinets. Each cabinet sported a pair of doors that opened from the center. A little half moon had been cut into the top of each door for decoration. The room to the right, located under the kitchen and just barely glimpsed from where they stood, appeared to contain laundry equipment and more floor-to-ceiling cabinets.

"We have a set of cabinets just like these at the farm," said Mrs. Hornish, admiration in her voice. "Jacob's father built those. Jacob built these here for me from the same design. I like to put things up, you see."

"Put things up?" Xander was unfamiliar with the phrase.

"Preserves, jellies, pickled vegetables, butters of various kinds. Didn't your mother put things up, dear? I suppose not. People buy what they need at the supermarket these days, don't they. But it doesn't taste as good. And you can't buy pickled watermelon rinds at the supermarket."

Mrs. Hornish undid one of the simple metal clasps on one of the cabinets. The doors fell open revealing what was to Xander a magical assortment of gleaming bottles and jars set back row after row after row.

"We have some catsup here," said Mrs. Hornish as she grabbed one of the bottles. "There's nothing too special about homemade catsup but you might as well have a bottle. This is how H.J. Heinz started, you know. He didn't start with catsup. He started with bottled horseradish. But it's the same thing."

She opened Red Riding Hood's basket lids.

"Keep them open, dear."

"You made all these?" Xander asked, astonished.

"Oh, yes. And there's much more, as you'll soon see. Each one of these cabinets is filled to capacity with pickles and preserves."

"Even the cabinets in the next room?"

"Yes, sir, even those. Filled to capacity."

Mrs. Hornish softly shuffled from cabinet to cabinet, gently undoing each clasp. Hundreds of neatly arranged jars, free from dust, radiated like crystal from the shelves. Once all of the doors fell open, Mrs. Hornish stood back and, clutching her breasts, admired the wonder of her own creation.

"Wow," said Xander. "You put all these up?"

"Yes, I did."

"My mother put Stouffers boxes up into the freezer. That's about it." Xander used his own mother as the model for the mythological Mrs. Redwing. "She had a career. When she was alive."

"Oh, dear, I see." Mrs. Hornish said a silent prayer for all the poor unfortunate children of career mothers. "Well, young man, you won't go home empty handed today. We'll load up this basket. Then we'll find a good, strong box and we'll load that up, too."

———

Jeff shook from even the faint breeze that drifted across the water in the middle of the lake. His shoulder and arm muscles ached from rowing. If he and Hornish had an accident out here in the middle of the lake they would never make it back to shore. Jeff fervently hoped that the justification for all this intense discomfort, the secret story Hornish wished to convey, was not a long one.

Mr. Hornish told this story:

I was a young man when I began my career with Cleveland Pharmaceuticals. They were a small firm then, twenty or so employees. I started out in sales. Sales were mostly local. Thanks largely to my initiative, we branched out to other cities in Ohio, then into Pittsburgh, then Michigan. Eventually I opened markets in Philadelphia, Baltimore, Washington, Norfolk. Took my truck down to the Carolinas.

Sales were door to door, city to city back then. It was my shoe leather, my handshake that built that business into a world class concern. And everyone knew it. The bosses were happy to have me. They acknowledged my work with regular, substantial raises and with promotion. When the time came I brought my kids into the business. And I want you to know, my children did not slide by on my reputation. I raised them to work hard. In due time they proved their worth to the company and moved into management positions. Together we made Cleveland Pharmaceuticals an even greater success. The firm went public.

In the mid-eighties one of Mr. Reagan's cronies staged a leveraged buy out of Cleveland Pharmaceuticals. In short order a flock of MBAs descended upon us. I found myself reporting to a suit from Texas we'll call Raymond. Raymond smiled a lot, he patted me on the back, took me into his confidence. He convinced me he had the interests of the firm at heart. I welcomed him into the family. We all welcomed him into the family.

Then one day a friend of mine, who happened to be a secretary in the front office, invited me to lunch. In a very private restaurant in a dining room in the back she whispered, "Don't turn your back on Raymond."

"What do you mean?" I asked.

"He's no friend of yours, that's all. And you might want to collect your messages three times a day instead of just once. President Bennett has been busy sending memos detailing important company policy changes. These changes are based on Raymond's recommendations. A select number of people don't seem to be receiving their memos. I put them in their mailbox, but by the end of the day those memos have been collected by someone else. Only three people have access to the back of the mail slots: Bennett, Raymond and myself. To report that memos are being stolen from your mail slot you'd have to accuse one of us."

I understand everything is sent by e-mail these days, Jeff. In those days we communicated through paper. I reported a mix up in my mail and asked to see copies of the memos. There were big changes in the offing indeed. I saw that Raymond had taken credit for many of my own ideas. The wording of these memos suggested I was resisting implementation of my own suggestions.

It became clear to me over the course of the next few months that I had been targeted for termination. Well, I had always been on excellent terms with the president of the company, so I scheduled a meeting. We discussed my outstanding record. I laid my suspicions about Raymond on the table. I let him know some of the anger and frustration I was feeling over Raymond's behavior. Bennett brushed it all away with a sweep of his hands.

"Raymond is a miracle worker," he claimed. "He gives me reports, a thorough black and white analysis of every department in this firm."

"I'd like to see the reports on my department," I told him.

The president dismissed the idea as if letting a department head read reports relating to his own department was not done in the business world.

"Your work isn't all it could be, Jake," he insisted. "The figures are all there."

"Let me see the figures."

Dismissed again.

"You and I go back a long way, Jake," he told me. "I want to be fair."

"There's nothing fair about it," I said, angry now. "This suit from Texas has obviously been sent here to get rid of people. It's clear that even though my work is excellent, a case of incompetence is being fabricated against me. What's the problem? Am I paid too much money? Are you looking to get someone half my age for half the price?"

Bennett says, "Look, Jake. I'm on your side. But there's a whole new Board now. I report to the Board. Raymond also reports to the Board. It doesn't all go through me. You understand?"

I understood that Raymond had him by the balls.

Raymond continued his assault on good people in the firm. Several people jumped ship, took jobs elsewhere. One fought, threatening legal battle. I know they wanted me to just quit, take an early retirement. But the lack of integrity shown by the company, the simple lack of gratitude pissed me off. I forced them to commit a direct act of betrayal.

Raymond filed an endless barrage of reports filled with snide remarks and accusations of incompetence. Every single day I received at least one note of complaint from Bennett's desk detailing my shortcomings, my failures, my lack of sound business judgment and my refusal to implement mandated changes. I suffered through two incompetency hearings. At the conclusion of the second hearing, Cleveland Pharmaceuticals reluctantly and with deepest regret terminated my employment.

I was fifty-two years old, not really ready for retirement. I don't need to tell you the shortage of jobs at equal salary available for someone my age. It was happening all over town, Jeff. Good, hard working people being forced out of their jobs by suits like Raymond. Oh, Mrs. Hornish and I didn't have it so bad. We owned our own home, we had some money in the bank. Other people in our position weren't so lucky. Some people lost their homes. Some people got sick and couldn't afford a doctor.

This predicament saddened Mrs. Hornish and me. We wanted to do something about it. But what could we do? Then that bastard Raymond started going after my children. The same process he put me through. The set-ups, the slanted reports, the stolen communications. He created impossible goals for them and when they didn't reach those goals accused them of incompetence.

I woke up sick every morning, Jeff. Sick in my soul as well as my body. How could I let this man, this compassionless embodiment of evil, destroy the lives of my children? Mrs. Hornish and I prayed on it every day. Every day we asked to be touched with the light of the truth. Give us direction, Lord. We will be Your willing emissaries. We will charge the world with the light of Your word.

And God spoke to me, Jeff. Yes, He did. Clear as mountain water His words poured into my ears. Like a second baptism, He owned me body and soul for a new purpose. He told me exactly and in detail what I must do.

———

Drifting from cabinet to cabinet, dragging his fingers across the glass cornucopia, Xander found magic in all that food. He read some of the labels. Blueberries 1994, Cherries 1997, Baby Cucumbers 2006, Mincemeat 2007, Beets and Onions 2003, Tomato Butter 2005.

Mrs. Hornish placed jar after jar into Xander's basket.

"I'll just bet you've never tasted pickled watermelon rinds," declared Mrs. Hornish.

"No, ma'am."

"They're delicious. Wait until you try them." To herself she mumbled, "Should have had some for lunch."

"What are those large jars in the back?" Xander asked, craning his neck.

"Oh, those." Mrs. Hornish removed several rows of smaller jars and extracted one of the large ones from the back. The contents looked familiar to Xander. He had seen jars like this on display in an Italian restaurant in Pittsburgh. It featured an artistic arrangement of layered vegetables in some kind of brine. White beans on the bottom, then carrots, then black olives, then red beans, string beans, green olives, red peppers, and so on. In the odd light of the basement it took on the look of exposed strata at an archeological dig.

"Wow," he said, holding it, stroking the strange object's cool glass. It had the allure of a fetish for him. Then he remembered where he had seen jars just like this one. Empty jars.

"May I have one of these?" he asked.

Mrs. Hornish laughed. She so enjoyed giving gifts. And she liked this little boy. So bright, so aware. And it was clear the poor thing hadn't had a decent meal in years.

"You may have two," she pronounced.

———

Mr. Hornish continued with his story:

I studied Raymond. Like a detective I gleaned information about him. Like a thief I watched his house, observed his habits. Raymond liked to fish, you see. Every weekend he took his boat out on Lake Erie. Sometimes he took friends along, but mostly he fished alone. Hour upon hour of solitude, just Raymond and his line and the great open lake.

He drank expensive bourbon when he fished. He often returned to shore a little intoxicated. Sometimes I myself rented a boat and, keeping my distance, observed him out on the lake. All summer long I observed his fishing ritual.

Fall arrived. The water out on the lake turned bitter cold. Still Raymond fished. This is just how the Lord said it would be, Jeffrey. Every evil creature has one thing they do to excess. Find that one thing and you have found their most vulnerable spot. Attack them there and you will purge them of their evil.

One day early in October I followed Raymond out onto the lake.

The temperature was only forty-two degrees that day. The water was too choppy for fishing. Yet the man took his boat out on the water. Far, far out.

As far as he had ever gone. I followed from a safe distance, keeping him in view through binoculars. I watched him drink three quarters of a fifth of bourbon. The water threw his boat around, the alcohol made him swagger. Clearly this was the sign that the time had come.

I allowed my boat to drift up alongside Raymond's boat.

"I thought I recognized you," I shouted to him.

He squinted at me, not believing his eyes. He had always smiled at me, always behaved in a charming manner, even as he stuck the knife in my back. It was all just modern business practice, you know. Nothing personal. Personally he liked me, you see. He was a good Joe deep down.

He welcomed me like an old school chum.

"Jacob Hornish of all people," he said, nodding toward his liquor bottle. "It's the only way to brace yourself against the cold, old friend." Raymond eyed my much smaller boat. "Why don't you moor yourself up to the side here and come aboard?"

I did as he suggested.

For a time we talked pleasantly. I drank a shot of his brandy. This was how it had been at work. The goodwill, the enthusiastic exchange of information, followed days later by reports in which my words had been twisted against me. We drank to the bottom of his bottle. He kept a store of brandy below deck. He produced a second bottle and we drank from that as well. I sipped while he indulged.

At one point he took a deep drink, ran his tongue across his lips, and closed his eyes, savoring the effects of the golden liquor. A sudden sound broke his reverie. A sound from God. It was the sound of his reel, spinning wildly.

"Probably a fucking wall-eye," he said, taking up his line.

The fish was strong. Raymond's equipment was maybe just a little too professional, maybe just a little too heavy. Each time Raymond let out his line, the fish pulled his uncertain legs closer to the edge of the boat. The fish himself was engaged in holy battle. He pulled Raymond ever closer to the water.

A moment came when the fish pulled exceptionally hard on the line. Raymond jerked forward. I joined with the fish in God's holy battle. I gave Raymond a little push. It wasn't much. Just enough to send him somersaulting over the boat's guardrail. Raymond tightened his grip on the rod—a reflex reaction, I'm sure. The fish pulled Raymond further out into the water.

It took him a moment to realize what had happened. Once he heard the sound of his anchor cranking up into the body of his craft, I'm sure he remembered the feel of my hands on his back.

"What the hell are you doing?" he screamed.

"You are an incompetent sailor, I'm afraid," I answered. "Although it grieves me to do so, I'm filing a report against you."

"It's cold in this water!"

"Sailor consistently failed to take note of adverse weather conditions. For a considerable number of weeks now Sailor has failed to consider the adverse effects of alcohol in the bloodstream vis-à-vis hypothermia."

"You bastard!"

"I'm afraid, despite a long and distinguished record of service, I have to recommend you for termination. It's a shame, really. Just when you thought you had your life all worked out."

Raymond swam toward the boat. As if we could change the process once it had started! I was on a mission. I had goals to accomplish. I pulled a gun out of my inside coat pocket. Raymond stopped swimming toward the boat.

He laughed in a peculiar, staccato fashion. Perhaps it was the chill of the water.

"Okay, okay," he said. "You made your point. Obviously we have something to discuss. Let me come on board."

It was beautiful, really. As if on cue, the boat started drifting away from him. I tossed a life buoy far out behind him so that he would have to choose between swimming after the buoy or swimming after the boat. Taking note once again of my gun, he swam toward the buoy. At least from the buoy he could still practice the art of the deal.

"Okay, Hornish. You have my attention. What do you want? Name it. Only do it quickly, please. I'm freezing."

"I want the truth from you."

"The truth?"

"Why me? Why did you target me?"

"It was already decided," Raymond shouted up to the drifting boat. "It was my job to implement the decision."

"I worked faithfully for that company all my life. I made that company a success. I had no place to go, no way to earn a living."

"It's not my job to take personal considerations into account. Please, I'm cold. Please."

"I considered that company my second home. I considered those people my family."

The teeth of the snake chattered. It affected his speech. Through the clacking of porcelain against porcelain, he said, "Look. We wanted to bring in our own people. We have good people in Texas."

"You already had good people in Cleveland. People with many years of experience. People who worked long and hard for the company."

"Please! For Christ's sake, Hornish. Please!"

He had not answered me truthfully. I knew that. I screamed this time, at the top of my lungs, "Why did you target me? The truth, now. The truth! Or I'll shoot you dead in the water."

"You want the truth?" he screamed back, teeth gnashing. "Because they hate you family bastards, that's why. It's a job, not a home. It's your employer, not your father. The people you work with are business associates, not brothers and sisters. To make a business profitable all you family bastards have to go."

Raymond waited, but not too long.

"There. I told you the truth. Help me, please. For the love of God. I don't want to die."

I posited a thought.

"It's just my nature, you see," I explained. "It's my nature to create family wherever I go. I make a point of introducing myself to my neighbors, my grocer, my banker, my coworkers. I take a personal interest in them. Their well being becomes tied up with my own. In time they become a part of my extended family. This way everywhere I go I see family. Every transaction I make is with a family member. I find that life is so much more satisfying when I am surrounded by family."

The evil one's limbs must have crackled like tinder in an icy fire. He drifted into numbness.

"I...I have to come out now," he stuttered.

"First I require a confession," I said. "You must confess to me before God that you are an evil, back-stabbing shit. I want you to say it in just those words. Evil, back-stabbing shit."

As best he could, in a low sibilant voice, he muttered, "I am an evil —back-stabbing—shit."

"Um," I said, disappointed. "You mouth the words, but I detect insincerity. For a confession to work, it must come from the heart. It's not too late for you. To repent."

"You mother fucker."

"I see your dilemma," I assured him. "How can you speak clearly from your heart when you have no heart. No human heart."

"Murderer!" he hissed.

"Come now. Give it another try. Evil."

"Hornish."

"Back-stabbing," I prompted.

"Please..."

"Shit."

The boat drifted further away. The evil one shook. He turned crimson, then purple, then blue. His eyes took on a doll's gaze.

"Murderer," his last word.

I waited an hour or so. I let Raymond's boat, empty brandy bottles wedged securely, drift to be found by the Coast Guard. I took my own boat back to shore.

God's will be done.

———

"Are you cold, son?"

Jeff glanced slowly around at the still, icy waters of the lake. The man had a way of making a point.

"Just a little."

"We'll go back soon," Hornish assured, apparently not touched by the cold. "They call me St. Patrick. Do you know why?"

Jeff shook his head.

"St. Patrick rid Ireland of all her snakes. There is not a single snake in Ireland. Did you know that?"

"No, I didn't."

"I'm ridding America of her snakes."

Part of Jeff wanted to laugh. "It's a big job."

Hornish smiled. "I don't have to do it alone." He indicated the oars. "Why don't you head us on back?"

'So he's not going to kill me out here,' Jeff thought. He gratefully took up the oars. The physical motion of rowing warmed him up somewhat. His heart raced, partly from the exercise, partly from fear.

"So you have a snake in your lair," said Mr. Hornish.

"Yes. What you said. What happened to you—"

"No need to say it, son. It's the same everywhere. Fortunately, you've come to me in time. Your situation is correctable."

They talked about many things on the row back. Names. Times. Places. Price. Method of payment. Once on shore, Hornish gave Jeff a fatherly bear hug. Jeff could smell the flesh of the man, the smell of fireplace smoke in his hair.

Almost in a whisper, Hornish said in Jeff's ear, "Don't you give a thought to his immortal soul. God will attend to that. You and I, we will concern ourselves with this earthly life."

———

Mrs. Hornish helped Xander load two large boxes and the picnic basket full of bottled preserves into the back of the Subaru. Xander insisted on carrying the picnic basket himself, though it was a little heavy for him. The lid of one side of the basket popped up as Xander walked, showing just a hint of black fur each time.

Mr. Hornish inspected the basket. His wife had packed the jars and bottles carefully with handmade tea towels and pot holders—little extras for her guests. Topper languished among the folds of the towels as if awaiting his close up.

"You rascal you. I swear I have to watch you every minute." Mr. Hornish lifted the almost escapee out of the basket. Holding the pup eye level in the palm of his hand, Hornish teased, "You must be trying to get yourself adopted."

Jeff said quickly, "I'm afraid they don't allow pets in my plan."

"Oh," Mr. Hornish laughed, "you wouldn't get this one anyway. You can have your pick of the others. This little guy is special. He's keeping me company in my old age. Ain't you there, Topper?" He gave the puppy a silly kiss.

'Only if they allow pets on death row,' Jeff thought.

"Call me soon, now," said Hornish after they got into the wagon. "And bring your boy any time. We like visitors, don't we Mother?"

Mr. and Mrs. Hornish stood side by side in front of their cottage, smoke trailing out of the chimney top, baby basset in tow. They smiled and waved as the Subaru bid a rapid departure.

"Jesus Christ," said Jeff, looking back at them in the rear view mirror. "That guy's a scary bastard."

"What did you find out?"

"He told me everything. Confessed to it all out on the lake."

"He confessed to killing Roman and Chester?" Xander asked, astonished.

"No. He confessed to killing over three hundred middle management executives and consultants up and down the eastern seaboard. Killed the first batch himself, then hired a network of people to kill the others. It costs thirty-thousand dollars to get rid of your boss. It's just as I thought. Roman was one of the henchmen, Chester was a customer. Chester hired our Norman Rockwell dad back there to kill Greta Fields."

Jeff continued, "First Hornish told me this long story about how he killed the first poor sucker, some guy from Cleveland Pharmaceuticals named Raymond. Raymond got Hornish fired after years of loyal service, then started in on the rest of the Hornish clan. He killed Raymond in Lake Erie."

"He told you that?"

"Yes. Told me this in the middle of icy cold Rock Creek Lake, I might add. It was a point well taken."

"Why would he tell you things that could incriminate him?"

"It's my word against his," said Jeff. "If I go to the police and they contact him, he gets me killed. If I say nothing, I become a co-conspirator, part of the family. He wanted me to know all about it. He encouraged me to ask as many questions as possible. That's how I found out Chester paid him to kill Fields. I asked him, he told me."

Xander shivered. "Did you ask him if he killed Roman and Chester?"

"I put it another way. I asked him if he knew who killed them. He confessed something went wrong with Roman and Chester, but he wouldn't say what. He told me to let him worry about that."

"So he wouldn't tell you."

"No."

They drove in silence for a number of miles, each deep in his own thoughts. Jeff interrupted the silence. "You told me Chester siphoned off twenty thousand dollars from his bank account."

"About that. I was adding it in my head."

"Hornish charges thirty thousand for his services. Where's the other ten?"

"You think maybe Roman kept it?"

"Maybe. Maybe Chester didn't pay it. Maybe they conspired together to cheat Hornish out of a third of his money."

"Or," said Xander, "maybe Cone did something with it and blamed Roman. Maybe they had a falling out and Cone set Roman up."

Jeff added, "Hornish told me he had to have all the money up front. No revolving charge for murder. I bet he let Chester slide on a payment plan. All those kids. That would have touched a soft spot with Hornish."

"Sounds logical."

"Um." Jeff made a side comment, "I'm not going to be able to see you for a couple of days."

"No way. Forget about it. Why?"

"I don't want an argument this time. It's for your own safety. I'm going to be in the hot seat for a while. See, I kind of made a verbal agreement to have somebody killed."

Xander sat upright. "Not me!"

"Of course not, you idiot. I'm having Archie Hammer killed."

"Who's Archie Hammer?"

"Some guy I hated in high school. It's the only name I could create off of the top of my head. Hope to hell he doesn't work for Digital these days. The point is this: Hornish has investigators. He's bound to investigate me. If he finds out who I really am before I can turn him over to the police, my hairy assed is fried."

"What do you mean fried?"

"Dead, my friend. Dead. This man takes no prisoners. He's killed several hundred people by his own admission. I'm sure he killed Roman and Chester. I know it in my bones. He won't hesitate to kill me."

Xander wrung his hands. It had always been a game, a puzzle, up until now. It hadn't occurred to him that the stakes could get real.

"Mrs. Hornish wouldn't let him kill you. She's a nice lady. She can't be in on it. She—"

"She's about as innocent as Lady Macbeth." Jeff said slyly. "She's pleasant, not stupid. Consider the low-life characters her husband brings home for business meetings. Consider Cone and Roman. That Franklin Baum guy. Those aren't the kind of people she was used to in their old life. Even if he tried to keep it from her, she'd figure it out. It's a family thing. Family is very big with Hornish."

"I just can't believe that she knows."

"These people are dangerous, Xander. Trust me on this. The Hornish's are on a holy mission. They consider themselves to be doing God's work." Xander shook his head. "That's right. That's how he justifies it. He calls himself St. Patrick because the real St. Patrick chased all the snakes out of Ireland. Hornish considers himself to be on a holy mission to rid American business of her snakes."

"But how can you turn him over to the police? You just said it's your word against his."

"I just have to get hard physical evidence that links him to the Roman/Chester murders. The way I see it, I've got a couple of days before he can verify my story. Even if the Digital offices are normally open on weekends, they won't be open this weekend because of the snow. It's tight, but I have some time to come up with irrefutable physical evidence."

"Well, not much time. What happens if you can't find any physical evidence?"

Jeff looked solemnly into the eyes of his young friend. "Then it's a countdown to death, my friend." He held Xander's terrified gaze. Jeff shrugged. "Well, there's nothing else to do. I'll get the evidence.

38.

Jeff dropped Xander off at home around 9:30 p.m.

"We called from the road," he explained to Sally. "But you weren't in. We left a message on the machine."

"Newspapers don't stop publishing because of snowstorms," announced Mrs. Pooka. She was tired and snippy. Too much tedious work for too little recompense. "I'm not sure I appreciate you hauling him all the way to Ohio in weather like this."

"He insisted on coming," Jeff justified. "You know how he is. He would have stowed away in the trunk if I hadn't taken him voluntarily."

Jeff graciously donated all the preserves to the Pooka larder. Sally smelled the ham through the aluminum foil. "Real ham," she said, juices gushing in her mouth. "Oh my God, and biscuits."

"And pie," said Xander. "A real one made with real dough and real cherries."

"Do they still eat like this in Ohio?" Mrs. Pooka asked.

"This is an old fashioned couple," answered Jeff. Without even realizing he had done it, he kissed Sally good-bye on the cheek. "Bon appetite."

Hands in his pocket, Jeff slinked away in the snow.

Sally watched him go, mystified. She couldn't remember if he had ever touched her before. She couldn't remember even so much as a hand on her shoulder. She fought the impulse to wipe the kiss away. Instead she concentrated on the sensation of his surprisingly sloppy wetness.

Just as he reached his car, he turned back to say, "I've got a lot of work to do in the next few days. Mind if I give your son back to you for the weekend?"

"It will give us a chance to get reacquainted." 'Shit,' she thought, 'I didn't mean for it to sound like that. Sounded a little sarcastic. Did he notice?'

"We'll keep close to the home fires. Maybe I'll make my way through a box of these preserves." 'Why did I say that? He'll think I'm a cow. I'd like to trade minds with some smarter, better woman for just one day. Lauren Hutton. What a vacation that would be. Rich fashion model, beautiful all her life, who goes off on exotic adventures around the world between shoots. Must be nice to think her thoughts. My life sucks.'

Jeff waved. Sally waved back. Sally thought, 'You cannot fall in love with this man. He's gay. And you've suffered enough.'

Jeff popped in the car and drove off.

————

Jeff reluctantly dragged himself up to the Cloisters. These days it was essential to check his messages. Good thing, too. There was an urgent message from Dottie Hatfield. She sounded breathless and hurried.

"This is Dottie, hon. Look, I'm in trouble. They tore up my place. Rose and I were out shopping and when we came back I found all my furniture destroyed, all my clothes ripped to shreds. Vernon must have done something really bad to piss these people off. I think they're after that little black book I gave you. Please, please, please keep that little black book safe by your side. They're going to kill me, I know it, and that book is the only bargaining chip I have. I'm on the run. I'll have to call you when I get a chance. Please, please, please stay at home.

"I have to meet with you and get that book back. Bye for now."

Jeff searched madly through his house for the little black book. He found it in one of his desk drawers. 'Thank God,' he thought. Of course, there was no reason for it to be missing. No one had invaded his house. The Hornish people couldn't have connected him with this business. Not yet. Although it was possible someone saw him entering or leaving Dottie's apartment building.

"I need some sleep," he said to the walls.

He took himself downstairs and flopped on his bed, shoes and all. REM sleep came upon him with enough speed to astound even Russian scientists.

————

At twenty past eleven in the morning Jeff finally stirred. Winter sunlight filled his room. A borderline wet dream erection pressed against his pants. The phone was ringing.

"Hello," he muttered, shielding his eyes from the light. "Jeff speaking."

"Thank God, thank God, thank God you're home," came Dottie's voice from the other end. "I called you a hundred times yesterday. I was afraid to leave a message. Then I thought I'd better. Are you so popular you have to gallivant all over town in a snowstorm?"

"I went to Ohio yesterday," he managed.

Dottie audibly sucked in her breath. "You met St. Patrick? What does he look like? I've always imagined him as a cross between Jabba the Hut and the Wizard of Oz."

"Who's Jabba the Hut?"

"Oh my dear. You don't see many movies, do you?"

"Not many modern ones." Jeff started to come awake. "Where are you?"

"Never mind. I'm on the road. I can't talk long. Do you have my book?"

"Yes, I do."

"Keep it in your pocket. Don't let it out of your sight. I've decided I don't want to die young after all."

"Understandable," said Jeff. "How can I get it to you?"

"Meet me at the Webster Hall in Oakland tonight at nine o'clock. Do you know where it is?"

"Been there many times."

"They have an over twenty-one dance tonight. Big band, spinning mirror ball, a singer like Dinah Shore. You can't miss it."

"Nine o'clock."

"Yes. Meet me at the entrance to the ballroom. Bring the book. And for Christ's sake, look over your shoulder. These people are dangerous. Larry Cone will kill you for a Timex watch and he's the best of the clan."

"I'll be careful."

"Dress nice. You don't get in without a tie."

———

The old Webster Hall, located in the heart of Pittsburgh's university center, opened in the late 1920s as a club for unattached men of means. The Depression cut pretty deep into the pool of wealthy young men of the unattached variety. The club couldn't make a go of it. The Webster Hall metamorphosed into a hotel and later condos. There was still a restaurant and several meeting rooms —including a full-sized ballroom—on the ground floor.

To Jeff's knowledge there had always been a classy restaurant of some kind in the building. In his college days he frequently dined there at a restaurant called the Chez Maurice with his best friend Roger.

The elegant red carpeted hallway brought back memories of that time. Roger. Poor Roger. Chose the ultimate luxury major in school: philosophy. His point of view leaned toward the skeptical, the morose. Jeff remembered sitting with Roger hour after hour at one of the small tables at Chez Maurice, talking across starched white cotton table cloths, antique Limoges dinner service. They discussed Heidegger, Kant, Sartre—never anything personal. Jeff's childhood and adolescence was too freshly painful for table talk. As for Roger, there was something fundamentally sad about him.

Roger. Those years in college. Talking philosophy over rich food, holed up in the privacy of the library archives, debating with professors; those were the best years of Roger's life. It was his period to bloom. The post-college world held nothing for him. After all, there were no careers available for philosophy majors, unless you considered a career in law. Roger considered the study of law to be pedantic and for provincials.

For a number of years Roger languished in the elephant graveyard of liberal arts degree majors: retail. Without school, without Jeff, without their talks at Chez Maurice, Roger slipped into a state of lethargy. Then depression. He developed (or inherited, Jeff was never sure which) a form of diabetes. Roger neglected his disease in favor of chocolate and pastries and a rather deep immersion with booze. He lost one of his legs, became legally blind.

Toward the end Jeff treated Roger to a dinner at the Chez Maurice. Over clams in a white sauce, Roger argued, as he had in college, that all death is a form of suicide. "My dear Jeff," he said. "We kill ourselves with food, we kill ourselves with habits and addictions, we kill ourselves with our past—our personal past and our genetic past. Why not kill oneself deliberately when the jig is up? I was never meant to live past college."

We mention this, Dear Reader, because Roger was quite possibly the first love of Jeff's life. Oh, they never had sex. Nothing like that. Each understood that the other was gay, though it was not discussed. There was a gentle love between the two men. It wafted in the space between them. And frankly, Dear Reader, Jeff dodged a bullet with this one. Roger was simply too dark for our man Jeff. Jeff, for the best imaginable reason, which is no good reason at all, has maintained an optimistic outlook. And I suppose in one's thirties that's all that one can hope for. After all, upon examination, what does Jeff have? A good brain, a handsome appearance and a past with which he has made his peace.

Gone now, Jeff thought. Such a sweet man. (And that's how he'll be remembered.)

Jeff took a deep breath as he continued walking toward the ballroom.

Faint strains of Benny Goodman beckoned him to the appropriate corridor. Jeff loved the Big Band Era, loved swing music. "Dance, Dance, Dance." He had the sheet music at home.

By the looks of the attendees, this was more of an over sixty-one dance than an over twenty-one dance. Most of the women passing through the entrance wore evening gowns; the men sported suits, even a few tuxedos.

At a table outside the ballroom door an elderly woman with a die-black page boy haircut took money and dispensed tickets.

"That's seven dollars," she told Jeff. "Five with Senior ID."

"I seem to have left my Senior ID at home," Jeff said, winking.

"Sorry, hon. Force of habit." She laughed. "Didn't even look at you."

"Understandable. Listen, I'm supposed to meet someone here. A younger woman, about my age. Beautiful. Stunning dresser. Her name is Dottie Hatfield."

"Oh, Dottie!" page boy exclaimed. "We know Dottie. She's a regular. She's not here yet, I know that for sure."

"I'll just wait for her here."

———

Jeff felt a tap on his shoulder. A woman with a familiar voice, dressed floor to neckline in an imitation sable stole, whispered, "Pay for me, honey. I didn't bring my money."

A massive, yet elegant, fur hat obliterated a third of the woman's face. Jeff might have looked right at her and not recognized her.

"Were you hiding behind the schefflera?"

"Actually, I've been hiding behind other people," Dottie answered, eyes darting nervously here and there. "The most effective way to hide is in a crowd. Let's go inside."

Jeff paid for two tickets. Page boy looked Dottie over. Obviously head to toe fur was not Dottie's customary fashion statement. The ticket lady looked at Jeff as if to say, "What gives?" Dottie virtually pushed him into the ballroom. She ushered him over to a small, two-chaired table at the edge of the dance floor. Despite the suffocating warmth of a thermostat set to the low eighties for the seniors, Dottie remained wrapped and hidden within the stole and hat.

"Do me a favor," she said. "Don't look any further into Vernon's past." She fanned herself, sweeping the room with her eyes, a fretful searchlight. "There are special birds who fly in during a crisis to make certain all of Hansel and Gretel's breadcrumbs have been eaten. They're here now, scouring for crumbs. You don't want to look like a tasty morsel." More manic glances from Dottie, as if she expected feathered flocks to materialize out of dark corners, from beneath tables, from within stylish pocketbooks. "They're everywhere. It's best they don't learn about you. Especially now that you've seen His Worship the Saint. You really are a fed of some kind, aren't you? Order a drink for us, honey."

Jeff hailed a waitress and ordered the best they had, a Glenfiddich. The lady desired a sloe gin fizz. After the waitress departed, Dottie asked, "You brought the book?"

"Of course." He moved to retrieve it from his inside pocket.

"Give it to me when we leave," she said. "How close are you to finding my baby's killer?"

"I have a few leads," he replied. "I'm pretty sure who did it. What I need is concrete evidence, something I can take into a court of law."

"I want his head back," she said, dismissing the concrete evidence request. "Remember that. So who do you think did it? St. Patrick ordered those murders, didn't he. I knew he did. I knew the moment it happened. You know why?" Jeff shook his head. "They all lose their heads, that's why. It's the modus operandi."

"What do you mean, they all lose their heads?"

The waitress brought their drinks. Dottie took a long hard draw on her straw, then sat back dramatically in her chair, as if pierced through the heart by the alcohol. Jeff waited, took a sip of his Scotch. (Just a sip. He planned to stay sharp.)

"Vernon told me," she said, looking away. "He wasn't supposed to tell me. In fact, it meant his ass if he ever told anyone. But he thought I should know. Just in case."

"In case what?"

She leaned in. "In case his head went missing. I would know who did it and I could take steps to protect myself. He loved me, you see. He genuinely loved me." She sucked deeply on the red straw. "No illusions. He knew what he was getting into. He knew what they could do."

"Tell me about the heads."

"This is off the record."

"Certainly."

Melodramatically she added, "I will never testify."

"Understood."

Dottie gestured with her right hand, a toss in the air, as if she were about to impart everyday gossip. "St. Patrick has a thing about Ireland. The ancient Celtic warriors used to cut off the heads of their vanquished. They hung these heads outside their tents or huts or whatever. Trophy heads. They brought strength to the warrior, refreshed the warrior's masculinity. For our St. Patrick it served a double purpose. It refreshed his masculinity and it proved that his warriors had done their job. That's when they got paid, you see. When they delivered the head."

"Vernon told you this."

"After his first big payoff he took me on a vacation to Disney World. My whole life I wanted to go to Disney World. It was like a honeymoon. He was so paranoid that someone would overhear our conversation, he waited until we were alone in the Pirates of the Caribbean to tell me. In the dark, guns and cannons firing, he told me the details about his new line of work. That's when he told me about the heads."

"Do you think St. Patrick found out he told you?"

"I never told a living soul about it. Until now. I kept all Vernon's secrets."

"Then why did they kill him?"

"I don't know. Maybe he told someone else. Mr. Buster Brown shoes."

"Who?"

"Your friend," she said. "That Chester guy. I could never remember his name, you see, so I called him Mr. Buster Brown shoes. That guy was so schmaltzy American Dream I swore he wore his Buster Browns to school every day. I knew that guy would get my baby killed."

Jeff took another sip of Scotch, another small one. He reminded himself, Not too many small ones.

"How could you know something like that?" he asked.

"Listen honey, clean people don't mix with street people. Sooner or later their naiveté, their lack of street smarts, gets us into trouble. They don't know what to shut up about. They think it's all a cute game. Let's play Street Scum. Would you get me another drink, dear?"

Jeff summoned the waitress and ordered another sloe gin fizz. The band eased into a soft ballad. A tall woman in a pink chiffon dress stepped up to the microphone. Eyes closed, as if off somewhere in a romantic dream, she sang *Red Sails in the Sunset*.

Dottie continued, "When shit happens—shit they caused—their lawyer extracts them from any legal entanglements. They go home to wifey, reputation still intact, money still in the bank. It's treated like a mistake, a small indiscretion. They fell in with the wrong people. Could happen to anybody. People like Vernon and me, we lose our money, we go to jail. Do you see how it works? I knew something bad would happen to my Vernon because of that Chester guy. Mr. Buster Brown shoes."

Even though he'd never actually met Marshall Chester, Jeff felt a bit of an affinity for him, maybe for teachers in general. Chester didn't need to be denigrated quite so severely. "You know," he said, "some people think very highly of Marshall Chester. A first rate teacher. I've seen his awards."

"Look," Dottie said sharply, "some dickhead named him after swamp land and he allowed himself to be called swamp land his whole life. Didn't have enough initiative, enough spark, to change that dreadful name. Dragged it with him right through to the end. A life lived without imagination.

"Look at me," Dottie continued. "I changed my name. I changed my hair, I changed my nose, I changed my clothes. I didn't like how God created me so, screw God, I created myself. It wasn't so hard." Dottie snapped her fingers above her head like castanets. "Nothing excuses mediocrity. Nothing."

The waitress brought Dottie's second drink. Dottie sucked it down in a single draw. *Red Sails in the Sunset* drew to a tearful close. The alcohol kicked in, leveling Dottie out. She smiled for the first time that evening. The band launched into *Begin the Beguine*.

She let out a long sigh. "Oh, what the hell," she said. "Let's dance."

"I'm not a very good dancer," Jeff protested.

"Honey, with shoulders that broad you don't need actual dancing talent. Just stand somewhere on the floor and you'll look just fine."

Dottie stood, removed the Russian hat. She struggled a bit with the coat. The thing buttoned all the way down to the floor. Jeff helped her with the bottom buttons. Finally it peeled off. The over twenty-one patrons gasped. Many knew Dottie Hatfield personally. Many more knew of her. Dottie always looked good. Always. But she looked especially dazzling at that very moment in her eggshell white Victorian wedding gown.

As she came out onto the floor, people touched her, touched the dress. "Dottie," they whispered, awestruck.

"Nice inconspicuous outfit," Jeff quipped.

"They tore up all my other clothes," she said. "This was all I had left."

"I thought it was too small for you."

"Honey, I'm a mess of burst seams. When they turn up the lights at midnight me and my pumpkin need to be the hell out of here."

Dottie led her handsome, dark-haired partner around the floor. The other dancers continued to sneak glimpses and quick touches. They murmured, "Dottie," as if rubbing an icon or spinning a prayer wheel.

"They all think I'm married to you," she laughed. "I'm sure they don't connect my Vernon with the man they've read about in the papers. They think I've dumped my old boyfriend on a whim and came up with a looker. You don't dance half bad."

"I'm a little stiff," he said.

"Honey, when you're a lot stiff let me know. I'll break out the champagne."

"Dottie—" Jeff started to protest.

"Oh, don't get your hopes up. It's just an old joke. And I'm still in mourning."

Inaudibly Jeff said, "Thank goodness for that."

The wedding dress inspired the band to play a string of romantic ballads. The old people loved to slow dance. Easier on the joints. Cole Porter led to Harold Arlen who segued to Johnny Mercer. Then, they eased into the penultimate romantic ballad, the one that left no dancers in their seats: *Laura*.

Jeff moved to sit down. He cared little for the dancing, even less for the intimacy (not to mention the subtle groping) of Miss Dorothy Hatfield. But she pleaded, "We can't sit down now. It's *Laura*. This song breaks my heart. We can't sit down now or I'll cry."

"All right, all right." Jeff took a deep breath, looking up at the ceiling as if he might find some relief from slow dancing there. "One last dance. But this is it."

She pulled in kissing-close to him, resting her head on his shoulder. She closed her eyes and indulged for just a moment in a special fantasy. She imagined it was two weeks earlier. She was dancing in the arms of her Vernon.

While they danced Jeff broke into her reverie. "Tell me where to go from here, Dottie. Time is running out for both of us. I need concrete evidence. Something I can take to the police."

Slowly, resignedly, she lifted her head. 'Such a handsome, dark face,' she thought. 'Savage black beard stubble. Radiant blue eyes. A thousand guilt-free carats. Waiting for an answer. Waiting for an answer from me.' "Dorothy, my dear," she said. "You've had the answer all along."

"What do you mean? The address book?"

"No, you oaf. You were just there. Think about it. The costumes, the armoire."

It was so hot in that ballroom. A trickle of perspiration ran down Dottie's back and over his fingers.

"St. Patrick," she said.

People stopped dancing. They stared at Jeff and Dottie. She drank too fast, Dottie realized. She was feeling insecure on her feet. She felt held up by Jeff, not by her own strength and will. A trumpet player in the band put down his instrument mid-song. Other band members caught his open mouth stare. The music skidded to an awkward stop.

A woman in a blue sequin gown screamed. She screamed and pointed. Everyone in the room turned their attention to Dottie and the back of her dress. And Jeff. Holding her in his arms without the music playing. Holding her up.

"Mrs. St. Patrick," she managed to say.

Dottie slipped out of Jeff's embrace onto the floor. He noticed his hands. They were dripping with blood. He had blood on his hands. Not an insubstantial amount. He felt the hot liquid slip under the white cuff of his shirt sleeves and warm his wrists. It all happened very slowly. What could it mean?

"I've been hit by a bullet," Dottie said to Jeff as he bent down to her. "I didn't even feel it."

People gathered around Jeff and the wounded Dottie. They pushed in cautiously, concerned.

Jeff knelt down close to her, disbelieving, afraid to touch her. Dottie grabbed the lapel of his jacket and pulled him down into her face. She was losing her voice. She could only whisper. In his ear, inaudible to the crowd, she said, "Keep the book. Don't stay here. Say you're running to get help. Get as far away as you can. Run! Do it now!"

Jeff glanced around at the peering faces. A woman in peach chiffon stepped up and identified herself. "I'm a nurse," she said.

"Good." He pulled her over to Dottie. "She's been shot in the back. Tend to her please. I'll run and get help."

And run he did.

Jeff sprinted out to the garage and into his four wheel drive. He hit the gas and sped recklessly through busy Oakland, cheating lights and stop signs. He dodged the siren stricken ambulances and the angry, racing police cars as they weaved their way through busy Saturday night traffic. Away.

Away.

39.

Just past midnight.

Two detectives in a county issue Taurus drove too fast through the ice encrusted, snow bearing streets of Wexford.

"Christ, don't they ever salt out here?" Detective Carlton Lyons cussed to his partner.

"You drive too fast," Rosalyn Winters calmly replied. Fast driving didn't bother her. Accidents in automobiles didn't bother her. Bad habits bothered her.

"I'm in a hurry," Lyons spouted. "Excuse me, but we're after a witness. A witness who is probably, almost certainly, up to his Cherokee ass in guilt."

"He's a computer information specialist, Carlton. Where's he going on a Saturday night?"

"Huh! You don't know him. He'll disappear on you like a magician. Or a Spirit Walker. Or whatever Indians got that disappears."

"Carlton. You're not going to tell me he shape shifts into a wolf."

"Nah, nah. But I'm telling you, he looks like a nice guy, like a college boy with a responsible job. In reality he's a sly, slippery son of a bitch." Lyons shook his head for emphasis. "You go to grab him and he's not there. And he lies! Lies come out of his mouth like kisses. Just about the time the smile wears off your face, you know he's tricked you."

Detective Lyons hit the gas harder. The back end of the Taurus swung out dramatically, narrowly missing the driver side of a snow-abandoned vehicle. Without skipping a beat, Winters asked, "Are you telling me you kissed this man, Carlton?"

"Don't even go there." Carlton pointed an index finger at his partner, who smiled just a crack on the side of her face he couldn't see. "Detective Carlton Lyons has never kissed no man. Not even in the line of duty. And Detective Carlton Lyons never will. And if I did, it wouldn't be that slippery Cherokee."

"Nice language, Lyons. Is this what you treat them to in court? Slippery Cherokee? No wonder all our perps go free."

"Hey. Don't blame that shit on me." Gas pedal. Vrooooom! "It's the system sets those people free. Not no testimony from Detective Carlton Lyons. I am not a bigot."

"Um-hum," muttered Winters.

"I'm a black man. You understand that? I'm a black man. My people been strung up on trees. Ain't no black man a bigot. I love all people, including slippery Cherokees, bitches like you, and the niggers from my own tribe. I pass my love all around. Equal opportunity lover here."

"Um-hum," Winters muttered once again.

"And I'm telling you this particular Indian pisses me off. Not all Indians everywhere. This particular one. He's slippery and he's slimy and he's going to wish he moved out west with the rest of his people while he had the chance."

Calmly, Winters added, "Cherokee's don't come from Pittsburgh, Carlton. The Iroquois come from Pittsburgh. His people never left here because they didn't come from here. Just a fact of history, Carlton."

"Cherokee, Iroquois. Who gives a shit. He's part Irish, too. I'm going to make this Mick wish he'd taken a boat back to the Emerald Isle while he had the chance. Does that work better for you?"

"Oh, that's lovely. Just let me do the talking in court." Calmly, while Lyons steamed, she added, "By the way, you're driving too fast."

"Fast! Fast! You think this is fast?"

Lyons flipped on his brand new, shit-kicker, rooftop emergency lights. They blazed, they sparkled, they hurt your eyes. His fired off a machine gun round of flashing orange and red and white across the charming snow cast lawns of Wexford. The siren from the Taurus wailed through the streets like a wounded animal, waking the sleeping peace of forested suburbia.

Few of Jeff's neighbors missed the arrival of Detectives Lyons and Winters.

———

They found lights on in the Redwing abode, but no sign of human inhabitants. Lyons rang the doorbell several times, politely for the neighbor's benefit, as if making a social call. His partner peered through the vestibule window at the long hallway that led to the living room. Lyons pressed the doorbell more insistently.

"Let's face it," said Winters. "If it was you, would you come home?"

"Tough call on the Redwing guy. He has a high I.Q. but he's not too bright."

"Witnesses said he had blood all over him. He has to come home sometime to clean up. Unless he's got a friend."

"That little boy," Lyons remembered. "Doesn't he live around here somewhere?"

———

Earlier that evening the little boy, watching the eleven o'clock news in bed instead of sleeping, heard the report of the Oakland shooting. Dorothy Hatfield from the Shadyside area shot twice in the back while dancing with a man reported to be her groom. Ms. Hatfield was taken to Presbyterian Hospital in her blood soaked wedding gown. Her new husband, as yet unidentified, fled the scene. The police are trying to locate a man described as being six-foot, 170 pounds, black hair, blue eyes, wearing a tweed jacket with suede patches on the elbows.

Even without the charcoal drawing of Jeff's distinctive face, flashed for an extended period on the TV screen, Xander knew the fleeing groom could only be Jeff. The man only owned two jackets: a classic blue blazer with brass buttons and an old college tweed with elbow patches. Jeff could be identified from a satellite in space wearing that sorry old tweed jacket.

For emergency purposes, Mrs. Pooka kept a set of Jeff's house and car keys in a cookie jar on top of the refrigerator. Xander snuck downstairs (his hard-working mom fast asleep) and silently extracted those keys. Jeff might need his help. It's just possible Jeff called home to leave a message for Xander to find. He might have come back for supplies before escaping to a hiding place. So it was Xander, in fact, who had turned on the hallway lights duly noted by Detectives Lyons and Winters.

For at least an hour Xander kept a vigilant watch from Jeff's bedroom window for the familiar burgundy Subaru. But the police arrived first. Xander recognized Carlton Lyons, the detective who last year made it clear in no uncertain terms that Jeff was to stay out of police business. Of course, Lyons would have recognized Jeff from the charcoal rendering.

As Xander followed the progress of the two detectives, so did many of Jeff's neighbors. Some watched, like Xander, from a window while others watched from the safety of doorways. A few people ventured boldly out into the street. Old Mrs. Wightman chose just that moment to take her cat for a walk. (A walk that the cat neither wanted nor appreciated.)

The detectives rang the doorbell a second time. Xander was torn. Should he let them in, explaining Jeff's absence in a positive light? Or should he continue hiding out in the house, waiting for further developments? Maybe they'd get tired of ringing the doorbell and just go away.

Then he remembered. He hadn't locked the front door behind him.

"Look," he heard Lyons say. "It's open."

"Do you think we should go in? We don't have a warrant," reminded Winters.

"He's a witness in a homicide investigation. We're concerned for his safety. Besides. How do we know he wasn't the intended victim?"

"Because it was a professional hit?"

Winters stuck a little too close to the book for Lyons' style of policing. With barely concealed impatience he pointed out, "The door is open. No one answers. He should be here, right? Maybe he's lying on the living room floor in a pool of his own blood."

Well. A handsome man lying helpless in a pool of his own blood was an image Detective Winters found particularly abhorrent. Besides, she wanted to see the inside of Jeff's house. Last year she didn't get to see the house. She had to hear about it from Carlton. The idea of a handsome man that kept a neat house appealed to her.

"All right," she said. "We go in."

Of course, thought Winters, the suspect's involvement with Bartholomew Postwaite suggested he might be into kinky stuff. That was no reason to give up on him, though. Handsome, single man of means who kept a neat house was not easy to come by. It occurred to our Rosalyn that with a revolver in one hand and a whip in the other she just might transform this Jeffrey Redwing into marriage potential.

Out loud she said, "I don't like all these single men. Something's got to be done about it." She knocked on the hallway walls as she proceeded toward the living room. "Hey Redwing! Jeffrey Redwing! It's the police!"

"It's the police!" echoed Lyons. Softly, he said to his partner, "He doesn't seem to be here."

Peering around the top of the stairway, Xander followed the two detectives as they proceeded further into the house. He heard Winters say, "When does the furniture arrive?"

"He spends most of his time upstairs," Lyons informed her.

"He lives in the bedroom?" Winters preferred a man with more ambition.

"No. He's got a workspace up in the attic. He calls it the Cloisters. He has computers up there—a fucking mainframe."

"No shit."

"Yeah. Electronic gizmos, a microscope, a telescope, recording equipment. It's like a mad scientist factory up there."

"Is this neighborhood zoned for electronic gizmos?"

"How the hell would I know? It's probably okay. Didn't look illegal."

Winters thought about it. "I'd like to get a look up there. Do you think we'd be violating any important Constitutional Rights?"

"Probably," her partner replied, moving into the kitchen. "But then again, he might be lying up there in a pool of his own blood."

Winters laughed. "That's right. We'd have to check that out."

Once they moved into the kitchen Xander could only hear murmurings. He had to decide what to do.

Outside, Mrs. Wightman's cat leaped up into the woman's arms to get its paws out of the snow. The binoculars brigade, Sharon Beineke and Sheila Romney, joined Mrs. Wightman in her vigil. Other neighbors edged away from their doorways and moved cautiously toward the police car's flashing lights.

'What to do. What to do. Oh God,' thought Xander, 'what to do.'

He tip-toed down the stairs. From the last step he peered into the living room toward the kitchen. A small light above the sink cast long, eerie shadows of the two detectives. They couldn't see him. Perhaps it would be better, all in all, if he simply left the house while he had the chance.

Xander dashed to the front door on tip-toes, then casually walked out like someone in complete control. Isn't it time for school?

"Xander Pooka," Mrs. Wightman called from across the street. "Come here to me."

Xander meekly crossed the street to deal with the neighborhood's self-appointed crime watch official. "Yes, Mrs. Wightman?"

"What's going on in that house?"

The other neighbors drew close to hear the answer.

"One of Jeff's alarms went off," Xander answered matter-of-factly. "Jeff is out on a date, so I came over to check it out."

"Out on a date," remarked Mrs. Beineke. "With whom?"

"It's Saturday night," answered Xander. "He always goes out on Saturday night." Let her think about that.

Mrs. Wightman didn't fall into Xander's little subplot.

"If his alarm went off, why don't we hear it? I don't hear any alarm. And why are the county police here? We have our own police."

Xander thought fast. "It's not a house alarm, Mrs. Wightman. It's an alarm on one of his computers."

"A computer alarm? I never heard of such a thing." Mrs. Wightman squeezed her cat with emphatic skepticism. She wielded quite a bit of power in her upper arms. The cat let out a scream.

"Well, you see..." Xander hedged. Make it believable. "He wouldn't want me saying this, but Jeff does a lot of sensitive work for a variety of government agencies."

"Then why isn't the FBI here?" Mrs. Wightman demanded. "If he does such secret work for the government. What's the matter? All the FBI cars in the shop?"

"He does work for the city and county also," said Xander. "And I'm just a little boy. He doesn't tell me everything."

This stopped Mrs. Wightman for a moment. One thing she knew for sure: there was a juicy story here somewhere and this boy knew more than he was telling. Mrs. Wightman raised a thick, stubby index finger and pointed it in Xander's face. It was a menacing, grandmotherly gesture used with considerable success to scare confessions out of her grandchildren. Before she could launch into her next line of interrogation, however, a familiar Subaru wagon rounded the corner.

———

Detective Lyons pulled a kitchen chair up to the open refrigerator and took a seat.

"What are you doing, Lyons?" his partner asked.

"This guy's a killer cook. I'm gonna see what he's got to eat."

"And how are we going to explain this in court?" she asked. "I don't think he's lying in the vegetable bin in a pool of his own blood."

"Don't bother me now," Lyons teased. "This is serious business. Look, we got spinach lasagna, green beans with sesame dressing. What is this here?" Lyons opened a Rubbermaid container. "Looks like Chicken Kiev in a bed of wild rice. I'm telling you, the last good meal I had came out of this refrigerator."

Rosalyn Winters peered into the array of neatly stacked, gourmet leftovers. "Why is this guy single? That's what I want to know."

"I want to know what the hell you're doing in my house," Jeff's voice bellowed from the kitchen doorway. He had washed the blood off of his hands, but the tweed jacket, the white shirt, the rep tie, all a loss. He wasn't wearing a winter coat, having left that behind at the over twenty-one dance.

Lyons stared at Jeff's bloodstained clothing. "Well, Mr. Redwing," he said with patronizing amiability. "Been out dancing tonight?" Then by way of explanation, "The front door was open."

"I never leave my door open."

"It was open," Winters told him with a smidge less condescension. "Your hall light was on. We were concerned for your safety."

Jeff didn't respond. His fingers shook through his hair. Had Larry Cone paid him a visit? Jeff had bad memories of Detective Carlton Lyons. On the other hand, a police presence might just keep Cone or Baum or God knows who at bay. Almost mechanically, Jeff crossed the room to the flatware drawer. He retrieved a fork and handed it to Lyons.

"Is she all right?" he asked quietly.

"Second time in a year we find you in the middle of one of our investigations," said Lyons, stabbing the Chicken Kiev. "You remember what the lieutenant said he would do if he ever caught you meddling in police business again?"

"I'm not in the middle of anything," Jeff protested. "It's all very innocent on my part. I went to the over twenty-one dance—"

"Prosecution." Lyons threw his authoritative, husky voice around the kitchen. "He promised to prosecute next time. This time."

"I don't know what I have to say to convince you," Jeff wrung his hands

He thought, as he was saying this, Dear Reader, that his acting was improving.

"It was all very innocent on my part."

Winters looked Jeff over while Lyons chomped down his food. Not a bad looking man, she thought. Not bad at all. Neat, except for the blood stains. Likes to cook.

"Are you hurt at all?" she asked.

Jeff shook his head. "I'm all right. How is the woman?"

She chose not to answer just yet. "Tell us what happened," she said instead. "From the beginning."

"Not very much to tell," Jeff started, fingers through the hair once more. "I happened to be in Oakland this afternoon. I had cabin fever from the snow. I decided to go to the museum. Then I took a walk through the Phipps Conservatory."

"A little late for the Spring Flower Show, wouldn't you say?" asked Lyons.

"They have shows year round."

"Let him tell his story," Winters objected. Good cop. And besides. He was well spoken. She liked a well spoken man. Detective Lyons shrugged.

"I went back to the museum and had dinner in the museum cafeteria," Jeff continued. "After that I hung out in the library for a while. On my way home I drove past the Webster Hall. There was a sign outside advertising an over twenty-one dance. I thought, 'What the hell? I'm over twenty-one.' I decided to check it out."

"And then," interjected Lyons, "your date just happens to get shot in the back on the dance floor."

"She wasn't my date," Jeff protested. "I was on my own. Actually, the woman approached me at the door. She said she'd accidentally left her money at home. She asked if I'd mind paying her way in."

"And you said, 'What the hell?'" said Lyons skeptically.

"She was a beautiful woman. I'm a single man. Why shouldn't I pay her way in?"

"There's a problem with that scenario," said Lyons. "The woman selling tickets claims you asked specifically for Dottie Hatfield."

Without batting an eye, Jeff countered, "Not true. I didn't learn the woman's name until we were inside the ballroom. Your ticket seller must have confused me with someone else. Maybe the assailant."

'Good point,' thought Winters. "Witnesses say you spent all of your time with the victim. You two sat at an intimate side table and talked like old friends. In fact, most of the people at the dance were under the impression that you and Hatfield had gotten hitched."

"That's because when she got up to dance and took off her coat she was wearing a wedding dress. Excuse me, I need a drink of water." Jeff crossed in front of the two detectives and poured himself a glass of water from the tap. "I don't know why she was wearing a wedding dress."

"Didn't you ask?"

"She said she had been burglarized just that day. All of her clothes except for her wedding dress had been destroyed. It was strange but, what the hell? It was just a dance."

Lyons swallowed a bit of wild rice.

"I'll tell you what my problem is, Redwing. You tell me, what the hell. What the hell this and what the hell that. See, I know you. You are a man who is extremely well organized. I bet you have the recipes to everything in this refrigerator written down on alphabetized index cards." ('Index cards!' thought Jeff. 'What is this, the sixties?') "I bet you write out an agenda each morning of everything you are going to do that day." (Good guess.) "I bet you organize your clothes in separate closets according to the seasons." (Doesn't everyone?) "Forgive me, but I don't see a spontaneous kind of guy standing before me. I bet What the Hell comes out of your mouth about once every four or five years."

"What can I say, detective? I don't mean to be disrespectful, but perhaps I'm more complex than you originally thought."

Carlton laughed. "Oh, that's for sure, Jeffrey Redwing. You're definitely more complex than I originally thought. I'm just wondering how much of that complexity is legal."

To catch him off guard, Winters threw in, "Just what is your relationship with Bartholomew Postwaite?"

She studied him. No reaction at all. And for good reason.

"I beg your pardon."

"Bartholomew Postwaite," she repeated.

"I'm afraid I don't know any—" he stuttered.

"Bartholomew Postwaite," Lyons said impatiently. "The man who died in your arms this evening."

Jeff closed his eyes. He hadn't known that Dottie was a man, but if he had given it any thought he might not have been blind sided. Nonetheless, he had become quite fond of Dottie. He fell back against the wall.

"So she died," he muttered.

"You are such a liar, Redwing," said Lyons. "You stood there bold faced and told two officers of the law that you'd never met the victim before. You can stop with the teary eyes. She's not dead yet. She's in critical condition at Presby. I knew you were lying. Just had to test you."

"I didn't know her," Jeff said. "Not really."

"Is that your thing, Redwing? You like drag queens?" asked Lyons.

"No, of course not. I thought she was a woman. She looked like a woman, moved like a woman, spoke like a woman."

"She come on to you?" asked Winters.

"A little flirtation. More subtle than most of the women I meet. She said she was in mourning."

"In her wedding dress," said Winters.

"I believed her."

Lyons interjected abruptly, "You a customer of hers, Redwing?"

Jeff knew, of course, what Lyons meant. Still, he thought it best to play innocent.

"Customer?"

"So how do you know her? Him?" Winters asked. "Let's hear the story. She's not exactly a member of your social circle. I understand you're something of an intellectual, a computer whiz. How do you come to be dancing on Fifth Avenue with Pittsburgh's most notorious drag queen?"

"Tell us the truth now, Redwing," Lyons warned. "This was attempted murder. The perpetrators took serious risks getting to Postwaite in that crowded ballroom. Maybe they got a look at you, too."

Jeff sighed. "I knew Marshall Chester."

"So that's it." Lyons smiled.

"I didn't know him well. We crossed paths at Carnegie Mellon. I don't know how, but this Dottie person knew about my little indiscretion last year with the police. She got the idea I was some kind of private detective."

"How did she get that idea, Redwing?" asked Lyons. "You weren't poking around police business again. Tell me you weren't. You know the consequences."

Winters ran down the list, "Incarceration, financial ruin..."

"You don't have to tell me. Dottie Hatfield, as I knew her, has connections. I don't know who her people are but she was able to find out that I have done some work with the FBI. She put that information together with the incident last year. She decided I was some kind of fed."

"And what did she request you do in your role as a federal agent?" asked Winters.

"She wanted me to find out who murdered her husband. Boyfriend. Whatever he was."

"Old Vern," said Lyons, exchanging a look with his partner.

"She was convinced he had been executed by one of his business associates."

"And you could do a better job of tracking his murderer than the police."

"She didn't feel she could go to the police."

"So you started nosing around police business," accused Lyons.

"No, no. Definitely not. I told you. I would never do that. You put the fear of God in me last year. I've learned my lesson."

Lyons moved in close to Jeff's face, way past the social comfort zone. "Fear of God," he snarled. "I'll tell you what, Redwing. I wish I had you hooked up to a lie detector right now."

"So do I," said Winters.

"I'm telling you the truth," Jeff said. If he hadn't been so scared he might have cracked a wicked smile.

Lyons poked him. "You know what I think the truth is? I think you've been fucking this drag queen up the ass and paying for it. I think you've been using your gizmos upstairs to secure confidential materials for her. I think you're up to your hairy Cherokee ass in trouble."

"Honest Injun, officer," he said, holding up two boy scout fingers. Jeff tried to smile. It wasn't going over. "I was trying to put her off as delicately as possible. She knows people. She could be dangerous. I couldn't just be rude. But I certainly, as I said, learned my lesson last year. I will never interfere with police business again as long as I live. You have my word."

"The word of a pathological liar," said Lyons.

"The word of a good, decent, law-abiding citizen. I swear I had no idea who she was. I thought she was a woman named Dottie Hatfield. A wronged widow."

"She never gave you a blow job," said Winters.

"Certainly not," refuted Jeff. "I've been living lately like a monk."

"A monk, a saint," said Lyons contemptuously. "You listen to me, Redwing. I was disappointed hearing your name again. I don't like the fact that you have a personal connection to our friend Bart. My instincts tell me you are in this like Jonah was in the whale."

"Your instincts are wrong, officer."

"Detective."

"Detective. Sorry."

Lyons waited, then: "You keep out of this Postwaite business. You understand me? You make sure you keep your nose out of this business. And stay indoors! I don't want you leaving this house until I figure out what's going on."

"Am I under some kind of official restraint?" asked Jeff.

"No," barked Lyons. "You are under the considerable restraint of my advice. Keep your nerdy little ass out of this. You hear me?"

"Yes, sir. Actually, I was thinking of hibernating for the rest of the winter."

"That sounds good," said Lyons.

"You hibernate until this case is closed. That will make me a happy man." Lyons turned to his partner. "Will that make you a happy woman, Detective Winters?"

Winters seemed more perplexed than satisfied with the result of the Redwing interview. She was about to agree conditionally to being a happy woman. Then, abruptly, she decided to speak her mind.

Sticking the long, boney finger of the law in Jeff's face, she said, "You listen here. You don't need the love of a drag queen. There are plenty of lonely, unattached real women around." Carlton looked up hopelessly at the ceiling. "And this is something else I have to say. You better not be living like a monk. That's not why mother nature made you. You're a strong, vital man with a brain in his head. Good genes, good baby making material. It's your duty to find a good woman and make her happy. Give her children. Fulfill her destiny."

"Don't you forget it, Redwing," Lyons laughed. "She'll be back for a date."

"I just might be back," Winters asserted. These men pissed her off. "There are too many single men in the world. And I don't like it."

Lyons cracked up. He pulled his crazy partner away.

"Come with me, girl, before this man has you up on sexual harassment charges." They started to leave. Carlton called back to Jeff, "Remember what I told you, Redwing. Keep your nerdy ass in this house."

———

'I am not a nerd,' Jeff thought. 'And I don't have a little ass, I have a big ass. And I still have some Christmas shopping to do, so I will definitely be leaving the house at some point. Restraint of your considerable advice.'

Lyons and Winters paused dramatically at Jeff's front door and looked out over the neighbors. In due time they plodded on back to the police vehicle, heavy with the leaden yet mysterious authority of police business. Although neither one said, "It's all over folks. Go back to your homes," the neighbors felt it somehow.

Xander's explanation of events had been chewed upon by the neighbors but not digested. Most, however, went back inside. Excitement over. Mrs. Wightman stayed for quite some time to her cat's distress. She stared at Jeff's house as if willing answers from its snow dusted bricks.

Jeff, who had moved out of the city to escape social involvement, would now have to do something he loathed: explain things to the neighbors. That would not be easy because at that very moment a *Post Gazette* reporter was typing these words:

> "Notorious Liberty Avenue drag queen Bartholomew Postwaite, alias Dottie Hatfield, was shot twice in the back late Saturday night while attending a dance at Oakland's Webster Hall. Her apparent date for the evening, computer information specialist Jeffrey Redwing of Wexford, ran fleeing from the scene. "Blood dripped from his hands," described Harriet Martin, 61, a Webster Hall regular. "He said he was going for help but he never came back," claims dance veteran Chip McMahon, 74. *Post Gazette* readers will remember Jeffrey Redwing from an incident involving... "

This article, appearing on the front page of the Sunday morning edition, complete with color photo of Dottie Hatfield bleeding in her wedding dress, would later present quite a challenge to Jeff's quick thinking story creating abilities.

Just at that moment, however, leaning up against his kitchen wall, Jeff still possessed a small window of time free from the specter of his neighbors' concern. He could deal later with his standing in the community. Right now he was more concerned with the small matter of saving his life.

He ran a tired, gritty hand over his stubbly face. Between the lattice of his fingers he spotted Xander.

"It's on the channel eleven twenty-four hour news service," Xander announced with considerable glee.

"Great."

"What happened?"

Jeff explained about the call, the little black book, the dance, the wedding dress, the perspiration on his hands that turned out to be blood.

"It had to be a professional hit," said Jeff. "I didn't hear any shots. Dottie didn't even know she'd been hit at first. The police just confirmed it. The police know something about all this, Xander. I don't know how much."

"They said on television that Dottie is really a man," said Xander excitedly. "His real name is Bartholomew Postwaite. Wow."

"Can you believe it? A drag queen." Jeff shook his head. "I must be really naive."

"Naw, she was just good. She fooled you. She even fooled me and I've seen lots of TV shows and movies about drag queens."

"Have you?"

"Oh, yes. *Priscilla, Queen of the Desert*. I love that movie. Dottie was also a prostitute. Think of all the men she fooled over the years. She fooled everybody. The David Copperfield of gender benders."

"Yeah, well. I'll tell you something Xander," said Jeff. "I do sense the presence of a master illusionist behind this series of criminal acts, but it's not Dottie Hatfield."

"Who do you think it could be?"

Jeff sighed. "I don't know. Here's something I learned, though. Vernon Roman did something terribly wrong. Dottie is certain that St. Patrick had Roman killed."

"Why does she think that?"

"Because she knows that St. Patrick's henchmen always take the heads of their victims as proof of the kill. Think about it. Greta Fields' head is taken from her tomb, that bank manager in Kitty Hawk was decapitated in an automobile accident. Then a samurai appears in a Wendy's parking lot and slices off Roman's head—which cannot be found."

Jeff continued, "It harkens back to the ancient Celtic warriors. They cut off the heads of their vanquished. These warriors then hung the heads outside of their huts as proof of their manliness. The more heads, the greater the warrior. At least that's what I remember from my readings of Celtic history."

"Why didn't they take Chester's head?"

"Chester wasn't the intended victim. He just happened to be there. See, it's vengeance. Vengeance is the motive behind these killings. Chester had to be killed because he knew too much about St. Patrick's organization. But it was Roman they wanted. It was he who did this bad, bad thing."

"What bad, bad thing?" Xander asked.

"I don't know yet. Something really bad. St. Patrick killed him and went after Dottie tonight."

"Do you think Cone did the shooting?"

"It's possible. Or Franklin Baum. You know what else occurred to me? Hornish told us his daughter lives in this area. What if she's his representative in Western Pennsylvania? What if she is the puppet master? Think about it. He's got a successful organization operating up and down the eastern seaboard. He's got five children."

"So if St. Patrick's daughter is head of his organization in this area," said Xander, "then Cone and Baum work for her."

"Maybe she's the shooter," said Jeff. "I noticed Hornish didn't want to say much about his daughter." Jeff thought about it. He loved the idea of a daughter puppet master. Who could the daughter be? "Roman betrayed them. If I could figure out how or why I might get the evidence I need. These people know who I am now, Xander. I can't wait for the police to close in on St. Patrick and his gang. I've got to find the evidence myself or someone will be taking shots at me."

Xander, choked up, didn't know what to say. He looked down at his feet. "It's so sinister. Honest to God, Jeff. When I saw that report in the newspaper last week I never thought it would turn out like this."

"Neither did I." Jeff looked down at his blood soaked clothes. How did it get this far? From such innocent inquiries? "But we can't think about that. St. Patrick is motivated by a sense of justice, of righting wrongs. But his solution is cruel. Think of all of the people he has killed."

"All those heads," said Xander. "How did the Celtic warriors live with the stench of rotting heads hanging outside their huts?"

"I wonder what St. Patrick does with the heads," Jeff said almost without thinking, only half conscious of the implications. A chill ran up his spine. "Oh my God!"

"What? What is it?"

"I just realized what Dottie was trying to tell me." Jeff pulled himself together quickly in the midst of a plan. "I want you to go home. Now. It's too dangerous for you here. Stay away from me until this business is over." Xander started to object. "Don't argue with me or you're going to end up like Marshall Chester."

"What are you going to do?"

"First thing, I'm going to get out of this house. I am a standing target as long as I'm here. You need to go home. Immediately. Go."

Xander wanted to argue with his friend. Jeff's penchant for walking directly into the path of danger alarmed him. They were supposed to be a team. At the same time, he knew it wouldn't do any good to argue.

"All right," he said. "I'll go. You take care of yourself!"

"Come here to me," Jeff said. "I need a hug."

Xander paused at the sight of the blood on Jeff's jacket and shirt.

"Don't worry. All the blood is dry."

Xander held fast to Jeff. Jeff's body felt overly warm, his clothes sticky with dried perspiration.

"You look tired," Xander said. "You should get some sleep before you do anything else. You can sleep at my house. It will be safe. I'll sneak you up to my room."

Jeff smiled just a little. "That's kind of you. Don't worry about me. I got two or three hours sleep last night. I'm all set."

"Two or three hours!" Xander protested.

"You know me. Two or three hours is enough. Really, I'll be fine. There's just one thing." He stroked Xander's hair and laughed a tiny laugh. "Promise me you'll go to college."

40.

XANDER TRAVERSED THE TWO WINDING STREETS TO HIS HOUSE WITH the speed of a gazelle. As expected, his stressed-out mother lay fast asleep in her bed having missed all the excitement. Probably wearing earplugs, Xander thought. He tip-toed around her room. Locating his mother's purse, he withdrew her car keys quiet as a jewel thief.

Periodically his mother let him warm up the car in the morning while she put the finishing touches on her makeup. Their Camry started with a simple twist of the ignition. To tell the truth, he was just a little too short to reach the gas pedal and at the same time see over the dashboard. To follow Jeff he needed to create a lift of some kind for his shoes.

With electrical tape from the basement he managed to strap several stacks of paperback novels to his Nikes. James Michener and Stephen King added a good eight inches to his stretch.

His mother never threw a telephone directory away. Xander grabbed two of the ancient ones and used those as a booster seat so that he could see up over the dashboard. Unfortunately, this extra boost meant he once again needed extra stretch to reach the gas and brake pedals. Xander retrieved a couple of Sally's Nora Roberts novels and hitched those to the Micheners and Kings. In this way he transformed himself into the smallest imaginable person who could drive a car.

For the first time ever he got to do something he had often begged his mother to let him do: he eased the car out of the garage and down the driveway. Except his mother had parked head in, so he had to ease it out backward. This experience did not fill him with an adult-sized sense of accomplishment—it scared him half to death. He applied the brakes and the car skidded in the snow dramatically to the left.

"Shit! Shit!" he said. "Do I really want to do this? But I have to. I have to protect him. It's my fault he's in this situation. We could have gone to the museum. We could have gone to a hockey game. No, I had to get us involved with drag queens and professional killers."

Slowly Xander lifted his foot from the brake pedal. He let the car drift backward and maneuvered it into the street. His heart beating like an African drum chorus, he put the car in drive and ever so gently hit the gas. The car lurched forward, sliding to the right this time in the snow. He screamed until the car drifted into some semblance of alignment with the road.

Xander remembered a trick Jeff sometimes used in the snow. He put the car in second gear, then edged it forward at approximately half-a-mile per hour. That at least kept the Camry from sliding into his neighbor's parked cars.

He made it as far as the entrance to Jeff's street without incident. Sticky with sweat, hands shaking on the wheel, the sound of his own pulse overwhelming the urgent warnings of the voice in his head, he finally turned off the engine. I can't do this, he thought. This was so much harder than driving the simulation vehicle at the mall. And Xander knew that Jeff, in his current manic state, would be racing the Subaru at metal rattling speeds. He would never be able to follow in the Camry.

As snow fell in fat, flat flakes on his windshield, Xander thought of another way to protect Jeff.

Thankfully, it would not require the use of Stephen King wedgies.

———

Jeff, more tired than he wanted to admit, indulged the welcoming sensation of steaming hot water showering down over his aching body. He surrendered to a number of metaphorical indulgences as well. For instance, he imagined himself in a computer game, the new SONY thing with the improved graphics.

In this game he played the role of an insect trying to avoid being captured and eaten. At first he navigated through the attack path with great agility, but then he made a sudden turn and a cliff edge surprised him. He tumbled over the edge out of control, landing in a sticky web. Through his insect eyes he saw them coming for him. Cone and Hornish and even the illusive (and dead) Greta Fields.

They charged nimbly down the silk grid. They stung him with scalding hot venom discharged from the tip of tubular serrated legs. "Let them take me," he said out loud, watching thick soapy water swirl down the drain. "I just want to be clean."

Over thermal underwear he donned Bean chords, a Bean Oxford shirt, a Bean fisherman's sweater, Bean thermal socks and Bean water resistant hiking boots. Over this ensemble he immersed himself in a dark blue, down filled Bean parka, its thirsty pockets filled with such survival essentials as a

Swiss army knife, a baby crowbar, a palm sized flashlight, wooden matches and assorted bandages in case he got shot.

Thus attired to challenge the forces of evil, he drove off in the direction of evil's source: Rock Creek, Ohio. Maniacally transfixed, he failed to notice Sally Pooka's car parked awkwardly near the entrance to his street.

Once outside of Wexford, Jeff found the highways wet but relatively clear. Even so, he drove faster than he should, at times reaching a speed of ninety miles per hour.

He talked to himself intermittently.

"I lost too much sleep," he admitted. "Not enough quality REM. It's affecting my judgment, I know that. I'm bound to create a major error in judgment soon. This trip is probably a major error in judgment."

About half an hour later he observed, "My coordination is diminishing. It's just a matter of time, really. I'm probably hungry, too. When was the last time I ate? The last thing I put in my body was alcohol. That's not good. I'm probably living on body fat right now. Body fat that I created at that heavy meal in Ohio yesterday. That's ironic. But not good."

Twice he stopped at turnpike toll booths, each time throwing handfuls of change at the exact change coin catchers. Shortly after the second toll, Jeff crossed the state line between Pennsylvania and Ohio.

"That didn't take long," he said. "I must be driving at breakneck speeds. Woe! Ninety miles per hour. They should paint a skull and crossbones on my bumper. No. Really. I should have a bumper sticker that reads: 'Watch Out! Danger! Man Deprived of Critical REM Sleep! If you object to my driving, call Detective Carlton Lyons.'

"God, that woman he had with him was strange. What was her name? Detective Winters. Lyons and Winters. The Lyon in Winters. I bet they get a lot of jokes about that. But listen, Jeff, wasn't Winters strange? That speech about my civic duty to make single women happy. No, single lonely women. She said that word several times. Lonely, lonely. She's probably lonely. She probably wants a date. She'll use this case and my sorry ass predicament to blackmail me into a date. Ha!

"Then I'll be forced to explain my philosophy of life. I hate that. My philosophy has a lot of holes in it. Anyone trained in logical thinking could bring my philosophy to its knees. That woman looked like she could put Plato in a headlock. It comes to personal preference really. I prefer muscled creatures with hairy bodies. And penises. Penis is essential. I'm sorry, Detective Winters, but I am not in the vagina business. I choose to remove myself from that particular field of play.

"It's very St. Francis of me. And here I am charging into battle as St. Francis. It's St. Francis versus St. Patrick. It's the battle of the saints. They could make a Japanese monster movie out of this. Hornish stomps around eating gross quantities of comfort food, lopping off people's heads. I chase after him, a laptop in my hand, screaming, 'Stop that, you!' while thousands of Japanese citizens run with no sense of direction through the streets of Tokyo."

Jeff thought he heard something. Giggling. Was that giggling? He must have been laughing at his own jokes. How Red Skelton. His mother used to love Red Skelton. He could never understand it. The man always broke up laughing just as he got to his punch line. Maybe that's what she liked. Maybe she liked laughing along with Red. Not many laughs in his mother's life. Poor Betsy. Betsy Redwing. What a peculiar name. Betsy Redwing. Mrs. Betsy Redwing.

What did his own name sound like to other people? Jeffrey Redwing. Jeff Redwing. Mr. Jeff Redwing. Should he change his name like Dottie? Perhaps one day, out of the blue, he might change his sex. Seemed to be happening everywhere. 'God, I'd have to wax my chest. That would hurt. Anyone with this much chest hair should remain a man. It only makes sense.'

He started singing, "I'm so tired. I'm such a stupid git. Although I'm so tired, I'll have another cigarette..."

'That reminds me. I wonder how the Eggman is doing. I'll have to call him when this is over. If I'm still alive.'

"What exactly are you going to do when you get there, Jeff?" he asked himself out loud. "You've got to have a plan. You're a capable strategist. Except nothing leaps to mind. Well, let's consider the scenario. I'll arrive at approximately 3 a.m. No street lamps, so it will be pitch dark except for a tiny bit of moonlight reflecting off of the snow. How are the batteries in my flashlight? Quite fresh, thank you. Should last a couple of hours.

"Of course, we'll have to park the car far enough away from the cottage to avoid detection. Maybe I could park on the other side of the lake and row somebody's boat over. Naw. Nix that idea. Nothing in this world is getting me out on that lake again. That scary bastard! How dare he make me row all the way out to the middle of the lake and then tell me that horrible story. He's very cruel for someone who calls himself a saint.

"We haven't come up with a plan yet, have we? No, I'm afraid we haven't. Well, what about this, Jeff. Why don't we sneak up on one of the windows and pry it open with the baby crowbar. The Hornish's are bound to be asleep. I can creep silently down to the basement. It will be like I'm invisible. I'll creep and I'll gather at least one piece of incriminating evidence. Do I need more than one? No, one is enough. It's vitally important to get in and out without detection. Vitally important. Vital.

"You're forgetting about the blasted dogs. Bassett hounds are pretty good intruder detectors, aren't they? Yes. Anything called a hound makes a good detector. Shit, shit, shit. There goes plan A. On the other hand, she's an old Bassett. A mother with a brood. Teats sucked round the clock for weeks now. She's probably too tired to pay any attention to me. She'll probably sleep through my little Watergate escapade. And besides, I'll be invisible

"I should have brought a gun. Why didn't you? Well, for one thing I don't own a gun. And for another I wouldn't know how to load it or aim it or fire it. What kind of American are you, Redwing? I'll bet all the Cherokees on the reservation know how to fire a gun. Yeah, but I've never been to the reservation. That's too bad. A gun with some knowledge of how to use it would be useful at this moment. Happiness is a warm gun. Bang, bang, shoot, shoot.

"Which reminds me. I should have left a message for the Eggman. I should have let at least one person in this world know where I was going. I could end up another headless body somewhere.

"I'm getting punchy. Maybe I could hum a Zen chant. I have to piss, too. Maybe I should pull off to the side of the road. No, don't do that, Redwing. The piss pain will keep you awake. Use it to stay sharp.

"Almost there. Christ, you're a madman. An Almost Reality Avenging Angel." Waving an imaginary cowboy hat over his head, Jeff shouted at the top of his lungs, "The Almost Reality Avenging Angel rides again! Yahoo!"

41.

A GENIE'S LAMP OF SMOKE CURLED UP FROM THE HORNISH CHIMNEY. It scattered into grey filaments against the cloudy night sky. An unkind wind whipped around the stone cottage. Jeff spotted a strange car, a Peugeot sedan, in the driveway closest to the kitchen entrance. It's Pennsylvania plate read: Pie X2.

Retrieving his flashlight, Jeff peered into the car. A pair of black leather driving gloves rested neatly on the driver's seat. He noticed an empty CD jewel case: *Elvis – 50 Million Fans Can't Be Wrong*. On the back seat he spied a tidy pile of textbooks. Math textbooks. So...

Was this an emergency meeting? Or were they here to cool off after the shooting in Pittsburgh? Or was this just some sort of weekend soiree—just the middle management murderers and their dates?

Several lights were on inside the house. The drapes were drawn, but enough light filtered through to illuminate the immediate grounds. Silhouettes shimmered like dancing spirits against the drapery fabric. Vague murmurs and vestiges of words leaked through the window glass. There was a loud discussion taking place, maybe even an argument.

Jeff crept around the back of the cottage and tried his hand at petty breaking and entering. The windows were locked. His baby crowbar fit snugly under the sash of the bedroom window, but snapping the lock would make a forbiddingly loud sound. A shot of pain crossed Jeff's loins. He had to piss really badly, now. The bitter wind sharpened his bladder discomfort. He wanted to just break the glass, declare himself. Let them deal with it.

But that would be stupid. He didn't have a weapon. Confrontation was not a good option.

Jeff crept back around to the kitchen side of the cottage. Here a curtain over a small sink window was only loosely drawn. He could see inside. An orange nightlight cast a Halloween pall across the room. The handmade maple table and chairs, the mountainous crust of Mrs. Hornish's apple pie. He noticed a detail he had somehow missed on his earlier visit. On the wall nearest the doorway hung two plaster reliefs: the little Dutch boy and the little Dutch girl. They faced each other, feet poised for a little Dutch dance. 'God these people and sinister, too,' he thought. I definitely should have brought a gun.

Jeff wondered if perhaps the kitchen door might simply be unlocked. It was closed against the cold, of course, but with guests so recently arrived and so few people living in the plan, why lock it? Jeff tried the door. It opened easily.

Jeff spotted the dogs resting in the corner against the wall near the sink. Mother Bassett raised her head, made a motion as if to howl. Jeff raised his fingers to his lips. That seemed good enough for the tired mother. She lowered her head and sighed, her pups fast asleep tucked under her side. Except for Topper, of course. Topper was off somewhere getting into mischief.

Jeff shined his flashlight across the kitchen floor looking for the pup. He didn't want to step on the little guy, after all. Topper did not appear to be in the kitchen. Jeff sidled up to the door that led into the next room. He cupped his ear to pick up the conversation of the people in the living room.

For a while he didn't hear any sound at all, not even the percussive sound of china teacups settling into saucers.

Then Larry Cone spoke: "I'm not trusted," he said angrily. "I'm not trusted and I don't like it. After all I've done for you. Fuck you, old man. Just fuck you."

"We want to trust you, Larry," Mrs. Hornish said in her motherly way. "It's just that we don't understand. Help us to understand."

Before Larry could help them to understand, Mr. Hornish interjected flatly, "I trust those who deserve to be trusted."

"Fuck you, old man."

"Mr. Hornish," Penny English cajoled. "I'm close enough to Larry to be his wife." Jeff imagined she cast a sympathetic glance toward Mrs. Hornish. "If he had ordered those killings, I would have known." The wrong thing to say. Other people were forbidden to know, that's what Dottie had said. "Marshall Chester was my dearest friend in the world. If there had been a problem of any kind we would have worked it out together."

As if asking an unanswerable question for the hundredth time, Mr. Hornish asked, "Then where is his final installment?"

"I told you," said Cone. "He died before I could get it. What am I supposed to do? Go to the widow and ask for the balance of the hit money?"

"I don't buy it," Mr. Hornish declared. "We don't do business that way. We always get our money up front."

"He couldn't sneak that much money out of his bank account without his wife noticing," said English. "He removed twenty-thousand slowly over six months. He needed a couple more months to ease out the last ten. I personally vouched for him. I promised Larry I would pay the last ten myself if Marshall couldn't. And I'll keep that promise. For Christ's sake, the man has only been dead a week."

"Lovely lady," began Mr. Hornish, "I don't want your money. Money is not the issue here. Sound business practice is the issue here. Communication. Trust. It's a madhouse in Pittsburgh. I have an employee and a client executed in our signature style. I have another employee taking over a nationally televised press conference to confess to these executions. I have a payment of ten thousand dollars missing. And we have yet another execution, a shooting no less, in a crowded public ballroom. Pittsburgh is out of control."

"I told you I had to shoot her," said Cone. "She was talking to that fucking fed. She was dancing with him, talking and talking and talking. And she was drinking. Who knows what she told him."

"What fed?" asked Mr. Hornish. "What are you talking about?"

"This guy. He was at Vernon's funeral. He was at Chester's funeral. This guy has been everywhere talking to everybody. He broke into my house. You understand? This is serious shit."

"How do you know he's a federal agent?"

"He's an agent all right. He has a specially trained kid works with him. An eleven-year-old boy."

Mrs. Hornish gasped.

Cone continued, "My neighbor told me how this smart as shit kid talked his way into my house. He pretended to be my fucking nephew or something and popped the lock on my front door. Eleven-year-old kid."

"So," said Hornish. "Jeffrey Redwing is a federal agent."

"That's him," Penny said quickly. "That's his name. Or the name he goes by. He passed himself off to me as one of Marshall's old college friends. Said he was writing a story about him for the alumnae magazine."

Vehemently Cone added, "You tell me things are out of control in Pittsburgh. We have a federal fucking agent up our ass."

"Well," said Mr. Hornish. "This is very serious. This is serious indeed. It's too bad. I liked that young man. We'll have to kill him, of course. Do you know where he lives?"

"Oh, we know," said Cone. "I would have popped him tonight but the cops were all over his place."

"We'll have to kill the boy, too," Mrs. Hornish added.

Kill the boy? I don't think so.

It was perhaps a rash act. With a little more sleep and a visit to the proper toilet facility, our man Jeff might have cogitated upon his dilemma. He might have invented for himself a slightly less dangerous solution. Oh, the might have beens in life. How they haunt our later years.

Jeff threw open the swinging door.

"Special Agent Redwing," he said menacingly. "And you're not killing anybody. Anybody else."

They stared at him, shocked. There was silence for a moment, then Jeff picked up his cue.

"Every police officer within the surrounding three hundred school districts knows I'm here. We have it all on tape. And you're surrounded. So." He shifted from side to side on his feet. His perps weren't attempting to escape. On the other hand, he didn't know what to do with them. "So. I'll just take those slivered heads if you please. Severed heads," he corrected. "Severed heads. I'll be taking all your severed heads as evidence."

"He's drunk," said Cone.

At that very moment the power went out. The room turned dark as an underground cave.

Someone yelled, "Get him!"

Jeff heard a scramble of footsteps and a clattering of chairs. Teacups went flying. Something whizzed past his head. Someone grabbed hard onto his body and pushed him into the swinging door. He fell onto his back, half in and half out of the kitchen. The person who pushed him fell on top of him. He could tell from the smell of cologne it was Penny English.

"I just want to get out of here," she said. She pulled herself up and ran into the kitchen. After stumbling into the kitchen table, Penny made her way to the outside door. Jeff saw the door open. Penny ran outside, ran fast, into the snow.

Jeff got up quickly, checked himself. He seemed to be all right. The others had apparently left the living room area. He stood still and listened. He heard thumping sounds, heavy shoes on wooden floor boards, on wooden steps, coming from some distant place in the cottage. With his pocket flashlight he scanned the room. No one.

The outside door opened again. Penny stepped inside.

"Don't hurt me," she said. "I just want my keys."

'It's all so maddening,' Jeff thought. 'It's all so absurd.' He shined his light on her purse. She retrieved it, fumbled through it, and extracted her keys.

"It will be bad for you if they kill me," he assured her. "You're the perfect choice for state's witness. You could get out of this. Of course, you won't be able to teach. But if they kill me there won't be any deals."

"What should I do?" Penny appeared amazingly collected for someone in her position.

"Get the police. Get them here immediately."

"I thought the police were surrounding the place."

"Bad choice of words. They're not surrounding so much as converging.

But they're not converging fast enough. Things weren't meant to develop this quickly. Go! Please!"

Penny paused. Should she turn state's witness or trust to Cone and company? Well, she'd seen what Cone and company could do. And the relationship seemed all but over anyway.

"All right," she said. "I'll call the police. I'll have to drive out of the area. My cell phone won't work here." Getting into her role as witness for the state, she added, "Larry has a gun. They've probably gone upstairs. Hornish has a semi-automatic stashed away in one of the bedrooms."

"Great."

"What you want is in the basement," Penny whispered. "Go. Quickly." She nodded toward the basement door.

Jeff heard another series of thumping noises. They did, indeed, appear to emanate from the second floor. Jeff edged toward the basement door. As he did so he watched Penny English walk cool and collected across the room. Then he saw what she saw: a telephone on a lamp table. It was a land line phone. Penny dialed 911.

"I'm calling from Rock Creek," she said to the 911 operator. "The Hornish house on Rock Creek Drive. There has been an attempted murder—"

A series of gun shots fired across the room. The bullets tore into Penny's body with such fierce velocity that she jerked upright. The phone's receiver fell to the floor. Jeff scurried down into the basement, hissing, "Shit, shit, shit," as he went. He didn't get to see Penny shot through with over twenty rounds, collapse into a heap on the floor.

———

Jeff stepped slowly, softly along the floor of the basement. Blind in the dark and afraid to turn on the light, he inched along. Footsteps crossed the room above him. It sounded like two sets of feet.

"Here Mother," he heard Hornish say.

The reflection of a flickering light scattered across the top of the basement steps. Candles maybe. Or a lantern.

"He's in the basement," Mrs. Hornish informed.

An arc of light illuminated the stairwell. The light descended slowly, one cautious step at a time. Jeff found the first of the jelly and jam cabinets. Extending his arms, he felt his way from cabinet door to cabinet door.

'Maybe,' he thought, 'it would be a good idea to get out my Swiss Army knife.' Admittedly, it wasn't much of a defense against a semi-automatic weapon. But maybe, just maybe, a split second before they opened fire on him, he could hurl the knife across the room at Hornish. Maybe, just maybe, the knife would drive straight into Hornish's nose and up to his brain before a single round could be gotten off. Jeff wasn't a practiced knife thrower. But a miracle could happen. Under intense, life-threatening pressure he might uncover secret knife throwing abilities. Something always happens to save the hero. The strength to lift a bus is found, hidden archery skills revealed. Sometimes, to everyone's astonishment, God takes an active interest in human affairs.

'Fuck,' he thought, 'I'm going to die.'

———

Mrs. Hornish's warm, fleshy voice wafted down the steps toward him.

"Jeff, we don't want to hurt you," she said. "We want to strike a deal."

Jeff backed further away. He wanted to turn his flashlight on for just a moment, just to find a hiding place or perhaps another room. Or better yet, an exit. But he didn't dare.

He found the cement floor uneven in places. The jelly and jam cabinets tipped forward just a little bit. Jeff took hold of one of the cabinet handles, accidentally turning it open. Several jars slid forward, crashing to the floor. Before he could get his bearings he slipped on preserve goo. Attempting to right himself he opened another door, spilling its contents as well. Three shots rang out in his direction. He heard one of the missiles whiz past his ear. The bullets flew into the cabinet behind him, cracking wood and shattering glass. Instinctively Jeff dropped to the floor and flattened himself.

Two more shots flew over his head into the cabinets. These did not come from the direction of the steps but from the opposite direction across the basement. Jeff realized that Cone was on the basement floor with him. He had been all along.

"He's down here," Cone yelled toward the steps. "Near the cabinets."

Faintly, as if from a great distance, the sound of multiple police sirens encroached upon the sound of Jeff's thundering heart.

"Mother," Mr. Hornish warned.

"We'll get him," she said with a certain meanness.

The Hornish's carried lanterns down the steps. In a flash, Jeff spotted Cone across the room. Jeff leapt like a frog away from the steps and out of the light. Cone fired, once again missing. Jeff leapt yet again and rolled into the next room.

Just as he did so Mrs. Hornish let go with a great sweeping arc of bullets. Wood and broken glass exploded in all directions. She continued to fire, spraying a mélange of tomato butter and pickled peppers and preserved cherries. She hit Cone multiple times. Blood spurted like a geyser out of his neck.

"You killed him, Mother," Hornish said.

"He's worthless," Mrs. Hornish replied. "The police are here. Where is that cock sucking Indian?"

"He must be in the next room."

"We haven't time. Here, give me your lamp."

Jeff heard a loud shattering of glass and a whoosh as the oil lantern broke against the wall of wooden cabinets, setting them ablaze.

"Mother!" shouted Mr. Hornish in astonishment.

"It's the best thing," she declared. "Let them burn. Let's get the hell out of here."

Mr. Hornish's highly varnished, handcrafted wood went up like tinder. A tidal wave of fire spread across the roof of the basement. It rolled effortlessly into the room where Jeff huddled in a corner. There was plenty of light now. He could see quite clearly that there was no way to escape.

The blaze in the next room set off a firecracker display of flying bullets, probably from Cone's gun. Several of these seared past Jeff's head. He flung himself up against one of the cabinets in that room, trying to make himself as small a target as possible.

The earsplitting sound of police sirens mixed with the crackle and roar of burning wood. Jeff screamed as loud as he could for help.

Fire from the ceiling ignited the tops of the cabinets in Jeff's room. In a panic he opened the doors and hurled bottles at the encroaching flame.

"I'm down here!" he cried. "Help! I'm down here! I'm down here!"

A single hatchet broke through the plane of the overhead rafter. Water poured through the hole. Then more hatchets broke into the wood. A gush of water poured into the room. A wave of it lifted Jeff up and threw him across the cabinets. He cried out again and again to let them know he was down in the room, he was alive. He wanted out.

Water crashed into the cabinets with such velocity it forced open all the doors. Jars spewed everywhere throughout the room. Jars broke against each other, jars broke against walls. Several jars smashed into Jeff's body; one hit his head. He lost his balance and fell.

He knew if he passed out he would drown in the pool of water now rising in the basement. He struggled to remain upright. He reached both of his hands up into the air. A red coated savior reached down to grab onto his hands. Jeff looked up into the swarthy, water beaded face of a fireman and he could swear, he could just swear, that for a split second, he saw Xander standing at the fireman's side. Then Xander disappeared. He was losing it, losing consciousness. He reached up a little higher for the fireman. One last try.

Before the fireman could grab Jeff's hands, a final imposing cabinet toppled down into the water. Out came the giant jars, the same size jars he and Xander had found in the armoire at Roman's apartment. First five, then ten, then twenty-five, then so, so many. Hundreds. Hundreds and hundreds. Heavy mason jars, each filled with a human head, labeled across the bottom. Jackson Levy, Newport 1992...Angelica Dane, Freeport 1994...

Suzanne Porter, New York 2005...Domenic Sparta, Philadelphia 2003... Todd Masterling, Cambridge 2000...Greta Fields, Pittsburgh...2007. Heads. Hundreds of heads. Jar after jar after jar of pickled heads.

It was then, bobbing among the hideous heads, that Jeff finally lost control of his bladder.

————

The firemen pulled him out of the basement. Jeff, badly bruised, bleeding in several places. It was thought he might have broken a couple of ribs. Two firemen laid him as gently as possible on an ambulance stretcher.

Xander had directed the rescue operation knowing his friend was trapped in the cottage. They tried to hold him back, but at one point he ran into the burning building.

Anxious and scared, he followed Jeff's body in the stretcher and waited until Jeff opened his eyes.

Jeff tried to speak but couldn't get anything out. He wanted so desperately to say, 'What the hell are you doing here?'

Two gun shots echoed out from the area of the lake. Mr. and Mrs. Hornish had escaped in their pontoon. The police pursued them in a neighbor's pontoon. Firemen and police officers worked together to remove the bottled heads from the cottage basement. The jars rested neatly in the snow, markers in a bizarre dream. Someone was puking.

"I climbed up the utility pole and cut the power," Xander explained. "I didn't know how to call the police, so I pulled the fire alarm. I figured when the firemen got here, they could call the police. It was a good thing, a bit of synchronicity don't you think? Because the house caught on fire. I was so scared."

A fireman attending Jeff told him, "You're damn lucky you wore that parka. It has a couple hundred shards of broken glass imbedded in it. If that had been your skin, there wouldn't be any flesh left."

Jeff wanted to thank the fireman but he couldn't make his mouth move.

"I saw your silhouette through the window," Xander said excitedly. "I saw you break into that room. Just sheer guts. You're the bravest man in the United States of America. And I know you. You did it, Jeff. You caught them. Wait till Mrs. Wightman hears about this."

Jeff rolled his eyes. He struggled, struggled so hard, to say, once again, 'What the hell are you doing here? And don't tell Mrs. Wightman a thing!' But all he could do was settle his hand on his little friend's head. As he did so, a tiny Bassett snout popped out of the flap of Xander's coat. A wet puppy tongue reached up and gently licked the underside of Jeff's wrist.

Jeff passed out.

42.

Jeff suffered more from fatigue and hunger than from the myriad cuts and bruises that ranged over his body.

Not a single scar to that gorgeous face, Dear Reader, which I believe demonstrates that God does indeed, on occasion, interfere in human events. God loves a good face.

At the Cleveland Pavilion of Internal Medicine they performed an MRI, ran a number of blood tests, pumped him full of antibiotics and, that done, pampered him silly. His hairy chest, which became the talk of the nurse's station, received any number of ointment treatments and light finger massages, including one he enjoyed from Nurse Danny.

Xander stayed by his friend's side, refusing to leave. The law enforcement community—at least in Ohio—owed a debt of gratitude to the civilian who risked life and limb to expose the murder-for-hire ring responsible for the killing of his old college buddy. Not a soul had bothered to check the college attendance records of either man. Due to Jeff's considerable heroism (and his equally considerable celebrity) hospital administration gave special permission for Xander to sleep in the second bed in Jeff's semi-private room.

Police and federal investigators retrieved nearly four hundred heads from the Hornish cottage in Rock Creek. They found an unspecified number in bean fields adjacent to the Hornish farm house just outside of Cleveland. (These bottles dated from the late eighties and were thought to represent the ring's earliest murders.) The labels on the bottles helped to facilitate identification of the victims.

The local press and later the national press identified Jeff as a computer information specialist with ties to the FBI. Jeff did not describe himself so. In fact, so many case files closed after Jeff's exposure of the Hornish ring that it is entirely possible the F.B.I. itself leaked the connection. An agent from the D.C. office, a young man with a beaming smile, even stopped by to check on Jeff's recovery and to thank him for his efforts on behalf of the Bureau.

"I'm not an agent," Jeff reminded him.

The agent smiled wickedly. "That's not what we say around the office." 'Oh-oh,' Jeff thought. 'Somebody talked, probably Gregory.' "As you might know from the news reports, Jacob and Marion Hornish committed suicide out on the lake. We might like to talk with you later when you come around. Just to fill in our reports."

"Actually, I feel fine. I could talk now."

The agent shook Jeff's hand. "We'll talk later," he said, winking.

Shit.

———

Sally Pooka awoke that fateful Sunday morning to find herself living in interesting times. The phone rang persistently until finally, in disgust, she hauled herself up out of bed and answered it.

That's when she discovered, courtesy of the Ohio State Police, that her son, an Alexander Pooka, was not in his bed where he belonged but in some place called Rock Creek. He had stowed away in the back of a station wagon owned by one of her neighbors, a Jeffrey Redwing. Saturday evening Mr. Redwing drove to the Ohio community of Rock Creek where he became embroiled in a gun battle with a ring of professional criminals thought to be operating a murder-for-hire scheme.

Her son saved Mr. Redwing's life by climbing an electrical pole, cutting off the electricity to the residence thought to house said criminals. He then alerted the fire department to the presence of a dangerous blaze. Her son, though shaken, survived the incident unharmed. Mr. Redwing, suffering from smoke inhalation and multiple wounds to the body, was rushed to the Cleveland Pavilion of Internal Medicine. He appears to be recovering.

Would she like to speak to her child?

Once in Cleveland, Sally got the story first from Xander and later from Jeff. Remarkable as it sounded, it kind of made sense. She understood the elaborate, if strange, process by which Jeff took an interest in solving the murder of an old college friend. The rather wild story concerning a dance floor shooting of a notorious Liberty Avenue drag queen/prostitute sounded plausible in a certain light. Lack of sleep affected his judgment when he decided to drive to Rock Creek to confront Marshall's killers—in an extremely isolated place in the dead of night in the next state over. Okay. Maybe, just maybe, she could buy all that. What choice did she have? It was the story being offered up. The police seemed to buy it. Even the FBI seemed to buy it.

Her son's behavior surprised her not one tiny bit.

And yet, Sally was no fool. A mother could sense a lie instinctively. She knew in her heart that the big child and the little child had conspired together in a lie. She just couldn't prove it. There wasn't much she could do about it. So there it was.

She couldn't forbid Xander to see Jeff. Her son clearly idolized this man. And Xander did not worship alone. During Jeff's stay in the hospital Sally sat by his side. She watched while Jeff, sitting upright in his bed, received nurses and doctors and reporters and well wishers and stray hospital patients, even an FBI agent, like some kind of hairy-chested Buddha. People were drawn to him. They longed to stay with him and touch him.

She felt it herself sometimes. The man possessed a certain magic. It filled her with admiration and a sad kind of love. This made her a forgiving person when she ought to have been a dubious person.

'It must be his looks,' Sally thought. 'People are drawn to a handsome man, especially when he has an innocent, winsome quality. Disarming. That's it, disarming.' A disarming, handsome man could be a dangerous thing, Sally realized. This one bore watching.

———

At one point during Jeff's hospital stay, Xander left to play with Topper in the kennel. Mrs. Pooka, alone now with Jeff, decided she herself would apply Jeff's Vitamin E salve to his face and torso.

"I'm tired of these nurses coming in here feeling you up," she declared.

Jeff teased, "So you thought you'd do it yourself."

"Watch it, Redwing. I'll give you a couple more bruises."

"Yes, Mrs. Pooka."

He closed his eyes while Sally slowly pressed the oily salve into his face.

"It's a shame all those dogs died in the fire," she said. "Poor innocent things. Just that one pup survived. Xander found him running around outside."

"He's an adventurer, that little dog," Jeff replied quietly. "He wasn't with the brood when I entered the kitchen."

"How could you tell? Did he look that much different from the other pups?"

"He didn't sleep with the other pups. He liked to climb on top of his mother's back and sleep there. That's why they named him Topper. I looked for him on the floor because I didn't want to step on him."

"Very considerate of you under the circumstances."

"I didn't want him to yelp and give me away. Although, I don't know why I bothered. Two minutes later I burst in on them like Zorro. That was so stupid."

"Was it the lack of sleep? You weren't thinking clearly?"

"Yes, that. Also I heard them talking. They said they were going to kill me. Which I expected, really. But then they said they were going to kill Xander. I don't know. I just lost it."

"You love him more than his father ever did," said Mrs. Pooka. After a slight hesitation, she leaned forward and kissed him on the forehead. He didn't crack a smile or acknowledge her act of affection in any way. He just allowed it. The gall of that man!

"Incidentally," Sally said. "You get the dog."

"C'mon Sally. You see how Xander loves that dog. He wants it so badly."

"I don't care. I'm allergic to animal dander. Pet hair makes me itch." Jeff lifted open his left eye and examined Sally skeptically. "I break out in hives."

"You're a mean mom."

"That's what everybody says. I'm still not taking the dog. Xander can play with him at your house."

————

After being home a few weeks Jeff received a commendation from the Mayor's office. On his way to the podium, Jeff made a point of vigorously shaking the hand of Detective Carlton Lyons. Ellen Coffey, just a few seats down from Sally Pooka, shook her head in amazement. She felt deeply touched when Jeff turned and gave his commendation to Xander for saving his life. 'Yes,' thought Mrs. Coffey, 'he came so close to death this time. So close.' She could not shake the image in her mind of Jeff, blue on a slab in her laboratory.

In time Dottie Hatfield recovered from her nearly fatal gunshot wounds. She kept the lacy Victorian wedding gown, two holes in the back, drenched in dried blood, as a souvenir of her brush with death. She put it right back on the wire dress dummy in her apartment.

Along with Rose, Dottie waited and prayed for a call from the police. Vernon's head had not been among those found at the cottage. Dottie assumed the head never made it to Ohio. There hadn't been time to transport that particular trophy to the Hornish lakeside abode. Where was it?

When questioned, Franklin Baum feigned mental illness and denied all knowledge of the Roman/Chester murders. "I don't know nothing about no heads," he complained. "I seen pickled pig's feet, I seen pickled herring, but I ain't never seen no pickled heads." Remarkably, authorities were never able to tie Franklin Baum to any of the murders or murder suspects. His name in Roman's little black address book was not enough to charge him with association or conspiracy, much less murder.

The Hornish clan often used costumes and always decapitated their victims. The pattern of the Roman/Chester killings matched the pattern of all the other Hornish killings. Roman was clearly affiliated with Hornish.

The Allegheny County Sheriff's Department felt justified closing the book on the murders of Vernon Roman and Marshall Chester.

43.

THE EGGMAN ALLOWED JEFF A RESPECTABLE AMOUNT OF TIME AT HOME before ringing in with their special Beatles tune.

JEFF
I was wondering when you were going to call.

EGGMAN
Howdy partner.

A cowboy in chaps appeared on Jeff's screen, a big letter J in the center of his chest. On the other side of the screen a group of lowdown good-for-nothing cowboys (wearing bandanas) appeared. The cowboy in chaps moseyed on over to the good-for-nothings and drew on them, blowing them away. Toy gun sounds accompanied the action.

JEFF
Very funny.

EGGMAN
Hey, partner. I made you a star on the Internet. You done us hackers and nerds proud. One day we'd like to grow up to be just like you. Have our own shoot out.

JEFF
I didn't shoot anybody. I didn't have a gun.

EGGMAN
So I read. I put all your newspaper clippings, along with
a few personal comments, on my Website. Sound effects, too.

JEFF
Thanks. I need more publicity.

EGGMAN
You're entirely welcome. In Japan you're bigger than
Madonna. A guy in Norway named a cow after you.

JEFF
A cow?

EGGMAN
Yes. There's a cow in Norway named Jeff Redwing. Think
about it. You're an inspiration. You're also just a teensy bit
dumb. What were you thinking?

JEFF
They threatened to kill Xander. I went off the deep end. I
burst into the room shouting, "FBI" Told them I had a lot
of back up.

EGGMAN
Did they buy it?

JEFF
For about twenty seconds. Then...

EGGMAN
Whew! Glad you're still with us, buddy.

An egg shaped face, beading with perspiration, appeared on the screen.
A cartoon hand wiped the perspiration off of the egg's forehead.

JEFF
Thanks. Glad to be here myself. Glad they're all dead.

EGGMAN
I noticed the FBI stepped in and took a lot of credit.

JEFF
They're welcome to all the credit. An agent came to visit
me in the hospital. He said they call me Special Agent
Redwing around the Bureau. He meant it sarcastically.
I might be in trouble with the Bureau.

EGGMAN
How so, Walrus?

JEFF
I'm supposed to meet with them in D.C. early next year.
They're either going to commend me or inform me I'm in
deep shit. If I disappear shortly after my D.C. visit you'll
know it was deep shit.

EGGMAN
I vote for commendation. You're a hero. If they do anything
but erect a bronze replica of your ass in the lobby, let me know.
I'll send a virus their way.

JEFF
I'll have to cure the virus. Don't do me any favors.

EGGMAN
On a lighter subject...how was your Christmas?

JEFF
A lot of fun. Sally (that's Xander's mother) and Xander
spoiled me. They gave me a wooden crate, stamped Maine on
the side, filled with goodies from L.L.Bean. I gave Xander
an iMac.

EGGMAN
How do I sign up to have you as a Big Brother?

JEFF
The kid deserves it. He's brilliant. His real dad ran out on him.
Sally can barely afford to pay her bills.

EGGMAN
Did you give Sally a Christmas present? Or is that a touchy subject?

JEFF
I gave her a year's supply of beauty treatments and massages at Elizabeth Arden. Actually, Dottie Hatfield gave me the suggestion.

EGGMAN
Loved those headlines, Walrus. Drag queen shot at over-21 dance in the arms of computer information specialist. Ooo-la-la. I want to have your children. You'll be getting letters soon. I put the newspaper articles on my site.

JEFF
Oh, thanks. My address, too, I suppose.

EGGMAN
I wasn't that tacky. But let's face it, how many Jeff Redwings can there be in Wexford, PA? I bet they have a special bin for you at the post office.

JEFF
You bet right. My correspondence has been keeping me entertained throughout my convalescence. I've even received nude photos. From men, women and drag queens.

EGGMAN
Well, that covers the waterfront.

JEFF
As it turns out, that only covers a part of the waterfront.

EGGMAN
Oh? Never mind. I won't ask.

JEFF
So how was your Christmas?

EGGMAN
I'm Jewish. We don't do Christmas. I did spend the holidays with my family. Let's just say I was so pleased that next year, as a special Chanukah present, I am thinking of giving each and every one of them the Lizzie Borden award.

JEFF
Now, now. Be nice. At least you have a family.

EGGMAN
I like yours better. They give nice presents. So, Walrus, what's next? Any plans for the future?

JEFF
Xander and I are spending the rest of Christmas vacation watching all the great movies I've never seen. Sally joins us after work. They can't believe I've never seen these movies. Last night we watched *Star Trek VI.*

EGGMAN
Loved the great floating blobs of Milk of Magnesia blood.

JEFF
That was cool. Also liked *Close Encounters.* When the long awaited spaceship turns out to be a hotel chandelier—that was the first good laugh I'd had since everything happened.

EGGMAN
Careful, now. *Close Encounters* is sacred. And spaceships really do look like hotel chandeliers. Can't believe you haven't seen these movies before. Too much time in the Cloisters. You need to get out more.

JEFF
No comment. Sally brings new movies over every day. Tonight we're watching *Gandhi* and *The Last Emperor.*

EGGMAN
Why hold back? Throw in *Lawrence of Arabia* and cover that whole region of the map. Hope you have lots of popcorn. A three foot high bag ought to do it.

JEFF
Well, that's it. That's all I'm doing. I'm not even going to leave my house if I can help it. Sally brings in food, Xander brings in the mail. I'm just going to sit on my couch, recuperate and avoid as much reality as possible.

EGGMAN
Sounds like a good plan. Glad you're okay, Walrus. I
was worried about you.

JEFF
Ah, shucks.

On the screen an egg shaped face blew Jeff a kiss of musical notes.

EGGMAN
Goo-goo-ga-choo.

JEFF
Later, Eggman.

———

Sally and Xander practically lived at Jeff's house from the time he returned home until Xander resumed his formal education on the third of January. Sally shopped for groceries and movies (with Jeff's credit card). Jeff busied himself with the preparation of lavish meals. In the afternoons while Sally worked, Jeff and Xander played computer games, tinkered with the synthesizers and recording equipment up in the Cloisters, and watched whatever shows were on the Sci-Fi channel. At night Jeff and Sally and Xander watched two, three, even four movies.

Sally enjoyed a good movie, but four in a row was a bit much for her. Somewhere into the third film she either fell asleep in her chair or excused herself to one of the guest bedrooms. Xander, accustomed to secretly watching television in his room until the wee hours of the morning, held up pretty well through Jeff's holiday film marathon.

Though he wouldn't say so, Jeff didn't want to be alone in the house. No matter how tired he became, he just couldn't sleep. He jogged on his treadmill, lifted weights, did ab work along with a DVD, cooked elaborate meals, watched three or four movies. Nothing helped. If he laid down in the quiet of his bedroom he thought about the heads, rowing out into the lake, the exhumation of Greta Fields' corpse, the pitch dark of the Hornish basement, Larry Cone firing shots from across the room, Penny jerking upright with the phone in her hand.

All these scenes played through his head over and over. And more.

Even Xander fell asleep eventually. When that happened, Jeff comforted himself with a sip or two of Macallan. He watched infomercials or ran one of the movies again. Every couple of days he actually fell asleep for a few hours, waking with a nightmare.

The day of the Chester burial, Jeremy Richer had compared Jeff to Alec Baldwin. Jeff thought he would like to see an Alec Baldwin movie. Sally rented *The Hunt for Red October*. When Jeff caught sight of the handsome actor on the screen he felt embarrassed—and grateful not to have mentioned Jeremy's comparison.

Watching the movie, sipping Scotch, Jeff thought about Jeremy Richer. He recalled the graceful movement of Richer's body as he opened chairs at the gravesite. Jeff remembered the dark, handsome face greeting him at the entrance to the funeral parlor. The voice on the phone. Jeff wondered how long Jeremy might be staying in Pittsburgh to take care of his sister. How appropriate would it be for him to call for a date. Was he, Jeff, ready to date?

The killer of orchids. That was how Jeremy Richer described his brother-in-law. The killer of orchids.

'Alec Baldwin is far too handsome,' Jeff thought. 'How could Richer make such a comparison? My complexion is darker for one thing. Well, I'm part Cherokee. My cheekbones are wider. We share a similar body type. Maybe that's what he meant. If I painted my face white, put makeup on my cheekbones that made them appear closer together, wore a Navy uniform, then maybe, in a dark room...'

"Shit!" he said out loud.

Xander, sleeping in Sally's arms, stirred but did not wake.

'Shit,' he thought.

Because, Dear Reader, he knew.

He knew.

Should he take action? Should he tell someone?

After all. He had put so much work into this. He risked his life, for Christ's sake. And there was such a thing as justice. There was such a thing as morality. Two threads in the fabric of the law, of civilized behavior. Aren't these things important? Aren't they more important than my personal well being?

"No," he said finally. "I'm done with this."

Sally roused and stretched. Squinting at him, she asked in a groggy voice, "Did you say something?"

"I'm done with this," said Jeff. "I'm going upstairs to bed."

Jeff turned off *The Hunt for Red October*. He climbed the stairs and turned down his wonderful, warm, goose down blanket and slid his naked, aching body into high count Egyptian cotton sheets. He slept the sleep of a man who has been pardoned.

44.

By the time the crocuses bloomed in May, a major page turned in the Chester household.

Scott Chester, graduating in the top 2% of his class, accepted a scholarship from Washington Jefferson to study Russian. His stated long term goal: move to Russia, help ease that struggling nation's transitional difficulties. His secret long term goal: get as far away from his family as humanly possible. With any luck he'd never see Pittsburgh again. When he died they could bury his body in Moscow.

Young Jason Chester planned to build a model city in Scott's room. Plans included a magnetic high speed transportation system that started at the airport (his room) and culminated in Dream City (Scott's room). Total immersion in blueprints and design details took his attention off of his mother's big move to New York. Without him.

———

A white Cadillac limousine drew up to the Chester residence. Scott and Jason stood in the doorway of their home. They watched Uncle Jeremy, now their guardian, load suitcases into the limo's trunk.

Jane Lund got out of the limo to see if she could help. When she realized there wasn't anything she could do, she watched Jeremy shift suitcases around to make more room. Jane laughed.

"We could have sent a few things UPS," she said.

Jeremy looked up from his organizational duties.

He hadn't quite adjusted to his sister's relationship with the dark and frail Ms. Lund. It surprised him. But then, why should his sister be alone? Jane Lund made a much more appropriate companion than Marshall

Chester. Jane was at least interesting. Jeremy certainly approved of Elenora's move to New York to resume her acting career. The orchid, thought dead, blossoms once more.

"I wonder," he said smiling, "how the two of you are going to get all these suitcases up to your apartment?"

"Elenora says if you've got money, there is always someone in New York willing to carry your bags."

"That's true." Jeremy laughed. "How pragmatic of my sister to say so."

"Oh," said Jane, "she's the Saint Teresa of pragmatism. She's got me digesting food now. I've even promised to give up cigarettes once the move is complete. What will I do without anorexia and cigarettes?" Jane laughed her signature hiccup laugh. "How will I fill up my day?" Hiccup. Jane shook her head, smiling. "That remains to be seen." She looked down at the street as if a picture of her future resided there.

Jeremy looked back at the doorway, where his beamingly beautiful sister hugged and kissed Scott.

"You'll be all right," Jeremy said. "She's raised seven boys. I don't imagine she'll have much trouble with you."

Scott, trembling with suppressed anger, produced one well rounded tear. He felt betrayed by his mother, though he couldn't say why. He understood her need to create a new life. He certainly understood her need to get the hell out. But a part of him thought she should wither purposeless until death in the Chester homestead.

"I'm so proud of you," she said.

Not his way, the complete surrender. He hugged his mother, but stiffly. She nuzzled him on the neck like a lover.

"Jane and I have a fabulous apartment in New York with a view of Central Park. Plenty of guest rooms. New York is a magical city. You'll see when you visit. Anything can happen. Even my tired old self can build a new life."

Jeremy approached them.

"You're all set," he said.

Elenora took Jason's hand.

"Come walk with me," she said, wanting to speak privately to her youngest, most vulnerable child. Jason walked in fearsome silence. He had witnessed his mother's troubles with drugs. Many times he cried himself to sleep, not knowing what was wrong with her. He never wanted to see her back on those pills sleeping her days away. But he didn't understand why she couldn't take him to New York.

"Your Uncle Jeremy will take good care of you. You know that."

"Yes," he replied.

"It's important that Mommy goes to New York. I'm going toward something I very much need. I'm not leaving you. It would break my heart if you thought that."

"I don't think that," said the wizened boy. "But why can't I go with you?"

"For one thing, you have to finish your school year."

"It's almost done."

"Mostly I need time to get settled. I need time to get used to New York. I'm an old woman now, Jason. I know you don't think of your Mommy that way, but I am. I don't have the natural courage of a young woman. And. I'm going back to school. When not in school, I'll be auditioning for parts. I'll be busy all the time. I don't want you growing up alone. I'm afraid that might happen if you came with me to New York."

"Jane will be there. She could look out for me."

Elenora smiled.

"Honey, your Aunt Jane is more of a child than you are. I'm afraid you would be looking after her."

Jason looked down, suppressing tears. He didn't want her to stay; he didn't want her to leave.

"Your Uncle Jeremy loves you to pieces," Elenora said. "You'll have so much fun with him. Uncle Jeremy has been alone all of his life. Now he'll have you for company. You can do lots of things together. You'll see lots of movies, I'll promise you that. And you know what else?"

"What?" Despite his best effort, he shook. Tears started falling.

"One day I'll be an actress on television. You can tell all your friends that your Mommy is a famous actress. Won't that be fun?"

Jason nodded, still looking down.

"And once I get settled you can come to visit. You can spend the summer in New York. You can come up for weekends. And I'm always just a phone call away. You can call me every day if you want. Okay?"

Jason nodded.

"So you're not losing me, little man."

Elenora held him close to her. She smelled his hair, the skin around his neck. She wanted to burn his little boy smell into her brain so that she could recall it in an instant.

"Now I've got to let you go or I'll never leave."

Jason let go of his mother. She straightened up, walked back to the limo. Jeremy walked with her.

"It's hard," he said, as she wiped tears away with her sleeve. "But it's the right thing to do."

"I'm scared," she said.

"You'll be fine. Acting is just another profession. And you're very good at it. There is a demand for actors in your age group to play smaller roles. You can start there. Remember, Danny Aiello started in his forties."

"That's right," she said, laughing just a little. "Don't think I haven't been collecting late-in-life success stories. And it's not like I'm starting from scratch. I am a graduate of the highly esteemed Carnegie Mellon drama school."

"Second only to Yale."

"First in my day," she said.

"There you go."

Well," she said, collecting herself. "I've kept this limo driver waiting long enough." She started to turn from her brother.

"Sis?"

"Yes?"

"Thanks for, you know, the financial support. And the opportunity to be Jason's guardian. I know I haven't been a model of stability. You could have chosen someone else."

"Nonsense," she said. "We're like twins, you and I. You're a hero to me. I trust you implicitly."

Jeremy, Scott and Jason watched together as the Cadillac drove Elenora away. Soon it disappeared around a bend.

And so it was done.

Scott asked if he could take Jason to Eat 'n' Park for a sundae. Jeremy, grateful for the opportunity to be alone, told them to take their time.

———

'Is there such a thing as justifiable murder?' Jeremy wondered.

He climbed the stairs to do what he must do. Time to burn a little sacred cloth. As he ascended, he thought about the matter of Greta Fields. She clearly, deliberately, and wickedly destroyed the well planned lives of deserving people. No gray matter. She did this. She earned her living doing it.

Was killing Greta Fields the same as killing a terrorist? If we knew she had destroyed ten lives, would that be justification enough to murder her? What about five lives? What about the planned destruction of just one life? At what point does it become the same as stopping a terrorist?

In the second floor hallway Jeremy reached up for a piece of rope suspended from the ceiling. Pulling the rope released a compact set of collapsible wooden stairs that led to an attic storage area. Jeremy squeezed up these stairs and entered through the small opening. He choked at first on the stale air and dust of the hot, dry space.

Marshall had made that decision, Jeremy realized. Marshall decided at what point he felt justified arranging the murder of Greta Fields. Marsh lived with that decision for a short time, then, on that unseasonably warm December evening, died from it. It wasn't Jeremy's place to pass judgment on his brother-in-law. What if she had attacked me? Jeremy asked himself. What if she attempted to bring to an end my own cherished way of life? Would I have killed her?

Might have. Of course, Jeremy didn't have a career he cared anything about. He had almost become a priest. He almost cared about that. Almost.

In the very center of the attic he stood up straight. There was an old Louis Vuitton steamer trunk back by one of the windows. What a wonderful contraption, riddled with secret compartments and locked chambers. One such compartment held bottles of liquor. The lid of the trunk opened to form a writing desk. His mother purchased it at auction for five dollars in the sixties. It would fetch thousands today.

Jeremy took a key from his wallet. With it he unlocked one of the larger compartments. His cassock and collar, stolen from the seminary so many years ago, lay neatly stored inside.

"Old friend," he said, rubbing the familiar black cloth against the smooth skin of his cheek. "The Halloween parties. Mardi Gras. All the sex I had in this costume. Brothers and sisters, we are gathered here together to celebrate the body of the host. Old, old friend. I hate to do it."

Jeremy took his cassock and collar down to the nicely appointed sitting room where Jeff had once sipped tea in fine china with Elenora. In the fireplace he arranged three Duroflame logs and set them alight.

'No more Jeremy the Priest,' he thought, laying the cassock into the fire. 'Pittsburgh can be a small town. I just can't risk running into that Redwing character dressed in this costume. It's amazing he didn't recognize me at the funeral parlor. Well, I didn't recognize him either. Not without the little boy.'

He remembered the call he got from Scott that frightful night.

"Father has been murdered in the city," Scott said with a strangely impatient intonation, as if getting murdered was the kind of thing that happened to suburban people who wandered out of place. "Mother asks that you come right away. Fly in if necessary."

Jeremy hurriedly packed every stray bit of clothing. He remembered hesitating over the priest's robes. Why take them? For what possible use? Perhaps the presence of death inspired him. Someone in the family had died. Perhaps the opportunity for high theater will arise. In a flash he packed the cassock and collar.

At four in the morning he discovered the Chester household surrounded by news trucks and police vehicles. His sister ran to him, threw her arms around him. Her body was hot to the touch. Tears streaming down her cheek burned against his own skin. It was a terrible thing to think, but he thought it anyway. 'That mediocre man is dead. Finally.'

But his sister had loved the mediocre man. She needed comforting. And he, Jeremy, would tend to all the arrangements on her behalf, intercede with the media, act as a liaison with the police, tend to the children. Offer solace. Yes, solace. He had trained for it, however briefly.

Imagine his surprise when the next morning, after everyone in the house had gone and they were finally alone, Elenora took him upstairs to the attic. 'Quiet, quiet, I have something to show you.' And then the Louis Vuitton trunk with its secret, locked compartments.

It was like when they were children. She, the older and wiser sister, knew things about the grown up world. Whenever she found something interesting or revealing she took him by the hand and led him to it. 'There! There it is! Evidence of how they really are. Didn't I tell you? Aren't you shocked (yet pleased)?'

That afternoon in the attic she removed the nun's habit from one of the locked compartments. Modern nuns no longer wore this kind of garb. They dressed like civilians. But the older orders still wore the black cloth, the tightly wrapped head piece. German nuns, eastern European nuns. What could it mean? What role did this antiquated nun's habit play in her husband's demise?

She withdrew another costume. She showed him the blue and gold silk, the black trimmings, splattered with dried blood. While his mind raced with forbidden thoughts, Elenora opened a false bottom in the trunk. From it she removed a long, curved, beautifully ornamented ceremonial sword. Stained with the same dried blood.

"I have the head, too," was all she said. "I hid it in a safe place. But I have a problem. The belt. The samurai's belt. I think I left it in the confessional at the church."

What could he do but help his sister?

Jeremy stuffed his cassock and collar into a plastic Giant Eagle supermarket bag and drove to St. Stephen's church. What a lovely old church it turned out to be. Nineteenth century robber barons had poured their gilt-laden millions into a monument of sandstone, stained glass, gold and mahogany. The place was open but empty, a sad reflection on the state of city churches.

He found one functioning confessional (the others were being used as storage)! He searched for but did not find the samurai belt. If the police didn't have it already, it was still in the church somewhere. To poke around the offices and back rooms, he would need to look like he belonged there.

That was why he had taken the cassock and collar along. He changed into his costume right there in the confessional just as his sister had done the previous evening.

The offices and back rooms were locked. Well, this was the city and not a very nice neighborhood at that. He couldn't very well break down the doors, not with the police haunting the scene of the crime just next door. What difference did this belt make anyway? The police couldn't connect it with Elenora. Could they?

It was then, emerging from the back, he encountered that handsome man and his little boy. Or not quite his boy. What was the story? He couldn't remember. Anyway, there they were, playing make believe in the confessional. Blasphemes. Jeremy enjoyed having his little joke with Redwing, obviously a lapsed Catholic. And that Xander was a hoot. Private investigator indeed. What private investigator took his son, or pretend son, along on an investigation?

Then the man tried to pass himself off as one of Marshall's old college chums. Anyone could see that Redwing was in his early thirties. But if he wasn't an old college chum and he wasn't a private investigator, what was he? The FBI took half hearted credit for him. Special consultant, they called him.

Well, in the end Redwing did a good job, whoever his employer might be. A good job, but not a perfect one. A few details eluded his detection. The matter of the costumes. I mean really. Costumes link to actors. Don't you think? Perhaps they don't understand, these law enforcement types, that an actor never stops acting.

My sister took on the role of wife and mother for twenty some years. Even though she played that one role, and only that role, for such a long time, Elenora remained an actress without parallel. Her performance on that fatal night proved it.

Redwing missed something else, something that even a lapsed Catholic should have noticed. At one point during their conversation, Jeremy glanced up toward the pulpit. There, laid ever so neatly across its slanted surface, was a lovely piece of blood stained black silk. To the casual eye it looked perhaps like part of a vestment or ceremonial cloth. But such a piece would not be black. It would be gold or white.

Jeremy knew in an instant that upon the pulpit rested his sister's incriminating samurai belt. Some conscientious church-goer obviously came upon it and determined it belonged to the church. It looked perfectly placed, almost invisible.

The completed samurai ensemble along with the nun's habit was now enroute to New York. Elenora planned to sell them or donate them to a theatrical costume outfitter. Within a few months Jeremy planned to drive the sword to New York as well. He would rather burn his sister's incriminating costumes along with his own. He wanted to bury the sword in Cook's Forest or, better yet, melt the thing down.

Elenora wouldn't hear of it. Years from now, after her death, she wanted people to know she did it. She wanted people to trace the costumes and the sword. She thought she might write a play about the Chester/Roman murders. The costumes and sword could be used in the production.

"Wouldn't that be a delicious irony," she said to her brother.

Jeremy chose his sister over justice. She knew he would. She counted on it. He did her bidding without requiring an explanation.

One quiet afternoon after all the madness had settled, Elenora made a pot of tea. She invited her brother into the nicely appointed sitting room. In front of a roaring fire, she told her story.

45.

ELENORA TRACED IT ALL BACK TO HER PREGNANCY WITH JASON.

During that pregnancy Marsh stopped having sex with her. That wasn't entirely unusual. During the later stages of her previous pregnancies they had refrained. But this time, after Jason's birth, they did not resume. This was by mutual, though unspoken, consent. Even though they were only in their late-thirties, sex had long since ceased to be arousing or exciting. It had devolved into a form of dispassionate physical release.

"When he mounted me," Elenora confessed, "I imagined men from my college days. I imagined television actors. One of my favorites was the aluminum siding guy from the next street over. He's chubby and a little bald but nonetheless possesses a certain masculine élan."

"I know just what you mean," said Jeremy.

"Marsh must have imagined himself with other women. It just became less and less satisfying. After Jason we just gave up the pretense. But something else happened. I think we stopped caring about each other as well. We became a functioning family unit with no underlying purpose.

"I realized, Jeremy, that without the sex and without the love, I became essentially a housemaid and a nanny. This tortured me. I had once been a person with dreams."

"I'm so glad you're saying it," said Jeremy.

"I didn't have the courage to overcome my circumstances. Divorce without good cause meant giving up my children, because I knew Marsh would fight for them. And then, from a financial perspective, how would I survive? I still had a little money from father, but that was earmarked for college tuition. How could I justify taking my children's tuition money?"

Elenora worried all the time. Possibilities, scenarios. Her whole life became about dreams and imaginings.

She comforted herself with compulsive masturbation. In her imagination she fucked every man she ever found attractive in high school, in college, in the neighborhood, in retail stores. Even her children's teenage friends. She purchased a dildo during this period, one with a special clitoral stimulator. Of course, she had to hide the thing. It's difficult to hide something in a house full of children. That's when she rediscovered the Louis Vuitton trunk. Elenora experienced some of the best orgasms of her life up on the attic floor.

The masturbation sessions, and especially the fantasies that went with them, made life tolerable. They kept her from screaming out loud; they kept her from taking action. They enabled Elenora to ride out her time in a life without purpose. For a while.

Then she found she couldn't sleep.

"God, Jeremy, night after night lying in bed with Marshall. Not sleeping, trying to sleep, not sleeping. Sometimes I stared at him while he slept. He looked like an alien creature to me. Do you understand? I would lie there and think to myself, 'I've never gotten a good look at this man. He looks strange. I've had sex with this man thousands of times. Let him inside my body. Why? Who the hell is he?' I'll tell you something, Jeremy. Sometimes I'd stare at him for an hour, maybe more. After a while he didn't even look human to me. He'd look like some other species I'd mistaken for human."

On and on it went until Elenora talked the family doctor into a prescription for sleeping pills. Later Valium. That's when she discovered the great release of sleep.

"If you've failed your dreams, Jeremy, sleep can be a powerful and most welcome balm. Better than booze. You simply drift away. No pain, no consequences. After a while no lunches to fix, no husband to launch. Mommy's tired. Leave Mommy alone. Did the phone ring? I was sleeping. Did you already make dinner? Sorry, I was asleep. Sleep, sleep, my dear. The elixir of failed dreams.

"During what I now call My Sleep Period, Penny English slept with my husband and, worse, Vernon Roman entered our lives."

Of course, Elenora had heard many stories about the great and wondrous Vernon Roman—especially the story of his inexplicable parachute escape from a promising academic future.

The man Marsh brought home was at best seedy and vile. They had accidentally run into each other. After all those years. Wasn't that amazing?

Elenora tolerated his presence on that first day. She studied him as actors will do. She fed him a sandwich while he told stories from his scabrous street existence. It was all very amusing. Marsh drove Vernon home. She didn't expect to see Vernon again. After all, whatever relationship Marsh enjoyed with him in high school, they shared nothing in common now.

"Why on earth," asked Elenora, "would we choose to socialize with a street hustler?"

Yet Vernon returned. Like the flu you can't quite shake. Back at her house. Eating her food, saying filthy things to her children, making inappropriate sexual comments to her. He wasn't coming on. It was just dirt for dirt's sake. It had become his way of life. This is how he lived. This is how he expressed himself.

"I don't begrudge anyone their lifestyle, Jeremy," said Elenora. "But he did not belong in my house with my husband and my children. What was he doing there? Why did Marsh extend the invitation again and again?"

Elenora and Marsh discussed, then fought about it. This was Marshall's old and cherished friend. There was nothing wrong with him that a little TLC wouldn't fix.

"TLC, Jeremy. This street crud. He had been a hustler. You understand? While Marshall and I built a home and brought children into this world, he sold his body on the street to men. Bent over for truck drivers. Who knows what he did. Then I heard the name Greta Fields."

Marshall didn't want to tell her at first. All this trouble at school. In all fairness to Marsh, maybe he thought he couldn't talk to Elenora about it. She had become something of a problem. Valium alternating with sleeping pills. Still. Vernon Roman knew about Greta Fields and Elenora did not. That's when she became suspicious.

A notion crept into her brain. Greta Fields was the reason for the sudden emergence and persistence of Vernon Roman. Something was going on. Something very important and, given Vernon's involvement, probably sinister. Elenora decided it would be in her best interest to stay awake.

She pretended to take her pills; she faked sleep. Her inability to sleep without medication became for the first time as asset. She noticed, for instance, that her husband kept strange hours. After the kids went to bed for the night, he checked to make certain Elenora was sleeping, then slipped out. He often did not return until 5 a.m. The kids must have noticed something, given how kids are. But they didn't mention it. Elenora began to feel like there was a conspiracy going on. Everyone was in on it but her.

Then it happened. One night Marshall brought Vernon to the house around 2 a.m. Marsh entered their bedroom to check on Elenora. He whispered her name several times. Elenora kept her eyes closed and her body still. Marshall returned downstairs to Vernon.

There is a small sewing room just over the dining room. A carpet covers an old heating vent. Elenora lifted back the carpet and listened at the vent.

She heard Marshall say, "What guarantees do I have?"

Vernon answered, "You don't need guarantees. This is a business. If we don't come through, word gets out. We go out of business."

Elenora heard the sound of a cupboard door closing, then the clinking of crystal.

"I can't sleep at night," Marsh said. "I never used to drink this late."

They moved around a bit, away from the vent. For a while Elenora could only make out mumblings and an occasional word. Then Vernon moved back nearer the vent. She heard him clearly say, "It's done. It's in motion. You'd be stupid to try to stop it now. For one thing you'd be out ten grand. Then you'd still have to live with your problem."

Elenora's heart beat so loudly she wondered if they could hear her downstairs. The house was ultra quiet. What problem did Marshall live with? Was Elenora his problem? Was she listening in on plans to do away with an unwanted spouse? She had seen so much of that in the news lately. Seemed everyone was doing it. What undercover agent would come to her rescue?

"I have a conscience," Marshall said. "Will I be able to live with myself afterward? What kind of life will I have?"

"The life you deserve," Vernon firmly replied. "The life you were living before that bitch came along. Look, man. You studied hard, you got your degrees, you gave a hundred percent to your school and your students. You did all the right things. You're a good man, right? Hey, listen, you were always the nicest guy in school. I could never compete."

A jumble of noises ensued. The two men moved around, fixed additional drinks. Marshall said something; Elenora couldn't make it out.

Then she heard Vernon say, "If a burglar comes into your house, what do you do? The man's a threat to your family, a threat to your life. You blow him away. Am I right? What can he say? He's a burglar. He knows every time he breaks into a house there's a chance he'll get blown away. Another burglary, another chance. This Fields woman. She makes a career out of busting people's ass. She fucks people over. Seems to me if you fuck people over for a living, you run the risk that one of your victims will fuck you back. Am I right?"

"Yes, yes," said Marsh. "It's all very logical. But for Christ's sake, Vernon. I'm a Catholic. Murder is a mortal sin. I've been raised to believe that life is sacred."

"What else have you been raised to believe?" countered Roman. "Come on, Marsh. You were raised to believe if you worked hard, if you were an honest man, you could accomplish anything in life. Along comes this psychopathic bitch. She targets you. She gossips about you, spreads lies about you, sets you up to look bad. Soon your colleagues don't like you as much as they thought.

"Then you hear that word. Incompetence. Your work has always been the best. Still you hear it. Once the word incompetence enters the discussion, she has won her campaign. She can even afford to say something nice about you once in a while, just so she can appear to hold a balanced perspective.'

"But her campaign of slander and insinuation means professional death. Once she gets you fired from this school, your career is over. You've invested your youth and your middle age developing this career. You don't have a second life's worth of time to build another one. It's over. Your livelihood, your reputation, your future, your dreams, your family's dreams, your health. All over. Because of one psychopathic bitch named Greta Fields. Hey, I say you're lucky you found us."

A long silence followed this speech.

Then Marshall said, "How will it be done?"

"Cone will do it."

"Penny's boyfriend. How did he get involved?"

"He's been involved," answered Roman. "Penny talked to him about your situation. Cone talked to our people in Cleveland. They talked to me about this guy in trouble named Marshall Chester. I think, 'How many Marshall Chester's can there be?'"

"So our meeting wasn't coincidental."

"I look at it as an unscheduled business meeting. What's that word? Synchronicity. I owe you. From that time back in high school. I turned my back on you. My life-long friend. I shouldn't have done that."

"So you owe me a life-saving murder."

"That's exactly what I'd call it. A life-saving murder. Hey, I could have left you hanging out there. But I said to myself, 'This guy was my best buddy at one time. He needs me now. I should take care of him.'" Vernon moved about, mixed himself yet another drink. "But it's probably not absolutely too late. If you want to spare the bitch, we can take our finger off of the trigger. You won't get your money back."

Marshall asked resignedly, "How will Cone do it?"

"Better for you not to know. There are a thousand ways to take somebody out. It will look perfectly natural. The beauty of it is: she will die doing something she loved."

"If it looks like a natural death, how will I know your people did it?" Marshall asked.

"We'll show you her head in a pickling jar."

Elenora heard her husband laugh, a nervous laugh. Vernon laughed as well.

"That struck me funny," Marshall said.

"It won't when you see it."

"Are you being serious?"

"Oh, yeah. Cone or me—probably me—will bring you Greta Fields' severed head in a large glass jar filled with pickling solution. It's supposed to be an old Celtic tradition. St. Patrick insists on it. You won't get to keep the head."

"Thank God."

"St. Patrick keeps all the heads."

———

The Fourth of July picnic.

Elenora met Larry Cone for the first time. It was a major indiscretion for Penny English, a high school teacher, to be seen among her colleagues with that man. What would you call him really? Is that what people call white trash? Her fellow teachers must think her depraved or desperate. There was certainly no reason for a woman of Penny's striking beauty to be desperate.

This is when Elenora realized that Penny English had seduced her husband. Penny English was the kind of woman who must intimately know the important men in her life. She must sample them, drink from them, must know their full measure. It probably happened during Elenora's pregnancy with Jason. The other teachers at the picnic knew. Even the more perceptive students would have guessed.

Penny English scooped a modest spoonful of macaroni salad made with low fat mayonnaise onto a royal blue plastic plate. As she nibbled this sorry fare, Elenora pictured her in Marshall's office, bent over his desk, her trendy suit skirt tossed to one side, her slip lifted up over her back.

Greta Fields arrived with her lover, Jane Lund.

Jane wore a black strapless bathing suit that advertised her undernourished condition. The bony, pale white woman nervously crossed her breast plate with her hands as if to hide the exposed portions of her body. This outfit couldn't have been Jane's idea. Why should Greta parade the shocking thinness of her lover? What satisfaction did it give her to watch her colleagues cringe?

Elenora behaved cordially to the pair—one might say more cordially than her position as host required. The other teachers thought her a fool for chatting so congenially with her husband's enemy.

But Elenora knew something they didn't know. Elenora knew Greta Fields was about to die. She didn't know how it would happen or when it would happen, but somehow during the course of that day Larry Cone meant to kill Greta. It would not appear to be murder. It would appear natural, brought on by something Greta loved.

Greta suffered from an urgently terminal condition. As such, Elenora thought it only Christian to treat the dying with kindness.

Jane gravitated toward Elenora. In social circumstances people didn't bother much with Jane. When she sensed a sympathetic soul, Jane latched on. She barely left Elenora's side the whole afternoon. She helped with refreshments, carried potluck dishes to the picnic tables, even fanned Elenora with a paper plate when the teacher's wife happened to complain of the inexorable heat.

"I'm anorexic," Jane confessed without prompting. "And bulimic. Sometimes I don't eat at all. Other times I overeat and have to throw up." Jane chronicled the list of forbidden foods taken and surrendered: whole bottles of maple syrup, whole bags of potato chips, entire sheets of birthday cake, gallon containers of ice cream. After thus detailing her gastronomic history, Jane continued with a series of outrageous, often funny stories from her life as a prostitute. Elenora found that she liked this strange woman.

Jane moved on to tell some very frank stories about Greta and their love life. Elenora considered how, in a certain light, Jane's skinny body might be viewed as attractive. The spirit inside the woman imbued her pallid skin with an ethereal quality, an aliveness not at first glimpsed. Elenora drifted off as Jane spoke. She wondered what it would be like to touch a woman's naked body. Jane's body, for instance. Could two women touch each other in a way that transcended pornography? She wondered.

Greta Fields loved to eat, that much was apparent.

She ate discreetly at first, then abandoned herself to the abundant picnic food with a zealous sloth. She ate thick, grilled hamburgers, topped with several slices of cheese, lathered with mayonnaise on top and drenched in pools of ketchup on the bottom. She hog bit her way through ears of steaming corn that virtually dripped with melted butter. Twice she returned to replenish mountain high portions of macaroni salad, potato salad, ziti salad, ambrosia salad.

People gathered around to watch her. It was a marathon, like one of those State Fair events in which extremely fat contestants eat their way through twenty or thirty pies. During a break to gulp down a 16 oz. bottle of Diet Pepsi, Greta explained, "I love picnic food." Burp.

On to the desserts.

There were at least fifteen desserts laid out on the dessert table. Greta glopped a generous portion of each one onto a series of plates. Marshmallow Gook Surprise, brownies topped with icing, chocolate chip/pecan crunch cookies, rhubarb pie, coconut rum cake, apple strudel, blueberry cobbler.

"Jell-O?" she exclaimed in mock astonishment "Well, we only live once."

Strawberry upside down cake, raisin spice cake, raspberry pumpkin soufflé cake in a pool of heavy cream. And, of course, the dessert of the Gods: cheesecake. Chocolate cheesecake, chocolate vanilla swirl cheesecake, Chambord cheesecake, Mount Gay rum cheesecake, even Mexican hot chili cheesecake. "Whoever made this is perverted," she turned from the table to address the crowd, "but I love you."

There was one more slice of cheesecake. Just one more. It featured a brown sugar, cherry crumbly sort of thing on top. There was just one slice. Elenora hadn't even seen it on the table before Greta's march on the desserts. It sat on its own little paper plate. Cheesecake a la Cone.

Greta spooned the messy mixture into her mouth. She moaned all through the eating of it. She moaned the way Penny English must have moaned having sex with Elenora's husband. Red cherry goo from the topping left a mustache. Greta smiled, almost innocently, perhaps as she might have smiled when she was a little girl, before anything really bad had happened to her. She said, "What's an extra two thousand calories?"

Then her face changed.

A troubled look came into her eyes. She glanced about her, taking in the smiling, contemptuous faces of her colleagues. A terrible sharp pain cracked across her chest. It was like a break in the ice.

'Where was Larry Cone?' Elenora wondered. He had been in the vicinity of the dessert table mere minutes ago. He should be on hand to catch Greta as she fell to one knee. He could play the role of the helpful, manly guest, setting the stricken woman on the ground, calling loudly for an ambulance. But Larry Cone was nowhere to be seen. He had drifted away, in the background now, the invisible guest no one really wanted to know, a forgettable patch of drab black and white in the calico quilt of the teachers' picnic.

'So this is how murder works,' Elenora thought.

A crowd gathered around the struggling creature, on her back now, clutching her side, gasping for breath, her lips moving silently like a hooked fish tossed onto land.

It was then that Elenora decided. Before Greta Fields was fully dead; while the paramedics with their piercing sirens broke the peace of the hot afternoon; while Greta thrashed about in the grass, clutching herself, writhing. In that moment, looking on, almost coldly detached, observing Jane's dread horror as professionals examined and pounded and asked pointless questions about the one person in the world who had ever loved her, in that moment Elenora decided to kill her husband.

She had to do it. It was a matter of standards.

———

The paramedics put Greta on a stretcher and installed her in the ambulance. Jane gasped, "What are they doing?"

"Why don't you go with her," Elenora said softly, kindly. "You can ride up front. They'll let you."

Jane looked helplessly at Elenora. This required the taking of responsibility, something Jane did poorly. And it meant she would be alone. Alone in the hospital with medical personnel, answering difficult questions. And Greta had all the money. How would she get money for cigarettes? She couldn't get through all this without cigarettes.

"Just go," Elenora said in her best comforting tone. "I'll come in the car. I'll see to it you're all right."

Jane nodded reluctantly, gratefully. One of the paramedics literally lifted her up into the cab of the ambulance. Jane looked back at Elenora, stricken, confused. Just then the first tear emerged.

"I'll meet you there," Elenora called as the ambulance raced away.

Elenora drove alone to St. Clair Hospital. Marshall begged off, claiming responsibility for his guests and the house. That was a good enough excuse, Elenora supposed, but he really ought to be at the hospital to reap the fruit of his labors.

On the drive Elenora imagined Marsh in the car with her. She spoke to her imaginary passenger, working it all out for herself.

"It's a matter of standards," she reiterated. "Standards are important to a man like you. You used to be a good man with very high standards. It has always been one hundred percent with you. One hundred percent to your career, your family, your romance. But you know how standards work, Marshall.

"One day you're just a little too tired to give one hundred percent. You give ninety. You get away with it. Soon ninety percent becomes the new standard. Then an unfortunate circumstance gets in the way of the execution of ninety percent. Let's say your wife becomes unexpectedly pregnant with your seventh child. You bend to circumstances and give maybe seventy percent. You get away with it once again. Seventy percent becomes the new standard.

"Then something truly tragic occurs. Let's say the School Board hires Greta Fields. You can't let this woman destroy everything you've spent a lifetime building, so you take action. You associate with street scum, murderers. You arrange to take Greta Fields' life.'

"At that point, Marshall my love, you've no standards left at all. No human association will be beneath you, no action beyond consideration. Every lie will be just one more lie, every perpetration just one more added to the list.

"This new Marshall Chester," she said, glancing at her husband's ghostly visage, "will resent me for being the woman who married the old Marshall Chester. My presence will remind you every day of your fall from grace. And in the course of eating with me and talking with me and sleeping beside me, you will come to know. You will come to know that I actually know. The conspiracy, the missing money, the contract killing—a killing financed with money earned teaching school children. Teaching school children the importance of standards. And what about these children? Will they, also, instinctively know? Will they respond with their old enthusiasm or will they sense how dry and hollow you've become inside?

"You hoped to save your beloved Vernon from a life of lowered standards. But it is he who reached across the chasm of the twenty-five years between you. He grasped you in his talons and took you down with him. You live where he lives now."

Elenora drove mindlessly, hardly knowing where she was going.

"I can see it quite clearly, Marshall," she continued. "There is no place for me in this new scheme of things. Eventually you will decide that, like Greta Fields, I will have to go. It might take a year, maybe two. But sooner or later you will find a way to justify the murder of your wife. And it won't be a pleasant wait for me. Someone will have to pay for the burden of your guilt. I will pay, the children will pay, because we are the markers of your past."

She spotted the sign for hospital parking.

"We're having this talk," she said, "because I've decided, just today, that I want to live. I want to see my children married. I want to dance at all their weddings. I want to live long enough to play with my grandchildren. And here's something else. I want the acting career I gave up for the man you used to be."

Elenora pulled into a good parking spot near the elevator. She turned off the engine, then faced the empty space in the car.

"So you see, it's like this," she said. "One of us has to go. And I've decided it's going to be you."

46.

"Sleep proved a good foil," she told Jeremy.

Marsh and Vernon felt free to talk while I slept on the couch or slept in my room. This was my first bit of real acting, too, you see.

I discovered that Vernon kept two apartments—a run down thing in Polish Hill for the benefit of the I.R.S. and a luxury affair in a security building on the edge of Shadyside. By piecing bits of conversational scraps, I tracked down both addresses.

Don't ask me why, but I wanted to see these places. I couldn't get in at first, but I spied on him all the same. Saw that Dottie Hatfield a couple of times. I wondered about her. What kind of woman would fall for a man like Vernon?

It was an enlivening experience, Jeremy. I felt like a bloodhound that has been given a sniff of clothing. I studied Vernon's environment, ferreted out his weaknesses, his idiosyncrasies. The Wendy's across the street from his Shadyside address, for instance. He stopped there three or four times a week. From outside I watched him go through the ritualized behavior of eating burgers and fries at a fast food restaurant. It was just like being back at Carnegie Mellon, studying civilians, copying their mannerisms. At last, a role that excited me.

I learned how to break into the Polish Hill apartment. I did it several times. It was a two story house built into a hillside. The landlady blasted her television at ear splitting levels all day long. Judging from the graffiti inscribed on the back of the building, I guessed that the neighborhood kids hung out there at night. During the day, however, I had the place to myself.

The first day I chickened out. I sat on the hillside staring at what I suspected were Vernon's windows. I got the shakes. How would I explain myself if I got caught? He was a dangerous man, after all. And I had to wonder, was I going too far? Have I crossed a line? Am I insane? I didn't have the courage to break the law.

That night, all through dinner with Marsh and the kids, I felt nauseous. It was all I could do to keep down my food. Look what I had almost done. I, Elenora Richer, was using my intelligence and my finely tuned artistic sensibilities to contemplate murder. I had almost broken into someone's home—an action totally out of character. I chastised myself over and over as I watched my family eat, while I listened to their idle chatter. 'How lucky,' I thought, 'to be safe at home.'

Then I remembered Greta Fields lying on the ground, clutching her side, gasping for air. My husband did that. My husband paid an old high school friend to steal that woman's life from her. It could easily have been me gasping for breath. I reminded myself, Jeremy, one day it will be me.

Oh, truthfully, I am not a strong woman. I knew that evening, with all the sickness in my stomach, your sister Elenora did not possess the strength to carry out the necessary murders of Vernon Roman and Marshall Chester. I, personally, am much too sensitive, much too kind, to deliberately inflict pain or harm. Conspiracy, duplicity, calculation are all outside my realm of experience.

But, as an actress! As an actress I could take on the role of a character who possessed the necessary qualities. I could assume the persona of a character for whom conspiracy, duplicity and calculation are as natural as a spider's secretion of silk. I thought on it. I needed someone cool and cunning, someone capable of scaling walls, risking personal injury, even risking death in pursuit of justice. Guess whom I chose to portray? You'll like this part, Jeremy. It will appeal to the culture freak in you. I chose Emma Peel of *The Avengers*.

I bought myself a pair of black tights and a black top. I aerobicized with videos every day. Over several intense weeks I progressed from a basic workout to a workout challenge to an advanced course.

In between workouts I studied old *Avenger* episodes. That Diana Rigg was an amazing woman. Her performance pushed me forward, urged me on to the next level of fitness, the next plateau of commitment. I became strong, Jeremy. No one, but no one, will ever play Emma Peel better than Diana Rigg, but I felt I could give the character a spin of my own. There was just room enough for a second interpretation.

One morning I got my husband and kids off to school and returned to the Polish Hill apartment. The landlady was playing *The Price Is Right* loud enough for them to hear it on Mars. After first checking to make sure I was alone, I scaled a nearby tree, then shimmied to the edge of the limb nearest the most accessible window. I reached out my arm as far as it would go, which was just far enough to lift the sash. With cat-like Peelish agility I leapt onto the ledge and slid into the room. There. Easy.

It was a bathroom. Old looking. Pedestal sink with separate hot and cold faucets. The cold faucet dripped, creating an orange-brown stain on the porcelain. A comb containing a few hairs Vernon's color rested along the edge. The dingy brown toilet scared me a bit. I lifted the lid. No water in the bowl. Probably evaporated. No toilet paper either. The towel rack held an old dish towel, its fleece thin in patches. It was obvious the bathroom hadn't been used anytime recently.

Next I found a small bedroom with a mattress on the floor. The furniture was strictly Goodwill, probably left behind by the previous tenant. There was a tired old dresser, looked like its handles had been sold for scrap in a desperate hour. I wriggled a couple of the drawers open. They were neatly lined with newspaper from the sixties, otherwise empty.

The living room was a bit more interesting. A threadbare rug in the middle of the floor sported the remnants of an absolutely enormous Art Deco sofa. You didn't need a microscope to see the dust mites crawling all over it. The bugs on that thing could have traced their lineage to the Roaring Twenties.

What else? A wooden mantle covered with a thin layer of undisturbed dust. An old bean bag chair with a tear in the plastic patched with electrical tape. Oh, and next to the bean bag chair we had an answering machine with a built in telephone—not exactly the latest model.

Here's the best part.

Amidst this squalor, against one wall, set a gorgeous, mint condition nineteenth century armoire. Two sided, as most of them are, with a door on the left and a door on the right. No handles on the doors. A pair of ornate skeleton keys opened each door and functioned as handles as well. Mother had one, do you remember? Except the keys weren't in the armoire.

Well, the incongruity of this exquisite piece of furniture intrigued me. I had to get a peak inside. Mrs. Peel and I scavenged around the room, examining the undersides of the armoire, the sofa, even the bean bag. Nothing. This puzzled us. We retreated to the suburbs to ponder the matter of the locked armoire.

Over the course of the next few days, I made the rounds of the junky antique stores on the South Side. The shop owners loved me in my Emma Peel tights and I do believe that I became, if only briefly, something of a South Side character. With just a little bit of money I managed to acquire a box full of keys—keys to doors, keys to chests, keys to clocks, all kinds, all sizes. Not one of these keys fit Vernons's armoire.

One afternoon, while the landlady launched *Columbo* up to the stars, I laid down on the floor to give this problem my deepest thought. I felt something hard and sharp under the throw rug. Slipping my hand underneath, I first encountered more orange newspaper from the sixties, then I found something a little more interesting. It was a plastic, legal paper sized transparent sleeve. Tucked carefully inside I found four newspaper obituaries.

Curiously, these obits were not all Pittsburghers. One described the life and death of a paper products executive from Philadelphia; another detailed the unfortunate skiing accident of a native New York resident. Another, someone from Maryland. Another, someone from Michigan. Hadn't heard of any of these people.

Reaching further toward the center of the rug I found several more plastic sleeves, each one filled to capacity with obits. Except the last one. This one held the lone obituary of one Ms. Greta Fields. And, low and behold, this sleeve held, within a tiny plastic pouch, a set of bronze skeleton keys.

I'm sure you read in the newspaper, the left side of the armoire held some thirty theatrical costumes. This intrigued me. I understood the policeman's uniform, the Honeywell Security uniform, the fireman's uniform. Vernon and his cohorts wore these costumes to commit crimes. But what possible use could they make of a Renaissance gentleman's outfit or an Edwardian suit or a samurai's robes? What crime would they commit in a nun's habit?

It had been twenty years since I'd run free in a wardrobe room. I loved Vernon's costumes. I spent any number of afternoons trying on outfits, acting out scenes. I almost lost track of my purpose.

Almost.

You see, the other side of the armoire presented a mystery to me. It consisted of five wooden shelves full of oversized mason jars. In the back of one shelf I found a stash of lids. It should have been obvious. After all, I overheard Vernon tell Marshall about the heads and the pickling solution. But I didn't really believe him at the time. It was just too bizarre.

Each time we visited Vernon's apartment, Mrs. Peel insisted we check the jars. Sure enough, one afternoon while the landlady sonically immersed herself in *The Guiding Light,* I opened the right side of the armoire and noticed the jars had been moved. Something caught my attention. I pulled out a few of the jars and inspected the back of one of the shelves. There was something white back there. Something white against the glass and the mahogany.

I let Mrs. Peel pull it out because I knew, I knew. And I didn't want to overreact. I didn't want to scream or drop the jar onto the floor.

"It's Greta Fields," Mrs. Peel surmised.

"How did they do it?" I wondered.

"Broke into her mausoleum, got her down from her shelf and—" Mrs. Peel traced an index finger across her throat. "In the jar she goes with a little pickling solution. Voila!"

"How unseemly."

"You know what you must do." Mrs. Peel withdrew the samurai's robes from the costume side of the armoire. "There is no time left to lose."

"There is no sword with the costume," I said.

"Think what you've got in your attic."

"But that's an ornamental sword I won during a stage combat competition. Is it as good as samurai's sword?"

"It is if you say it is. Remember, you're an actress."

"Well…" I thought, imagining my special award in it's hiding place. "It's made of hammered steel. I have an electric knife sharpener at home. I suppose I could use that to sharpen my sword. It sharpens shears."

"There you go."

"But I can't kill anybody," I said. "I thought you would do this for me."

Mrs. Peel shook her head. "Not my area of expertise I'm afraid." She held the samurai's robes up from the tips of her fingers. "But he can help you."

———

Do you remember, Jeremy, how I bitched and bitched about being forced to take stage combat? Especially fencing and sword work. Most of the women complained. When were we ever going to be called upon to do battle on stage with a saber? Never, that was our argument. But Dr. Bunny challenged me. Remember Dr. Bunny? You thought it was so funny that the stage combat instructor's name was Dr. Bunny.

No one ridiculed him, I can promise you that. He was a tough character. And he challenged me.

"What's the matter, Richer," he said. "No athletic skills? Two left hands? I forgot. Your Daddy got you into this place."

Well, that did it. I was bound and determined to show him.

I spent every spare moment in the gym, sword in hand. I got so good, I started sparring with the guys. I beat the guys. Remember that? Daddy was so proud of me.

Dr. Bunny sponsored a competition. The winner was awarded a genuine sword. Not a stage sword, but a genuine, impressive shiny steel item, hammered and put back in the fire and folded back on itself and hammered again. Back in the fire two hundred times to give the blade super rugged strength. Beautiful, ornate handle with ebony inlay and a crest with lions.

The only man in school I couldn't beat turned out to be Dr. Bunny himself.

Isn't it ironic that years later I finally acquired a role that demanded not just competence with a sword but mastery? Don't you just hate it when your teachers turn out to be right?

Of course, I'd never studied samurai sword technique.

I rented Japanese samurai movies and learned. It's not just physical, Jeremy. The mental state is crucial. The samurai were noble beings, charged with the protection of more than just people and villages. They were charged with the preservation of an entire way of life.

Each day after Marsh and the kids left for school, I retrieved the sword. It had been honed to an exquisite sharpness by the electric Chef's Choice tool. I donned the samurai costume, charged around the room, wielding that magnificent instrument. My spirit filled with justice and honor. What a role, Jeremy. So exhilarating.

The samurai required more strength, physical and spiritual, than Emma Peel. It took a while to develop that strength. I did some weight training. I adopted *The Way of the Samurai* as my Bible. One day, with the samurai's instinctive knowledge of such things—I knew I was ready. The time had come for action.

———

I called Vernon's number and left a message. Marsh needed to see him urgently. Call me as soon as possible. I figured he checked his messages periodically from his cell phone. He called me a couple of hours later. 'Hey, Elenora, what's up?' I told him Marsh is worried about something. He was stuck in meetings all day, but it was critically important that Vernon meet him this evening. Five-thirty in front of the old Homeopathic Hospital. Don't speak. Walk in silence to the Wendy's on Center Avenue. He'll talk to you there.

"I know this sounds clandestine," I said. "But he says it's really important."

"No problem, Elenora. You tell old Marsh I'll be there."

Then I called my husband at school. This is Mrs. Chester. I have a bit of an emergency. Can you call my husband out of class? A couple of minutes later Marsh picked up the phone. 'Elenora, what's the problem?' Vernon Roman called, honey. He sounded worried. I wrote down what he told me to tell you. Meet him tonight at five-thirty in front of the old Homeopathic Hospital. Don't speak. Walk with him in silence to the Wendy's on Center Avenue. He'll talk to you there.

Jesus, Marsh. This sounds really scary. What do you think he wants?

As Elenora I drove to Schenley Park. In the woods I changed into the nun's habit. Then, as Sister Anna Marie Beck, I drove to Bloomfield and parked the car a couple of blocks away from St. Stephen's church. St. Stephen's is next door to the Wendy's. I had specked it out earlier. It's an old city church with a dwindling congregation. There was a good chance I could get in and out unseen.

I entered one of four confessionals. There I changed into the samurai's costume, leaving the nun's habit behind in the confessional. I proceeded down to the basement. There is a door in the basement that opens to a set of stone steps that lead to the side lawn of the church. I crept out this door, leaving a piece of wood between the door and the frame so that I could get back in.

I snuck along a row of hedges, keeping an eye out for passersby. It was almost dark. St. Stephen's lawn ends at a three foot wall that borders the Wendy's parking lot. I jumped down onto the blacktop and hid behind a large van.

I said a little prayer, Jeremy. You see, I was so frightened I was beginning to break character. The samurai said a prayer. The samurai remembered all of Elenora's sacrifices, remembered Elenora's children, remembered Greta Fields gasping for breath. The samurai remembered poor Jane Lund, left helpless and without love. The samurai watched and waited, waited and watched.

Vernon Roman and Marshall Chester rounded the entrance to the parking lot. The two men walked solemnly together, heads down, saying not a word. They approached the blacktop. As the samurai I hardly recognized Marshall Chester. That was Elenora's husband. Their history was gone now, gone from this place. Marshall Chester was just a man, a once good man who had been tempted away from cherished virtues into something sinister and devoid of spirit.

The samurai crept slowly along the edge of the van, following the two men with his eyes. Before they could stop to think, the samurai leapt out at them, suddenly and dramatically. The sword flew up into the air. Despite its great weight, the samurai swung the sword with alacrity. Vernon and Marshall, momentarily transfixed, watched as the samurai brought the sword down swiftly onto Vernon's neck.

Despite the sharpness of the blade, Roman's neck proved dense and resistant. The samurai filled with rage. He struck again and again. In a universe without time he struck again and again until finally the sword cut through the bone as well as the flesh.

Vernon's head lifted up off the plane of the glimmering steel, up, rotating. It fell to the ground and rolled, face frozen in pain and shock. It rolled hideously toward the wall near the church.

The other one, Marshall Chester, watched it all, stunned, unable to move. The samurai turned toward this man. A realization crossed his face. Strength came back into his legs. Energy filled his body. Just a split second away from a speedy escape, poised on the very brink of motion, the samurai brought the swift sword crashing down onto the cap of Chester's left knee. Turning the sword in a blinding arc of speed, the samurai reached behind Chester and cut the hamstrings of his right leg.

Marshall Chester fell to his knees. He looked up into the face of the samurai, but he didn't see his lover there. Instead he saw a kindness, a recognition. He had been a good man once. A loving husband and father. He had been honorable. The samurai did not want his head, only his death.

"I am an innocent," the man said.

"I will be merciful."

The sword went in through the man's solar plexus, through the center of his being. Chester hung there on the blade, suspended for just one moment of grace by the beauty of the samurai's justice. The samurai withdrew his sword. Quickly, before anyone could act, the samurai collected the head, vaulted up onto the lawn of the church, then disappeared into the basement.

While police sirens wailed outside, the samurai raced to the confessional. I broke character, Jeremy, coming away slowly from the samurai. I took off his blood stained robes. I removed his porcelain white makeup. I placed

Vernon Roman's head in a plastic bag, nothing more ceremonial than that. I put the costume in a black canvas tote that match the nun's habit remarkably well. I changed back into Sister Anna Marie Beck. I spent a few moments getting into character, then calmly proceeded outside.

The place was surrounded by police cars and news vans. A reporter stopped me outside the church and asked if I had seen anything.

"I saw a man wearing some strange sort of Halloween costume. He ran down Liberty Avenue in the direction of Bloomfield. It looked oriental, the costume, although he ran so fast I can't say for sure. I was amazed, of course. It's not a sight you see every day. He ran remarkably fast, as I say, then just seemed to disappear. It was almost like magic. He disappeared into a building or a side street. I was too far away to tell. I'm getting old, you know. The eyes aren't as sharp as they used to be."

Sister Anna Marie Beck then calmly walked the next few blocks to her car, got in, and drove back to Schenley Park. There I broke character once again, reverting back to Elenora Chester. Before they could discern Vernon's identity I drove to his Polish Hill apartment, climbed the tree, broke in, then stole his answering machine. I didn't want the police finding my message there.

Rush hour traffic had mostly abated. I raced home. The kids were out, as had been planned. In the attic I quickly hid everything—the costumes, the makeup, the sword, even Vernon's head—in the secret compartments of the Louis Vuitton trunk. That's when I realized I didn't have the samurai's belt. There was nothing I could do about it. I couldn't very well go back for it. Tomorrow I would have to find a way to cover my tracks.

I took a long, hot shower, making sure to wash every bit of the makeup off of my face and out of my hair. Fresh clothes completed the transformation. Fixing myself a well deserved pot of herb tea, I settled back and waited for the police to call.

During the wait my real emotions emerged. I realized the magnitude of the acts I had just committed. I wondered, once again, as you might well imagine, if I was insane. I wanted desperately to call you, Jeremy, but it would have given things away to call before the arrival of the police. I decided to take a pill. In fact, I took several. It was the best thing, really. Elenora would normally have been asleep on the couch, steeped in the emptiness of her drugged out life.

I was out for the count when the police arrived. Scott called you at my request. 'Tell him to get here quickly, even if he has to take a plane,' I told Scott in front of the police. I didn't want to involve you with it, Jeremy. I wanted to keep you guiltless, free of all knowledge. But you see, I had to get the samurai's belt back. The police would be watching me. I couldn't very well change back into Sister Anna Marie Beck and go fetch it. You were the only person in the world I knew I could trust. Please forgive me.

That Redwing man almost ruined everything. He got closer and closer to the truth and then, just at the end, diverted all suspicion to Vernon's gang in Cleveland. Of course, I planned it to look like one of Vernon's own killings. It fit the modus operandi of the Hornish clan, as I later learned they were called. It made perfect sense to the police that Hornish killed Vernon over a money dispute or some similar clan squabble. They reasoned my poor husband was in the wrong place at the wrong time.

Years from now, my dear brother, after I am dead and you are dead and the children have children of their own, this house will be sold. The new owners will one day decide to clean out those cluttered storage areas in the basement. So many cans of mostly used paint, spray bottles of expired weed killer, boxes and boxes of old nails and rusty hinges and metal tools of indescribable function.

They'll come to the jars of food I put up so many years earlier. They'll wonder why I didn't eat these preserves. Jar after industrial sized jar of piccalilli and stewed tomatoes and peppers in oil.

Way in the back, behind all the other preserves, these new owners will discover something quite bizarre. It will shock them, maybe even fill them with horror. For tucked behind the lovely round apricots and elderberry jam, they will find the head of Vernon Roman in a large mason jar full of pickling fluid. And they will know. These new people will know the whole story of the horrible murders that darkened the lives of the family who lived here before them.

Taped to the jar, in a transparent plastic sleeve, they will find the newspaper obituary of one Vernon Tiberius Roman. And just below the obituary, on a piece of acid free paper, they will find this note:

I killed him
Eleanor Richer (actress)

THE END

Ralph Ashworth grew up in a neighborhood where many of the boys joined gangs, hustled downtown or otherwise engaged in illegal activity. He escaped this world by retreating indoors where he passed time creating characters and stories. At Carnegie Mellon in Pittsburgh, Ashworth studied with historical novelist Gladys Schmitt and had the opportunity to attend a unique master class with such writers as E.L. Doctorow, Stanley Elkin and Frank Herbert.

Ashworth has written feature articles for numerous city publications, including *Pittsburgh Magazine* and the *Pittsburgh Tribune Review.* In 1994 a small press specializing in Americana published his first book: *Greetings From Pittsburgh.* The antique picture postcards from this book are part of a permanent video exhibit at the Heinz History Center.

Fiction remains Ashworth's true passion. *The Killer of Orchids* is his first novel and Jeff Redwing is his favorite character so far. Ashworth lives in Pittsburgh with his partner of thirty-two years where he is currently plotting the second Jeff and Xander mystery.

Photo by Michael Beigay